CONVERGENCE

Nicole M. Ahles

This is a work of fiction. The characters, organizations, and events portrayed in this novel are either products of the author's imagination or are used fictitiously. Any resemblance to actual events, places, or persons, living or dead, is entirely coincidental.

CONVERGENCE
By: Nicole M. Ahles
Paperback – 1st edition 2022

Copyright © 2022 by Nicole M. Ahles. All rights reserved.
Except as provided by the Copyright Act (title 17, U.S. *code*) Jan. 1978, no part of this publication may be used or reproduced, scanned, or photocopied, recorded, uploaded, distributed, or transmitted in any form or by any means whatsoever without the prior written permission of the publisher or author with the exception of the initial intent of obtainment and in the case of brief quotations embodied in critical articles and reviews and properly cited.

NicoleAhles.com

NAB Publication
Cover design copyright © 2022 by Britani Christenson, Casey Christenson
Image copyright © 2022 Eezy Inc. All rights reserved
Interior design by Nicole Ahles
Printed by Ingram Spark

ISBN 978-0-9911126-4-7

For Kristin,
who first believed.

CONVERGENCE

ONE

Tala's eyes opened slowly. She was lightheaded, her mind filled with a thick fog. Her body was warm and wet from what she assumed was night sweat, and her eyes struggled to focus. Something strong was pulling her back to sleep. She closed her eyes, a scorching heat enveloping her body, and began to drift off.

She awoke with a start, her body moving quickly through the house, faster than she ever had before, yet her feet did not touch the ground. She felt arms around her. She must be dreaming. Through drowsy eyes, she saw fire burning around her. The large flames licked the walls, higher and higher, reaching the ceiling. She tried to take a breath, but the air was too hot, too thick with smoke, and she coughed. Her lungs began to burn in her chest. Before she could try for another breath, her body burst through the back door, flung onto the concrete patio. She skinned her knees, elbows, and palms, but she hardly noticed. She turned just in time to make out the hazy shape of a person heading back toward the house. Her house. Her house was on fire.

Taking in gulps of fresh air, Tala crawled breathlessly across the rough patio to the lawn. The grass was cold on her skin, and she collapsed into a heap. Groggy, her surroundings once again began to slip away from her. She tried to fight it, but the darkness was heavy and overtaking her. She blinked erratically to keep it from consuming her.

Where were her parents? Her brother? He was staying with them for the night. Smoke billowed from the house, and she coughed, her lungs still burning. Her mind was in a thick haze. A sudden boom filled her ears, her body recoiling, leaving behind a high-pitched ringing that echoed in her head. Debris fell around her, but her body couldn't move. She lay paralyzed in the grass, damp from the nighttime dew, the inferno before her hot on her face.

From somewhere in the distance, she picked up the faint sound of a new ringing. It started to grow, louder and louder, and it took her cloudy mind a minute to realize it was the sound of approaching sirens. She covered her mouth with her hand, shielding herself from the falling ash as she took in deep breaths, coughing in between. Her head spinning, she glanced around. Startled, she made out the darkened figure of a man, the flames burning behind him. Their eyes locked as her breath caught. She stared at him, trying to focus, but her mind only seemed to be pulling her into a long, dark tunnel. She tried to call out to him, but when she opened her mouth, nothing came out. And then suddenly, he was gone.

A moment later, people swarmed the yard, and she recognized them immediately as Republic firefighters. They pulled long hoses past her as she struggled to her feet, heavy streams of water dowsing what was left of her home. Her heart fell.

"Tala!" a voice called through the darkness. She turned to see Thias racing toward her, panic across his face.

Thias, she thought. Her brother was alive. Relief washed over her like a wave as he pulled her to him.

Her mind was trying to piece reality together. Who was the stranger? Was that how she'd gotten out of the house? And how, she wondered in confusion, had Thias gotten out? Where had he just come from?

♦♦♦

11 years later

"What do you mean you're taking me off the case?" Tala asked. In the five years she had been a Militia Forces agent for the Republic of Columbia, not once had she had a case taken away.

"It's not you, Agent Alexander," said Captain Kole. "This case has been classified above your security clearance." He spoke above her, his body turned away, and didn't make eye contact.

Tala glanced around his office; it wasn't often that she was in it. It was minimalistic. Not surprisingly. It was sleek and clean with simple white furniture: his interactive desk and a large chair behind it. White paneled walls, the triangle of the Republic behind his desk, and a portrait of President Royer II hanging on the wall. Nothing personal.

"It's just that I'd like to finish what I've started. I'd like to debrief the suspect. My suspect," she said.

Kole turned on his heel in quick precision, his dark eyes stopping on her. Her body stiffened, and she swallowed hard.

"He's not a suspect, Agent Alexander. He's a Rebel. And the matter is done," he said. His stone-cold face fixed fiercely on her for another moment, the silence in his office deafening. She was sure he could hear her heart pounding inside her chest.

"Now," he said, not losing his edge of intensity, "you're being tasked for a different assignment." Kole gave a nod, and the door to his office opened behind her. She didn't dare move to see who it was.

"Since Director Alexander, here," Kole said with another nod, "will be taking over this case, we're in agreement with how to use you in our proceedings." Tala cringed slightly at the mention of his name, and a moment later, she caught his scent, a subtle combination of patchouli and black pepper, as he brushed past her. He gave not so much as a glance in her direction. He walked to Kole's side of the desk before he finally turned toward her.

"It certainly has been a while since I've seen you," he said coolly, a smirk curling at the corner of his mouth. But Tala knew that was no smile. That wasn't a pleasantry. That was an accusation.

"We'll be using you for tonight's National Statement," Kole said.

Her brows furrowed and her mouth gaped slightly.

"You're confused," said Director Alexander as he scrutinized her. "Let me explain. The reasons are two-fold." He took a seat in Kole's high-backed leather chair, and Kole immediately stepped slightly back, a deferential expression on his face. "First of all," Director Alexander continued, "this plot foil, and the subsequent arrest of the Rebel behind it, shows strength on behalf of the Republic's Militia Forces. You serve both as a face of protection as an agent and the face of the legacy that built this nation. People know your name and respect you. This was your takedown. It's fitting you be the one to assure the public of their safety. Secondly, this Statement will serve as a warning to all Unified Rebels throughout the nation, and to the schisies sympathetic to their cause. A crackdown is being instituted on all traitors, regardless of their citizenship status. Not even the Preferred will be immune. Punishment will be severe. There is unrest building throughout the country."

"Unrest?" she asked in surprise. She could practically feel Kole's knowing glare on her. She may have been the granddaughter of one of their founding fathers and first elected leaders, but she was never in a position to be in the know on sensitive matters. This was completely new information to her.

"Yes, unrest," Director Alexander said. "The Substandard citizens, hell even the Standard citizens, are up in arms over the tithing hike. Crime rates are skyrocketing all over the country from the Nameless population. And the UR and the schisies helping them are only growing stronger. People need to be reminded of all the Republic does for them. We need to demonstrate our strength and reinforce loyalty to our country and its leadership." He folded his hands neatly in his lap and gazed at her through his steel blue eyes. It made sense now. He only wanted to use her because of her name, not because of anything she'd actually accomplished. She resented him.

A beep came from Captain Kole's pocket. He swiftly pulled out his palm pad, stared at it for a brief moment, then looked up. "Please excuse me, Director, duty calls." Kole briskly left the room, leaving Tala alone with Director Alexander, still seated at the desk, his hands still folded in his lap. He smirked at her.

"Thias," she said, using his first name once she was sure that Kole was out of earshot. "Surely you can accomplish the same thing if you address the nation," she said. "Don't you think it's a little underhanded to use me simply because of our family's position? Besides, you're an Alexander too. You address security frequently. Or what about Wynn Davison? She does the weekly National Statements. Why not her?"

He straightened in the chair. "Because she's not an Alexander. It's my job as the director of Militia Forces to ensure the safety of all our citizens. And part of my responsibility is to invoke loyalty to the Republic. These are precarious times, dear sister. We are a formidable nation, but these are threats to the vision of peace our country was built on. I'm sure you don't need a repeat history lesson on the devastation of war, which we will only be doomed to repeat if we are to lose control of the people.

"And so yes, I will use you and not Wynn, and what you represent to fortify fidelity. Our citizens respect you, not just because you are an Alexander, but also because you are one of the few female MF agents. They see you as strong. Something good must come from all the years of enabling your independence and non-conformity to what I want for you. If not, it was all for nothing." Thias rose from the chair, straightened his pressed suit coat, then rounded the corner of the desk toward the door. He stopped, shoulder-to-shoulder with Tala. "Your ride will be here in a few minutes to take you to the State Media building. Don't keep it waiting."

And then he was gone.

Feeling defeated, she made her way from Kole's office to the rotunda, the heart of MF Command. Tala knew she looked as unstrung as she felt. Many of the other agents eyed her carefully as she entered the oversized room. From the corner of her eye, she spotted her partner, Ronin, approaching her.

"Forget all of them," he said quietly, nodding to the on-lookers around them. "They're only interested in how this is all going down. This was a big case, and it was your lead that started it," he said, and he put his hand gently on her arm. A show of solidarity.

She felt herself take a breath, and her shoulders dropped slightly. She looked up at him. "I've got to get going," she said.

He cocked an eyebrow in confusion. "And where is it that you're going?"

"I'm being tasked to make the National Statement," she said, hearing the spite in her voice.

"About the arrest and plot foil? Why you?"

She sighed. "Apparently, they have their reasons," she said, glancing over her shoulder in the direction of Kole's office. "I just don't understand why we're being taken off the case, why I don't have the clearance to lead the debrief. That part is just as important as the arrest itself."

"I was mad too. I get it, it's frustrating. But you know what insubordination will cost you," he whispered, then pursed his lips, his expression hardened. "Drop it."

She glanced around them, relieved to no longer be the spectacle in the room. "I just… I want to go back to that warehouse. To look for more evidence. There's more to this than meets the eye. Why don't you feel this way too? This can't be the end of it."

"Stop. Just stop." Ronin put up his hand. "There are a million reasons why you can't do that. And you know every single one of them. So actually, this is the end of it. Let it go."

Tala's palm pad gave a small vibrate from inside the side pocket of her pants. She pulled it out to see the alert that her car was out front.

"Listen, I've got to go. Watch me on the Statement?" she said and gave him a knowing smirk.

"I couldn't miss it if I wanted to."

It was a cloudy fall day, cool but not cold, as the luxury autonomous sedan took her through the streets of Columbia City, the Republic's capital. The affluence of the Stoughbour borough was evident in the grandiosity all around. Sleek high-rises stretched into the sky. There was a splendor in the innovative architecture, buildings with smooth curves, skyscrapers that twisted as they rose through the air. On Grand Avenue was Tala's favorite building, a towering arch with a waterfall cascading down its center.

Some buildings were made of polished metals and gleaming glass, making each appear to be lit up simply by their own reflections, while others had hard, rough surfaces of wood, steel, and concrete.

The Republic of Columbia, built on the ruins of part of the former United States after the Great War, prided itself on its supremacy and opulence. The Militia Forces, their once small civil army evolved into an elite military power, reinforced its strength and position while artists and engineers created architectural masterpieces that made the world marvel. And the Republic's advancement in technology was rivaled by few others around the world.

The sidewalks were crowded with masses of people moving in all directions. Tala's car slowed more than once. With over twelve million residents, the capital city, divided into six boroughs, was bursting at the seams. Jobs were hard to come by for Substandard citizens, and those living under the radar, classified as the Nameless and stripped of all citizenship, had an even more difficult time earning an income. But even with its over-crowding, constant noise, and strange smells, the city was home. It was all Tala had ever known, and for that she loved it.

Tala gazed out the backseat window as the State Media building came into view. It was a large building, not in height but in breadth. It was sleek and striking, taking on a C-curve, like an isolated wave in the ocean. The glass panels that comprised the exterior mirrored the sky, giving the structure a light gray tint. On clear days, it was always a crystal blue, majestic and beautiful.

Across the street from the State Media building was the Central Government building from where President Royer II ran the country. It was also where her brother Thias, director of Militia Forces, operated. It was one of the most glorious buildings in all of North America. Three towers twisted like spirals into the sky, glass bridges spanning between them. One hundred stories up, comprised of steel and glass, was a black cynosure that sat in the heart of the three towers. The president's chamber. It was as if the building held within its grasp a giant, obsidian pearl. To add to its elaborate and inventive design, the entire structure stood in the middle of a vast reflective pool. The bottom and sides were lined in cerulean blue tiles that made the water always appear pristine and clear. It was striking. Marble platforms reached across the pool, accessing the building in nine locations. All of it was arresting, even to someone who had seen it often. It was the showpiece of the Republic.

As a team of stylists at the State Media building busied themselves getting things in order for her, Tala gazed at her reflection in the mirror. She had never considered herself an unattractive woman, but certainly not a glamorous one either. Even when she was required to dress up for Thias and his endless dinner parties and social events. She avoided them as best she could.

Between her jacket and thick cargo pants, she looked bulky in her uniform. She unzipped her frag jacket, engineered to resist bullets and shrapnel, and slipped it off, letting it hang at her side.

Tala seemed to only ever be seen in one of two ways. As an MF agent, she was masculine because of her career choice. She was a woman in a man's world. But with Thias and the city's upper class, she was a pretty face. Her high-profile name earned her the title she despised most of all: the princess of the Republic. She often wondered who the real Tala was, and if she would ever be valued outside of people's opinions and labels of her. She was an Alexander; there was a prestigious legacy in her name that she couldn't escape, and Thias made his expectations of her very clear. He was determined and intentional with her, and it was inevitable that the day would come when she would have to fall in line with his vision of her. Marry well and have a silent but visual presence. Uphold her family name.

"Miss Alexander," a woman said as she approached. "We're ready to get started. Please follow me," she said kindly.

Tala was submerged in a hot sulfur tub, her skin scrubbed until she was certain it was raw, waxed on nearly every surface of her body, and plucked in every remaining spot. Her eyes were given drops that made them burn for several minutes, though she was assured it would subside after a short bit.

"It's to enhance the blue of your eyes for the broadcast. It's so rare to have blue eyes," one of the stylists said to her matter-of-factly.

Tala felt exposed as the three women worked simultaneously about her nearly naked body. She tried to cover herself, but as soon as she did, a stylist took her hand and went to work on her nails, trimming and filing. And then came the polish, a light shade of nude, keeping a natural look. It was a strange sensation to have the gel lacquer on her nails. It made her fingers feel heavy.

Finally letting her slip on a robe, a stylist washed her hair, scrubbing harshly, using product that tingled and stung on her scalp. But the women who worked on her were unmindful of her discomfort.

When they were finished revitalizing her, as they called it, Tala stood in front of the mirror, once again gazing at her reflection. It was her, but a version she hardly recognized. Her skin looked fresh, nearly glowing. Her eyelashes were long, black, and bold, her lips defined yet subtle in a light shade of pink. Her hair was sleek, and although it was naturally straight, it seemed even more so after being styled, and for the first time in a while, she felt the long locks sweep along her back. Her natural shade of blond seemed lighter, brighter, invigorated, and renewed. She studied the reflection staring back at her; she was beautiful, she conceded. She was exactly as her brother wanted her, and her heart fell.

A stylist appeared beside her, a black garment bag laid across her arms, and she gave Tala a wide smile.

Tala was dressed in a tapered trouser that accented the curve of her hips and a white button-down shirt with an open V to reveal her collarbone. Then they slipped on a lightweight jacket to match the pants, letting it hang open in the front. She stepped into a pair of shoes, strappy across the top of her foot, yet still covering her toes. She felt uncertain of herself in heels that high.

She was rarely a face for the country but rather a name. After the Statement, she knew more people were likely to recognize her than ever before. That thought alone left an unsettled feeling in her stomach.

Lastly, one of the stylists placed a thin necklace around her neck, the delicate chain cold on her skin. She glanced down to see the symbol of the Republic falling into the open collar of the shirt: an upright, equilateral triangle, though the bottom side was incomplete, broken, a small gap in the middle. This seemingly simple icon symbolized the master race of the nation, the triangle signifying the social hierarchy of the Republic of Columbia. The president and leadership were at the tip, and the disconnected bottom represented the mass's inability to master truth, knowledge, and awareness. As long as there was human imperfection, the triangle could never be complete, and nothing could parallel the highest point, which demanded obedience and reliance upon the greatest authority.

Tala thumbed the necklace charm as she was ushered out of the room by a team in gray suits and a single MF agent down a long corridor of white paneled walls and a black, solid-surface floor, her heels clacking along with each step. People passed in all directions, their faces staring at their palm pads or tablets. It was strange to Tala how no one seemed to interact. Not so much as a glance at each other. Everyone went about their business completely independently.

"Through this door, Agent Alexander," the agent said as he entered a code into a small digital panel. The door opened, and a second man held it for her while she walked through.

She stepped into the backstage area of the press room from where the National Statement was broadcast, two MF security agents standing nearby, along with Agent Grant, Thias's personal detail. Ahead, she spotted a brightly lit podium, familiar to her from all the National Statements, perched before a crowd that she only heard, not saw. Thias lingered in the shadows off stage, waiting for her.

"Well, well," he said as he approached. "Don't you clean up nicely?" He handed a tablet to her. "This is your statement. Do not stray from it. Do not answer any questions," he said.

Tala nodded as she quickly read the script. She let herself skim it for a second time, then looked up to confirm she was ready.

"We've got sixty seconds before we go live," someone said as they walked past and gave Thias a nod.

A man ushered Tala toward the edge of the stage, and she wobbled unsteadily on her heels as he hurried her along.

"Get it together, Agent," Thias said under his breath as he appeared beside her.

Tala swallowed hard. Her stomach was swarming from her nerves as the seconds ticked closer to when she had to step out in front of all those people, in front of the nation.

"Now," a voice said, and someone gave her a nudge. Tala followed Thias as he strode across the stage to the podium. He was an expert at this. Bright lights hit them, blinding the crowd from Tala's view. She forced herself to take a deep breath as Thias stepped up to the podium and raised his hands to quiet the room.

"Good evening, people of the Republic of Columbia." He gave a suave smile to the cameras that were on him, broadcasting him throughout the country. The National Statement aired automatically on every palm pad, tablet, and TV monitor. Every residence, workplace, and public location were required by law to have screens, some so large they covered the sides of buildings, to broadcast over. Tala's stomach flipped as her ears grew deaf to her brother's words. It took her a moment to realize everyone was watching her, Thias giving her a severe look. She snapped out of her trance and stepped up to the podium.

"Good evening," she said, then cleared her throat. "At approximately eleven o'clock last night, due to a collaboration of Militia Forces, a raid on a warehouse along the East River on the upper west side of the Ganbury borough was carried out. MF apprehended a suspect, whose name is not being disclosed at this time, who had in his possession a little over two hundred pounds of cocaine and fifty pounds of explosives. This man has been identified as a member of the Unified Rebels. At this time, Militia Forces are certain that this case is not associated with any plots of terrorism against the Republic. President Royer emphasizes vigilance and calls on all of our nation's citizens to always put the Republic first. Anyone who commits treason against our great nation will be punished to the highest extent of the law. We will have no tolerance for any Rebels within our borders, nor their sympathizers. Sleep safe tonight, everyone, as this is a victory for the Republic of Columbia. Thank you."

Tala quickly stepped back from the podium, forcing deep breaths through her nose while still maintaining a look of confidence on her face.

"Director Alexander, was your sister part of this raid?" a woman from the crowd called out as Thias stepped back up to the podium.

He gave that smile again, the one he used so well to charm those around him, and he nodded. "It is mostly in part due to Agent Alexander's work that this raid was conducted at all," he said.

"Would you say that your sister's ranking within the MF is due to your position as director?" a man asked loudly above the crowd.

Tala saw Thias's hand clench as it hung by his side, obstructed from the view of the crowd by the podium. Although all news throughout the country was subject to government review and official approval, questions that came during a live broadcast could rarely be censored.

"Agent Alexander is a committed agent to the MF force. It is her excellent track record and hard work that has earned her a spot where she is. I hold my role as director of our nation's Militia Forces very seriously, as its sole existence is for the protection of our citizens. And I would never entrust the responsibility of our national security to someone who has not earned it. There will be no more questions." Thias stepped back from the podium, his charming smile gone, his jaw now set in a rigid line, as if chiseled from stone, and he walked off stage. Tala followed, reminding herself to hold her head high while she hurried behind him.

Out of view of the cameras and the crowd, Thias turned to Tala, taking a slow breath.

"Not bad for your first time. Maybe I'll use you in the future," he said.

"I'm not sure I'm cut out for this on a regular basis," she said.

"We'll just have to see how things go. Now, on to other things. Chancellor Adams is coming to dinner tonight. It would be nice if you could be there too. He said you canceled the date I arranged."

Tala shuffled her feet unsteadily. "I did. Things came up. And I'm not up to socializing tonight," she said, bracing herself for the backlash.

"Tala," Thias said with an audible sigh. "You're nearly twenty-seven. It's time you settle down. You can't chase criminals forever. I'm sorry I ever encouraged it. You are a prominent figure in this society and the chancellor will only bolster your position. You can't be young, wild, and free forever."

Tala fought the urge to roll her eyes, she was all too familiar with the tirade. She wasn't sure there was a point in arguing anymore. "I know what you want from me," she said. "But these are choices I need to make for myself. Despite your good intentions," she added quickly, if only to avoid a quarrel later. He would never have an argument in front of other people. He would undoubtedly save that for a time behind closed doors. "I'm really just not up to it tonight," she said.

"Fine. I'll let you off for tonight. And tonight only," he said. "Mostly because I don't have it in me to debate with you about this again. But next time, you won't have this option," he said with a severe expression that told her he was serious. "Now, I've got a meeting to get to. Enjoy the rest of your night," he said with a nod, then swiftly headed for the door, Grant on his heels. A moment later, he was gone, and with the exception of a single security guard near the door, Tala was left standing by herself in the dimly lit area off stage.

In the absence of everyone, Tala's mind went back to her crime scene, to the warehouse, and the same unsettled feeling in her gut returned. Her training had taken her so far, and now it was her intuition that was trying to take her further. Something, she was certain, was being missed. And she was determined to find out what it was. After all, it was her job to protect her city. It was her responsibility as an MF agent to dig deeper, to find the answers.

❖

Kane stared at the large screen on the wall long after the broadcast ended and everything had gone black. It had been so long since he'd seen her.

"She looks different," he mumbled.

"Looked the same to me. Maybe a little older, though. When was the last time the public saw her?" Max asked as he nudged his glasses and swiveled around on his chair to his desk, his back to Kane.

"I don't get it," Kane said, turning around on the couch to face Max, ignoring his question. "Why wouldn't Thias do the broadcast? He's the one who does anything national security-related. Occasionally Wynn. All Thias is going to do is put a target on her back."

"Whose target?" Max asked.

He shrugged. "The Rebels. The Nameless. The schisies. Random thugs around the city. Nobody messes with Thias. Too many mysterious disappearances of those who've tried. But Tala? People won't hesitate," he said.

"I'm not sure I agree with you," Max said as he finally looked up. "She's still an Alexander. Thias's sister to be exact. People like her more, so they'll soften to her mission statements.

"Not everyone knows her face like they do his, but they know her name. She might be considered the princess of the Republic, but she's also regaled as a hero. She's an MF agent. And a good one. People respond to those kinds of heroics. And that is why," he said with a nod, "they tasked her for the Statement, I assume, anyway," Max said.

Kane considered this for a moment. "Maybe," he said as he stood up and crossed the room. He reached for his leather jacket tossed over the back of a chair, worn and broken in from years of use. "I'm going for a walk."

"Stay out of trouble," Max pleaded. "No fights. I don't care how good your intentions are."

Kane eyed him for a moment, gave a single nod, then headed for the door.

He stepped onto Harvey Street, the narrow street outside Max's front door, which was always heavily shaded by the buildings that towered above, all with old and crumbling brick facades and fire escape platforms with ladders stretching up each floor. These were buildings from before the Great War. Almost all of Stoughbour had been rebuilt over the last several decades, and it was where the grandest buildings in the country stood, but the other boroughs of the city, like Oxwick, where he lived, still had many old and intact buildings. It was a mix of old and new.

Harvey Street, which was more like an alley than a street, lined with broken and cracked sidewalks barely wide enough for two-way foot traffic, smelled of burnt fried food, most likely coming from Mrs. Knox's pod next door. With Kane's senses always in overdrive, the smell was nauseating. It was the worst when she made fish. That smell lingered for days.

It was later than Kane thought, and the street was darker than he expected, the distant sun nearly set. Fall was undoubtedly in the air, and by that time of day, the temperature began to drop. It was particularly chilly, and he lifted the collar of his jacket, shivering slightly. It would be completely dark soon. He always felt more comfortable roaming around after dark. Until the city curfew at midnight anyway. Although that rarely proved to be the same problem for him as it was for others.

As though his thoughts summoned her, Mrs. Knox emerged onto the street as he passed her door. The empty cloth sack in her hands suggested she was going to the market. There was a small one just around the corner that sold most of the basics, though they were often more expensive than the bigger grocery stores.

"Not getting into any trouble?" she asked and eyed him with a half-smile, brushing a loose strand of gray hair away from her face.

Kane gave a low laugh. "Trying," he said. "How's Ezra?"

"He doesn't agree, but I think his cough is only getting worse," she said. "Got some marshmallow and ginger roots to ease it a bit."

"Well, hope it works," he said as he shoved his hands deep into the pockets of his jeans and shuffled his feet, not knowing what else to say. He knew, and she knew, that it was only a matter of time for the man. Too many years were spent in the coal mines west of the capital. Late at night, before climbing down into his bunker, Kane could hear Ezra's fits, sometimes lasting hours.

"Yes, well, you have a good evening," she said meekly and with exhaustion.

Kane gave a nod of his head, then continued down the street to Highland Avenue, one of the main thoroughfares through Oxwick. From there, he could go north across the East River Channel into Ganbury or go west across the river to Stoughbour, the heart of Columbia City. Tonight, he chose to go north. It was easy to get lost in the city, but not for Kane. He'd been wandering the streets for eleven years. He knew every corner of the city. And he was an expert at hiding.

By the time Tala emerged from the State Media building, her workday was over. Ronin would have left Command long ago, and Captain Kole would only find tedious work for her to do if she returned. No, she would go home and change, then head back out. Dressed as she was, she was sure to stand out along the docks of the East River, and it was imperative that she blended in.

Tala was relieved to come home to an empty pod, which meant she wouldn't have to dodge any questions from Mila, her podmate. Mila was also her closest friend and would undoubtedly know that she was up to something. Tala couldn't risk anyone knowing she was going back to the warehouse.

She quickly changed back into her MF uniform, this time foregoing the bulky frag jacket, then pulled her freshly styled hair into a tight ponytail. Securing her duty belt and plasma gun, she set off down Fergus Avenue to the nearest subtrain station. She kept her palm pad powered on just long enough to board the first train to Ganbury, then, as a countermeasure, quickly turned it off, removed the battery, and stowed it in the side cargo pocket of her pants.

A public passenger car would be the fastest mode of transportation for her, but the train provided more anonymity. While the public cars were autonomous without drivers, they were closely surveilled, each one outfitted with geotracking, which could be traced back to her.

Tala carefully chose a seat in the back of the half-crowded train car, and while no one seemed to pay her any attention, she kept a hardened expression on her face. She wanted people to avert their eyes, she couldn't afford for anyone to pay too close attention, because if they did, they would notice what was amiss. A partner. MF procedure dictated they work in pairs. The last thing she needed was to spark curiosity in someone and draw any unwanted attention. In addition, keeping a low profile was essential if she was going to avoid being recognized, though in uniform she looked nothing like she had during the Statement broadcast.

Tala exited at the sixth stop in Ganbury and made her way topside, where she was met by the cool fresh air of the night. With the moon as her guiding light, she briskly made her way toward the river and up to the fishing docks, careful to avoid city surveillance cameras, which, fortunately, were notoriously unreliable in this part of the city. In the distance, across the river, the cityscape of the tall high-rises of Stoughbour lit up in the darkness. She had an hour and a half before curfew and the nightly rolling blackouts would begin. But she was confident she had more than enough time to investigate and still get back to her sector with time to spare.

The cold air near the water was damp, sending a chill deep inside as she made her way north, dodging freight crews still on the clock, and eventually, the warehouse they had raided the previous night came into view. Posted notices and neon flags indicated it was an MF investigation site.

Tala ascended the concrete staircase to the entrance. With a glance around, she tugged at the heavy metal door, and it let out a loud squeal as it opened. She checked her weapon at her waist and grabbed her flashlight. Clicking it on, she stepped inside.

Apart from a small pile of busted wooden crates in a back corner, the large warehouse was only steel I-beams supporting the roof and a cold concrete floor. Without windows, it was simply a black void in an already dark night.

As she moved along the interior perimeter, a rat scurried at her feet. She gave it a hard kick and continued with her sweep, the white beam of her flashlight the only light in the room. Her back bumped into the handle of an ajar office door that had been jimmied open the previous night. She stepped with caution into the small office and scanned the room with her light. Aside from an outdated and oversized metal desk, the room was empty. She circled the desk and opened each drawer. This had already been done, and she knew she was being redundant, but she couldn't help it. Something inside her told her that something had been missed. There was more to this case than just their suspect, some drugs, and the small cache of explosives. She'd never known the Unified Rebels to deal with drugs, and it was unlikely that their sole suspect had been working alone, even if her superiors were convinced he was. UR worked in teams. They were efficient and methodical. It wasn't like them to have any amount of explosives guarded by just one person. The agents on her team may have been satisfied with the single arrest, but she was not.

With the office and warehouse once again coming up empty, disappointingly, Tala started making her way back toward the exit. The figure of a man, tall with broad shoulders, suddenly filled the open doorway. Lit from behind, his face was shadowed in the darkness. Tala's breath caught, then she heard hurried footsteps, more than one set, approaching her from behind. She tried to focus on the sound each foot made on the concrete, brisk and light, though one seemed to drag more than the others. Aside from the man in the doorway ahead of her, she was certain there were at least two others behind her, most likely three.

Her hand moved instinctively to the handle of her gun, and she swallowed hard, taking in the room around her, gauging her distance to the exit. But even if she could get to it, she knew she likely wouldn't get past the man that stood in it. He looked almost twice her size in height and breadth. She could hear heavy breathing coming from someone behind her as the strangers closed in, and an uneasy feeling settled into her bones.

"I wouldn't do that if I were you," said the man in the doorway in a deep, husky voice as he nodded toward her gun.

Tala continued with slow, cautioned steps, her heart pounding rapidly, the hair on her arms standing on end, her hand still firmly on the handle of her plasma gun.

"You're going to want to let me pass. I'm Militia Forces. There will be consequences if you hurt me," she said, keeping her voice steady.

Sudden laughter erupted behind her. All men. Tala felt her chest tighten.

Less than ten feet to the exit, she came to a stop, her hand dropping from the handle of the gun. She could feel the presence of the men behind her and carefully turned her head from side to side, making out the figures of two of them. Both were larger than her but not quite as much as the man still standing in the doorway.

"What's an MF doing out here, by herself?" the man before her asked, and the others let out low, throaty chuckles.

In their brief moment of distraction, Tala thrust her elbow into the chest of the man to her back right, then turned quickly on the ball of her foot and leveled a kick across the jaw of the man to her back left.

A pair of arms wrapped around her from behind, clutching her tightly in their grasp. She sucked in a deep breath, bracing herself, then threw her head backward. She heard the break of a nose as the man yelled out, and she slipped out of his grip.

Tala charged at the man in the doorway, pushing him backward, out the door and onto the landing. He punched her hard, and instant pain spread across her cheek and behind her eye. She grabbed her gun from its holster and slammed the butt into the side of his head.

For a second time, a pair of arms came from behind and wrapped firmly around her body, knocking her gun from her grip. She watched it fall the fifteen or so feet from the platform to the ground below. She bucked and thrashed wildly, but the arms that held her were strong, and they did not falter. Reaching her hands behind her, she grabbed fistfuls of hair and tugged hard.

One of the men emerged from the warehouse, blood streaming from his nose, and he clasped his hand on Tala's jaw, squeezing her face as he turned her head, forcing her to look him in the eye. His look was dark and cold, his face screwed up with rage.

"Bitch," he spat.

She grunted as the arms around her tightened, and the fourth attacker appeared from out of the warehouse.

"You have no business snooping around here," sneered the largest of them, a bloody gash on the side of his head from her pistol-whip.

In one moment, it was just the five of them standing on the landing at the top of the stairs, Tala and four men she didn't stand a chance against. And then suddenly, without knowing how, a sixth person appeared and plunged his fist into the face of the man who had Tala in his grip.

His hold released, and she lunged at the largest man for a second time, her fist finding his pudgy face. He punched her in the rib cage, pain shooting through her chest, but she managed a second punch, knocking him off balance. As he stumbled backward, he reached for Tala, grabbing a fist full of her jacket, and together they crashed down the stairs, Tala's head slamming hard into the concrete.

Landing in an intertwined heap on the pavement below, pain burst through her body. Looking down, she saw the unnatural angle of her leg below her knee. She winced as she slid her leg across the gravel, separating herself from her attacker.

She coughed, an acrid metallic taste in her mouth as she spit blood. Her head was pounding, and a warm trickle of blood slid down the side of her face. Her attacker rose from the ground and grabbed Tala by the hair. He punched her once across the cheek, and more pain surged through her. Her surroundings were growing fuzzy. In the distance, she could hear a man crying out, but unable to orient herself, she was unsure where it was coming from. Tala coughed again as the man crawled over her, pinning her to the ground. With her good leg, she jerked her knee up, meeting him in the groin, and he fell to her side, grunting loudly.

Breathing hard, Tala forced herself to her knees, the pain in her broken leg spreading like hot fire as she crawled toward her gun lying in loose gravel, tangled up in weeds that had sprouted from cracks in the pavement.

Two hands clasped firmly around Tala's throat, jerking her backward, her fingers only inches from her plasma gun. The grip tightened around her neck, and her body began convulsing as her breath restricted. She clawed, to no avail, at the hands clutched around her neck, black spots forming in her peripheral. Desperate to take a breath, she slapped behind her at the man's face, but he only squeezed harder. Tala reached again for her gun, stretching her body as far as she could, her strength dwindling. The tips of her fingers brushed the butt as the man tried to pull her back. She told herself to fight; this couldn't be the end. With a burst of panic and adrenaline, she reached again, her arm extending as far as it would possibly go, feeling as though it would tear from the socket. Her hand finally clasped around the cold butt of the gun. Tala felt herself growing faint, the world around her dimming into a blackened tunnel. She bit hard at the inside of her cheek to ground herself. With a surge of the last of her strength, she turned the gun and fired it over her shoulder.

The grip around her neck instantly slackened, and she gasped for air that burned as it filled her lungs. The world was slipping away from her. Tala collapsed onto her back as the shape of a man, shadowed in the darkness, approached her. Feeling faint, her body growing weaker, she felt her gun drop from her grasp, her fight fading away. She tried to blink away the darkness as it closed in, but it was heavy, and a moment later, the blurry shape of the man was all that was left in her head. Perilous to stop it, her mind fell away, the darkness swallowing her, leaving her limp body in its wake.

TWO

From somewhere in the distance, Tala could hear her name called out. She felt heavy and exhausted, and her body was riddled with pain. In her ears, she could hear the wheezing of her labored breathing.

She heard her name again, echoing in her head.

"Open your eyes," a deep and unfamiliar voice called to her. "Tala," it repeated.

Tala felt something warm brush along her cheek and slowly, everything began to come back to her. The warehouse, her four attackers, the fight. She was suddenly aware of the cool air on her skin, the hard pavement beneath her, the smell of the river lingering on the breeze, and the faint sound of lapping water.

Taking a deep breath, she opened her eyes. For a moment, the world around her was foggy, and she blinked to bring her vision into focus. She saw the river, a barge floating by, and the partially lit cityscape across the water.

Something beside her moved, and she turned her head to see a man on his knees beside her. A look of relief seemed to come over him when their eyes met.

"Are you okay?" he asked with genuine concern.

Tala stared blankly at the stranger. The light from a nearby lamp post washed warmly over his brown skin and reflected off his shaven head. He was in jeans and a heavy leather jacket. His dark eyes stared back at her.

Tala tensed and shifted away from him. Instant pain soared through her, and she let out an agonizing cry.

"You're hurt. Badly," he said as he rubbed his thumb across the scruff on his chin. "I'd say a broken cheekbone, maybe fractured ribs, your leg is dislocated at the knee, possibly a concussion by the looks of that gash on your head." His eyes moved down her body. "And your neck is already starting to bruise."

Even the small nod she gave him jarred her body, and she willed herself to breathe steadily until the sharp edges of the pain subsided. Who was this man?

"Okay," he said with an audible sigh. "You can't go anywhere in this condition. Not without an ambulance, which isn't advisable. I have the feeling you're not here on official business. Or you wouldn't be alone." He shook his head. "I'm going to do something. I can help you, but you need to stay calm."

Tala's pulse quickened, and her eyes flared. "Wha… what?" she stammered.

"I'm not going to hurt you. I promise," he said in a deep, husky voice, his eyes not leaving hers.

Tala's breath hitched. She didn't know him, didn't know what was about to happen, yet there was something reassuring in his eyes as he looked down at her.

He could've simply killed her or left her, and since he hadn't done either, maybe he really was able to somehow help her. Though how, she didn't know. She was fully at his mercy, and she swallowed back her rising panic.

"I promise," he said softly.

Out of options, Tala gave a small nod with apprehension and fear. He was right, an ambulance wasn't an option. There was no one to call. "O… okay," she whispered, her words almost inaudible, her voice hoarse, and her throat sore.

He took a deep breath as he placed his hands gently on her face, his hand large enough to cover half of it. She winced at his touch and squeezed her eyes shut. Her cheek began to grow warm beneath his hand. It quickly grew hot, and then hotter yet, and then finally, she felt the pain begin to subside. As the heat in her cheek, along her hairline and into her temple intensified, the pain was becoming a mere distant memory. Unsure of what was happening, and her heart thumping wildly in her chest, she willed herself to lay as still as she could until finally, there was no more pain in her face, and he pulled his hands away.

Tala's eyes fluttered open, and slowly, she brought her hands to her cheek. In disbelief, she found there was no lingering pain. None at all. She touched her face repeatedly, bracing for a spot tender to her touch.

"What did you…" she exclaimed hoarsely as she looked up at him. Her chest tightened, and she swallowed hard, which only hurt her throat. What had just happened?

He said nothing, but there was a curl at the corner of his mouth.

"How'd you do that?" she asked, her voice cracking, her head racing in confusion. "Did you just…" She couldn't bring herself to even say the words they were so preposterous. And yet…

"I'm going to put my hands around your neck now," he said calmly. "I promise not to hurt you," he assured her once again.

Tala sucked in a breath of cold air and shut her eyes. She flinched as he put his hands on her throat, his fingers warm to the touch. Fear rose up like bile. Her neck began to grow warm under his touch, then hotter and hotter with each passing second. Like it had with her face, the pain began to suddenly recede.

When he removed his hands, she opened her eyes and looked up at him with bewilderment and uncertainty. She glanced around, her eyes catching his as she tried to push everything into the internal hard drive of her mind. But it was too much to process. As if the information and her brain were incompatible, unable to be reconciled. She brought her hands to her neck, and to her amazement, there was no pain.

"What's going on?" she asked, the rasp of her voice dissipating, though she could hear the traces of fear when she spoke. Her pulse thumped in her temple and fingertips.

"I can keep going if you want," he said, gazing down at her, his dark eyes piercing through her.

How was this happening? Who was this man? Maybe she hit her head harder than she thought.

"I think so," she said with apprehension, her voice thick and swollen. She did want him to continue, right?

He tilted his head. "I'm sorry to ask, but can you lift your shirt so I can do your ribs?" he asked timidly as he awkwardly readjusted his body. "I… I," he said, stumbling over his words. "It's harder through clothing."

Tala stared blankly at him for a moment. Feeling unsure of everything, she unzipped her jacket, then tugged at the hem of her shirt. If only she'd worn her frag jacket. Pain spread through her with every move she made, and she let out an involuntary groan. Carefully, she pulled the fabric higher, exposing her stomach, then her rib cage. The air was cold on her skin, sending goosebumps down her body. He kept his gaze averted, and once she reached the middle of her torso, he didn't push her to go any higher.

Tala winced in pain from even the smallest movement but fought the urge to cry out. Instead, she focused on her breathing.

Apprehensively, the man placed his hands over her ribs. The pain at his touch was excruciating, and she grunted loudly, her fists balled at her sides.

After the pain in her ribs was gone, he gently pulled her shirt back down, covering her stomach, and Tala, not realizing she had been holding her breath, exhaled.

"You still doing okay?" he asked.

"By okay, do you mean completely freaked out because I have no idea of who you are and what the hell is going on? Then, yeah, I'm doing okay," she said with a nervous and hurried breath.

He let out a low laugh. "I thought I told you not to do that."

"I'm trying. Really, I am," she said.

"Your leg is going to be the hardest. And I'll have to lift your pant leg, which is going to hurt," he said bluntly.

She looked down at her leg, the unnatural angle it was bent at below her knee, then shook her head. "No, you won't be able to." Now that there was no longer any pain in her chest, she was able to sit up. Tala reached for the side of her duty belt and pulled a knife from its sheathe. With a brief hesitation, she handed it to him. "You'll have to cut it," she said as she motioned toward her pants.

The man took the knife and carefully sliced the cuff of the pant leg, and with a swift motion, he tore the heavy fabric up to her thigh with ease. He set the knife on the asphalt and slowly pried the fabric away from her skin. Gentle with every move he made.

All the muscles in her body constricted as Tala braced herself for his touch, and she still groaned loudly through gnashed teeth as he snapped her leg back into its joint.

She screamed in pain. "How do you know you're even doing it right?" she asked through shallow, rapid breaths.

"That's why your leg is the hardest," he replied. "I pop it back into place and hope the rest will be enough."

"How can you even do this?" Her fear was waning, though her incredulity was rapidly increasing. Her mind was desperate for understanding.

He hesitated before looking up at her. "I just can," he said. Tala knew that was all he was going to give her.

This time, she didn't close her eyes but instead watched as his face grew hard and serious, fixing his gaze on his hands as they pressed down around her knee. She suppressed a scream. The heat began to grow warmer and warmer, a tingling sensation spreading through her knee, from her thigh to her ankle. Tala's breath shook as she watched, but he didn't break his focus.

The pain was intense, bringing tears to her eyes. Then suddenly it began to recede. He closed his eyes for a moment, his body bent over hers, and when he opened them, he seemed even more focused.

Tala's leg grew hotter, the tingling deepening into her bones. His hands quivered as he pressed his palms harder against her, his fingers curling around her knee. And then he pulled away and all at once, the heat dissipated, and the pain was gone. He took a heavy breath as he looked at her, and she saw small beads of sweat dotting his brow. With a single nod, he backed away, giving her space, then reached down to offer his hand while she tried to stand.

Tala took it in hers, still warm to the touch, and he pulled her up with a swift tug that she was not expecting. She took a wavering and uncertain step, then steadied herself. She waited for the pain, but it did not come. She moved her body, pressed her fingers to her throat and face, took steps, shifted her weight in different directions, and inhaled deeply. To her astonishment, there was no pain.

Her mind searched its deepest recesses for a word, something to say to him, but not even one seemed substantial. There simply were no words. Tala turned to him, unsure if she should thank him or fear him. "Who are you?" she finally asked.

He was silent, and Tala felt herself staring at him in shock, disbelief, and even wonder. Then from the corner of her eye, she spotted the lifeless body of the man she had fought, a gaping wound in his shoulder and up into his neck where she had shot him with her plasma gun. Tala spun on her heels and found the other three attackers lying at the bottom of the staircase, all of them dead. She turned back to the stranger.

"Did you do that?" she asked. The details of the attack were fragmented in her memory. She remembered how he seemed to have come from nowhere. One minute he wasn't there, then somehow, he suddenly had been. "How did you… why?" she asked. A flicker of light in the distance caught her attention, drawing her eyes away from him to a darkened sector of the city across the river.

"Oh no," she gasped. "What time is it?" Tala scrambled to find her palm pad, still tucked safely in her pocket, miraculously unharmed. But it was still in two pieces, the battery removed, and she didn't dare power it on. Judging by the darkened sector, she guessed it had to be at least one in the morning. The subtrains had all stopped at midnight, at curfew, and she was miles away from her pod. If she left on foot now, she could maybe make it by sunrise. *Maybe.*

"Tala, I can get you home," he said.

Her head snapped in his direction. "How do you know my name?" she asked, her eyes growing wide. Her heart lurched in her chest as she took a step back and glanced around at her surroundings. She shouldn't have come. And now she had four dead bodies to explain. She looked back at the stranger. "Tell me who you are. How do you know my name?" she demanded, her voice rising. Now, despite herself, she was beginning to panic.

"A lot of people in the capital know who you are," he said calmly. "I mean it, I can get you back to your pod. And I can take care of this," he said, gesturing to the mess around them. "I'll make sure none of it can be traced back to you."

She cocked her head and stared at him, her mind spinning, dizzying her. She was uncertain of everything around her, with one exception: if it was discovered that she had played any part in this, her life would be over. She cringed as Thias's face flashed through her mind. She looked back at the stranger, who hadn't moved so much as an inch since she'd stood up.

"I know you're trying to decide if you can trust me. But if I'd wanted to hurt you, I would have. Or I could have just left you," he said. "I'm your only chance."

"And how do you plan on getting me all the way to Stoughbour? The bridges are closed. The subtrain isn't running anymore. And there are MF patrols. If we're caught, we'll both be arrested," she said.

He cracked an unexpected smile and let out a small laugh. "Trust me when I tell you that I don't want to be caught any more than you do."

Tala considered this for a moment. "Somehow, I believe that. But how are you going to get me back? What's your plan?"

His head tipped slightly to the left, a smirk still on his face. "I'm going to run," he said flatly, as if it was obvious.

"Run? That's your big plan?" she scoffed. "You fixed my leg. I can run too."

"Not like me, you can't," he said, reaching down and picking up her knife. He walked to the dead body beside them and carefully cut around the open wound from her gunshot. "We can't hide that he's been killed," he said, glancing up at her, "but we can make sure they don't know it was a plasma charge." Unlike a traditional gun with a bullet, plasma guns left behind something akin to a laceration.

Tala shifted on her feet as she watched him cut through the flesh of her attacker. Only MF agents were allowed plasma guns. It was illegal for anyone else to own them. It was illegal to own any gun. If it was discovered that he had been shot with a plasma gun, it was sure to spark a major investigation. The stranger took the flesh and tossed it into the river. Tala was surprised by his calm demeanor.

"Now, do you want me to get you home, or do you plan on camping out here for the night? And then somehow explain all of this tomorrow," he said, motioning around him. He handed back her knife, then slid her gun out from the back of his waistband. "Sorry, I couldn't take any chances," he said. "I'll get you home. Unseen." He straightened his back in confidence.

Tala hesitantly took back her gun and knife, not even having realized she hadn't had the gun on her. "I don't know why," she said, eyeing him carefully, "but I believe you."

He gave her a small smile.

"But first," she asserted, "your name. At least give me that much."

He studied her for a moment, his eyes holding her gaze. "Kane. My name's Kane. But that's all I can give you."

Tala nodded. "Thank you."

"All right then, hop on," he said, gesturing to his back.

"Are you serious?" she asked.

"Yes, I'm serious," he said as he glanced over his shoulder. "Every minute you waste here is one less you get to sleep tonight."

Tala approached him slowly.

"I'm not going to bite. Now get on," he said, a hint of impatience in his voice.

"This feels weird. You're not an animal," Tala said.

"You sure about that?" he asked as he eyed her. He let out a low laugh. "Get on."

Tala hooked her arm around his neck, and he swiftly, without effort, lifted her onto his back. "Now," he said as he spoke over his shoulder, his face near enough to hers to feel the warmth of his breath, "hold on."

Without hesitation, Kane took off in an effortless run with Tala on his back. With every step he took, he gained speed, and soon they were traveling at a pace paralleled by the subtrain. Then faster. Tala's heart pounded, and her mind raced. None of this should be possible. Yet it was happening. She never would've believed it had she not seen it with her own eyes. And even then, she was uncertain of it.

She tucked her head low behind his shoulder to shield her face from the cold and biting nighttime air. She gripped him tighter but knew his grasp was better than hers; he wasn't about to drop her. The city blurred around her as they sped through it, and she closed her eyes, an unsettled churning in her stomach.

When Kane's pace slowed, Tala perked her head up as she looked around. Her sector had gone dark, and it was difficult to get her bearings, the moon now hidden behind thick clouds.

"I'm on Alexander Avenue," she whispered as they came to a stop. It felt unsafe to make noise. MF could be anywhere. She couldn't help but notice that Kane's body seemed unaffected by his intense exertion. He wasn't short of breath or perspiring.

"Ironic… Tala *Alexander*," he whispered back. "It's two blocks that way."

"I can walk," she said as she slid down his back. Her feet back on solid ground, she shifted awkwardly as he turned toward her.

"You okay?" he asked. She could barely make out his features in the dark.

"I just… we shared a fairly intimate experience with me on your back, and well, I just met you," she said with a quiet, nervous laugh that surprised her. "I've not been known to just hop on anyone's back," she said. She gave him a small smile.

Kane smiled back. "Come on. Let's get you home," he said as he headed down the street.

"Is it even worth it to ask about your, er, skills?" she asked, jogging to catch up to him.

He shook his head. "Nope."

Tala nodded expectedly.

They rounded the corner, and Tala's building came into view. Tall, over a hundred stories, known as a vertical village, housing thousands while also being environmentally sustainable. After the Great War, infrastructure was destroyed in many parts of what was now Columbia City, and many of the original buildings had crumbled or burned to complete decimation. People, in desperation, turned to the select few who stood up and declared they would rebuild what had been lost. Tala's grandfather was one of those people.

Due to the lack of fuel and water resources, creative and innovative architecture was necessary. It was through this need that the vertical villages, now built all around the city, were developed. These villages were also designed with aesthetics in mind: white, rectangular segments, each ten stories, were built and stacked on each other and interlocking, pivoting out from one another in a wide expanse, building layers upon layers.

Each village was erected with water efficiency, daylighting, and eco-power in mind. Roofs and walls incorporated living material to help with insulation, climate control, and retention of storm run-off. Photovoltaic technology was integrated into exterior building panels and windows to collect and generate solar power. And each pod's external balconies were suspended botanical oases in condensed form.

"Well," Kane said, "back, safe and sound, with time to spare before sunrise."

Tala's eyes narrowed as she studied him. Her mind was boggled with confusion, gratitude, and still a little fear. Although she was fairly confident he wouldn't hurt her.

"What about—"

"Surveillance?" he asked, as though reading her thoughts. "My friend will take care of that," he said with a shrug.

Despite herself, and maybe naively hopeful, she believed him. "Thank you," she whispered. Her eyes lingered on him for a moment before he gave her a nod, turned, then walked away, leaving her alone in the complete darkness. He rounded a corner and quickly disappeared.

Confounded, Tala made her way up to her pod. It would be morning in only a few short hours.

Kane tried to slip into Max's pod as quietly as he could. But the hinges of the front door squeaked, and Max, a light sleeper already, was on the couch and woke as soon as Kane opened it.

"Where the hell have you been?" he asked in a half-wakened fury.

"It doesn't matter," Kane said dismissively. "Is there still water in the tank?" he asked as he glanced at the dried blood on his hands from cutting around the plasma wound.

"It refilled at midnight," Max said curtly as he fumbled for his glasses. "Just like always. Now, tell me where you've been."

Kane sighed, knowing he'd have to tell him. It was Max who he needed to hack the city surveillance. "I was with Tala," he said flatly.

"Oh, please don't say Alexander," Max pleaded.

"She needed help."

"Help? Help? What in the world would Tala Alexander need help from you with?" Max asked in exasperation, his mouth agape.

"And since we're on the topic, I need you to manipulate some surveillance footage," Kane said, shifting on his feet, bracing himself for instant backlash.

"Oh, this just gets better and better." Max sighed.

"The docks along the East River."

"I'm going to get an ulcer," Max said and took a seat at his desk, which was completely interactive, with a computer screen built into its surface. Having experience with this already, it took him only minutes to hack into the city's surveillance, and with a few drags of his finger, a 3-D image from the cameras near the docks rose from the surface of the desk into the air, as if it were something he could reach out and grab hold of. Max played the scene from one of only two cameras to catch anything, engrossed by the footage of the fight.

"I have to say, she held her own quite well for a bit there, considering she was up against four men," Max said generously, still watching the footage, now from the second camera, which showed a better angle of Kane's fight on the entrance platform. "You had to kill them?" he gasped as he looked up at Kane.

"What was I supposed to do? I don't think they were in any mood for a rational conversation," Kane said defensively. "They would've killed her."

Max sighed. "I can see that. But did you have to snap their necks like that? And then toss them over the railing, off that landing like they're dead rats or something? This is the kind of thing that attracts suspicion, drawing unwanted attention. Normal people can't do that."

Kane gave a guilty shrug. "How else should I have done it? It was quick. And I tossed them aside because they were rats. It's not like anyone can trace it back to me."

Max rewound the footage, making a digital copy of an earlier timestamp, then spliced it over the actual footage. With a few smaller manipulations, he moved on to the footage from the second camera, repeating the same process.

"You really make that look too easy," Kane said as he stood above him, watching closely.

"That's because after nine years with you, I've gotten good at this," he said as he rolled his eyes. "Anything else I need to review?"

"Maybe outside her pod. I don't think we were seen on anything, it was too dark, but I'd rather be safe than sorry," Kane said. "Corner of Alexander and Fergus."

Max pulled up the location, scanned the images, and when they were both satisfied there was nothing to see, he reduced the image back to the desk surface and put the computer to sleep. "Now," he said with heavy irritation,

"I am going back to sleep. In my actual bed, since I have an actual job that I need to get up for and be at in only a few hours. It's how I support the two of us. Remember? Unless, of course, there is anything else I can do for his Highness."

"Does it help if I say I'm sorry?" Kane asked, trying to hide the smirk on the corner of his mouth.

"No," Max said flatly as he stood up, passed Kane without so much as a glance, and made his way down the hall.

Kane sighed as he watched him disappear around the corner. He washed his hands, scrubbing hard at the dried blood, then he opened the hidden hatch in the floor, which accessed an old fallout shelter from the war, and climbed down to his bedroom. He paced the room for a minute, his mind racing and full of Tala, beautiful, smart, and strong Tala. His head was beginning to throb from the physical exertion of healing her and then blurring them through the city.

In the stillness of his room, the reality of everything he'd done came back to him, and it started to weigh on him. Worry beginning to gnaw at him from somewhere deep inside. He'd been reckless, and in that moment, he couldn't understand what had implored him to reveal to her the things he could do. It was a risk that he knew would cost him his life if the wrong person discovered him.

But he couldn't stop himself, and she didn't feel like a threat. Though he didn't quite know why.

Lying in bed, images of Tala played through his mind. But not images from tonight. No, these were images of a younger Tala, groggy and in a half-sleeping stupor while smoke billowed into her bedroom, flames burning at the threshold. She looked so small, curled tightly in her blankets, her blond hair splayed across her pillow. All that had gone through his mind that night was the same that had gone through his mind on this night: she needed his help.

❖

Tala woke to a loud beeping. Groggy, she took a moment to find its source. Her palm pad buzzed wildly on her nightstand, and lazily, she reached out for it, fumbling it in her hand. Prying her eyes open, squinting in the bright sunlight that streamed into her bedroom, she saw that it was Ronin calling. She answered, his face filling the screen.

"Are you still in bed?" he gasped at the sight of her.

"What?" she moaned.

"Tala. Wake up! You're late."

Tala shot upright. Late? She glanced at the time. It was nearly nine. She was supposed to report by 7:30.

"Damn it," she muttered. "Okay, give me ten minutes, and I'll be on my way."

"You've got five. Come to Ganbury. The warehouse," he said.

Tala felt her chest tighten. "Why the warehouse?" she asked in feigned surprise.

"There was a murder last night. The team is down here. Captain Kole too. You need to get here and fast. I'll cover for you the best I can," he said.

She nodded, then hung up, the screen going instantly black.

She flipped the covers off and rushed to her closet, throwing on a clean uniform, then pulled her hair back into a smooth ponytail. She moved to the mirror, checking her neck and face for bruising. She lingered before her reflection, the previous night suddenly washing over her like a wave full of shock and disbelief. For a moment, she struggled to catch her breath, her mind spinning, searching once again for an explanation.

How?

It felt like a dream; none of it could have been real. Yet she knew it was, her memory conjuring the events like a reel playing a movie in her mind.

Slowly, she turned her head from side to side, letting the sunlight fall over her, and pressed her hands to the places her injuries had been. Not even tender to the touch.

She sighed with relief to find there was no indication of her trauma from the attack. Closing her eyes, she forced her mind to come back to her, back to the present. She had a new task to focus on: making sure she wasn't discovered.

Hustling from her bedroom as she secured her duty belt, she found Mila sitting at the counter in the kitchen, toast in hand, a steaming cup of coffee beside her.

"I didn't realize you were here," Mila said in surprise at the sight of her, a mass of bedhead gathered into a messy knot at the nape of her neck.

"I completely overslept," Tala said as she rushed to the cabinet near the refrigerator and grabbed a small, white bottle.

"No time for coffee?" Mila asked.

Tala shook her head. "Looks like it's a Vitality pill for me this morning." Tala didn't like to take them. They were filled with supplements meant for stimulation that would last for hours, but they tended to make her shaky. Today, she was going to have to tolerate it. Most people lived on the pills rather than coffee, which was an expensive commodity. She popped the pill, swallowing it down without water, double-checked her gun, grabbed her palm pad, then rushed out the door. "See ya!" she yelled over her shoulder just before the door slammed behind her.

It was a cloudless day, the sun warmer than it had been in days, and Tala hustled from the subtrain platform in Ganbury, the very one she had been at less than twelve hours earlier. As she made her way along the river, up to the docks, she realized her mistake, knowing she should've hailed a public passenger car. Though it was too late now.

As the warehouse came into view, she felt panic rising in her chest, her hands becoming clammy. It was going to be her moment of truth. Would they know that it had been her who made the mess? Had Kane, a stranger who had no business helping her in the first place, been true to his word and covered up the surveillance?

"You're late, Agent," Kole said sternly with both irritation and anger laced in his voice, and he folded his arms across his chest.

"I'm sorry, Captain. I have no excuse," she said, knowing that it wasn't worth it to explain.

"Ashby!" Kole called to Ronin. "Update Agent Alexander on this situation."

Ronin jogged over to them. "Glad you could make it," he said, eying Tala carefully.

"So, what's going on?" she asked, keeping her voice even. Ronin knew her well, and he'd been trained in interrogation, in how to look for the smallest of tells in someone. Deceiving him would not be easy. Her hands trembled, and she hoped it was only from the Vitality pill that was kicking in.

"We've got four dead bodies," he said.

"I don't understand," she said, her heart racing as he continued to eye her. She felt the color drain from her face and looked away.

"Civilian called it in this morning," Kole said.

"Three of them have broken necks. Looks like they were snapped cleanly and swiftly. Whoever did this was strong. Knew what they were doing," Ronin said. She could still feel his eyes on her, and it was making her increasingly nervous.

"And the fourth?" she asked, steeling herself and meeting his gaze.

"That one is a little more baffling. There's a fatal wound near the heart and up to the neck," he said.

"What kind of wound? Bullet? Knife?" she asked with a cocked brow, her eyes flitting to her captain. He was easier to look at in the moment.

"We suspect a knife. But this isn't a typical stabbing. His flesh was cut out of him," Kole said.

"Well, well, if it isn't the princess of the Republic," Agent Bishop said as he approached, and Tala cringed at the sight of him. "Nice National Statement last night. I was almost reminded you were a woman," he sneered, lifting his chin. "So nice of you to finally join us."

"That's enough," Kole snapped.

"Agent Kassis and I are thinking the fourth one was shot," Bishop said, referring to his partner. "And that's what was cut out of him." Bishop straightened his back as he looked at their captain.

"Find any shell casings?" Tala asked, trying to shift her mind into detective mode.

"No. No shell casings," Bishop said with a glaring look.

"What makes you think it was a gunshot?" Ronin asked.

"That would be part of the mystery, now wouldn't it?" Bishop said. "But my guess, to hide something. It's no ordinary stabbing. Something was intentionally cut out of this man. Nobody loses chunks of flesh otherwise. There was something there that someone didn't want us to find."

"Ink," Tala offered, knowing quite well there was no ink there, but she had to steer things in a different direction. "Or maybe he had some kind of marking that would've been identifiable."

Kole and the other agents were silent for a moment.

"I'd say it's a theory worth considering," Ronin finally said.

"I want this perimeter sealed off, and every square inch of the area searched," demanded Kole. "I want these guys IDed. They were here for a reason, and I want to know why. They were looking for something or hiding something. I want to know what. And I want to know who else was here to do this kind of damage. We're likely looking for a team. Bishop, Kassis, one of you contact Command and have them pull surveillance from last night. Everything in a four-block radius of this warehouse."

"Got it, Captain," Kassis said as he pulled out his palm pad.

Tala felt heat rush to her cheeks. Her heart pounded, and her palms began to sweat. She knew she had blindly trusted a complete stranger, and her head swarmed with nervous uncertainty. She clasped her hands together to keep them from shaking.

"You two," Kole said with a nod to her and Ronin, "time to stop standing around." He gave them each a once-over, then turned to walk away.

Tala started toward the warehouse, Ronin coming up behind her.

"You going to tell me what's up?" he asked, keeping up with her hurried pace.

"Not sure what you mean," she said with a shrug.

"Come on, Tal. You overslept. And something's off with you now. I can tell by your voice. You've barely even looked at me since you got here. No one knows you better than I do."

"It's just the Vitality pill I took this morning. You know how they make me feel," she said. "But I didn't have time for coffee. I didn't sleep well last night. It happens to all of us at some point or another."

She felt Ronin's eyes on her, studying her, but she focused her attention ahead.

"Fine," he said. "But if something's up, you can talk to me."

"If something comes up, I'll be sure to let you know," she said with an edge in her voice.

Tala approached the three dead bodies at the bottom of the stairs, now laid out beside each other and covered by a plastic sheet. She lifted the corner. Their necks were undoubtedly snapped, each turned at an awkward angle, each with a protruding bone on one side, though not breaking the skin. She tried to picture Kane doing this. She knew he'd had no trouble single-handedly taking on the three of them. Despite herself, her mind wandered back to Kane, and her hand went instinctively to her throat. The sense of an impending wave of conflicting emotions came over her, and she swallowed hard to suppress it.

"Too bad they're dead," Bishop said as he approached from behind. "Could've had yourself a boyfriend."

"And yet he's still a better option than you," she said, rolling her eyes. He was maddening. If there was someone who could get to her, it was him. Always Bishop.

He huffed. "Don't know what you're looking for. It's obvious. They're Unified Rebels."

"I'm inclined to agree," Ronin said. "Our suspect from the raid is a Rebel, it makes sense that these guys would be too."

"Actually, we don't know that he was. We didn't even get to intake before the case was taken from us," she said, her voice clipped. "They're just telling us he's a Rebel."

"Tala…" Ronin said quietly, cautiously.

Ignoring him, Tala knelt and lifted the sleeve of one of the bodies. It was bare skin. She reached for the other. Bare skin. She checked his neck, torso, legs, then rolled him over to check his back. All clean.

She pulled back more of the plastic and checked the other two bodies. They were both clean as well. "No ink," she said flatly, as if it was obvious. "Blows your theory out of the water. The Rebels are always inked. It's their mark."

Bishop furrowed his brow. "Okay, so what's your big idea then?"

"I need more information. A true detective doesn't jump to conclusions on a whim just because he doesn't want to do the investigative work," she said as she draped the sheet back over the bodies and turned to take the stairs to the warehouse door, striding coolly past Bishop.

Tala stepped into the warehouse where a draft sent a small chill over her after having been in the warm sun. Like she had the night before, she walked the perimeter, using her flashlight to light the darkened space.

She made her way to the broken pile of wooden crates and one by one, tossed them aside. Reaching the bottom and finding nothing, she kicked a few scraps in frustration, then headed for the exit.

Back in the sunshine, she took a deep breath. Standing on the platform sent memories of the night before racing through her mind, the images flashing at her like a bad dream. Shaking her thoughts away, she made her way back to the ground below.

"There's nothing in there," Bishop said, still standing over the dead bodies. "Maybe if you'd been on time, you'd know we already searched the warehouse."

"Something has obviously been missed. These guys were here for something. Don't be so dense. Do your job," she said, turning her back to him as she walked away.

"You heard her," Ronin said with an air of amusement in his voice.

Tala made her way to the river and around the back of the warehouse, unsure of what she was looking for, hoping something, anything, would stand out to her. She knew in her gut they were missing something, but she couldn't put her finger on it. Her mind played over a dozen scenarios, and she resented Thias for not allowing her to interview her suspect. Somewhere were the answers she was looking for. There were a half dozen agents on site, and they were all missing it. But there was something. Of that, she was certain.

Her eyes wandered, scanning her surroundings closely, and she heard a quiet whistle, so hushed that she nearly missed its faint hiss. She perked up, glancing around her, and saw a brief flash of clothing and dark skin as it appeared, then disappeared just as quickly from behind an oversized fuel tank.

Without needing to see a face, she knew who it was, and her pulse quickened. He was another piece of the puzzle she couldn't put together. She gave an inconspicuous look around, and when she was sure no one was watching, she slipped behind the tank.

"What're you doing here?" she whispered to Kane. "You realize there are agents everywhere, right?"

"No one will see me," he said confidently as he waved his hand dismissively. "I've been dodging you all longer than you even know."

"I've never seen you my entire life, and now I've run into you twice in less than twelve hours. I don't understand why you're even here," she said curtly in a hurried breath. She knew she shouldn't be insolent with him. He had already helped her more than she could ever repay.

He seemed unfazed by her tone. "I was here early this morning. We didn't have much time to scope anything out last night, you know, between the intense fighting, repairing all your injuries, and the hurry to get you back home. Not to mention the surveillance I had to have tampered with," he said flatly as he ran down the list.

She exhaled loudly, her shoulders sinking as relief came over her at the mention of the surveillance. "Really, what're you doing here? Who are you?" she asked, her voice softening.

"Under the desk in that office, there's a hidden door in the floor. And I suspect it's got firearms in it," he said.

"Firearms? How do you know that?"

"I found the door when I slid the desk away because I was picking up the acrid and sour scent of the saltpeter and sulfur. Then your pals showed up, so I had to move the desk back and make an abrupt exit. If you know what I mean."

"You could smell that?" she asked skeptically. "Another special skill of yours?"

Kane cocked his head and smirked.

"Where would they come from? Why would they be there in the first place? The drugs and the explosives were just in the corner of the warehouse.

Exposed. So why have those so easy to find but hide the guns?" she asked, more rhetorically to herself as her brain played through the information. More puzzle pieces.

"You're the agent. You tell me," he said.

"Tala?" a voice called out from the distance.

"I've got to go. Thanks for the tip," she whispered. She lingered for a moment, taking him in, equally bewildered and fascinated, then emerged from behind the tank to see Ronin looking for her.

"What're you doing?" he asked, his eyes narrowing.

"What everyone else is doing," she said with a wave of her hand. "Looking for anything that would suggest what's going on here. You know, evidence? I was thinking," she said, a thought coming to her, "with the river here, maybe we won't find anything on surveillance in the area. It would be the perfect way to come and go from here without being spotted." Covering up the surveillance footage to cover her tracks, she realized, could also mean she was covering the tracks of her attackers, and she chastised herself for not thinking of it sooner. Everything about this was sloppy for her. Maybe, though, the river was a real possibility. A boat could easily have taken her attackers to the docks. But that would also mean there was someone unaccounted for. A driver. Because there certainly was no boat now.

Ronin was quiet, the look on his face telling her he was processing what she had suggested. "It's a possibility. One we should consider, anyway," he said. His eyes didn't leave her.

Tala shifted uncomfortably.

"Did you find anything back there?" he finally asked with a nod toward the fuel tank.

"No. But I'm going to look through the warehouse again," she said, hoping to draw attention away from the tank. It took everything she had not to glance over her shoulder at it. She couldn't help but wonder if Kane was still there.

"You were just in there," Ronin protested. "We all have been. There's absolutely nothing in there. Except for some old-ass desk and broken crates, it's empty. Not sure what you think you're going to conjure."

"Since when do you doubt my instincts?" she snapped. He looked taken aback, but she didn't let her gaze falter.

"Fine. You're right. Let's take another look," he said with resignation.

She nodded and made her way back to the front of the warehouse just as a black sedan was approaching the scene which could only mean one thing: Thias had arrived. Her mouth went dry, and she felt her chest tighten again as she watched Captain Kole make his way across the lot toward the car.

Tala reminded herself to focus on the job. It was the only way to keep her panic at bay. She looked away, then swiftly ascended the stairs and stepped back into the cool, dark building, losing track of how many times she had now done this. Her mind raced, searching for a plausible scenario as to why she would investigate the warehouse yet again. Ronin was already watching her with suspicion, she had to tread carefully around him. Having him so near set her on edge.

She bided her time before making her way to the office and went first to the center of the warehouse, stopping, sighing, and giving it another once-over, her flashlight roaming across the concrete floor, up the walls, and to the trusses of the ceiling.

"What're you looking for, Tal?" Ronin asked with impatience.

"I'm thinking," she said. She lingered for another moment, then set off toward the office. Inside the small, dusty room, she took another visual scan. She let her fingers trace over the cold walls as she walked the perimeter. Then her eyes moved toward the desk.

Repeating what had already been done a dozen or more times, she opened each drawer, making a thorough search of each one. Then she dropped to her knees, feeling around with her hands for something, for anything. Near its feet, she noticed small scuffs on the floor from where the desk had been moved.

"See this?" she said, running her fingers across the rough marks. She stood and gave the desk a hard push, its metal feet squealing loudly across the floor. Just as Kane had said, there was a panel in the floor.

"That was never found," Ronin said.

Squatting down, she ran her fingers over the seams of the door, then pulled her knife from her duty belt. Forcing the blade into the sides, the door loosened, and she and Ronin were able to slip their fingers under the lip just enough to lift it open. Inside was a deep, cavernous chamber. And as Kane had predicted, there were guns. Dozens and dozens of guns.

"Holy shit," Ronin gasped in disbelief.

Tala reached down, pulling out an assault rifle. She ran her hands over the cold steel. It was heavy to hold. She had only ever used a plasma gun, and this one felt foreign in her hands. She looked back down at the pile beneath her. It was a giant mix of handguns and assault rifles, all haphazardly filling the hidden chamber. She turned the gun over, looking for the serial number which had been rubbed smooth, making it untraceable.

"I'm getting Kole," Ronin said as he rose from his knees and jogged quickly out of the office.

Tala reached for a second rifle. Having never held one before, it was heavier than she imagined it would be. Plasma guns were lightweight. It was fascinating, this gun in her hands. Her fingers brushed over the scuffed serial number, possibly beginning with a 71, though she couldn't be sure.

Setting the rifle aside, she reached back into the chamber, pulling out a handgun, turning it over in her hand, the serial number of this gun also scuffed over, but faintly, less so than the rifles. She gave a quick glance around, making sure she was alone. Untucking her uniform shirt in the back, she slid the handgun into the tight waistband of her pants. She wasn't even sure what she was going to do with it. But the nagging pit in her stomach told her this gun held answers. If nobody was going to give her the chance to prove it, she would uncover the truth on her own.

Ronin returned a few minutes later with Captain Kole, Bishop and Kassis, and Thias following closely behind. As Thias stepped into the office, his eyes fell on Tala. They were cold and stern and seemed to burn into her. But she met his gaze as she stood. It was as if everyone around them disappeared, and in that moment, it was just the two of them. She didn't know what to make of his piercing stare. Cocking his head to the side, his eyes lingering for just another moment, he turned to face Kole.

"Well, Captain, it would seem your agent has made another large discovery," he said.

"Apparently impressiveness in their work runs in the family," Captain Kole said. Tala wanted to roll her eyes but knew better not to.

Thias let the corner of his mouth curl into a knowing smile as he nodded his head. "She is an Alexander," he said in a low voice, then let out a small, guttural chuckle. "Get this cleared out and cataloged," Thias ordered, then abruptly left the small, crowded office. "Agent Alexander, a word," he said while exiting.

Tala's eyes briefly met Ronin's as she passed him, and he gave her a nod of good luck.

"Looks like your work is on point again," Thias said to Tala once they were out of earshot of the others.

"Are you surprised?" she asked as she straightened her posture as not to appear small in his presence. If there was someone who could make her feel small, it was him.

He studied her for a moment. "No. No, I'm not."

"Now are you going to let me debrief the suspect I arrested?" she asked.

"No," he said, stopping, turning toward her. "It's above your security clearance." His jaw was set in a rigid line.

"But Thias, this is my job. I'm good at it, you just said so yourself. Let me see this through."

"Are you challenging me?" he asked. "I agree that you're good at what you do. I won't retract that. But I've already told you no. Don't push it. This is a situation of Unified Rebels, and I'll be the one to get to the bottom of this."

"No," she said brazenly. "It's not. These aren't Rebels. There is no ink on any of them. I looked for myself. And you know there is no Rebel without it. It's how they pledge their alliance to their cause."

Thias's icy blue eyes met hers. "I said no. End of story."

Tala sighed in defeat.

"I'll see you for dinner tonight. And that's not a request," he said, then turned on his heel and continued toward the exit.

Tala watched him leave, then slid her hand behind her, feeling the hard hilt of the gun she'd tucked in her waistband. *No,* she thought to herself, *not end of story.*

THREE

17 years earlier

Kane sat down at the table with a loud huff, his arms folded across his chest and a scowl on his face.

"Dad's only going to get mad at you if you keep complaining," Addox whispered as he leaned forward across the table. Only fourteen months older, Addox was patient and always compliant, especially where their father was concerned. The very opposite of Kane. Ismet, quick to temper, often clashed with Kane, who was frequently late for curfews, picked fights, snuck out at night, and had poor grades in school. He also had a sharp tongue, at least with his father.

But things were nothing like that with his mother. Dreya was a local schoolteacher and exercised great patience when it came to her youngest son. She saw in Kane a different need for love and understanding than in her oldest son. She was adored by many in their small fishing community. With long, curly blond locks and eyes blue like the sky, Kane thought she was the most beautiful thing in the world. And when she sang, her voice could calm him in even the wildest rages. It was with his mother that he sought solace. She grounded him.

Despite Addox's warning, Kane didn't wipe the scowl from his face even as Ismet entered the small dining room and took his seat at the head of the table.

"I better not catch any attitude from you out there tonight," he barked, his eyes glaring knowingly across the table at Kane.

Addox gave him a warning look. Kane wanted to say something. A million retorts came to mind, but he bit his tongue.

"That's what I thought," Ismet said.

"Sorry for the delay," Dreya said as she swept into the room carrying a pot of soup that she set in the middle of the table. "I cut the potatoes too large, and they took longer to soften."

"We're still okay on time," Ismet said, his voice gentler with her.

"Boiled potato stew again?" Kane whined when she ladled the dinner into his bowl. He eyed the clear broth with chunks of potato, carrot, and celery, no meat, with disdain.

"I'll not tolerate any complaining. You're lucky to have a dinner in front of you at all," Ismet said. "That boy Max down the street is lucky to have even one meal a day, trying to feed all those kids," he said, his voice booming through the room. "Besides, you need to be grateful for what your mother provides."

Kane's head dropped in shame at the idea of offending his mother. Quietly, he picked up his spoon and used it to cut through the large potato chunks, careful to get a spoonful with the floating herbs to ensure some flavor.

Both Ismet and Addox ate quickly, each taking seconds. But Kane stirred the food around more than he did anything else.

"Not hungry tonight?" Dreya asked quietly in her gentle singsong voice.

Kane looked up at her. Feeling his father's stare, he gave her a small smile, then dropped his gaze to his dinner again.

"That's all you get, boy," Ismet said as he rose from the table, his dinner dishes in hand. "It's going to be a long night and if you get hungry out there there's nothing for you," he said passing him. Addox was the next to stand, following their father into the kitchen with his empty dishes.

"Try not to sass him out there tonight," Dreya said. "Just focus on your task. I'll slip you the last of my bread that I was saving for my lunch tomorrow. You'll need it in a few hours." She offered a kind smile as she reached out and squeezed his bony shoulder.

The dinner dishes cleaned, Ismet and the boys, each layered with a thick pair of pants over their thermals and a warm flannel shirt, made their way to the front door where they slipped on heavy boots, balaclavas, jackets, and waterproof fingered gloves.

"Stay warm," Dreya said, almost pleadingly.

Kane was filled with dread. The temperature that afternoon had only been in the low teens. It was sure to drop to single digits by midnight, maybe below zero. And it was windy. It bit his face on his walk home from school that afternoon, and that had been with the sun still shining.

"Well," Dreya said once all three were dressed. She gave Kane a knowing nod to show she'd slipped the bread into his pocket, and he gave her an inconspicuous curl at the corner of his mouth. "Hope it's a good night and the whiteys are biting." She eyed Ismet, and Kane knew what it meant. Numbers had been low for months now, and his paychecks were small. Kane had even overheard a late-night conversation between his parents that their tithing to the Republic had been increased yet again. But Kane also knew they were hopeful things would turn around as it was the time of the year for the whiteys to move from the lake into the mouth of the river for spawning. For nearly a month, they would be able to fish off the pier rather than take their boats out to open waters. Boats came with expenses. And in a month or two, when the shoreline would finally freeze over, they'd be able to walk across the ice to stake out their fishing spots.

The three of them stepped outside, instantly met by the bitter cold and whipping wind. They grabbed their gear that had been sitting near the door, then set off on foot. It was roughly five blocks to Bedley Pier. Kane pulled his balaclava up to cover his mouth and tightened it around the sides of his face.

The frigid water, with big waves from the wind, sloshed up the sides of the pier. The biggest of them poured over the concrete form that stretched out into Lake Michigan, the mouth of the Hader River on its north side. A crowd had begun to gather, dozens ready to fish long into the night for the lucrative Michigan Whitefish. Kane trailed behind his father and brother toward the center of the pier, and the three of them wedged between two larger groups who each gave Ismet a friendly tip of their head in hello.

Ismet handed a baitcasting reel to Addox and the long-handled fishing net to Kane. It was the most boring job, but on this night, it would be a blessing to not have to stand at the very edge of the pier, where they would inevitably get soaked from the waves and the spray.

"Here we go," Ismet said as he dropped his jig into the dark, swelling water below, Addox following suit.

Kane adjusted his body behind the wall of fishermen that edged the pier to help block the wind, which made his eyes water. The fabric of his balaclava had frozen around his mouth from his warm breath, but he kept it covering his lips anyway.

Ismet, with brown skin and in a black coat, nearly disappeared in the darkness, becoming only a silhouette before Kane. Addox, on the other hand, who had gotten his fair coloring and freckles from their mother, stuck out in his red parka as he stood shoulder-to-shoulder with their father. Kane's color was a perfect blend of his parents, but he had gotten his deep brown, almost black, eyes and wiry, black hair from his father. When standing side-by-side, it was nearly impossible to guess the boys were brothers.

"Got one!" Ismet yelled out over the low conversation around them. "Kane! Net! Now!"

Kane fumbled the handle in his thick gloves, unable to get a good grip.

"Now!" Ismet yelled as his reel bowed with the weight of the fish. He tugged hard as the whitey fought from below the water. In one moment, it was thrashing wildly, and in the next, the line went still.

"Damn it, Kane!" Ismet hollered. "You can be such a worthless piece of shit! That was money right there that you threw away," he spat as he turned to Kane.

"I'm sorry, Dad. The gloves… they… they made it hard. I couldn't get a grip on the handle," he said, emotion rising in him as people in the crowd turned in their direction, though everyone knew of Ismet's temper.

"Well, I can fix that," he said breathily from fighting the fish. Ismet grabbed Kane's hand and ripped off the glove that covered it. In a swift motion, he tossed it over Addox's head and into the channel. He did the same with the second glove.

Kane swallowed hard as he looked up at his dad. He hated the tears in his eyes, but he refused to let his father win and quickly blinked them away.

"Now they won't be a problem, will they?" Ismet asked with a stern face as he glared down at Kane.

Kane didn't respond. Instead, he just met his father's baleful gaze.

Ismet's eyes lingered another moment, but not wanting to waste time with his jig out of the water, he quickly turned his back to Kane.

Anger heated Kane as it burned through his body. He felt his face and cheeks grow warm. In the worst way, he wanted to shove his father, just to watch him fall into the icy water and have to fight the large swells of the waves. A small moment of pleasure came over him as the image formed in his mind.

But instead, he propped the long pole of the net against his chest, still positioning himself strategically behind the wall of fishermen. He balled his hands up, tucking them neatly inside the sleeves of his coat.

When Addox's line went taut and then began to bow from the weight of his fish, Kane was ready. Ismet grabbed hold of the line for more force in the fight, and this time they were able to snag the fish into the net before it slipped away.

"It's a good one," Ismet said as he pulled it from the net, its silver body shimmering in the dim lights of the pier. "Clean hook. No lamprey markings. Well done, Addox," he said with a wide grin that Kane resented.

Someday, he thought, *I'll get away from you.* It would break his heart to leave his mother, but he knew she would understand.

Tala and the other agents filled two armored trucks as they made their way back to Stoughbour, and she was careful to keep herself pressed tightly into a corner seat. She was relieved when they made it back to Command. With the gun uncomfortably wedged in the back of her pants, she shifted awkwardly as she sat at her desk adjoined with Ronin's. She glanced up at him, finding him studying her again.

"What's up, Tal?" he asked as he rubbed his hand across the scruff on his chin. Despite his best efforts, he always wore a 5 o'clock shadow.

As Captain Kole approached, Tala straightened. "Captain!" she called eagerly.

"Yes?" he asked with impatience, stopping beside her. Tala noticed that his bushy eyebrows, heavily speckled with gray, were furrowed more often than not, and she guessed that the deep lines across his forehead were permanent after all these years. His eyes roamed the rotunda, distracted by something behind her.

"I'd like permission to make a trip to Jerez Island, to meet with my informant," she said in a hurried breath before she lost his attention. "He was my tip for the warehouse," she added quickly.

He looked at her for a moment. "Fine. Go." He gave a curt nod.

"I'd like to go alone, sir," she said and caught Ronin's surprised, and likely offended, look from the corner of her eye.

Kole glanced at Ronin, then back to Tala. "Permission granted. Ashby, you were with Agent Alexander in the office of the warehouse, I want a report from you by the end of the day. And Alexander, we're keeping today under wraps. No need to create any public hysteria or panic," he said flatly, then swiftly walked away, making his way across the room.

"What the…" Ronin looked stupefied as he rose from his chair, his arms outstretched.

"I'm sorry," she said solemnly. Her heart sank knowing her deceit. Ronin wasn't just her partner, he was her friend. But she could never explain to him what she had done. She couldn't explain it to herself. She had acted impulsively. And she wondered, who was this Tala?

The repercussions she would face if she were caught were insurmountable. She was sure that not even Thias could save her. There was no way she could drag Ronin into that.

"You're not doing anything illegal, are you, Tal?" he asked under his breath.

Tala felt her chest tighten. Sure, she was being aloof, but how could his first thought be that? How could he be so quick to doubt her loyalty? After all, it was her very loyalty that told her she had to dig deeper. It was her motivation for all the choices she made.

"Ronin," she said, unable to hide the hurt in her voice. "I'm doing my job. My informant is likely the only person with any information. It was his tip that started all of this in the first place. And he'll only talk to me. Just trust me on this. Let me do what I'm trained for."

He sighed in clear frustration, his thick waves of hair flopping to the side in a tousle and hanging over the top of his brow, which was creased tightly as a brief silence unfolded between them. "Fine. See you tomorrow," he said as he turned away, his back to her.

Tala reached her hand behind her, adjusted the gun, making sure her shirt was loose around the bulge it made, then abruptly left Command, dodging anyone who might stop her or slow her down.

Outside, the warm sun on her face, she took a breath of relief. She was treading on thin ice, surprising even herself with her rash choices. It wasn't like her to disobey orders. But her training taught her that protecting the Republic was always priority number one. It came above all else. They weren't one of the world's most powerful nations without the dedication of those who vowed to protect it. And she was doing just that, putting her country first.

But despite all her reasoning, she still couldn't shake the burdening weight of guilt lingering inside her. She could see the look of betrayal on Ronin's face if he knew. And every time she closed her eyes, she saw the look of anger on Thias's face, and it made her shudder.

Tala hailed a public car, which was something she rarely did, usually preferring the subtrain, even if it was always crammed with people and filled with a potent blend of perspiration, perfume, and other smells she couldn't quite pinpoint. But the gun was uncomfortable and digging into her skin, and she feared that the longer she was in public, the more likely it was that someone would notice something: her gait, the way she sat on the subtrain, or simply the bulge from under her shirt. She was lucky enough to get out of Command unseen. If someone on the street noticed a gun, there would be hysteria.

Tala was relieved to make it to her pod. It was mid-afternoon and Mila was still at work. Grateful to be alone, she pulled the gun out of her waistband and turned it over in her hand. It felt so different from her plasma gun.

Standing in the doorway of her bedroom, she scanned the room looking for the best place to hide the gun. Her room was minimalistic, and she had few options. She looked back down at the gun, her mind racing as she tried to connect the dots, but there were still too many unknowns. She had so many questions and virtually no answers.

Tala ran her fingers across the scuffed serial number. There would be answers in that number, but it was nearly impossible to make any of them out. Maybe 1118, or 1170?

She dropped her head in frustration. What was next? She had no plan. What had she expected to do with an illegal handgun that she had no way to trace? Her insubordination began to feel heavy as she held it in the palm of her hand.

She looked up at her bed, which was essentially an oversized, framed rectangular box. It had wide openings along the sides that contained built-in black-out blinds to be raised or lowered as needed, with a TV screen built into the foot of the bed. Synced with her palm pad, she also controlled speakers and high-efficiency lights in the headboard. The entire unit was a full-fledged multimedia center that stood in the center of her bedroom between a large window and a glass door to her balcony. All the windows of her pod were capable of alternating between transparent and opaque with simply a push of a button.

Tala gave the heavy bed a hard push, sliding it away from the wall, and slipping her hand under the headboard, she pressed on a panel, a small compartment sliding out to reveal itself. Using the hand biometric scanner, she opened it to find a second plasma gun and money she had been saving for years, a habit she learned from her mother, even though most currency was digital. Sometimes she wondered what the point of saving it was. Though this was not the time to consider it.

She dropped the handgun into the drawer and gave it one last glance before closing it, then she slid the bed back to its original place as if nothing had been moved to begin with. Until she had a better idea where to hide the gun, it would have to suffice. Although it couldn't be a long-term solution as it was a standard installation security compartment for all Militia Forces agents for backup weapons and anything else that needed to be secured. If MF were to suspect she had anything, it would be the first place they would search. The only thing to slow them down would be the biometric scanner.

With the gun now hidden, Tala left her pod and took the nearby subtrain across the East River to the security port in Oxwick, a borough at least twice the size of Stoughbour with a majority population of Standard citizens.

Tala waited less than ten minutes before catching the ferry, which was oddly vacant for a Thursday afternoon, and took a seat near the helm for the short trip to Jerez Island, a secure facility for prisoners located in the middle of the East River Channel.

Following procedure at check-in, Tala provided a thumb-scan to register herself as a visitor and turned her plasma gun over while in the prison. She was quietly led by a guard she didn't recognize to a small holding room.

Alone in the room, Tala took a seat and quietly waited for Watts to be brought to her. Watts, a Substandard repeat offender for petty theft and later the attempted robbery of a financial institution that left three people dead, willingly volunteered to be Tala's confidential informant within the prison in exchange for his family's protection from the leader of the failed robbery, who was still at large.

As the minutes ticked by, Tala was growing impatient. When the door finally opened, she was surprised to see Agent Mills, the prison warden, enter the room rather than the gangly Watts.

Mills was her superior, and Tala immediately rose to her feet. Standing erect, she gave her a salute.

"Relax, Alexander," Agent Mills said to her, motioning for her to sit.

"Not that it isn't nice to see you," Tala said to her former trainer and evaluator from the Militia Forces Academy, "but where's Watts?"

Tala knew that Agent Mills, despite ranking above her, had a high regard for her. Before coming to Jerez Island, Mills had been an MF trainer, and while at the academy, she had recognized early Tala's skills and took an interest in her training. She had insisted there were never enough women eager for military and law enforcement roles. Agent Mills encouraged her and pushed her hard, and Tala knew she was a better agent for it.

Agent Mills sighed, looking tired with dark circles under her eyes, as she took the seat across from Tala. "You won't be seeing Watts today."

Tala furrowed her brow. "Why not? It's imperative that I do."

"He was found dead in the yard late this morning," Mills said with clear regret on her face.

"What?" Tala whispered under her breath. She gave the room a sweep for security cameras.

"The room's clean." Mills waved her hand in the air. "No surveillance. No need to whisper."

"How? What happened?"

Mills pressed her mouth into a straight line.

"Look, something's going on. My case from the other night is bigger than some small cache of drugs and explosives. I'm certain something is being missed," Tala said, cautiously going out on a limb. "I'm only trying to do my job, hindered as I may be." She wasn't sure if Mills knew the case had been taken away from her, so she opted to leave that detail out. "Any information you have could go a long way. And I swear to keep your name out of it."

Mills was quiet for a few seconds, her gaze not wavering from Tala's. "He was gutted by a pipe during the morning field exercise. We have no suspects either. Seemed to find a small gap in security surveillance visibility," she said.

Tala's mouth fell open. "How? This is one of the most secure facilities in the country."

Mills sighed, distress etched across her face. "I'm more than aware of that. We weren't able to lift any prints from the pipe either. And there's more," she paused, turning briefly away. Tala saw her reticence. "Alexander," she said, looking back to Tala, "you have to keep my name out of this. I had to give a blood thumb-stamp when I signed the confidentiality agreements about this. But I agree, some things don't add up. You're a good agent, and I'm only telling you this because I'm confident in your instincts and abilities. After all, I trained you."

Tala nodded. The graveness in Mills's voice made her chest tighten with nervous anticipation. "No one will ever know where my info came from."

"The perp you arrested the other night at that warehouse near the river, he was identified as Gep Masters from Providence City, out near the western border. They're saying he's a Rebel, but I can't confirm that. His intake documentation was somehow corrupted in our system. And he's dead too."

Tala let out an inaudible gasp.

"One of my guards found him unresponsive in his cell only hours after his arrest. Medics declared him dead shortly after they arrived," she continued.

"And how'd he die?" Tala asked.

"This is where it gets messy," Mills said. "There were no signs of physical harm, and nothing came up on the autopsy and toxicology reports. Despite this, they closed the death investigation. The only time Masters left his cell was for his interrogation, which was classified level nine."

"Level nine?" Tala asked, unable to mask her surprise. It was the highest security classification level. "Why would a Rebel with this petty crime be considered such a security risk to warrant that elevation?" Tala asked, Mills's words circling in her brain as she tried to string together the new information.

"I asked myself the same question. And all surveillance was disabled because he was deemed a high-risk prisoner. They don't like to document the treatment of security risks like him," she said, brushing a wisp of gray hair off her cheek.

"Which means Thias was in the interrogation." Tala felt her pulse quicken as her mind raced. It was him who had classified the case above her security clearance in the first place, and now she couldn't help but wonder what it was that he knew.

"Masters was brought back to solo confinement after interrogation. He was alive when Director Alexander and the chancellor finished their interview."

"The chancellor? As in Vaughn Adams?" she asked, raising a brow.

Mills inclined her head and leaned in. "I'm not sure why he had any part in it. I don't think he's ever interrogated a suspect."

Tala took a sharp breath. "You think this could be some kind of coverup?"

"Don't know. But now you know everything I do. There's no reason for you to come back here again. And I don't want a single detail about what you know. Alexander, you need to tread lightly. Any whiff of insubordination and you'll find yourself in more than just hot water," Mills cautioned.

Tala nodded. "I appreciate all of this."

"Yeah, well, I just hope the risk was worth it. But now I'm recusing myself. You keep me out of this moving forward. You're on your own," she said, her mouth in a taut line. There were deep wrinkle lines in the corners of her mouth.

"Understood."

"I think this conversation is over," Mills said as she pushed away from the table and stood.

Tala felt a heavy weight pressing against her as she rose to her feet.

"One more thing," Mills said as she turned back to Tala, halfway to the door. "It's not just MF you need to keep an eye out for. If this case is connected to the Rebels, it's likely they won't want you digging around either. You best watch your back with them too."

"Got it." Tala swallowed a rising lump in her throat. What had she stumbled into?

Wandering down Alexander Avenue, Tala let herself be swallowed up by the heavy crowd, feeling safe as just another face in the mass. Her heart was heavy with uncertainty, and her head swarmed with confusion as she ran through the facts of her case, limited as they were. Her mind spun chaotically with the information she couldn't piece together. She had stepped into a web, and it was proving to be bigger than she imagined. And she was alone in her mission.

She couldn't help but think of Watts. He'd been her informant for over a year, and she wondered if she had inadvertently caused his death because of the information he'd given her. Though he had understood the risks from the beginning.

It was suddenly in that moment of distress that she thought of her mother and felt an overwhelming longing for her embrace. Missing her seemed to come in waves. With her mother, she hadn't just felt loved, she had felt cherished. But all of that changed with her death, the fire taking both of her parents. Raising her in their absence, Thias tried to instill in Tala the prodigious responsibility that came with being an Alexander. He had uncompromising expectations and exacting standards for her. He had graciously and proudly stepped into their father's role as director of Militia

Forces, despite being only twenty-one. He knew his place. But, even after all these years, she did not know hers.

Without having asked for it, Tala was tasked with representing and carrying on the honor of her family name. She had a responsibility to the ideologies of the country her family built and that she had sworn to protect.

It was with the Militia Forces where she felt most at home, most herself. But it was a difficult career path for a woman, always surrounded by men, always having to prove herself. There was enormous pressure to be twice as good at everything.

She had been created by both Thias and her family legacy. Even her position in the MF was overseen by Thias. He seemed to call the shots on nearly everything in her life. She wondered who she was without all of that. And, even more so, who was this person suddenly challenging everything?

Tala's pocket began to vibrate, her palm pad springing to life. She sighed at the interruption of her thoughts as she pulled it from her pocket to see the still image of Thias looking back at her with a subtle curl on the corner of his mouth and a penetrating stare. She ignored the video call and instead selected the audio.

"Hi," she said loudly as a truck roared past. Though her pod building was just ahead, she stepped out of the sidewalk crowd, around the corner of a building to give herself a quieter space to talk.

"Calling to remind you of dinner tonight," he said casually, friendly. No edge in his voice.

"Yeah, I'm still planning on it," she said without enthusiasm.

"Good." She could hear the pleasure in his voice. "Dress nicely."

"Are you suggesting that I usually don't?" she asked defensively. Her frustration was getting the best of her.

"No pants. And keep your hair down. Dressy. You know. We've been down this road a hundred times," he said.

"I hate when you make me do this. It's just us," she said almost pleadingly.

"Just do your big brother this favor."

"Fine." She sighed with resignation.

"Two hours. I'll send a car for you. I'm about to step into a meeting now. See you soon."

Their connection went instantly silent. She lingered briefly on the blank screen before shoving it back into her pocket.

"Well, good afternoon," Kane said, emerging from around the corner, stepping out of the crowd.

She was unable to mask her surprise at the sight of him. "What're you doing here?" she asked with more bitterness in her tone than she had intended. This man was just as baffling to her as her case. Maybe even more so.

"Did I catch you at a bad time?" he asked with slight amusement as he folded his arms across his chest and leaned up against the stone exterior of the building.

"What're you… are you stalking me? I've never seen you before, and this is now the third time since last night."

"You sure you've never seen me before?" he asked as he cocked his head and grinned, and Tala was taken aback. "No, I'm not stalking you. Okay, maybe I was waiting for you outside your building," he conceded. "But not this morning and not last night. Those were both happy accidents."

"Don't get me wrong, I'm grateful for… everything… last night, but I'd hardly call any of this a *happy accident*." She sighed, her shoulders slumping. "What do you want?" she asked.

"I want to know what happened this morning. I know you found the guns. I watched from afar as MF hauled them out," he said.

She gave a quick look around and then slipped farther behind the towering building, its heavy shadow enveloping them. "You were right," she said. "About the firearms. There were lots of them. We don't know anything about them yet," she said, her mind immediately going to the handgun hidden in her bedroom. The gun she still had no idea what to do with.

He tilted his head as he studied her. "There's more. What aren't you telling me?" he asked.

"I don't know what you mean," she said, sliding her hands into her pockets.

"Not true. Your voice got higher, you ever-so-slightly and uncomfortably shifted your body, your eyes are dilated, your breathing is heavier, and your heart rate increased," he said, cutting through her lie.

"You can pick up all of that?" she exclaimed as she took a small step backward, putting distance between them.

"And your heart rate is still increasing," he said with a growing smile. "You're not telling me everything. You're hiding something."

"I'm not sure what you are, but it puts me at a severe disadvantage," she said. "Who are you? What… how…" Her mind struggled to find the words.

Kane stood there silently, his eyes locked on hers, and it was once again clear she was going to get no answers from him.

"Fine." She exhaled and closed her eyes as she braced herself to admit what she'd done. It was one thing for her to know about it but another for someone else to. Yet here she was, going to tell someone she knew nothing about, practically as much of a stranger as those passing them on the sidewalk. "I took one," she said.

"A gun?"

She sighed. "A handgun. I slipped it into my waistband."

"And what exactly do you plan to do with it?" he asked, his brow lifting at the corner.

"The serial numbers on the weapons have been scuffed over, making them untraceable. But I think there's enough of the one I took to at least try to get a partial. Maybe. When I know where it came from, I'll have a better idea of what I'm dealing with," she said. She hoped he couldn't see through her, see how flawed her plan was. If she could even call it a plan.

Kane was quiet for a moment. "I've got a friend. A real tech guru. He'll be able to photograph it and digitally recreate the numbers. If it's at all possible, he'll be the one who can do it."

She eyed him skeptically, contemplating his proposal. Her pulse quickened. Maybe this was the break she was looking for. What option did she have? But that would mean she would be giving her one piece of evidence away, and an illegal gun no less. But it was just as illegal for Kane to possess it as it was for her.

"I'll take it and let you know what I find," he said.

"There's no way I'm giving you that gun," she said bluntly.

"You still don't trust me? I should've engendered at least some trust by now," he said, his voice deep and husky.

"Then I'm coming with you. To see your friend," she said.

"I'm not sure that's a good idea." He shook his head as he crossed his arms.

Tala tilted her head to the side. "And why not? Is he sketchy? A criminal? I can hold my own just fine. As long as he doesn't have your particular skill set," she amended.

"A criminal? No. He's the very opposite of sketchy. And of me," he said with a laugh.

"He can't be completely the opposite of sketchy, considering what we're asking him to do," she argued.

Kane sighed. "Fine, come with me. I'll meet you tonight. This spot. Nine."

"See you then," she said, her eyes meeting his. They were so dark they were nearly black, but despite the intensity in them, she didn't feel intimidated looking into them. There was something comforting in them, something almost familiar.

♦♦♦

Tala's car pulled into the drive of Thias's estate on the southern point of Stoughbour, perched perfectly overlooking the North Columbia Bay.

Thias approached the car as it came to a stop and opened the door for her. She slid across the leather and gingerly emerged from the backseat in one of the best dresses she owned: burgundy, with thin spaghetti straps and a fitted bodice. Fabric gathering at the waist led into a full skirt that tapered asymmetrically in the front to reveal a fitted tube skirt below. She searched his face for approval and felt a surge of delight with his pleased smile.

"Very nice," he said. He leaned in and gave her a brief peck on her cheek as he brushed away a long lock of hair from her shoulder.

"You don't look so bad yourself," she said as she gestured at his navy suit and smirked. Thias was rarely dressed in anything else.

"Come inside," he said as he motioned toward the footpath that led to the front door, following behind her after she passed. "I have a surprise for you."

Tala's interest was immediately piqued as she made her way up the walkway, which was lined with luscious greens and small lights to guide the way. Thias reached his arm past her for the front door, and she briefly caught his gaze before stepping into the house. The entrance of his home opened to a vast great room that showcased a sixty-foot-wide wall opposite her, made of custom electrochromic windows, like the ones she had in her bedroom, capable of alternating from transparent to opaque, that overlooked the bay with the lights of the boroughs of Walhurst and Burdale in the distance.

Thias's home was built to be both impressive and innovative. He wouldn't have it any other way. The estate, with over eight thousand square feet of living space, was rivaled only by President Royer's.

Thias's wife, Nina, was a purveyor of fine art and interior design. The open great room, with the kitchen and dining to the left and living room to the right, was clean and white, touches of light gray and dark blue displaced in the details of the art and furniture, with contrasting curved and straight lines throughout the room.

A serpentine water feature set in the floor divided the living space in the great room from the kitchen and dining, with a small bridge across it to bring the whole room together. In the dining room, a floor trough of glass edged the wall, lit with fire that splayed up the stone veneer behind it, the flames reflecting off the infused glass dining table nearby.

"Tala," a deep, smooth voice said, catching her off guard.

She turned unexpectedly to find Chancellor Vaughn Adams holding a cocktail and gazing across the room at her, a gleam in his eye at the sight of her.

Her breath caught as she tried to suppress her surprise and now better understood why Thias had insisted she dress up. He had been trying for weeks to set something up between her and Vaughn, and she'd already canceled once on him. It had been over a year since she and Keegan, a government engineer, had ended things, and Thias was eager to remedy that.

Though she felt a flare of irritation, Tala smiled kindly as Vaughn approached her. Leaning into her, he whispered, "You look stunning." She felt the warmth of his breath on her cheek.

"A drink, miss?" a small woman in gray, appearing from nowhere, asked.

"Umm, yes, please," she said, straightening herself. "Whatever Nina is drinking is fine."

The woman silently scurried away, disappearing out of sight through a discreet door off the kitchen.

"Tala," Nina said as she opened her arms in welcome. She was a tall and thin woman with jet-black hair. Draped in a deep green satin dress, she was the picture of elegance. "You look lovely," she said with a soft smile behind bold red lips.

"As do you," Tala said, embracing her in a tentative hug. They weren't an overly demonstrative family. "And where are the children?" Tala asked, though not surprised her nephew and niece weren't around.

"Oh, nanny has them in the east wing for the night. Thias," to whom she turned and looked at adoringly, "wanted just the adults for the evening."

Tala told herself to smile as she felt Vaughn's close presence. He was newly appointed to his position as chancellor, replacing the aging Fitz Lennon only six months earlier. Thias had lobbied hard for him with President Royer, though Tala didn't understand why. The two now worked closely, which is why, Tala suspected, he thought they could be a good match. Vaughn wasn't the first guy Thias had pushed at her over the years, and Tala found it infuriating, like she was a toy to be passed among the eligible men of Columbia City. But none of this, of course, was Vaughn's fault, and she reminded herself there was no reason to be rude with him.

The server reappeared with a glass filled with a golden bubbly that was sweet to the tongue when Tala sipped it.

"I hear you've been doing some impressive work," Vaughn said to Tala, his eyes meeting hers as he gave a coy grin. "I hear your name frequently these days."

She shifted on her feet. "Wow, my little name has made it all the way up to your office. I'm not sure I should be flattered or concerned," she said with a small laugh.

He let out a low chuckle. "I'd hardly say you have a little name. And they're all good things, I assure you."

"I hope everyone is hungry," Thias said, interjecting himself as he joined them with a drink in hand. "Our chef has prepared an exquisite dinner," he said, and Tala spotted Nina as she fretted about something with a kitchen staff. "Although I really have no idea what it is," he said in a hushed voice as he leaned in, like it was a secret, then let out a laugh.

Tala tucked a strand of hair behind her ear, and when she looked up, she caught Vaughn studying her, a look in his eyes she couldn't quite pinpoint, but it was enough to give her a small flutter inside.

"Yes, Tala," Thias said. "I was telling Vaughn about MF's last two big breaks, and how I can mostly attribute them to you." Tala thought she picked up an actual trace of pride in his voice.

"Why even have a team?" Vaughn laughed.

"Oh, that's enough work talk," Nina said as she approached. "Dinner is ready."

Vaughn motioned for Tala to go before him and fell in line behind her as they made their way to the dining table across the room, pristinely set with white porcelain dishes donning tiny silver flecks on the edges. Their plates, filled with roasted chicken and sautéed vegetables, steamed hot as the four of them took a seat.

Tala was quiet during dinner, satisfied to let Thias be the garrulous host of the evening. But despite her silence, she knew she wasn't going unnoticed as Vaughn's glances from across the table were frequent and lingering, and despite herself, she couldn't help but smile back. Then her mind went instantly back to her conversation with Mills earlier in the day. Vaughn, she reminded herself, knew something about Masters, and she wasn't entirely sure what to make of that knowledge. But she cautioned herself not to be hasty and jump to conclusions. After all, Mills had given her no evidence to support that he, or Thias, had anything to do with Masters's death. Watching him through dinner as he conversed with Thias and Nina, smiling at her, she couldn't help but feel there was something about his charm that was disarming, and she pushed away her thoughts.

Through her frustration with Thias, she had been quick to want to reject Vaughn, but sitting with him now, she couldn't help but think it was possible she'd been overlooking him entirely. He was tall and slender, but fit, with a refined taste that was reflected in his attire. Much like Thias, he, too, seemed to live in a suit. He was undeniably handsome, with thick dark hair and had a small dimple in his right cheek when he smiled and laughed. And by the continued looks he gave her, she was certain of his interest in her. It was the kind of match Thias had always wanted for her. It was likely the kind of match her parents would've wanted. Maybe he was even what she had imagined for herself.

"It's a nice evening," Thias said after dinner as he rose from the table, their plates having been cleared by the staff and their drinks refilled. "I'll light the fire outside, come join me."

"Oh, but it's a bit chilly," Nina protested as she grabbed her glass and followed after him.

"We can stay inside if you'd prefer," Vaughn said as he glanced at Tala. "I won't mind."

"No, it's fine," she said. She wasn't entirely comfortable to have it be just the two of them.

"After you." Vaughn motioned with his hand, letting her lead across the room.

Thias took his palm pad from his pocket, and with a few taps of his finger, the wide expanse of windows along the southern side of the home retracted, each panel folding together and disappearing into discreet pockets in the walls. No longer a separation between the patio and great room, a rush of fresh air from the bay came over them.

Thias sauntered onto the veranda, and with a few more taps of his palm pad, a fire sprang to life in a tear-shaped stone pit, then he took a seat and comfortably sipped his drink.

From Tala's seat, she could see the gardens of Thias's estate, and beyond that the ancillary residence for his security detail. The distant lights of Walhurst and Burdale twinkled in the dark from across the bay, and even though she couldn't see her in the darkness, Tala knew the statue of the green lady was standing out there on her tiny island. A remnant from another time.

"What a view," Vaughn exclaimed as he took a seat beside her. "It's amazing how close the boroughs really are," he said, motioning across the water. "We're a big city, but in numbers, not in size."

Thias nodded. "We tend to grow up, with taller and taller buildings, rather than out. We have the densest population in North America, and sixth worldwide," he said factually.

Tala felt the chill of the night wash over her, goosebumps raising across the bare skin of her arms and legs, and she gave a small shiver despite the heat radiating from the fire.

"Here," Vaughn said as he slipped out of his suit coat and draped it over her shoulders.

"Thank you," she said, her voice barely audible as she gazed up at him and pulled it tighter.

"You live in Stoughbour?" he asked as he sat beside her, then leaned close, tuning out the conversation Thias and Nina were having between the two of them.

Tala nodded. "Yes, but I'm north of here. Near the Oxwick bridge." She braced herself for an onslaught of questions about why she didn't live near the bay where the wealthiest in the city lived.

"Near the East River," he said with familiarity.

"Just a few blocks from it. You're in Stoughbour too?" she asked, though she already knew. He lived in one of the luxury residences not far from the bay. Less than a year earlier, she had been a security detail for a New Year's Eve party he hosted. It was clear he didn't recognize, or at least remember, her. When she was in uniform, she tended to just be another face. Which she liked.

"All my life. Although I did spend time on Stearns Point growing up. My family has a second home out there," he said. "It's nice that you've got your brother. My family is all over the Republic now. I'm the only one left here. They've all gone south for the warmer weather."

Tala briefly looked at her brother, a smile spreading across her face. She felt her earlier irritation with him fading. It was times like this, when they weren't in the public eye, and when Thias wasn't running security for the entire country that she felt a connection with him. Since her parents' death, when Thias took over raising her, it was these moments that she looked forward to the most. He was a busy man with a big job and a lot at stake, and she reminded herself to be gentler with him.

"Oh!" Thias exclaimed under his breath as he looked down at his buzzing palm pad. "Vaughn, we've got a situation," he said, his jovial expression quickly falling away as he rose from his seat. Adjusting his tie, he handed his drink to Nina. "I'm sorry, but we need to take care of some things," he said with urgency. He made his way toward the house, his palm pad pressed to his ear. "Grant, I need my car. I'll be out front in a minute."

Vaughn was quick to his feet, and Tala slid his suit coat off her shoulders, the cool air nipping at her skin.

"I'm sorry to do this," he said with regret as he took the jacket from her.

"Oh, I get it," she assured him.

He stepped in close to her, his shoulder pressing against her as he leaned into her ear. "Please tell me we can continue this," he said as he brushed a lock of hair off her collarbone, his fingers grazing her skin.

Tala, feeling a flicker inside, nodded. "I'd like that," she said when his gaze met hers as he retreated.

"Good." He gave her one last smile, showing off the dimple in his cheek, then turned and hastily followed Thias.

"Well, that was quite the way to end the evening," Nina said as she rose from her chair. "But I'm not all that sorry because it's chilly out here," she said with a small laugh and a shiver.

Tala nodded as she ran her hands down her arms and followed her to the kitchen, where she entered a code into a small digital pad built into the cabinet, along the edge of the counter, and the retractable windows began to close.

Once they were sealed shut, Tala could feel a discernable difference in temperature in the room and exhaled in relief as her body began to warm. She reached for her palm pad, realizing she hadn't checked it all evening, and in a moment of panic, she noted the time. It was five minutes to nine. In only a few minutes, Kane would be waiting for her halfway down the block from her pod. And she still had half of Stoughbour to cross.

"Is there anything I can help you with around here?" she asked Nina, knowing all too well there wasn't, but she felt the need to preface her exit.

"Oh no," Nina said with a dismissive wave of her hand. "That's why we have a staff."

"Then I should be going. It's been a long week," she said as she made her way toward the front door.

"Your car will still be in the driveway," Nina said. "Thias wouldn't have dismissed it. You should have no trouble getting home. No need to walk to the subtrain. I know how you are about heels," she said with a knowing chuckle as she motioned at Tala's shoes.

"Thank you," Tala called over her shoulder as she made her way down the front path, and relief washed over her when the black sedan came into view. She slid into the backseat, and the car immediately sprang to life. The dashboard lit up and the motor began to purr. After a few taps on her palm pad, selecting where she wanted the car to take her, it slowly began backing out of the driveway, and she sighed, dropping her head back against the headrest.

Minutes later, they were on the main avenue through Stoughbour, but traffic was heavy. A pit formed in Tala's stomach, and she chastised herself for losing track of the time. Vaughn had been wonderful, and it had been nice to get lost in someone for once, it had been so long, but the case was her priority. The gun was her priority. She silently hoped that Thias wasn't called away so abruptly on a matter that had any connection with her case. Or worse, any suspicions of her. She pushed the thought away.

Finally, Tala's pod came into view. When the car came to a stop, she slid out of the backseat as quickly as her dress and heels allowed, lingering only long enough to watch it drive away. Then she turned and set off in a hustle down the block.

The cold preying on her exposed skin, her heels clacking loudly on the pavement with every step, Tala felt a sigh of relief wash over her as she made out Kane's figure up ahead.

"I'm so sorry," she exclaimed breathlessly. "I completely lost track of time."

Kane eyed her carefully through the shadow of the towering building he stood beside. "You're going to get cold running around in that," he said, his arms folded across his chest.

"I know, I know, I look ridiculous. Give me two minutes. I'll run up to my pod, get the… er… thing," she said under her breath, "and then we can get on our way."

"I almost gave up on you," he said, his voice low and deep.

"Really, I'm sorry," she said and gave him a pleading look while she caught her breath.

He eyed her quizzically as together they made their way toward her pod, and as they approached the doors, he finally cracked a smile. "Go get it," he said with a wave. "I'll be here."

"Right back," she called over her shoulder, her heels clacking loudly as she hustled into her building.

♦♦♦

"Hey!" Mila said in surprised excitement when Tala stepped into their pod. "I wasn't expecting you home this early," she said, glancing at the time on her palm pad. "This is perfect. I decided to cancel on Cedric. I think I'm over him. You and I haven't had any time for just the two of us in over a week." She was burrowed under a blanket, stretched across the couch, her dark hair pulled into a loose pony.

"Actually," Tala said with regret as she scurried past her, "I'm not really back. I just have to grab a coat," she said quickly, cringing at the lie as she made her way down the hall.

"You're going back out?" Mila called after her.

"I'll be home by midnight, of course," she called back through the ajar door of her bedroom. She gave her bed a hard push away from the wall. Dropping to her knees, she retrieved the gun from the hidden compartment. Setting it on the bed, she stood up and gave the bed another shove to put it back in place.

Mila's head appeared in the doorway, and pushing the door open, she stepped into Tala's room.

Tala felt her chest tighten, the gun lying exposed on her bed, the black steel glaringly obvious on the white bedspread. She quickly sat down, using her body to shield it.

"What're you doing?" Mila asked, eyeing her with a raised brow. "I thought you were getting a coat."

"I am," Tala asserted. "It's just, my foot is sore. It's these shoes. Would you mind grabbing one from my closet?" she asked, massaging at her heel, feeling awkward with her charade.

"Umm, sure," Mila said. "Which one? You don't have anything for that dress," she said from inside the closet. "Not since the whole red wine incident. It's cold out tonight. I can't believe you're not wearing one now."

"My black one is fine," she called back as she slid the gun under her pillow.

Mila reemerged with the coat, thick woven material with an oversized zipper and large pockets near the hips.

"This is the coat you want for that dress?" Mila asked with obvious disapproval. She had far better taste than Tala, and unlike her, she loved any chance to dress up.

"Oh, it's fine. I won't be wearing it indoors anyway," she said with a wave of her hand. She thought of Kane, still waiting downstairs for her.

"Please use mine," Mila said as she tossed the coat on the bed beside Tala and abruptly left the room.

"Really, this one is just fine," Tala called out as she rose from the bed.

Mila returned a moment later with a thick white coat with a light fur lining.

"Oh, Mila, I can't wear that one," she said, knowing the money she had spent on it. Mila may be a Preferred citizen in the Republic, but she was a teacher, and her salary was far from generous. Although, much of her income went to supporting a large and varied wardrobe, with shoes and every kind of accessory to match.

"Yes, you can. If you're wearing a dress like that, you need the right kind of coat," she insisted. "Just promise me you'll cherish it."

Tala sighed. "Of course I will." She reached for Mila and pulled her into a hug.

"Okay, now get out of here," Mila said with a laugh. "I want details about him tomorrow," she called over her shoulder as she left Tala's room. She would swoon over the details of her night if she knew Tala had been with Chancellor Adams.

Hurriedly, Tala threw the coat on and slipped the gun into the inside breast pocket where it almost didn't fit. "There won't be any details," Tala said as she passed Mila, once again snuggled up on the couch. "See you," she said, then closed the door to their pod behind her. In the hallway, she exhaled in relief.

Retracing her steps, wondering why she hadn't at least changed her shoes, she made her way back outside to where Kane was patiently waiting near a tree, crispy fallen sleeves discarded at his feet.

"I'm sorry," she said as she approached. "My podmate was home. But I've got it," she said with a tap on the breast pocket of the coat.

"All right then. Let's go," he said, and together they headed back onto the street where they were instantly swallowed up by the pedestrian traffic.

Kane glanced over at Tala, a wide smile on his face.

"What?" she gasped, feeling heat in her cheeks. "I know, it's the outfit. Like I said, I look ridiculous," she said with an eye roll, glancing down at herself as she clacked along beside him, taking twice as many steps to his single stride.

"Yeah," he said with a nod, "it's the outfit. But," he averted his gaze, "I never said you look ridiculous."

FOUR

Kane and Tala emerged from the subtrain onto Wall Avenue in west Oxwick. Like everywhere in the city, the streets were busy and congested, and as they made their way down the sidewalk, he was keenly aware of her proximity to him. Despite the scores of people and the bustling city around them, he heard the rhythmic sound of her heartbeat above all the noise, finding it enormously distracting.

He knew she was nervous, picking up the small nuances as soon as she powered off her palm pad on the subtrain. Not that he blamed her. Her palm pad was her only lifeline. He would never hurt her, though she couldn't know that. But it was too risky, and she understood as well as he did why she had to turn it off.

It was dark, and the stars overhead were faint, the lights of the city polluting the sky. From five in the morning until midnight, Columbia City was alive, constantly in motion. It was always loud, the sounds of traffic, of car horns and sirens, construction, and endless chatter, all echoing off the tall buildings that lined each city block, playing it all back in magnified volume.

Traffic rushed past them, always in a hurry, yielding only for red lights, emergency vehicles, and pedestrian crossings. Together, as they strode side-by-side, they passed cafes, small markets and delis, a pawn shop, a locksmith, and a launderer. Not far ahead was Rose Park, filled with young children in the daylight hours. But they wouldn't go that far, turning down Highland Avenue before that. He'd lived in the city for over a decade, and maybe it was because his senses were always in overdrive, everything always overstimulated, but sometimes he couldn't help but want something different. Though his life had few options.

He watched as Tala pulled her coat tighter around her in the cool nighttime air. There was something about being near her that set him on edge in a way he couldn't pinpoint or explain. Distracted by her, he hadn't noticed how cold it had gotten since the sun set until he watched her give a small shiver.

Quickening their pace, he led the way, Tala and her heels clacking along beside him. "So, where were you that you're so dressed up?" he asked, trying to make conversation as he shoved his hands into the pockets of his jeans. She looked incredibly beautiful.

"I was at my brother's for dinner," she said as she followed him around a corner. "He always likes to go a little over the top."

Kane nodded. "I can see that." In his head, Thias was the biggest ass of all. He loathed him, finding him more arrogant than even President Royer, who was often difficult to read; it was the air of mystery around him that gave him his power. No one ever knew what to expect. Thias, though, was good at charming others. He knew just how to placate the Republic's citizens when he made the National Statements, which he did occasionally, mostly for security-related messages. Oddly, President Royer gave very few of them. Thias was an expert at playing on people's fears and portraying himself as the man to both impede and prevent any danger posed toward the Republic. The Great War, although many decades past, was still a lingering memory for a few, and its stories of horror and devastation were still recounted for each new generation.

In the Republic, they were taught there was no better life beyond its borders. The leaders of the Republic of Columbia spread fear by casting outside nations like DeSoto to their south and the Central Colonies to their west as lawless and wild, with high crime rates, few jobs, and low quality of life. Few people ever crossed the borders, leaving their neighbors an enigma. With little evidence to the contrary, people simply trusted what they were told. The Republic preyed on the prevailing and ubiquitous anxiety of the people to reinforce the idea that they *needed* it.

But Kane believed differently. He didn't know what lay beyond the borders, but he understood a side of the country that was never highlighted. Living as a Nameless, he saw the social injustices, the divisions in the people created by the oppressive hierarchy of the citizenship structure. He saw real struggle, the hard lives of many people with little opportunity for change. Outside the city, there were even fewer opportunities.

Thias was calculated in every move, and too many hung on his every word. Kane cringed at the thought of Tala being one of those people. But he already knew there was something that made her different. Tala would likely not see it the same way, but in defying orders and returning to the warehouse, by taking and hiding the gun, she was contesting his authority. Even if she didn't know it.

They passed a small market, Ned, a haggard-looking Nameless begging on the corner. It was his usual spot that time of day. Max was sometimes generous with him and gave him some money, but Kane doubted how much of it really went to food or shelter. The street was lined with old, nearly archaic brick buildings that, by some miracle, were still standing from before the war. The remaining bones of another city long gone, buried and rebuilt over by Columbia City.

"Your friend, what citizenship status is he?" Tala asked, interrupting his thoughts.

Kane glanced at her, her long, blond hair flowing behind her. "Does it matter?" he asked.

She shrugged. "I don't know. Maybe?"

"Max was Standard growing up. But poor as dirt. We grew up together. He excelled in school and was recruited to work tech for the government, so he was promoted. He's Preferred," he said proudly, though he had nothing to do with Max's success. "Has some money and a position for the first time in his life."

They rounded another corner, turning down Harvey Street, and Kane spotted Lora and Amelie approaching from the opposite direction, both in short skirts and small tops that showed off their belly piercings, despite the nip in the air. Amelie was a regret he liked to forget. Lora just hopelessly pined.

Their faces lit up at the sight of him, and he cringed inwardly.

"Hi, Kane," Lora said while she twirled a long lock of hair around her finger.

"It's been a while," Amelie said as she scanned him up and down. She glanced in Tala's direction and a scowl curled at the corner of her lip.

"Come to Charlie's," Amelie said, looking back to Kane, instantly dismissing Tala as if she weren't beside him.

Tala. He was suddenly aware that she could be recognized, which would undoubtedly raise questions.

"Sorry," he said. "Not tonight." He saw the look of disappointment on both their faces. Kane slipped his hand onto the small of Tala's back to hurry them past, but not quick enough to miss their glares at her.

From the corner of his eye, he saw Tala's amused smile, but he stared furtively ahead, avoiding her gaze. He could make out the giggles of Lora and Amelie long after they passed and intently listened to their retreating conversation. He was relieved they didn't seem to recognize Tala. Though they both certainly had plenty to say about her.

As Kane approached his pod, he saw Mrs. Knox outside her door, shaking out a rug, beating it against the brick wall. A plume of dirt and dust filled the air.

"Oh, good evening, Kane," she exclaimed with a beaming smile on her face as she stopped swinging the rug.

"How's Ezra? Did the ginger root help?" he asked, slowing his pace, Tala still close beside him. He wasn't as concerned about Mrs. Knox recognizing her. She was anything but a gossip.

When they stopped, Kane was overwhelmingly cognizant as Tala's arm brushed along his, sending a charge through his body.

Mrs. Knox gave a small tip of her head. "Maybe a little," she said with reservation and sadness in her eyes. "Are you a friend of Kane's?" she asked, shifting her attention to Tala.

Definitely didn't recognize her.

"Oh, umm," Tala said, clearly caught off guard. "Yeah, I guess so." She looked at him, and he was surprised by her grin.

"Well, you stay out of trouble," Mrs. Knox said with a knowing look and a shake of her finger in Kane's direction.

"We'll try," Kane said and gave her a small smile. He glanced back at Tala who was studying him carefully. "What?" he asked after Mrs. Knox disappeared into her home, the smell of fried food wafting into the alley when she opened her door.

"I'm just curious," she said with a pause. "You seem kind of popular. Do all of these people know about, well… you?" she asked quietly.

He looked at her, registering her expression, more curious than judgmental. He was surprised she didn't appear uncomfortable asking about what he knew was an absurd reality that he'd yet to give her any explanation for. He shook his head. "No one does. Well," he said, "except Max. And now you," he added as a car drove slowly past.

Her jaw gaped ever-so-slightly, and she shook her head. "I don't understand."

"The only way to contain something is to not let it out in the first place. I figure you of all people would understand that considering your line of work," he said.

"No. No, I mean, I don't understand why *me*."

He exhaled, shoving his hands into his pockets again. "What was I supposed to do? Just let you die?" he asked in a hushed voice though no one was around to hear them. He knew they were alone. Not even a car in sight.

She studied him again, and he couldn't help but notice that she always held his gaze, her eyes never wavering. He picked up no traces of fear in her when she looked at him. And that took him by surprise. She didn't know him at all. And yet she knew things about him that no one else did. She had no way to explain the things she'd seen him do, things no human should be capable of, and yet she was not afraid.

"You were willing to risk exposure because you didn't want some unknown woman to die outside a warehouse?" she asked. "You had no reason to trust me."

"Well," he said as he shifted his feet, "you have no reason to trust me, yet here we stand."

There was something about the way she looked at him that was unnerving. Not in a way that made him want to run, but rather in a way that made him want to simply be closer to her.

After a moment, she smiled. "Yes, and here we stand."

The corner of his mouth curled upward, and then he motioned just ahead. "We're here. White door," he said.

Tala followed behind him as he let himself into the pod, and he spotted Max working at his desk in the back corner of the room, who glanced up and gave a look of petulance when he saw Tala. Max adamantly did not want her in their pod. He wanted nothing to do with whatever she was doing, certain it would only mean trouble. Or worse, discovery. Max had protected and hid him for nearly a decade, and Kane knew he had every right to be wary. By putting himself at risk, he was simultaneously putting Max at risk.

"We don't bring people here. And she's not just anyone, Kane… she's Tala Alexander! You two couldn't be in more opposite places in life. She's a risk. No matter how much you think you can trust her, she's a risk," he had said earlier that day, his brows knit tightly behind his glasses.

Max was rarely a hot-head, but his anger had been seething.

But something about Tala was different. He hadn't let anyone else in in the last eleven years. He put up walls, keeping everyone at arm's length. Yet with Tala, he was voluntarily tearing down those very same walls that separated him from everyone else. And he couldn't understand why.

Tala gave the pod a sweeping look. It was dimmer than hers with smaller windows and dark, exposed red and brown brick walls. The building dated to before the war. It was bigger than hers and far more spacious. A kitchen to the left, with paneled cupboards and an oversized island that separated it from the dining room. Across the room were two large black sofas that faced an oversized TV screen mounted on the wall.

Her eyes fell on a man at a computer in the corner of the room. He looked annoyed as he stared at her. That, she thought, had to be Max.

She shifted awkwardly, knowing immediately that her presence was not welcome. But Kane was either oblivious, which she doubted, or simply didn't care, and casually led her into the pod.

"Max, meet Tala," he called across the room in his deep voice.

Max was silent as he rose from his chair and cautiously made his way toward them. He was a small man, dressed in jeans and a dark green hooded sweat-jacket, unzipped and open to a blue t-shirt that was taut around his midsection. His brown hair was wavy and shaggy, combed back, and his eyes were hidden behind thick, black framed glasses. She wasn't sure what she had expected, but he was not it. Kane hadn't been exaggerating when he told her they were complete opposites.

"Hi," she said with a warm smile, desperate to ease the tension in the room.

"For the record," he said in a slightly nasally voice, his thick brows furrowed tightly, "I don't think any of this is a good idea."

"Your opinion couldn't be more obvious than if it was written across your forehead," Kane said flatly.

"I appreciate you for doing this," Tala added.

Max sighed and lifted his hands in surrender. "Not like this guy ever gives me a choice. Do you have the gun?" he asked impatiently.

Tala nodded as she reached for it, pulling it from the breast pocket of the coat. The steel was heavy and cold in her hand, and it still felt foreign to the touch. Maybe, she thought, she should have brought her gun. Here she was, standing in a foreign pod, in a foreign part of the city, and alone with two men. One of whom she would never stand a chance against. She looked over at Kane as she considered what she knew he could do. But despite all that, something told her he would not hurt her.

She gave Max a once-over; he looked as non-threatening as a grasshopper. She handed the gun to him, and he studied it in his hand, both fear and wonder in his eyes. Without a word, he turned and retreated to his desk, Kane and Tala following him.

Max clicked on an overhead light. He nudged his glasses with his knuckle, lifting them to his forehead as he examined the gun without the lenses, rubbing his fingers over the scuffed serial number.

"So?" Tala asked after a long moment of silence.

"We'll have to see, won't we?" he said, looking up at her. "I'm good, but even I have my limits."

"What do you need?" Kane asked as he folded his arms across his broad chest.

"Time," Max said flatly. "Just time."

Tala turned toward Kane, unsure what to do next.

"Can I get you something?" he asked her, shifting awkwardly. He seemed as uncertain as she was.

"Water?"

Kane nodded and briskly headed toward the kitchen. "You can have a seat," he said, gesturing toward the living room. Tala glanced around, then headed toward a couch, taking a seat on the one along the brick wall. The pod, she noticed while she waited, lacked any personal touches. It was simple and minimalistic. And clean.

Kane brought her water and took a seat on the other couch, his back to Max.

There was silence between them, and Tala felt him avoiding her gaze. He was handsome, she thought. Very handsome, in a serious and bewildering way. He was casual, rugged, not pretty. He was undeniably attractive, and thinking about him like this made her face flush. He was tall, with caramel brown skin, and solidly built, though that seemed to be expected given the things he could do. There was definition in his arms, and she recalled his firm grip on her the previous night when he'd taken her back to her pod. His eyes were dark, nearly black. At first, they seemed hard, but when she looked into them, she saw something else, something gentle and deep. He had put up a shield, keeping everyone at bay, never telling his secret. Everyone but Max. And now, for some unknown reason, her.

"I take it this is where you live?" she finally said, interrupting the silence between them.

"What makes you think that?" he asked, looking across the vacant space between them, his eyes finding hers.

"Well, you said outside that Max is the only other person who knows the truth about you and the only person you trust, so reason would stand that he would be the person you would live with." From the corner of her eye, Tala noticed Max look up from the camera he was using to photograph the gun.

A smile curled at the corner of Kane's mouth. "Quite the observation," he said.

Tala cocked her head to the side, ever-so-slightly lifting the corner of her brow, challenging him to tell her it wasn't true. "It seems the most logical assumption."

"Yes, this is where I live," he admitted. "Over there," he said as he gestured to Tala's right.

Tala stood, unsure what she was looking for, and was surprised to see an opening in the floor, an open hatch resting against the wall. "Is that —"

"An old fallout shelter," he said. "From sometime around the war."

"So that's where you sleep?" she asked, turning toward him. "Down there?"

Kane shrugged. "Yeah. It's my own space. Max couldn't get a two-bedroom pod in the city as a single man, so this was the next best thing. It took a lot of hunting to find one that had a fallout shelter that wasn't registered with the government. At least we don't have to share a room," he said with a laugh.

"Tell me about it," Max scoffed from the corner.

"And if an emergency ever arose, I have the perfect place to hide."

Tala wanted to prod for more information. Who exactly was he hiding from? Who was he? How could he do the things he could? When it came to Kane, her mind was teeming with questions. But he seemed the kind of person who would reveal himself, as needed, in due time. And never earlier.

"Tell me something about yourself," he said.

She took a deep breath, exhaling loudly. "Like what? Everyone seems to know more about my life than I do."

"Sure, I know facts. Bullet points. I bet most people in the Republic do," he added quickly. "But tell me something that I couldn't look up."

Her mind ran through a list of possibilities. "I was close with my mom," she said after a moment. "She was my best friend really, which sounds soft, but when I lost her, I felt like I lost a piece of myself," she admitted quietly. That wasn't something she shared with many. But if she was open with him, maybe he would be open with her.

Kane was quiet as he looked at her. "I was close with my mom too," he said.

"What was she like?" she asked, surprised by his revelation. She wondered about his family. They didn't seem to be a part of his life.

"Kind. And gentle. She always gave me the benefit of the doubt, even if I didn't deserve it," Kane said, a look of remembrance across his face. "She died of cancer when I was twelve," he said as his eyes met hers. "But you know all too well what that's like. Losing a parent."

Tala gave a quiet nod of her head. "My brother raised me after my parents' death. Life with him was very different," she said, thinking back to the first few years when it was just the two of them. "My mother was rather demonstrative with me, but that couldn't be more opposite of Thias. At just twenty-one, he was propelled into leadership as my father's successor. He wanted so badly to be taken seriously that he just became stern and hardened. It's how he thought he needed to be as a new leader."

Kane didn't respond.

"He has moments when he shows a different side of himself," she said with a faint smile, though he looked unconvinced. "Sometimes, regretfully, I tolerate the stern side in hopes of glimpsing his softer side." Tala felt the room grow small as she realized she had admitted something aloud that she wasn't sure she'd ever admitted to herself. And maybe she shouldn't be sharing such personal information about her brother.

"Sorry," she said, shaking away her thoughts. "That was more than you asked for," she said, hearing the falter in her voice. "Tell me something else. Anything. Like, what's your favorite movie?" she asked, trying for a less serious topic. Tala couldn't remember the last movie she'd seen.

Kane let out a chuckle, deep and low. "You're going to laugh when I admit this. If you've even ever heard of it."

"Try me," she said.

"After my mother's death, I spent some time in a… facility, and it was the first time in my life I'd ever seen a movie. I loved it. I just watched it over and over again," he said with nostalgia.

"What was the movie?"

"It was called *The Wizard of Oz*. It's from a time before even the war," he said.

"I know the movie," she said in surprise. "My mom collected old films. I had a copy when I was a kid. I thought I was the only one. You've really seen that movie?" She couldn't help but laugh as she pictured a younger version of him watching the fantasy film.

Kane seemed to suddenly look uncomfortable as he shifted and readjusted on the couch. He glanced over his shoulder at Max who eyed him nervously.

Tala felt her joy quickly dissipate as she looked between the two of them. Something had just happened, though she didn't know what, and it was making her increasingly uneasy.

Kane turned back to her and readjusted again.

Her laugh long gone, Tala looked down, following the line of her bare legs to the points of her black shoes, unable to meet his eyes as the silence dragged on.

"Did I say something?" she finally asked, the awkward quiet growing too loud. She willed herself to meet his gaze.

His eyes were dark and steady as they looked back at her, and he shook his head. "No."

"Guys," Max said excitedly, "I think I've got something." He perked up in his chair and readjusted his glasses. "I am a genius!" he declared loudly.

Kane was on his feet in the blink of an eye, moving impossibly fast as he blurred past her, Tala following behind. They stood over Max's shoulders, looking at the 3D image of the gun that rose from the surface of the desk.

7116785012785

"You're sure that's the number?" Kane asked with some skepticism.

Max gave him an annoyed look over his shoulder. "Yes. I'm absolutely sure."

"That… that's a Republic serial number," Tala said, taken aback.

"How do you know that?" Kane asked, turning toward her.

"All non-plasma guns that were produced in the Republic of Columbia have serial numbers starting with 711, and they're all thirteen digits long. Like this one," she said. "It was their marker. It's how they could discern their weapons from anyone else's. It was illegal to have one from any other country," she said, both men staring at her.

"But all guns are illegal in the Republic," Max said bluntly.

"Right, but only in the last forty-five years or so. Before that, we made them in droves. It was how the Republic was strengthened in the early years," she explained. "The first President Royer banned weapons to all citizens halfway through his presidency. Unrest was growing, and it was feared that if the people were armed, conflict could erupt anywhere. There was a mass clean up across the country as guns were confiscated from every household. Massive fines and prison terms were given to anyone in violation."

They stared blankly at her, and she felt herself take a small step backward.

"You're saying there is nowhere else these guns would've been manufactured?" Kane asked.

"Yes. That's what I'm saying. DeSoto serial numbers start with either a three or a two, are nine digits long and end in a letter. The Colonies' are also nine digits long and start with three zeroes," she said. Tala thought of the west coast countries of Pacifica and Tahari. She didn't know anything about their weapons, but she still felt confident that this was a Republic gun.

"How do you know all this?" Max asked.

"The academy," she said.

"So, unless someone is illegally making guns that appear to be the Republic's, they're our own," Kane said picking it up from the desk, turning it over in his hands. "Why were they in the warehouse? Unified Rebels seems the obvious answer."

"No," Tala shook her head adamantly. "I don't think so. There wasn't a dot of ink on any of those men who attacked me. I looked them over myself."

Kane's eyes met hers, and she could see his mind was hard at work. "No, there was no ink. I looked this morning when I went back to the scene," he confirmed.

Tala shook her head. "My team wanted to dismiss it all and blame the Rebels, but UR all have ink—"

"It's how they pledge their allegiance to their cause," Kane said, finishing her sentence.

"You can't easily remove a tattoo," she said quietly as he looked at her.

"This gun may be the Republic's, but how do we know the others aren't from somewhere else?" Max asked.

"A valid point," Tala said.

"Could the Republic be doing something with them?" Max asked, craning his neck to look up at Tala. "Training or something?"

"Why hide them in an old warehouse if they were?" Kane said, turning to him. "Those guns were intentionally being hidden."

"My captain and my brother seemed just as surprised as the rest of us when we found them. If the Republic was doing something with them, Thias would've known about it," Tala said.

Both Kane and Max were silent.

"I hate to break up the brainstorming party," Max said after a moment, "but curfew is in thirty minutes. It will take you about that long to get back to your pod."

Tala sighed, feeling defeated. Once again, she had more questions than answers.

"Our search isn't over," Kane said as he placed his hand gently on her bare shoulder, sending a chill through her body. "But you should go." He reached for her hand, his fingers warm on her skin, and set the gun in her grasp. Tala closed her fingers around the grip as she looked up at him.

"Okay," she said quietly as she turned and crossed the pod toward the door. "One last question," she paused as she looked over her shoulder. "When you went through the surveillance footage around the docks, did you also see the men who attacked me?"

Kane and Max exchanged a brief look.

"No," they said in unison.

"I didn't even think about it," Kane said. "You were the only one we saw when we went to clear the footage. I'm sure of that."

"So, how'd those guys get there?" Max asked.

"The river," she said. "It's the only place there wouldn't have been surveillance cameras." She considered how this changed things. If someone brought those men to the docks via the river, then there was at least one more person out there that was unaccounted for. Just another missing piece to her puzzle.

She turned toward the door.

"I'll take you home," Kane said, following after her.

"That's really not necessary," she said as she slipped into Mila's plush coat. She returned the gun to the breast pocket.

"I know," he said, catching her gaze.

Tala felt her chest tighten and a swarm of fluttering low in her belly as he stood there, so near her, his eyes piercing through her with intensity. She swallowed hard and nodded her head. "Okay," she said in a small voice.

Kane reached for his worn leather jacket, and a minute later, they were on their way, back out on the dark and narrow Harvey Street.

"I'm sorry I made things awkward back there," she said.

He shook his head. "No, it was me."

"I just… I don't know what I said," she admitted quietly.

He sighed. "I don't usually talk about my childhood. It wasn't a very good one," he said through bated breath as they rounded a corner.

"But you said your mother—"

"Oh, she was," he said. "But my father was a real ass."

"You mentioned being in a facility after your mom died. Can I ask what that was?" she said, putting the words gingerly between them. "What kind of a facility? Why were you there?"

Kane was silent, his deep breathing and heavy footsteps on the pavement the only sounds he made. Staring ahead, he dropped his forehead and shoved his hands deep into the pockets of his jeans.

"You know what? Never mind. It's none of my business," she said quickly when she realized her mistake. There was something more there, she could tell by the way his entire countenance changed when she asked about it. She couldn't begin to imagine what he'd have been in a facility for, but seeing him now, she knew that whatever it was, it wasn't good.

Silence fell between them as they walked toward the subtrain. The crowd of people on the street had thinned, and their train car was nearly empty. With Kane beside her, Tala nervously picked at the polish on her nails.

When the train came to her stop, Tala quickly rose to her feet. "You can still catch the next train and make it back to Oxwick before midnight," she said. "I'm fine on my own." Tala headed quickly for the open doors and exited, when she turned, she was surprised to see Kane beside her, the same somber expression still etched across his face. They were alone on the platform as the train sped away.

"It was a medical facility," he said, breaking the silence between them.

Tala didn't dare speak, and she steeled herself to meet his gaze.

In stride beside each other, they made their way to street-level, where nearly everything was deserted. She glanced quickly at her palm pad, powered back on. She had seven minutes until midnight, and Kane hurried with ease down the street alongside her.

"My father couldn't care for me. Well, he couldn't put up with me," Kane admitted, his voice low and raspy with a tinge of emotion that Tala almost missed. "So, I was sent away."

"Kane," she said as she stopped and turned to face him. "You don't have to tell me anything you don't want to. I understand this is none of my business," she paused to gather her thoughts. "But if this was something that was done to you," she said, thinking about the things he could do, "I cringe at the idea of anyone hurting you. And whether you choose to tell me or not, just know that you can trust me." Her eyes looked into his, and even in the darkness, she saw his reticence. There was pain deep in his expression. He stood so close to her that she could feel warmth radiate from him, and for the second time that night, she felt a flutter inside her.

"Yes," he finally said, his voice low and hushed. "This was something that was done to me. I sometimes wonder if my father knew. And if he didn't, would he still have chosen to send me if he'd have found out?"

"It was a research facility," she whispered, more to herself than to Kane.

"For medical research," he said. "But not everyone there were as horrible as you're imagining."

"I find that hard to believe."

He grinned as he took her hands in his. They were warm, his fingers soft and his palms rough. For a moment after he met her gaze, there was silence and a sense of peace washed over her. Tala felt an overwhelming urge to lean into him, to press her face into his chest. But she stiffened, holding back the urge.

"And I do trust you," he said, his eyes steady on her.

Heat began to radiate through Tala, spreading wildly through her veins. She couldn't bring herself to look away from him. In the dark silence, the streets now vacant, Tala felt a sudden familiarity that she didn't understand. Those eyes, that gaze. It was so comforting looking up at him.

"It's midnight," he finally said, his voice low.

Tala swallowed hard as she took a step back from him, and he dropped her hands.

"I'll find you again. Promise," he said with a smile that didn't quite reach his eyes.

"Goodnight," she whispered. She lingered for a brief moment, then turned and began toward her building, her heels clacking loudly on the pavement. Reaching the doors, she glimpsed over her shoulder.

He was gone.

"Man, what the hell?" Max exclaimed as soon as Kane stepped into their pod. He had clearly been waiting for him as he sat at the island counter.

Kane sighed. "I don't know what you're talking about." Though he knew too well what he was referring to.

"You're toeing a fine line, my friend," Max scolded. "If the Republic has a princess, it's her. And you're not supposed to exist. So, tell me how it's a good thing that she knows about all your super-human crap, and now where you live. Where *we* live. We have rules for a reason, and one of them is that we don't have people here, let alone point out your bomb shelter to," he said with distress. "I put myself out there for you for a decade now, and even before that when we were kids. You're putting me at risk too," he said.

"That stuff when we were kids goes both ways. You can't pull that card on me," Kane said, running his hand over his bare head, feeling the roughness of the hair just starting to grow in. "But I know what you're saying," he said calmly. "Believe me, I know. But I trust her, Max."

"You don't even know her. You think because you pulled her from a burning house one night eleven years ago that you have some kind of connection to her, but you don't. She's an Alexander," Max said, his shrill voice finally coming down.

Kane took a seat beside him at the counter, and with a heavy sigh, he dropped his head into his hands.

"When I'm with her," he said, carefully considering his words as he tried to muddle through the chaotic thoughts in his head, "I feel like a real person. I do connect with her, Max, in a way I just can't explain.

"When I look at her, I see someone who can understand me," Kane confided. "Someone other than just you. And it's been just you for so long. I never realized what an island I've been until someone else showed up. She's seen what I am, and it hasn't sent her running. There's no fear in her eyes when she looks at me. It's like she can see right through the walls I've put up between myself and the rest of the world."

Max was quiet for a moment as he studied his hands. "And what about her mother? You gave away too much tonight, and she's going to ask more questions. Tala seems very astute, and she will find out the truth. What happens then?"

Kane's shoulders slumped. That had already crossed his mind, and he really just didn't know the answer. If he told her the truth, he risked either destroying whatever was building between them, or destroying the very memory of who she knew her mother to be, her mother, her best friend. He stood to lose everything with the truth, and he felt conflicted. She deserved the truth, after all these years, but now that he knew her, he wasn't sure he could let her go. He knew it was selfish, and he hated himself for it.

"I don't know," he mumbled honestly.

That night, Tala tossed restlessly in her bed. As she would drift off to sleep, the same image appeared repeatedly in her mind: a pair of dark eyes looking down at her, flames flickering in their reflection. Her surroundings were hazy, and she was overwhelmed with confusion. It was like being in a fog, unable to grasp reality. She could make out nothing other than the shape of a person. The silhouette of a young man. She tried blinking for clarity, but all she could see were those eyes, black and piercing, gazing back at her. They felt so real.

Arriving at Command, tired from the night before, Tala took a seat at her desk, opposite Ronin who was already at work on his computer.

"You and your coffee," he said with a smirk when she set her mug down. "You're never short of it." He seemed to be over his anger from the day before.

"Oh, zip it," she said.

"Perks of being a Preferred," he said, eyeing her knowingly. "And an Alexander."

Tala cast him a glare from the corner of her eye, and he laughed.

"Your meeting with your C.I. yesterday go well?" he asked, leaning back in his chair.

She let out an audible sigh. "Not really, but that's a problem for another day."

"You didn't come back after going to Jerez," he said.

"No, Thias had other plans for me."

"Professional or personal?" he asked, stretching his arms behind his head.

"Definitely personal," she sighed. "It was a set-up."

"Ambush. He's on the warpath to get you settled down and married again? Doesn't he know that I don't want another partner?" He chuckled. "Been too long since Keegan, huh? So, who was it this time? Another regional rep? How about a hospital director? Or maybe a financial manager?"

She shook her head. "Try chancellor."

Ronin raised a brow, perking up in his chair. "As in *chancellor* of International Affairs? As in Vaughn Adams?" His mouth was slightly agape.

"That'd be the one."

"He's pulling out all the stops this time," Ronin said, the corners of his mouth turned up. "So…"

"To my surprise, I liked him. I mean, I enjoyed his company," she said, feeling her face flush.

"Is he just as smooth in person as he is in public?" he asked. "You know he's like *the* bachelor of Columbia City, right?"

"Yes," she said. She used her hand to cover the smirk on her face. "But he seemed genuine. Not cocky or arrogant."

"The princess of the Republic snags the most eligible bachelor of the city," he said, then laughed.

Tala's eyes narrowed as she glared once more across her desk at him.

"Whoa. I was just kidding," he said, raising his hands. "And you're seeing him again?"

"Maybe," she said with a shrug and a coy smirk.

"Well, actually, you will see him again. Today," he said, his smile fading. "We got a special assignment."

"Special assignment? Person or event?" she asked.

He nodded. "Both, technically. They need additional security for a dignitaries' luncheon at the Central Government building."

"Upper-level officials? President Royer?" she asked.

"It's our turn in the rotation for support for the Presidential Protection Unit." His attention reverted to his computer, his hair falling across his forehead. "And the chancellor will be there," he said with a smirk.

Tala felt a tug in her chest. This time when she saw him, she would not be in a dress but rather her MF uniform: heavy black cargo pants, a black shirt, and a frag jacket. There was nothing feminine or attractive about it. The last time she had been in uniform around him, she had certainly gone unnoticed. She'd been just another face in that crowd.

"Agents," Captain Kole said as he approached.

"Captain," Tala said quickly as she rose from her chair. "Anything come back on the weapons we recovered?"

"Still being cataloged for evidence. As you know, there were a lot of them. I have no updates. It'll take at least a week, even with the rush on it. Now, I assume Agent Ashby filled you in on your assignment for today?" he asked, his brows furrowed like always.

"Yes, Captain," she said with a firm nod.

"Agents Bishop and Kassis will be assisting," he said in a flat, monotone voice. "There's a possibility you'll be in the room during this meeting with the president and, therefore, you'll need to sign the confidentiality and non-disclosure agreements. I've sent them to your computers, please review and sign them. You'll need to use your pricker for your blood thumb-stamp. I'm sure I don't need to stress the delicate nature of sensitive information. You'll be at the Central Government building for this meeting, there will be no deviations from routine security protocol for Presidential Protection. You won't be detailing the president himself, just providing additional security during the meeting and luncheon," he said. "Be ready in twenty."

"Yes, Captain," both Tala and Ronin said in unison.

Tala's finger absentmindedly rubbed her thumb where the pricker would stick her for the blood thumb-stamp.

Kole continued across the rotunda toward Bishop, who was intently studying Tala from across the room, a smug look across his face, and he lifted a brow to her when their eyes met.

"You going to be able to contain yourself with the chancellor?" Ronin laughed under his breath.

"I'm a professional," she said obstinately.

"I know, I know," he said with a grin. "I have no doubt in your capabilities. Now, sign and stamp those documents so we're ready when it's time to go."

Tala skimmed through her confidentiality agreements and non-disclosures, they all said the same thing, then swiped her finger across the computer with her signature. She finalized the documents with the prick of her thumb. A feeling of dread washed over her, and she couldn't understand why, in that moment, it seemed to matter so much to her what Vaughn would think of her.

Tala and the other agents showed their agency IDs at the main entrance security checkpoint of the south tower of the Central Government building. She stepped through the body scanner and turned over her palm pad, which would be locked away until her assignment was over, then they were all given temporary security badges to keep with them at all times while in the building.

The Central Government building was an impressive architectural masterpiece. Stepping into the grand and expansive foyer, she was met by an oversized marble staircase, lined with a magnificent golden railing and ornate balustrade that diverged into opposing directions halfway to the second floor. Prodigious crystal and gold chandeliers hung from the four-story-high ceiling with balconies on each floor above looking down below.

A woman, short and plump, approached them hastily, clutching a tablet firmly in her grip. Tala recognized her immediately as the Presidential Coordinator, though her name suddenly escaped her.

"Agents," she said curtly from behind thick glasses as she brushed a strand of gray hair away from her face, "I'm Agnesa and you'll be under my charge today while you serve as Presidential Protection support."

Agnesa, though unassuming at first glance, was not to be underestimated. She managed the president's schedule and security for a reason. A single negative report from her would be enough to ruin anyone's career.

"This meeting is rather impromptu," she continued, "and we have some agents who are unavailable today due to routine evaluations. We require an additional presence on the gallery floor. Follow me," she said with a wave of her hand, then turned quickly on her heel.

Tala followed after Agnesa as she made her way toward the grand staircase, her kitten heels clacking on the granite and marble floor in rhythmic beats. Once on the second floor, Agnesa handed an agent in a black suit her ID badge. He scanned it, then stepped aside to let her pass, and she waited, rather impatiently, her face glued to her tablet, while Tala and the other agents' badges were each scanned.

"Now," she said once all four of them had been permitted onto the floor, "I will need two agents outside the doors of the gallery where the meeting will be held, and I'd like two agents inside." Agnesa walked at a brisk pace through the corridors. "President Royer will have four agents that will join you inside the gallery once he arrives. You will be there in a support capacity only."

They made their way from one hallway to another, passing other security personnel along the way, occasionally needing to provide their IDs. With her terrible sense of direction, Tala was certain she was lost.

They came to a stop outside a pair of golden French doors open to a capacious gallery. Inside was an oversized, polished mahogany table that filled the center, surrounded by plush, white chairs and a single wingback at the head.

"Right," Agnesa said as she cleared her throat. "Agents Alexander and Ashby, please take a position along opposite walls in the gallery. Do not touch any of the artwork," she emphasized sternly. "You two," she said, tipping her head toward Bishop and Kassis, "you will take a post outside these doors. In addition, there are agents positioned at all points of entry to this hallway. And we foresee no problems," she said, eyeing each of them.

Tala stepped into the gallery after Ronin, her gaze roaming over the room, painted a lush dark green with mahogany trim and moldings to match the massive table. Paintings in varying sizes hung along the walls from thick cords suspended from the ceiling. They were detailed with precise brushstrokes and vivid colors, depicting images she was not familiar with. There were paintings of men seated at a long table, portraits of people, women sheathed in long, draping fabrics, luscious landscapes, and detailed battle scenes.

"Wow," Ronin whispered, and Tala nodded in agreement. It had been a long time since she'd been in an art gallery. Her eyes couldn't help but wander.

Tala quickly snapped to attention in her post as a cacophony of conversation approached the gallery, followed only moments later by an influx of men in pressed suits and ties. Tala recognized each of them, one by one, as they filtered in and took their place around the table: Associate City Representative Kavan Parker, Chief Justice Mikel Murdo, Republic of Columbia regional representatives Aiden Gray, Marshall Turner, and Vance Donovan, cabinet members Julio Martinez and Eli Valdi, followed by Chancellor Adams, and then finally, Thias, who paid her no attention as he strode in. Without a word to anyone, he took the chair beside the head of the table, Agent Grant slinking into a corner behind him.

Tala caught Vaughn's glimpse at her as he crossed the room, and she felt a small tug in her chest, but his expression was stern, his mouth pressed into a straight line, and she swallowed hard when he looked away.

President Royer was the last to enter, two agents flanking him and two following behind him. He was dressed as he always was, black slacks and a slim, straight-fitted topcoat with a stand-up collar that hung loosely to just above the knee. Tala could only think of three other occasions when she'd seen him in anything else. The first, when she was five and he'd been sworn in as president after the death of his father, Viktor Royer I. He'd worn a black and gray suit then. There were two other times, also when he wore suits, one burgundy and one navy, but she couldn't recall what they were for.

The room fell silent as President Royer let his eyes roam from person to person, the doors of the room closing behind him. When he finally took his seat in the wingback chair at the head of the table, the dignitaries each followed.

"Well," said President Royer as he folded his arms across the tabletop, "as you are probably aware, we are here to discuss the growing tensions with the DeSoto government. I'll get right to the point. President Pierce is limiting more and more trade exports from DeSoto to the Republic. In cohesion with their willful violations of our trade agreements, Mazanada, whom we know they have close relations with, is withdrawing from our agreements as well," he said in a low, dilatory voice with little fluctuation in his tone.

Although he was always slow to speak, he never appeared of lesser intelligence, and Tala thought it made him more intimidating. His calm and serene demeanor was always disquieting to her, knowing there was more going on in his head than what he ever revealed. She had never seen him smile, and his small, squinty eyes always seemed to be calculating.

He was much like Thias in this way: always anticipating his next move, intentional with everything he did. He was always cold and distant, and Tala wondered if he'd still be president of the Republic if he hadn't been his father's successor. If he would still have been chosen by the people back when government leaders were still elected. But free elections were short-lived in the Republic's history, having been abolished only four years after the first Viktor Royer was elected.

"Mr. President," Thias spoke up in his deep and firm voice, his jaw set in a hard line. "I think it would be more appropriate to discuss these details in private, without the presence of the additional agents in the room. Despite their signed agreements of confidentiality, I believe this is sensitive information that exceeds their security clearances," he said.

Tala tried to mask her confusion. She cast him a furtive glance, but he didn't look in her direction. From the corner of her eye, she spotted Vaughn beside him, sitting erect and rigid in his chair, and she was taken aback. This side of him was so contradictory to the Vaughn Adams she was familiar with. As a public figure, she'd only ever known him to be charming and charismatic. She tried to dismiss the discomfort she felt seeing him like this, telling herself that this was a completely different setting than anything she'd been in with him before.

"Yes, I am inclined to agree with you," President Royer said after a moment as he looked briefly in Ronin's direction. "Please resume your post outside the entrance. We will retrieve you if a problem arises," he said placidly.

Ronin gave him a small bow of his head, then quickly left his post, Tala following his lead as they swiftly exited the room.

"That was weird," Ronin whispered once in the hall and after the door closed behind them.

"What'd you two do wrong?" Bishop said, a pleased smirk on his face.

"You were dismissed?" Agnesa asked as she approached, looking up from the tablet in her hands. She slid her glasses off and, connected to a chain around her neck, she let them drop to her chest.

"They deemed the information for discussion too sensitive," Ronin said.

"Well then, you may take over here, while you two," she nodded toward Bishop and Kassis, "can resume your posts at the west entrance of this corridor. Please do not let anyone pass without my consent," she said in a stern, yet almost sweet voice as she reverted her attention back to her tablet and continued walking.

"Figures," Bishop said. "Give the princess the best positions. No nepotism going on here," he said with a scowl on his face.

"Make all the excuses you want," Tala said, "but I only get what I work for. I'm not going to defend my track record to you. It's not my problem if you can't measure up." She turned her back to him as she took her new post beside the double golden doors, meeting Ronin's eyes as he smirked discreetly.

Tala and Ronin waited for the better part of two hours before the double doors to the gallery opened, casual, rather than official, conversation carrying into the corridor.

Unsure how she seemed to always time it so perfectly, Agnesa reappeared, leading a line of servers bringing lunch. They filed into the gallery, one by one, and set a plate covered by a brushed nickel dome in front of each of the dignitaries. After the president's was removed to reveal his food, the other servers followed suit.

"You may resume your posts inside the gallery," Agnesa said curtly to Ronin, then gave a brief look at Tala.

They ushered back into the room, the smell of baked fish hanging in the air, and Tala resumed her previous position.

Vaughn caught her gaze, a softer expression as he gave her a nod. She quickly averted her attention, biting back the urge to smile at him. She caught Ronin's knowing look as he squinted just enough for her to see the small creases in the corners of his eyes from a suppressed smile. He hadn't been ignorant to her inconspicuous exchange with Vaughn, and Tala felt her cheeks flush.

Tala stood silently against the wall, her mind beginning to wander, President Royer's words lingering in the back of her head. She hadn't been aware that tensions with DeSoto had escalated. There was a common understanding throughout the Republic that their relationship with the nation sharing their southern border was not particularly genial, but that it was at least cordial. And it had never been alluded to that their relationship with Mazanada, the country to the south of DeSoto, was less than propitious. Tala was now overly curious about what had been discussed behind those closed doors.

As lunch concluded, President Royer was the first to make his withdrawal from the gallery, his agents leaving with him. In his absence, the other dignitaries divided into smaller groups of conversation throughout the room.

Tala spotted Vaughn making his way toward her, and her pulse quickened.

"Hello," he said softly.

She gave him the smallest tip of her head but knew she could not break rank.

He let out a small laugh. "So official," he said.

Suddenly, she couldn't help but feel he was mocking her.

"Would dinner tonight be possible?" he asked in a hushed voice. "You can blink once for yes."

Tala didn't want to seem overly eager, so she took a slow breath before giving a single blink.

Vaughn's grin was wide, showing perfectly straight, white teeth. "Pick you up at seven," he said. "Look just as lovely as you did last night." With one last lingering look, he turned and left the gallery, and Tala immediately noticed Thias's approving look from across the room.

FIVE

Tala could feel the overwhelming heat on her face. As she struggled to open her eyes, to keep them open, she saw the walls engulfed in flames as she moved through the house. Fire. Her head was thick.

Someone was holding her. She was flying. Or maybe she was walking. Her lungs began to burn, her head struggling to process.

Suddenly there was cold air. Fresh. She felt the concrete beneath her, rough on her palms. She crawled until she found grass. It was damp on her skin as her body collapsed, breathless, her mind groggy. She coughed hard. Through hazy eyes that fought to focus, to stay open, she made out a person, silhouetted by the backdrop of an inferno.

It approached her. Thick smoke billowed from the fire, pluming and curling in the still air around them, her mind slow and muddled, and as she gazed up, she met a pair of eyes, dark, black as night. Her mind began to fade, and she blinked hard, trying to bring it back, but the world was slipping away from her. The urge to sleep was strong. She took a laborious breath as she once again found the stranger beside her. He looked down at her with a penetrating stare, then turned away.

"No!" she tried to cry out, though no sound would escape her lips. "No," she tried again, but the young man was gone.

◆◆◆

Tala woke with a start, breathless, with a thin layer of sweat covering her body. Panting, she sat up and tossed the blankets off. Moving to the edge of the bed, she focused on her breathing, steadying it. Dropping her head into her hands, her dream played back to her in fragmented but vivid snapshots. They were the same memories that had frequented her dreams for years. Sometimes the details were foggy, her mind struggling to conjure them in complete form. Other times, the picture in her mind was so clear it was like living everything all over again. But despite what version filled her dreams, foggy or clear, one thing was always the same. Those eyes.

She'd dreamt of them a hundred times. Those deep, black eyes that had looked down on her while her world burned around them. They were the eyes of the person who saved her, despite what people said. No one had ever believed her.

Sitting on the edge of her bed, she felt a wave of familiarity wash over her, but she couldn't pinpoint where it stemmed from. Her head was a discombobulated puzzle, the details just fragments in her mind. Unable to string anything together, she failed over and over again to make sense of any of it. Who was the stranger that saved her all those years earlier? And why her?

Tala shuddered as she took a deep breath. Those eyes haunted her even more than the ghosts of her parents.

❖

17 years earlier

It was a frigid day, overcast with heavy, low clouds, and the wind was biting and harsh. It had snowed the night before, and the fresh layers blew with a fury across the ground and roads. Ice building on the bridges made them slick for the cars that drove over them. Kane blew off the bus ride home after school, opting instead for the long walk. It was payday, which meant his father would invariably be well into a bottle of brown liquor. But he knew his mom wouldn't worry about him when he wasn't home on time. He was beginning to suspect that maybe she, too, wanted him to stay away as long as possible.

Ismet, he thought, was a real son of a bitch, and when he was half-pissed, Kane just became a good punching bag for him. Although these days, Kane had started fighting back. He was now a moving target for his father, which often enraged him more. Kane found it immensely satisfying as he watched him stumble and fail trying to reach him. But when he finally did catch Kane, the repercussions were always disastrous. Instinctively, his tongue slid over the inside corner of his lip, healed just in time from the last hit to be a fresh canvas for his father again.

Kane turned off the road, stepping into the deep snow where he sank nearly up to his knees and made his way across an open field and then into the woods. Each step was slow and cumbersome, but this didn't bother him. This time of year, the sun set early, and he would soon be met with darkness. But it was an irrelevant factor for his walk home. He knew his way around Bedley and these woods like the back of his hand.

The crows called out to each other from high in the branches, an occasional squirrel hustled across his path. With every step, winding through the narrow avenues created by the heavy thicket, he disappeared deeper into the woods, the trees growing in thick. But the denser it became, the less snow there was on the ground, and it was easier to drudge through. It was now dark, and although hidden by the tree canopy, Kane knew the blackened sky above was filled with stars. On nights he had to escape the house, he'd head to the old fishing docks, and lying on the rickety, skeletal remains of them, he'd gaze up at those stars in wonder. All those hundreds of thousands of tiny, white specks, and he would think to himself that these were lights of hope; they were the possibilities of the world. As soon as he was able, he'd leave Bedley behind to chase those stars.

After a forty-minute hike through the woods, the snow deepened again as the trees thinned, and the lights of the back of the town's single hydrogen fuel station and convenience store came into view. Despite the cold, he had warmed enough on his walk that he'd removed his balaclava and shoved it into the front pocket of his coat.

"Hey, wuss, you're looking a little hungry!" a boy called menacingly somewhere in the distance. "But hey, guess what? So am I!" he jeered.

Kane picked up his pace and stepping out of the tree line, he saw a group of boys circling Max, a small, timid boy with glasses, like vultures around a pile of roadkill. Max gripped the edges of a brown paper bag that was likely carrying groceries from the convenience store.

"Please," Max begged in a small, desperate voice. "I need these. I need to get home."

"But I think I need them more," the boy said sarcastically. Kane could now see that it was Zak and his two cronies, Dean and Mikey, who went nowhere without him. In a swift movement that Max didn't see coming, Zak reached for his face, tearing off his glasses. "Oh, look at these boys, now wussy-pants won't be able to see while we beat the tar out of his ass!"

The other two boys roared with laughter.

"Leave him alone!" Kane hollered, jogging onto the scene. Kane wasn't a particularly large boy, but he was fast, and he did know how to pack a punch.

Kane stepped into the circle, sure to make eye contact with the boys to show they didn't frighten him. Adrenaline and excitement, and a little fear, were all building inside him.

"You get out of here, Ryan!" Zak yelled, calling him by his last name.

"Not a chance," Kane said, stepping closer. He knew he had to be smart, to stay one step ahead of the other three. "Give him the glasses."

"I don't think so," Zak said flatly as he cocked his head.

Max stood stiff and frozen with fear in the middle of the circle, clutching his bag of groceries tightly to his chest.

"That wasn't a question. Now hand them over before you won't be able to see for a week beneath the black eye I'll give you," Kane spat loudly.

Zak burst out laughing, but true to his word, Kane leveled an instant jab, strong and direct, into his right eye.

Zak immediately began to scream, dropping the glasses and bringing his hands to his face as he fell to his knees.

"What the hell?" Dean shouted.

"Who's next?" Kane asked as he brought up his hands in a ready stance.

Mikey rushed to Zak's aid as he convulsed on the cold asphalt, still screaming in pain.

Kane's dark eyes met Dean's, daring him to come closer. "I'll do it," he sneered at him.

"You fucking idiot! Hit him!" Zak yelled breathlessly at Dean as he shoved Mikey away, still clutching his face.

Kane saw fear in Dean's eyes as he took an apprehensive step toward him, but quicker than him, Kane's fist found his nose. Blood immediately sprouted from it, running over his top lip.

Dean screamed out, bringing his hands to his nose.

"Anyone else? You want it again, Zak?" Kane hollered, his voice loud and booming, even over the yelling of the two boys. "You going to give me the chance to do the same to you?" Kane asked, turning toward Mikey, showing he was more than ready to take him on too.

There was panic in his eyes, and Mikey threw his arms in the air. "I'm out!" he yelled as he spun on his heel and took off running around the corner of the building, his footfalls fading quickly.

"Get up," Kane said as he gave Zak a kick in the leg. "I have no problem getting the other eye too if you don't get the hell out of here."

With the one good eye, Zak peered up at Kane with malice on his face. "You're going to pay for this, Ryan. Don't think I'll forget this," Zak said as he fumbled to his feet. Grabbing Dean whose hands were covered in blood, the two boys staggered away, running after Mikey.

When he was confident they were gone, Kane exhaled deeply, his arms and legs trembling with adrenaline. He glanced around and spotted Max's glasses lying beside a nearby fuel tank. He walked over and picked them up, then gave them a close inspection.

"They don't look broken. Maybe a scratch on the lens," he said calmly as he turned toward Max, who still looked riddled with fear and shock. "Take them," he said as he shoved them toward him.

Max reached out in trepidation and took the glasses, then slid them back onto his face. "The…" he stammered, "scratch was already there."

"They're gone," Kane assured him. "C'mon, I'll walk with you home. Make sure those weasels don't come back. But pretty sure they're home and crying to the mamas," he said, giving Max a pat on his shoulder.

The streets nearly deserted, the boys started walking, Max still silent and in shock. The hard-packed snow crunched below their feet with each step, and the wind rustled the lingering dried leaves hanging on the otherwise bare branches.

"Thank you," Max finally said, his voice a mere whisper in the night. He clutched the grocery bag tight in his arms.

Kane shrugged. "Eh. It was no big deal." Although in his head he was thinking it was very much a big deal. He kicked ass. But he was also certain he had just planted a target squarely on his back. Zak wasn't the boy to drop something like this. But at least, he thought, the target was on his back rather than Max's.

"Why'd you do it?" Max asked, louder this time as he seemed to find his voice.

"Us underdogs got to stick together," Kane said.

"You didn't look much like an underdog back there," Max observed.

"Trust me, I am. More than you know," he said, giving Max a smirk. They fell in stride together and finished their walk to Max's in contented silence.

"I'm so sorry I'm late," Tala exclaimed as she entered her pod. Just being home was an instant relief.

Mila was sprawled lazily across their sofa, a long, L-shaped, white leather couch that took up nearly the entire living room, her legs stretched out and resting on the coffee table.

"Oh, I started without you," Mila said as she lifted the half drank glass of wine in her hand.

Tala laughed as she slid out of her heavy MF boots. Working on a string of robberies in south Walhurst had kept her on her feet for most of the day.

"Can we just stay in tonight?" Tala asked. After removing her frag jacket and duty belt, she stepped into the kitchen and poured herself a glass of wine from the open bottle on the counter.

"Up to you," Mila said. "Actually, no, let's stay in," she declared firmly. "I don't want to get dressed up. I'm happy right now in my leggings and t-shirt."

"You don't have to twist my arm," Tala said with a knowing smirk as she made her way to the living room. "What're you watching?" she asked as she glanced at the muted TV. She took a drink of the wine, a light, yet dry red, and her mouth puckered.

Mila shrugged as she sat up. "Just some lame biography on Seylah Esparza. I thought it would've been interesting since she's my favorite music artist, but it really isn't. I'm bored with it," she groaned. "If there's no theatrical drama, I don't like it. Apparently, not all Preferreds have exciting lives."

Tala chuckled and took another drink of wine. "I'm going to change. And take a quick shower," she called over her shoulder as she headed down the hall.

Setting the glass of wine on her dresser, Tala glanced around her bedroom. In her hurry that morning, after another restless night, she hadn't made her bed, and the blankets were tossed haphazardly around. The bed looked as fitful as her sleep had been. She blinked away the image of those eyes again. It had been months since she'd dreamt of the fire, and she couldn't understand why she was feeling so unsettled now.

Tala locked her gun and duty belt inside the safe in her closet, then slipped out of her uniform, goosebumps raising across her bare arms and legs. Stepping into the shower, steam fogging the glass panels around her, she caught her breath and held it until her muscles relaxed beneath the stream of hot water.

She let it wash over her body, taking her tension with it. Wracked with exhaustion, she felt her consciousness begin to ebb from the constant state of high alert that she'd been in all day. For many days now, if she thought about it. Since the first arrest at the warehouse, Tala had been firing on all cylinders trying to do two jobs simultaneously. And that wasn't even throwing into the mix both Kane and Vaughn.

Vaughn, she thought, her mind rewinding to the previous night.

"We're going out to Stearns Point," he had said with a gentle and handsome smile that showed off the dimple in his right cheek when he picked her up in his limited-edition J.D. Bradley. It didn't surprise her that he owned such a luxury autonomous car. Thias owned two. Vehicles weren't rare, but they were expensive, and in a city with such extensive public transportation, they were often considered frivolous for any citizen less than Standard. He glanced her up and down and gave her an approving nod.

"Beautiful," he said. "My family home is out there, on Stearns Point. I rarely get out of the city to it, but I thought it would be a nice surprise."

Living her entire life in Columbia City, Tala had only been to Stearns Point, the most eastern point of the outskirts of the city, one other time, when she was young and her family had gone with her grandfather to the first President Royer's second home along the water.

Vaughn's family home was stunning, not to the full degree of Thias's, but still extravagant. Windows along the southeastern face of the house looked over the ocean. Tala found it beautiful but oddly cold. There was something about the blackened water, a dark void in the night, that was uninviting, and she gave a small shiver.

While the car drove them back to the city, Vaughn toasted their night with champagne. He had taken her hand in his, stroking it gently with his thumb, holding it in his lap for most of the drive.

Vaughn's car pulled up to her building only a few minutes before midnight, but he showed no distress over the time, though he still had his drive home. He politely opened the car door for her and escorted her to the doors of her building. Tala had shifted awkwardly as they stood there in the dark, quiet night. But Vaughn was sure of himself. He stepped closer to her, and smoothing his thumb softly down the side of her cheek, he leaned in and lightly brushed his mouth across hers. Her heart had been racing, and she felt unsteady. Suddenly, Thias's face had appeared in her mind and she saw his approving nod, pleased with his adroit and masterful matchmaking skills. She didn't want him to be a part of that moment and irritation flared in her as she heard him whisper, "*I told you so… I always know what's best for you.*" His voice lingered in the back of her head long after their kiss ended.

Tala's shower timer beeped, telling her she had used her allotment of water. She lingered under the hot water for another minute, letting it clear the last of her thoughts, then reached for the knobs on the wall and turned off the shower. Cold air rushed over her immediately as she reached for her towel, then pat herself dry.

Tala was grateful she and Mila were staying in. She had never particularly enjoyed the club scene, which was Mila's scene, and usually required dresses and heels. She had been in them enough over the last few days. A casual lounge or upscale bar was better, but she still preferred to stay in.

In a pair of worn blue jeans and a t-shirt, her feet bare, she made her way back to the living room, collapsing onto the sofa beside Mila.

"I want the details," Mila said with a sly smirk. "All the details."

Tala felt her cheeks redden and took a drink of her wine. She gave a shrug. "There's not a lot to tell."

"I don't believe you for a second!" Mila cried, and Tala couldn't help but laugh. "Did you kiss him?"

"Only a small one," she admitted.

Mila's shoulders sank in disappointment. "That's not salacious. What else?" she asked. "What's he into? I mean, other than you." She grinned. "I only know of him as the chancellor, so formal. Who is he when he's not helping run the country?"

"Umm," she thought back to their conversations. *The Wizard of Oz*, she thought. No, she adamantly told herself, steering her mind back to Vaughn, surprised Kane had popped in at all. "He really talked mostly about himself, his work, his family a little. He mentioned Thias more than once, which was kind of annoying," she finally said.

"I bet he travels a lot," Mila said.

Tala cocked her head. "I would've thought that would be intuited since he's the chancellor of *international* affairs," she said. "Yes, he travels frequently."

"I think I would be terrified to fly in an airplane," Mila said bluntly. "Something about being thousands of feet in the air and looking down to see the ground as a distant memory."

Tala shrugged with a laugh. "It's not so bad," she said, thinking back to her incentive flight from the Militia Forces Air Guard while in the academy.

Although she imagined flying in a commercial or private plane like Vaughn would be drastically different than flying tandem in a military jet.

Tala drained her wine glass and stood to get more, grabbing Mila's empty glass from the coffee table. "Oh, finally," she exclaimed emphatically. "I thought you'd never finish that glass."

Tala glanced back over her shoulder. "You're seriously so lazy you couldn't get up and pour yourself another?" Tala chuckled as she refilled each glass, emptying the bottle.

"So," Mila said reticently as she took her glass back from Tala. "Been dreaming again?" she asked, eyeing her delicately.

Tala wasn't surprised by her question. They'd been podmates for five years, there was little they didn't know about each other, and Tala knew she groaned and yelled out in her sleep. But only when she dreamt of the fire. And those eyes. She'd never told anyone, including Mila, about that part of her dream. Thias had been so quick to shut her down all those years ago when she tried to describe a young man taking her through the burning house to the yard outside. Everyone insisted it had been impossible, that she had made it out on her own. Thias had arrived on the scene just after the explosion, and he assured her there had been no one else there. The fire department repeated the same thing. It was just her.

But Tala knew what she'd seen. Despite her foggy awareness of anything else. And for eleven years, those eyes haunted her dreams.

"Yes," she confirmed, hanging her head. In her mind, she could see Thias's reproachful glare. He would tell her it was time to get over it. It was time to move on.

"Do you want to talk about it?" Mila asked softly.

"No," Tala said, shaking her head and pushing her thoughts of her brother away. This was the second time he'd been in her head against her will in the last twenty-four hours. But it seemed he was always there, despite herself, always with a contemptuous eye watching over her in criticism of everything she did.

"Okay," Mila said. "Then tell me more about Vaughn. He's gorgeous," she said with a flip of her hair, and Tala was grateful she was so willing to change the subject. "What's his best quality?"

His eyes. Hard at a first glance, but deep and surrendering upon a second look. Kane's face flashed across her mind. *His eyes*, dark and seemingly endless, she thought, then shook the idea away dismissively before it fully formed in her mind. It wasn't possible.

"Tals?" Mila asked, waving her hand in front of Tala's face.

"Oh!" she gasped as she came out of her trance.

"You seem to be thinking pretty hard about something. Vaughn?" she asked playfully as she nudged Tala.

"Sorry," Tala said, reaching for her wine glass. "What'd you ask? His best quality?" It was just like Mila to want to gush like a sixteen-year-old. She forced her thoughts back to Vaughn. Tall, slender Vaughn. His soft brown eyes, his confident, suave smile, and that dimple in his right cheek. "I really don't know him well, but he's charming. Has a smooth smile. Like, when he looks at you, you know he's trying to disarm you," she said.

"Ohhh," Mila swooned. "I need a guy."

Tala laughed. "You have a different guy every week," she jested. She didn't see Mila settling down any time soon. In all the time they'd known each other, lived together, Tala never knew Mila to not keep her options open.

"Sometimes they're the same," she said defensively, a smirk curling at the corners of her mouth despite herself. "Do you know when you're seeing him again?"

I don't know, she thought, her mind still hanging on to Kane. She couldn't understand why she kept going back to him. She hardly knew him. But she hardly knew Vaughn as well.

"I'm sure in the next couple of days," Tala said, knowing Mila was asking about Vaughn. How could she ask about Kane? She had no idea he even existed. She couldn't know who he was. In that moment, Tala was surprised to realize, it wasn't Vaughn she wanted to talk about at all.

That night, when Tala crawled into bed, adjusting the mattress temperature on her palm pad to take the chill out of her bones, her mind wandered back to Kane. She felt his gaze on her, the way he left her unsettled, the way she didn't want him to look away in the moments they made eye contact. Surrendering. Yes, his eyes were surrendering, and it was like she was looking deep into his soul while he was able to see into hers at the same time. How could she understand someone she didn't even know? How could he understand her?

But were those the same eyes, she wondered, finally letting her mind settle on the thought. Both pairs of eyes were so dark and had a natural, calming effect on her. But could they be the same?

She rolled onto her side, closed her eyes, then waited patiently for her sleeping pill to kick in. She always envied people who slept easily. But she supposed that not everyone had lived nightmares that could haunt their slumber. Either that or they were able to simply lock those monsters up tight when they closed their eyes. Tonight, she was going to sleep. Kane, with his intense stares and subtle smiles, his smooth, brown skin and warm touch, his deep, rough voice and low laugh, was the last thought to hang in her mind before finally drifting out of consciousness.

Tala sat at her desk, nursing her second cup of coffee for the morning. Her sleeping pill had worked, but the last residual effects were hanging on while she was trying to focus on her job.

She hadn't dreamt during the night, but her mind was still playing with the possibility of a connection between Kane, those eyes that left her on edge, and those that had haunted her all these years. It was a nagging feeling that she couldn't seem to escape.

Keeping her work confined to her desktop surface for privacy, Tala searched and found Max in the Department of Internal Technologies database where he worked for the Republic. Max Cooper. He was easy to locate. She then pulled his public records. He was from Bedley, a small fishing hamlet along the shores of Lake Michigan. The son of a Standard citizen mechanic, he was the middle child of seven.

Tala typed 'Kane, Bedley' into her search field and found four public records for a Kane Ryan. The first was a birth record. This Kane was two years older than her. The second was an expunged juvenile assault charge when he was twelve. He served community service and the charge was dropped. The third was the mention of him and a brother, Addox, in a news article. They were listed as the sons of Ismet Ryan, who had been shot and his home burned in an unsolved murder-arson case with no suspects. A photo of Ismet accompanied the article. His skin was dark, much darker than Kane's. But she saw a resemblance in the face, though Ismet looked haggard and worn. She was confident she had found the right Kane. The fourth document was an adoption record. She was taken aback, reading then rereading the document on her computer.

Adoption?

Ismet's signature was scrawled along a bottom line, along with a second, a single name, typed, not signed: Stanger.

That wasn't really a name, was it? She wondered. Was it a surname or a first name? There was an address section that was left blank, and there was no phone number.

"Stanger," she whispered, the name hanging on her tongue.

"What's that?" Ronin asked, looking up from his desk. "You say something?"

She looked across at him. "For adoption records, can you sign with only one name? Can people only have just one name?"

"What'd you mean one name? Don't we all have just one name? Me? I'm Ronin Ashby," he said with a smirk.

"No, I mean just a first name. Or just a surname," she clarified.

"I don't think so," he said with a shake of his head. "That's a weird question. Why do you ask?"

She shrugged. "No reason."

Tala typed 'Stanger' into her search field, and the database yielded over nine thousand results. It was a far more popular name than she had anticipated. It was the third result that caught her attention. Stanger Research Lab. That, she thought, couldn't be a coincidence. She clicked the link, only to be directed to a page error. The site had been disabled or removed. She sighed in defeat. One more dead end.

"That expression on your face doesn't say *nothing*," Ronin said, and she looked up to find him studying her.

"Oh, I promise it's nothing. Really," she insisted with a dismissive wave of her hand. "Just something someone asked me to look into."

He eyed her curiously.

"Ashby, Alexander," Captain Kole said, interrupting them. "The autopsies came back on the men from the warehouse. Sent the files to your computers. Looks like we had some Unified Rebels on our hands."

"What?" Tala gasped. "How do we know that?" she asked, hearing the incredulousness in her voice. "Were they IDed? Captain, I checked those bodies, there was no ink."

Kole cocked his head at her as his eyes narrowed. "No IDs, they're not in the system. And I don't know how you missed their ink," he said flatly. "It looks more and more like they were there to retrieve their cache after we made our first arrest. Director Alexander has closed this case."

Tala's head was swimming in confusion. "So, then who killed them? And why were the guns so well hidden while the drugs and explosives weren't?" At least she was off the hook for their deaths.

"It's pretty clear they were a diversion, the firearms being their ultimate goal. Agent Alexander, your work is good and thorough, but I have the feeling you're questioning me," he said, a chill in his voice.

"No, Captain, not at all," she added quickly. "I was just thinking that there are still some lingering questions."

"Our suspect from the first arrest was able to provide us with a complete enough picture," he said.

Tala was startled by the revelation. "Really? You debriefed him?" she asked, knowing she was pushing her limits. It had been made clear to her more than once she wasn't going to get any info on that case.

"Of course not," he said. "Director Alexander debriefed him. The information he provided from an interview yesterday was what we needed. Now, as I said, this case is closed," he said resolutely. "You best watch yourself and how you speak to your superiors." He eyed her carefully for a moment, then briskly walked away.

"What the hell was that?" Ronin snapped in a hushed voice.

Yesterday? That was impossible, she knew. Masters was dead and had been for a week now.

Tala ignored Ronin and went straight to her inbox. She found the report Kole had sent and opened it. There was a detailed outline and itemized list of what had been found on each assailant, but Tala skipped all the jargon, scrolling to the last few pages where the autopsy photos were.

She fell back into her chair. Two had ink on their neck, the third on the inside of his bicep, and the fourth had one between his shoulder blades. This was all wrong. She knew, unequivocally, there had been no ink on any of them.

"Ronin, this isn't right," she whispered across to him.

"What?"

She stood up, motioning in the direction of the interview rooms. "Let's talk privately."

He hesitated a moment, then rose and made his way across the rotunda with Tala closely behind. Once inside the small room, she quickly closed the door.

"Why so secretive?" Ronin asked as he sidestepped the table in the room, folding his arms across his chest.

"That autopsy is wrong," she said. "I checked those bodies for ink. You know I did. You were standing right there."

"Tala," he said with impatience. "I wasn't paying any attention to those bodies. I was watching you, trying to figure out what was off about you. It's okay. You just missed them. You were rushed from being late, you were all jittery from the Vitality pill. No one is criticizing your work."

"No," she said adamantly. "Something isn't right, and our first suspect couldn't have—" she abruptly stopped herself.

"He couldn't have what?" Ronin asked sharply.

She swallowed hard. "Ronin, why don't you believe me? You were right there." She heard the desperation in her voice. "Things are not adding up."

"You need to drop this. Captain Kole and Director Alexander say this case is closed. If they're satisfied, well, that's all that matters. We did our job. Now on to the next one," he said.

"I'll pull all the files on this case. I'll show you," she said.

"Tala," he said sternly, his eyes leveling on her. "If you do anything that suggests insubordination, as your partner, you'll bring me down with you. That's a risk I'm not willing to take. You'd be putting my reputation on the line. So, believe me when I tell you that if you get your nose where it doesn't belong, you'll leave me no choice but to report you," he warned.

She was taken aback, like a punch to the gut, the wind taken out of her. Ronin had never spoken to her like this before. She saw the seriousness in his eyes and heard it in his tone.

"I don't mean to sound so harsh," he said, his expression softening some. "You're a good partner and you're my friend, but you know how the Republic handles people who defy their authority. It's not taken lightly. Maybe you think you can get away with this kind of behavior because Thias is your brother, but I can't. And I won't have my loyalty questioned. Now drop it," he repeated adamantly. Uncrossing his arms, he swiftly headed for the door, leaving Tala in his wake.

Alone in the interview room, she took a seat in an empty chair at the table and sighed in frustration, her head falling into her hands. The autopsy had been falsified, and not even Ronin gave her the benefit of the doubt.

She took in a sharp breath, willing her composure, then left the small room. As she made her way across the bustling rotunda, she spotted Vaughn standing with Ronin beside her desk.

As if he sensed her presence, Vaughn looked up, his eyes brightening at the sight of her.

"I wasn't expecting you," she said as she forced a smile for him, still unsettled from her conversation with Ronin.

"Well, I just found out I need to go west for some things. I'll be gone a few days. But I wanted to see you one more time before I left. Lunch?" he asked.

"Oh, umm," she paused as she glanced across the rotunda. Through his office windows, she spotted Kole as he sat at his desk, talking on his palm pad.

"I cleared it with your captain already. You're good," Vaughn said, giving her his suave grin.

"Okay," she said as she removed her duty belt from her waist and slipped it into a secure drawer in her desk. She felt Ronin's eyes on her, but she averted her gaze. She still felt stricken by his lecture, both angry and hurt that he could turn on her so quickly.

Oblivious to the tension between them, Vaughn slid his hand gently onto the small of her back as he escorted her past Ronin toward the main entrance of Command. She felt the eyes of her colleagues on her, making her feel uneasy, and she took a deep breath just as they stepped outside.

It was a cool, overcast day, and Vaughn's car sat parked beside the curb. Tala crawled into the backseat, and after the door was shut, he leaned into her, giving her a small kiss on the corner of her mouth. She smiled, reaching up and running her thumb along his smooth jawline, not even a hint of stubble on his face.

"I hope we're not going anywhere nice," she said as she looked down at herself in her uniform and suddenly felt self-conscious, thinking herself very unfeminine. Tala unzipped her jacket and slipped it off. She wore only a fitted black tee beneath it, though it did little to put her at ease.

When she looked up, she caught Vaughn's approving smile as he glanced her up and down. Despite herself, Tala's cheeks flushed. She was suddenly unsure of the look in his eyes.

They were seated in the back of the noodle parlor, Vaughn's back to the wall so he could see across the restaurant. Though they missed the lunch hour rush, half of the tables were full, and there were eyes from all around the room on them. Vaughn gave them no notice as he looked over the menu. Unlike him, she wasn't used to the attention. People knew her name, but she had managed a low-key visual presence for most of her life. At least with the general public. She didn't like to be recognized, although that was impossible to avoid entirely. There was always someone somewhere who knew her face.

She wondered if the attention on them now was because of Vaughn or if people recognized her as well. Gossip was likely to spread if she was, and that was the last thing she wanted.

With the rich smells of food wafting in the air, Tala hadn't realized how famished she was. When their food arrived, it looked so delicious, and she willed her voracious appetite to calm itself.

"You're going…" she said between small bites of long, curly noodles.

"West," he said ambiguously. "Yes. My flight leaves in a few hours."

She instantly got the sense that he didn't want to disclose any specifics. West could mean the western Republic of Columbia or beyond that to the Central Colonies or even the west coast countries of Pacifica or Tahari. She decided not to press him and instead took another bite of food.

"It'll only be a few days. A week, tops," he said. "I hope you'll miss me. Even if it's just a little bit," he said with a beguiling grin.

She gave him a small smile in return. "Maybe a little," she said with a flirtatious shrug, then felt a rush of heat to her face in embarrassment. She had never been a good flirt. Anyone she'd ever dated would say the same.

"I heard you've finally had some closure with your case," he said coolly.

"Which one?" she asked, cocking her head to the side.

"That warehouse up in Ganbury," he said.

Tala nodded her head. "That's what I'm told," she said, her frustration flaring inside. "Just curious, but what've you heard?"

"Just that your perp finally talked," he said with a wave of his hand. "He didn't give us a thing the night of his arrest. He was completely obstinate regardless of anything we said or did," he said, his eyes narrowing, his mouth in a taut line. He suddenly seemed distant. She'd never noticed the crease in his forehead before. But a moment later, it was gone, his bright smile returning as he let out a deep chuckle. "It all worked out though. Well, maybe not so well for him. But anyway. Enough work-talk."

Tala gave an amused smile to placate him but shifted awkwardly in her seat, unsure of what he was alluding to. Was he hinting at something more, or was she simply reading into it? She knew more than she should. Mills defied her orders when she disclosed the information about Masters's death. If Vaughn had been with Masters the night of his arrest, did it mean he had something to do with his death? Did Thias? She suddenly felt nervous in a new way as she looked across the table at him.

"Well," he said as they finished their lunch, "I've got a plane to catch, and I'm sure you've got a job to get back to." He quickly paid, then drove her back to Command.

Once again seated at her desk, Tala's head swarmed with information, uncertain of what was real and what wasn't. So many puzzle pieces, though none of them seemed to fit. Vaughn's words were heavy on her mind. When he was around her, she couldn't help but find him kind and charming. But she had at least glimpsed another side of him at the dignitaries' luncheon when he had looked so hard and stern, not at all a reflection of the man she was getting to know or the public figure she was familiar with. She was reminded of Thias. He was a master at playing both sides. He showed only what he wanted people to see. Was that who Vaughn was as well?

Tala sighed audibly from her desk, and Ronin looked up.

"Enjoy your lunch?" he asked with a light smile. His expression looked unsure.

Tala knew he was trying to mollify her after their last conversation. It wasn't just Vaughn who had left her feeling anxious. Ronin had her on edge as well. She hadn't known a time when she couldn't trust him. This was a side of him she never expected. This was a side of him she didn't recognize.

"Fine," she said curtly. She averted her gaze and looked at her computer, the autopsy photos before her again, the ink staring at her, mocking her.

"Tal," he said quietly. "I didn't mean to be so harsh. I was an ass. I've just never known you to ever question orders so much. You caught me off guard.

I know you'd never put me in a compromising position," he said with an apologetic, lopsided grin, his hair falling over his brow.

She met his gaze, but looking across the desk, she only felt disappointment. It wasn't just about him not questioning the unanswered details of the case. It was, she realized, that for the first time, he doubted her.

"I was being dramatic. You were right," she said to pacify him. "If Director Alexander is satisfied, then that's all the matters." Unable to sit across from him, not wanting to make small-talk, Tala stood. As she considered where to go to put some space between them, a thought came to her, her dreams suddenly bulldozing their way to the forefront of her mind. She knew she was likely to be haunted forever if she couldn't get any answers. The Records Department. It was time to pull the file on her parents' death. It occurred to her that she had never seen it before, and, she decided, it was time to change that.

Tala left the rotunda and made her way to sub-level A of Command and headed straight for the records and archives office. It was a small room filled with computer terminals along one wall. For security purposes, case records were kept on separate servers, accessible only from select locations. Agent Durham, a small, mousy man, sat behind a large desk that overlooked the room. He looked up briefly to acknowledge her presence, then went back to his computer. As he wasn't a field agent, she couldn't help but wonder what exactly he did all day. Overseeing computer terminals didn't sound exciting to her. Though she supposed someone had to do it.

Tala entered her agency ID number into one of the terminals. Not having a case file number, she input basic information of the case into the search field, and a moment later, a single file populated. She stared, unblinking, the names of her dead parents looking back at her. She didn't understand why, but in that moment, she was unexpectedly nervous. Taking a deep breath, she tapped the file on the screen with her finger.

A red banner flashed across the screen, the word **SEALED** blinking back at her. She stared in confusion and tried to open the file a second time, only to get the same alert.

"Excuse me," she said as she sauntered toward Agent Durham. He looked up at her through beady eyes. "The case I'm trying to access says it's been sealed. Can you look it up?"

"Case number?" he asked dully.

Looking back at the terminal, she read the case number to him as he typed it quickly into his computer.

"Yes, that case has been sealed," he confirmed, his voice as mousy sounding as he looked. "You'll need a level nine security clearance to access it."

Why, she wondered, would the case of a simple house fire be classified to the highest level? It didn't make sense.

"Can I ask who sealed it?" she asked.

Agent Durham glanced back at his computer. "Director Alexander."

Thias. But why? Her mind began spinning. There was only one reason to classify a case level nine… it had to contain sensitive information. What, she wanted to know, did Thias not want seen?

Tala's shoulders slumped as she approached the exit, feeling defeated yet again. Just another brick wall.

"Thank you," she said coolly. She gave Durham a nod of her head, then quickly left the room.

Confusion ran rampant like wildfire in her brain as Tala made her way back to the rotunda. She couldn't understand why her parents' case would be sealed. It had been all over the news for weeks afterward. And even after all these years, it was still whispered about. It was a great tragedy for the Republic, a bad gas leak. "*No one pulled you from the fire,*" she'd been told. Everyone had been wrong, and now she knew there was more to the case than she'd been led to believe. Level nine security clearance. There were only a select few in the whole country who had it. And she had to be one of them.

There was only one person she knew who could help her get what she needed. There was a chance he would refuse. In fact, she thought it was likely that he would. He'd seemed rather uncomfortable and irritated with her presence when she'd met him. But if there was one person she was confident could help her unseal those files, it was Max.

SIX

Lies.

Tala was swimming in them. Drowning in them. And she didn't know who she could trust. Her whole life, things had been black or white. Right or wrong. The ideal was simple: the Republic always came first because that was how she and her people were guaranteed safety, protection, and prosperity. And now she was being swallowed up by the gray. She wasn't sure where to turn for answers. She wasn't sure who to trust, and that brought a deep ache to her heart as she thought about the people she loved the most. What was the truth?

Tala's feet hit the pavement, not giving a second thought to where she was going. But they knew the way, leading her home simply through habit. Her mind was somewhere unfamiliar to her, and she stumbled through the congested chaos that filled her brain. She was so distracted that she didn't notice Kane as he approached her near the front doors of her building.

"Are you okay?" he asked.

She shook her head, bringing herself back to reality. She was surprised to see him and unexpectedly glad at the same time. It had been days since she had been to his pod, and she was relieved to know he hadn't given up on her.

"Just… overwhelmed," she admitted. "I've had a weird day."

Kane nodded as he shifted his feet and shoved his hands into the pockets of his jeans.

Tala tipped her head as she studied him. "Can you come up?" she asked bluntly, her words tumbling out of her mouth.

"Uh," he stammered. "Yeah," he said with hesitation.

"Mila, my podmate, isn't home," she added quickly. "So, there won't be any questions."

The corners of his mouth turned up. "I may be difficult to explain," he said with a small laugh. "I don't exactly scream Preferred citizen."

"You're probably the easiest thing to explain in my life at the moment," she said as she headed toward the doors, Kane in step beside her.

They took the elevator in silence, and Tala's mind wandered. Reaching the fifteenth floor, Tala made her way down the hall toward her pod, suddenly very aware of the security camera. But Kane either didn't notice or wasn't concerned about it.

Once inside her pod, she watched him scan the room. Kitchen and dining to the right, living to the left. "So, this is where you live," he said after a minute.

Tala nodded. "It's nothing fancy," she said. "But I didn't want some big, extravagant house along the south bay just so that I could live alone in a huge empty home."

Kane nodded, turning toward her. "Must be rough."

"Oh, sorry. That made me sound spoiled," she said, silently cursing herself. She felt her face flush.

"Maybe a little. But I was kidding," he said with amusement. "I'm fully aware that you're an Alexander."

She was suddenly struck by how attractive he was, in a very different way than Vaughn, and she couldn't help but think that with his rough and rugged features, she liked this look better. Clean-cut, clean-shaven, pressed suits and ties, good etiquette, that was how she was raised. Kane, with his worn jeans and cotton t-shirt, his shaved head, and the scruff on his face, his sharp cheekbones, and distinct jawline, his wide shoulders, and broad chest, gave her a flutter in her belly that she wasn't expecting.

"What?" he asked.

Tala realized she was both staring and grinning, and she quickly turned away. "Nothing," she muttered. She took a slow breath. "Anyway," she said, regaining her composure, "there was something I wanted to share with you." She motioned toward the sofa.

Tala was acutely aware of his proximity to her when they sat, and she felt her pulse quicken. She only hoped he didn't notice. And if he did, he didn't show it. "Okay," she finally said. "We got the autopsies back on my four attackers. And they're not consistent with what I saw."

"In what way?" he asked.

"The photos in the report showed ink. On every one of them," she said.

"No," he said, shaking his head. "I told you before the agents arrived on the scene, I looked them over. They were clean."

"Yes!" she blurted out in earnest. "Yes," she repeated, reining in her enthusiasm. "When I mentioned this at work, I was told I must've overlooked them. But I know for certain I didn't. I didn't miss them," she asserted. "The ink on the men in the photos was large. It wasn't something easy to overlook like a mole or birthmark."

"So, the evidence is fabricated. But why? And who did it?" he asked.

She shrugged and exhaled loudly. "When this all started, I just wanted to get to the bottom of it because I thought there was a real risk to the Republic. But," she said, her mind racing through her thoughts, "I'm not sure I trust Thias or Captain Kole. There's a coverup going on. I just don't know what's being covered up. And I don't know who's involved."

He was quiet for a moment.

"Vaughn said something today that sparked my curiosity," she added.

"Vaughn? Chancellor Adams, that Vaughn?" he asked.

She nodded and noticed his face give a subtle twitch. She didn't want him to know anything was going on between them, though she couldn't understand why it mattered. She instantly wanted to defend herself. But telling him there was nothing would have been a lie. There were enough lies.

"What'd he say?" he asked, his jaw tight.

"The day after the attack at the warehouse, I went to Jerez to talk to my C.I. He gave me my tip for my first arrest at the warehouse. But when I got to the prison, he was dead. Killed in the yard that same morning. Then I was told that the man I had arrested, identified as Gep Masters, had been killed too," she said.

He raised an eyebrow. "You never mentioned this before. How'd he die?"

She shook her head. "No known cause of death. He died in his cell the same night as his arrest. No signs of physical harm, and his toxicology and autopsies revealed nothing."

"That makes no sense," he said, leaning forward, his elbows on his thighs.

"He was interrogated by Thias and Vaughn shortly before his death. I can't say where my info came from, but it is a credible source."

Kane cocked his head.

"Today, Vaughn said something about not getting any information out of Masters the night of his arrest. But then my captain said that it was Masters who ultimately gave up the information that closed this case. *Yesterday.*"

"But dead men don't talk," he said, running his hand over his head.

"Then Vaughn said to me that it had all worked out in the end, except for Masters. I'm not sure what he meant by that, but I got the impression that he knew Masters was dead," she said.

"You're not supposed to know he's dead, are you?" he asked as he eyed her.

Tala's breath caught, and she was suddenly afraid she had divulged too much information. It was information she had sworn to protect. "No, I'm not," she conceded. It was pointless to lie to him. He would know, and she needed to have someone she had no lies with.

Kane studied her in silence, then a smirk curled on the corner of his mouth. "You certainly have a way of finding things you're not supposed to."

"It's my training," she said.

He shook his head. "I really don't think so."

"Life was easier before I learned all of this," she said quietly.

"But if learning this can make a difference, if it can save or prevent something, isn't it worth it in the end?" he asked earnestly.

Tala's gaze met his, her eyes lingering on him. "Maybe," she said.

"So, you think Vaughn Adams knows something?" he asked.

"Something, yes," she admitted. She let out a groan in frustration. "Damn it!" she yelled, her resolve snapping. "I feel like I'm spinning in circles. I tried to raise some of these questions with Ronin today and the next thing I know, he's threatening to report me for insubordination."

"Your partner Ronin?" he asked with a raised brow.

She nodded. Then she thought about her parents' case, sealed and out of her reach. But she decided to say nothing. If there was any chance at all that Kane had been involved, she didn't want to scare him off before she had answers.

Tala felt tears prick the back of her eyes, and she willed them to stay at bay as she took a deep breath. She looked away from Kane, embarrassed. "Sorry," she mumbled.

"Hey," he said gently, his voice deep and low. He reached for her hands, taking them in his. They were warm, and as he closed his grip around hers, he gave her a comforting squeeze.

She felt herself beginning to crack, becoming increasingly aware that she had stumbled into something bigger than she had imagined, and she was sure she was in too deep. She wouldn't be able to dig herself out now. She knew too much. She knew she had to see it through to the other side, wherever that was. She had a duty to her country, to the people she loved. But with the web of lies getting more complicated at every turn, she was feeling overwhelmed. Kane, she thought, might be the only person she could trust. She needed someone and was suddenly filled with hope at the thought of it being him.

She turned toward him, meeting his gaze, and before she could stop herself, she hurled herself into him, pressing her face against his chest. She felt him heave with a deep sigh as his arms slipped around her, and he pulled her close. He was warm, smelling of a subtle combination of soap and worn leather, and something that was entirely his own. As he held her, her emotions began to bubble at the surface and tears once again filled her eyes. She took a breath and closed them, feeling a single tear run down her cheek.

She couldn't do this alone. She had to trust someone. In that moment, her heart decided it was Kane. She only hoped she wasn't wrong in choosing him.

❖

16 years earlier

Kane slumped over in his chair as he swung his leg, kicking at a partially exposed rock in the dirt. It was easier to focus on the rock, with smooth shades of black and dark red swirled together. The voice of the pastor felt far away as he thought about his mother. She had looked so small and frail in her last days. But her voice was strong. And her faith even stronger. She had held his hand firmly, her fingers cold and slender. She wouldn't let him look away as she told him she loved him. *"There is no one who has filled my heart with more love,"* she had said, tears pooling in her eyes. *"Always be true to who you are, Kane Ryan. Don't let others break you,"* she said, and he knew who she was referring to, though neither said his name aloud. It was a silent understanding between them.

He'd been there at her bedside when she took her last breath, and he had felt his heart break. Things, he knew, would never be the same. He would never be the same. He thought of the stars in the nighttime sky, all those tiny flecks of light that he would gaze at in wonder. Each one a flicker of hope, and he was certain she had now joined them in the sky. Without her, he was uncertain of his future, but he put his faith in those stars to guide him on his way. And he knew he would never be truly without her.

Kane felt a sharp elbow into his side, pain stabbing him as he looked up at his father who glared through bleary eyes down on him. Ismet was half drunk. Kane watched him discreetly taking swigs from the bottle between friends who had come to offer their condolences before the service.

A slow chorus song began among the group of mourners as they rose to their feet. Unable to bring himself to watch her casket lowered into the ground, Kane picked at a loose button on his dress shirt. He heard his father take a raspy breath, his body shuddering.

After his mother's casket, a simple wooden box covered in white paint and lacquer, was settled on the bottom of the large hole that had swallowed her up, the crowd dissipated. But Kane remained behind. Leaving her alone felt like a betrayal. His eyes welled, and he heaved a loud sigh. Choking on emotion, he let his tears run down his face, soaking his cheeks, lingering on his jaw before falling onto the lapels of the suit coat that was too large and hung loosely on him.

"Are you seriously crying?" Ismet hissed.

Kane turned and looked up at his father, his dark eyes glossed over, and his brows puckered.

"This is your chance to show me that you're a man. And you're blowing it. Real men don't cry like little pussies. They channel it into hard work. Are you a pussy, Kane?" he spat.

Across the gaping hole in the ground, Kane could see the crowd of mourners now far off, then caught sight of Addox, who lingered nearby. He, too, was in a suitcoat too large for him, yet his pants were far too short. Addox was tall and lanky. It had been nearly impossible to find anything to relatively fit him.

Addox stared at Kane through vacant, sunken eyes. His shoulders slumped over, his soft brown hair unevenly trimmed and flopped over his forehead. He looked ashen and meek as he unassumingly hung in the background.

"No," Kane said through gnashed teeth as he wiped at his wet face and glared up at Ismet.

"You're a pussy," Ismet taunted. "You'll never be a man. We lose people all the time. We can't stop and cry to our mamas every damn time. And you," he sneered, "you'll never be able to cry to your mama again. And I won't put up with it. That's for damn sure."

Kane looked up at him through narrowed, defiant eyes, his jaw set firmly. Except for Addox, the crowd was now on the opposite side of the cemetery, near the road.

"You're going to be trouble for me," Ismet said with a shake of his head. "You better learn who's in charge right now. And you will yield to me."

Kane straightened his body, pulling back his shoulders as he stood taller, his gaze not dropping from his father's.

"You little fucker," Ismet spat as he pulled his hand back, then swinging it around, he made direct contact with Kane's face.

Kane staggered backward, pain exploding in his cheek. But he found his footing, straightened his body once more, and met his father's eyes again.

Ismet's nostrils flared as his eyes grew wide, and he punched Kane in the face, this time knocking him to his knees.

"That ought to teach you," he said as he lobbed a stream of spit onto him.

Kane steadied his breathing as his father walked away, stumbling on the uneven ground. From the corner of his eye, Kane caught Addox's pitying look as he watched quietly from across the gravesite, and he hated him for it.

Kane looked away as he stood, wiping the spit off the side of his face, then dabbed his finger on his freshly busted lip. When he glanced back, Addox was gone.

"Here you go," Max said from behind.

Kane turned to see his outstretched hand holding a tissue as he approached. He reached for it and pressed it to his bleeding mouth.

"Thanks," he murmured.

"Got you good," Max said matter-of-factly and without pity.

Kane was grateful for that.

"You want to get out of here? Head down to the old docks?" Max asked.

Kane gave a small nod. He spun on his heel and headed toward the cemetery gate, Max in stride alongside him.

They were quiet as they walked, but as they rounded the corner of Elm Street and the dilapidated docks came into view, Max broke the silence. "He's the real fucker," he said bluntly.

Kane looked at his friend in surprise. He was a small boy who was content always being in the background, who looked at you through thick glasses and shaggy hair that usually hung in his eyes. But he was Kane's friend. His only friend. And undoubtedly his best friend.

Kane smiled, his lip cracking open, beginning to bleed again.

"You can live with me," Max suggested, his voice high.

"You and the other eight people in your house?" he said with a low chuckle.

Max shrugged. "I'm sure there's room on the floor between the toilet and tub."

"I'll keep that in mind," he said and reached out, slapping him on the back. "Thanks," he said.

"Meh, it's no big deal," Max said, the corner of his mouth curling into a smirk.

It was dark when Kane had left her pod. Despite having no answers, Tala felt lighter. And although things were a mess, she felt she finally had some clarity, even if it was just a little. She knew she had found someone she could trust. And in finding a partner, she felt stronger. She knew she wasn't alone.

Tala only had a small window before Kane would make it back to Oxwick. She pulled out her palm pad and called Max. It rang so many times, she nearly gave up. But in the last moments of hope, he answered.

"Tala?" he asked in surprise when he saw her face on the screen.

"Yes, it's me. Look, I'm sorry to bother you—"

"Did something happen?" he asked in a hurried breath. "Kane okay?"

"Oh yes!" she exclaimed. "I'm sorry, I didn't realize… I can see how you'd think something's wrong," she said, stumbling over her words. "But nothing's wrong. Kane is fine."

Max's shoulders dropped in relief. He looked at her through narrowed eyes, his lips pressed together tightly.

He was irritated. She was very sure he was irritated.

"What do you want?" he asked.

"I need your help," she admitted, hoping there wasn't as much desperation in her voice as there was in her heart. "I need to access a case file in our records archives."

He shook his head. "I don't understand how this involves me."

"The thing is," she hesitated, "I don't have the clearance for it."

Max was quiet, and she saw the pensive look in his eyes.

"I'll pay you. Whatever you want," she added quickly, hoping that if he was ready to shoot her down that there was at least some incentive for him.

"Falsifying your security clearance is a major offense. For both of us. And is not an easy thing to do," he asserted.

"So, you wouldn't be able to do it?" she asked, disappointed.

"I didn't say that," he said flatly.

Tala was unsure how to respond.

"Tell me, why should I put myself on the line for you? And likewise, why would you trust me with this kind of inquiry?" he said.

Tala sighed. "I don't have anyone else to go to. I trust you because Kane trusts you. And I trust Kane," she said. "Look, I know you have no reason to help me. But this is important. It's so important," she pleaded.

Max was quiet.

The longer his silence dragged on, the more certain she was that he was going to refuse her. With no backup plan, Tala sighed in defeat and dropped her head.

"Fine," he grumbled. "I'll do it. But you don't have to pay me," he said, rolling his eyes.

Tala was unable to mask her surprise. "Oh… I…" she stammered. "I don't even know what to say."

"What level are we talking about?"

Tala sucked in a breath, bracing herself. "Level nine," she squeaked.

"Of course level nine. Why would it be anything else?" he said. "I'm going to need to access your agency identification information. But we'll have to spoof where you're sending it from so it can't be traced to either of us," he said.

Tala nodded fervently. She cautioned herself that this was a capital offense, and she would indefinitely be imprisoned for it. But even with that in mind, her excitement was alive inside of her.

"I'm going to send a virus to your palm pad," Max said. "When you open it, you'll be prompted for your agency information. Enter it, and it will spit it back to me. I'll write new code for a dummy account. But I'm going to put an expiration on it. A fail-safe. You'll have to get the file and upload it to the account before the clearance expires," he instructed.

"How long?" she asked, her mind racing through scenarios.

"Twenty-four hours. There are so few people with level nine security clearance, and the longer there is an additional, unknown account, the more likely you are to be discovered."

Tala nodded. "Got it. Twenty-four hours. I can do that."

Max's stare lingered for a moment. "I'll write it now and send it by midnight. You'll have until midnight tomorrow."

"You have no idea how—"

Max raised his hand to stop her. "Don't thank me yet," he said. "Not until the job's done."

"Okay," she said, biting back yet another *thank you*.

"Let me know how it turns out," he said. "Oh, and Tala, how did you get my number?"

"I looked you up. I, uh… wanted to learn more about Kane," she admitted, swallowing a rising lump in her throat.

"You found him, didn't you?" he asked, his voice tight.

Tala nodded. "When I searched your hometown and his name."

Max pursed his lips into a straight line, and she could see his cheeks turning red. "Please don't tell me this was from your work computer."

She took a sharp breath, not seeing her mistake until that moment.

"Shit, Tala! What if MF starts looking into you? You would be exposing him, his identity." Max's voice was bitter and angry.

"I didn't even think about that," she said feebly.

Max looked away for a moment, pinching the bridge of his nose, just beneath his glasses. "You have to fix this," he said, turning back to her. "I'll write a virus, hide it in a trojan. You have to open it from your work desktop. I will make sure any files with his or my information are corrupted. Jeez, Tala, you're giving me a lot of work."

"I'll be indebted to you," she said.

"No, I'm not doing this part for you. This is for Kane. Because my number one priority is to protect him. And that's what I'm going to do," he said. "I'll email the virus to you. Send me a message with your email address. Now, I've got to go. Suddenly a lot on my plate," he said with a bite in his tone.

Tala had just enough time to give an apologetic smile before her screen went black.

She had been senseless, and she needed to pull herself together. She couldn't be sloppy, especially with Kane's life in her hands. Max would fix this though. Of that, she was certain. Just like she knew he would get her access to that file.

She felt her body begin to quiver with nervous excitement. She was close now. She felt so close. Then a sobering thought came to her. She so desperately wanted answers that she hadn't considered that, depending on what she found, she might not want the truth.

No, she asserted to herself, the truth would always be the truth, regardless of how ugly it was. It would always be better than a lie.

Tala lay awake for most of the night, drifting in and out of sleep in short intervals, and even before the morning sun had come up, she was out of bed and ready for the day. Eager anticipation raced through her. Her palm pad nearly buzzed with the false identification as Tala held it in her hand.

"You okay?" Mila asked as she stumbled out of her bedroom, rubbing her eyes, her robe hanging open, the cotton belt dragging across the floor.

"Just ready for work," she said, trying to keep her voice level to keep her excitement from boiling over.

Mila eyed her skeptically. "A little unlike you." Her eyes wandered to the empty coffee pot. "No coffee?"

"Not today. Anyway," she said before there were more questions, "I'm off to work."

"Oh… okay." Mila wore her confusion on her face as she glanced at the kitchen clock.

Tala heard Mila's goodbye from the hallway as the door closed behind her, and she breathed a sigh of relief. She was too transparent.

Tala briskly made her way to the subtrain, which was only moderately busy that early in the day, then trekked the last three blocks to Command on foot.

The rotunda was quiet, mostly agents from the night shift still lingering. It was a shift that was typically uneventful because of the city curfew. Although it still had its exciting moments from time to time. It was too early in the morning for Agent Durham to be in the Records Department, so impatiently, she took a seat at her desk and glanced carefully around the room. She hoped she didn't look as guilty as she felt. Never had she ever imagined doing what she was about to do. She had fallen so far away from who she was only a week earlier. But oh, so much had changed in just one week.

She thought of Thias, what he would say if he discovered her. His menacing gaze burned in her mind. That image, frequently lingering in the back of her head, was a deterrent against many things in her life. The first few months following her parents' death were the most difficult. It was a time in her life she didn't look back on fondly.

At fifteen, she ran around with a boy named Kyler. She cringed thinking back to the trouble they caused. She had been convinced she was in love, and that made her eager to follow his every whim. In those days, she snuck out after curfew, slipped into bars and night clubs underage, and one wild night, they crashed Kyler's parents' car into a tree while joyriding in Baxtham. They were both lucky to walk away from that accident. Thias was quick to shut her down after that. He wasn't about to tolerate behavior like that from her. He needed to show his country he could be taken seriously as director of Militia Forces, young as he was, and being unable to reign in his little sister was not going to help him. It was at that time that Thias put her in an early program for MF cadet training. And to her surprise, she both enjoyed it and was good at it. It seemed to fill the void left behind in the aftermath of her parents' deaths. After that, the choice to pursue a career in the Militia Forces was an easy one, and she had found a confidence in herself she hadn't had before.

Now she was putting everything on the line in her pursuit of the truth. It was a true test of both her courage and training. She had often regarded those few months of disobedience as the result of misplaced emotional pain from her loss. She never considered that maybe she did have it in her to be defiant, to really challenge something. It was easy to follow Thias's lead. But in doing so, had she let herself become what he wanted rather than who she truly was? And now she couldn't help but wonder, who was the real Tala Alexander?

Tala watched Bishop enter the rotunda, and he gave her his typical jeering glare. She shook her head and rolled her eyes, turning to her computer. She loathed him, but seeing his frustration when his work was inferior to hers was all the satisfaction she needed where he was concerned.

Then she spotted him, Agent Durham from Records. He caught her attention as he quietly made his way across the rotunda to the elevators.

Busying herself, she gave him another few minutes to get down to sub-level A, to get the office unlocked and to settle in. She didn't want to seem too eager. She opened her email to find a message from an unknown sender, and she knew immediately what it was. Recalling her stupidity, she opened it and clicked the link in the message. A new window opened, numbers flashing across the screen, and she felt herself relax knowing that one thing was taken care of.

Ten minutes later, she rose from her desk. It was time. And surprisingly, her head was clear, and she let out a long exhale, steeling herself as she crossed the rotunda toward the elevator which was notoriously slow so, she opted for the stairs.

Without all the growing bustle in the rotunda from agents arriving for the day shift, it was quiet on the lower level. Reaching for the door to the Records Department, Tala's hand trembled, and she took a deep breath to steady herself. She entered the small room, Durham at his desk, briefly looking up at her. She gave him a small grin through pursed lips, and he quietly nodded, then turned to his computer.

Tala crossed the room to the terminal in the corner farthest from Durham. Her heart rate was gathering speed, and she was growing warm all over as butterflies swarmed in her stomach. She knew her cheeks were reddening, but she focused on her breathing which helped calm her trembling hands as she tapped the screen to wake it up. She was instantly prompted to input her identification number. She paused for a moment to let her head clear, then put in the false ID number Max had given her. She had committed it to memory, and holding her breath, she tapped *Enter*.

The terminal unlocked, and Tala's shoulders dropped in relief.

A fog began to gather in her mind, and her left leg quivered, but she bit the inside of her cheek to keep herself focused. She typed in the case file number, a tightness in her chest. This was it. It was either going to work or it wasn't. Feeling small beads of sweat gathering on her forehead, she tapped *Enter*, the case file opening before her eyes, the word **CONFIDENTIAL** in bold across the top. Eager nervousness washed over her as she tapped the red double arrow icon, and immediately, the upload to the offsite dummy account Max had created began.

Tala watched uneasily as the progress bar slowly crept along, showing the completion percentage of the upload. Time seemed to stand still.

The door to the office opened, and she spun around quickly, her heart in her throat. But the agent who entered paid no attention to her; he simply approached Durham's desk and began mumbling something to him. She studied them carefully for a moment, then looked back at the upload progress. It was taking too long. Until now, she had managed to keep herself relatively calm and steady, but with each passing second, she felt panic taking over, her mind wandering to worst-case scenarios. Thias's menacing face was in her head, his admonitory words in her ears.

She bit her cheek harder, the metallic taste of blood in her mouth. She gave a sideways glance at the agents who were still in conversation with each other, indifferent to her presence.

Turning back to the terminal, relief washed over her as the upload completed. Quickly, she closed the file and signed out of the terminal. Turning on her heel, she abruptly left the office, her heart racing in her chest. Once in the stairwell, she finally took a deep breath, willing her nerves to relax.

Her footsteps echoed in the stairwell as she made her way back to the rotunda, and as she rounded the corner, she was instantly met face-to-face with Ronin.

Her heart sank, and her mouth went dry.

"What're you doing?" he asked. "Bishop said he saw you come down here."

Of course he did.

Her body went hot all over as her mind raced for an excuse. She'd had so many planned for this very moment, and now her mind was blank. Her hands grew clammy as he stood there, waiting for her response, and once again, her face flushed.

"Tala?" he asked, his eyes narrowing, his brow furrowed as he studied her with confusion.

"I pulled an old robbery case from a few weeks ago," she said, finding her words. "The string of robberies from the other day got me thinking of an older one. I wanted to check and see if there were any similarities."

Ronin's eyes lingered on hers for a moment, and she knew he was weighing her story. Then his face softened. "So, what'd you find?"

Tala shook her head. "I don't think they're related. The witness statements contradict each other."

"Well, at least now we can rule out any connection. Good call," he said with an approving smile and nod.

As he turned and headed back up the stairs, Tala's relief was palpable, and she felt weak in the knees. She reached for the railing to steady herself as she exhaled slowly, calming her racing heart.

"You coming?" he called over his shoulder.

"Yep," she said, finding solid footing. With a sigh, she ascended the stairs.

SEVEN

When Tala returned to the rotunda, the room was bustling with activity, the daytime agents having edged out those from the night shift. Conversation traveled across desks, agents were on palm pads, tablets, and computers, the day in full swing. From the corner of her eye, she unexpectedly spotted Thias standing beside Captain Kole at Bishop and Kassis's desk. She watched in silence as the agents rose from their seats and set off in a quick pace on the heels of Thias and Kole, making their way to Kole's office, Grant slipping in after all of them. Thias approached the windows that looked out over the rotunda from the office, his eyes catching hers, his expression hard, then he pulled the blinds shut.

From the corner of her eye, she continued to watch Kole's office for signs of movement while she combed through endless frames of surveillance footage from around the crime scene of her burglary case.

Tala watched curiously as four more agents entered Kole's office, then abruptly closed the door behind them. Something was going on, and her heart couldn't help but beat a little faster at the thought of the crime she had just committed. Though none of them could know about it yet. But she had no regrets. She had been marked by the stain of a lie, but rather than feeling burdened by the weight of any guilt from it, she felt liberated in the knowledge that she had the case file.

"What do you keep looking at?" Ronin asked, startling Tala. She jerked her head in his direction.

"Something's going on," she said quietly under her breath with a nod toward Kole's office.

Ronin's brows arched.

"Thias is here, in Kole's office. They're with Bishop and Kassis and four agents from the tactical unit."

Ronin glanced over his shoulder at Kole's office, then shrugged as he looked back at Tala. "Yeah, I'm sure something's going on. But Tala, we're MF, there's always something going on somewhere."

It was true. But Tala knew from personal experience that when Thias showed up, it was never over something minor. She gave another glance at Kole's office, then turned back to her computer, resuming her work.

She busied herself by combing through what seemed like endless amounts of surveillance, if only to expend the frenetic energy building from her anticipation of what was to come. Her parents' case file seemed to be calling out to her in whispers, begging to tell the truth after so long.

Tala's mind wandered between her curiosity over the meeting in Kole's office, which had been going on for nearly two hours, and the illegal file she had just sitting on a server waiting to be opened. She was growing restless and watching the time tick by was doing nothing to settle her.

"You're not yourself today," Ronin said.

Tala looked up at him. "How so?"

"I can't quite put my finger on it. I can tell you're distracted," he said. "You're not still thinking about the other case, are you?"

"No, I decided to take your advice and drop it."

He nodded, a pleased grin on his face, and a knot formed in Tala's gut. They were trained to put the Republic first. They were trained to follow orders. But she couldn't help but think that in doing that, they, all Militia Forces agents, were blinded by their loyalty. She saw it in Ronin now. She could see it in her past self, maybe still in her current self. In that moment, she was no longer angry with him, but rather, she couldn't help but pity him.

Movement caught in the corner of Tala's eye, and she turned to see Kole's office emptying. Bishop, Kassis, and the tactical team wore trenchant expressions on their faces, followed by Kole who looked the same as usual, and Thias whose expression was stern but entirely unreadable. She watched as the agents left the rotunda, heading in the direction of the munitions locker, which meant only one thing: they were on assignment.

Thias caught Tala's gaze from across the rotunda, and he gave her a single nod of his head in acknowledgment. He turned to Grant, saying something she couldn't make out, then made a call on his palm pad while he headed for the exit. In a matter of only seconds, he was gone from sight.

"Agents," Kole said. In her distraction watching the other agents and Thias, Tala gave a small jump. "I want an update on your robbery case."

Ronin looked up at him. "We spotted a man, dressed in black, hooded, about half a block from the crime scene just minutes before the actual robbery, but we lost him on surveillance after that. So, nothing can prove that he's our suspect. He could be a person of interest though. But there's nothing discernable about him and his face is well hidden, so no way to make a positive ID."

"I saw what appeared to be the same person a few blocks away at the same time the emergency call came in, but again, visual was poor. The only thing we were able to determine was he is white, about six foot two, and male," Tala added. "Which is all we got from the victim's description."

Kole folded his arms as his eyes moved between them. "And this took place in the Legend Avenues district in southeast Oxwick?"

"Yes, Captain," Tala said.

"A Substandard neighborhood. Security cameras are typically unreliable there. They're vandalized faster than any of them can ever be replaced. What's our victim's citizenship?" he asked, his brows tightly furrowing.

"Substandard," Ronin said.

"And she had $5,000 stolen? Who has physical money anymore? And how would a Substandard have that kind of surplus?" Kole asked.

"She wasn't all that forthcoming in any of the statements she made," Tala added.

"Well, maybe it's time to wrap this up. If she's going to impede the job you're trying to do, then we don't need to go out of our way, expending resources that could be used for other cases. Mark it unresolved citing lack of evidence and catalog it," Kole said.

Tala and Ronin each nodded.

"You're both finished with your current rotation. See you back here in a few days," he said sternly, then turned on his heels and strode back toward his office.

"Ever noticed that we mark cases unresolved for Substandard citizens more than any other class?" Tala asked.

Ronin shrugged. "Maybe. But Kole's right. We can only do our job as well as the quality of evidence we have. If they're going to withhold information, well, then we can't fully do our job. I agree, it's time to move on. We've been at this one for days."

He had a valid point, but Tala couldn't help but think there was still injustice in it.

"Want to get a drink? Officially bury the hatchet of our disagreement this week?" Ronin asked, a flicker of apology, of regret in his eyes.

It wasn't just a disagreement, Tala thought. He had threatened to report her. His words were meant to be well-intentioned, stemming from his fear of repercussions from the Republic, something that strangely didn't seem to deter Tala now, but they triggered something in her. They were revelatory, if anything, about the relationship she had with Ronin: their friendship, their partnership. For the first time, a divide expanded between them, and it left her feeling disquieted. In her effort to break apart the lies in her life, she was keenly aware that she was simultaneously creating entirely new ones.

"I'm going to pass on the drink tonight," she said. "It's been a long week. Maybe tomorrow."

Ronin nodded, his shoulders sagging. "Yeah, okay."

Tala cleared and locked her computer. Grabbing her palm pad, she stood. "See you," she said, hearing the sadness in her voice as she gave him one last look, then turned and set off toward the doors.

"Your mission was a success?" Max asked, his face filling the screen on her palm pad.

"Yes," she exclaimed, excitement coursing through her as she made her way from the elevator to her pod. "I can't believe you pulled this off for me."

He sighed. "Tala, one thing you should know about me is that if there's a computer involved, there's not much I can't do," he said confidently, almost arrogantly, and she saw a pleased smile on his face.

She nodded. "Well, I didn't mean to underestimate you."

"What's in the file?" he asked. "Anything connected to this other stuff?"

"Sort of," she lied. This felt too personal, and she couldn't bring herself to say anything.

"Does Kane know?" he asked, giving his glasses a nudge back into place after sliding down the bridge of his nose.

"No. But I plan on telling him."

"I just transferred the file to your palm pad. You're all set," he said.

"Thanks, Max," she said, for lack of any better words. They didn't seem enough. She was thankful, but she couldn't help but think her excitement was premature. Despite herself, she was nervous about what she may find. What had he helped her with? What had they set into motion?

"And the other matter," he said, one of his brows arching.

"It's been taken care of," she said. "If your virus worked the way you said it would, all of that data should be corrupted or wiped clean. Whatever it was designed to do."

He gave a satisfied nod. "Good. From now on, if you've got questions for Kane, I suggest asking him personally. As for the other stuff, good luck," he said, then the screen went black.

Glad to finally be home, Tala carefully took a seat on her bed. The moment had come. Once the file was read, she'd never be able to go back; she'd never be able to unread it. Suddenly, every reason not to do it came washing over her, flooding the smallest cracks in her resolve, her courage slowly ebbing.

No, she yelled silently within the confines of her mind. It was time to meet the truth face-to-face, to look it in the eye. She hadn't come this far for nothing.

Her phone pulsed in her hand, a strident thrumming playing loudly. She glanced at the time, her heart sinking as she realized it was time for the National Statement. She felt the flash of annoyance as she let out a small groan. There was nothing she could do now but watch. Which was a requirement of all citizens. And her palm pad would do nothing until the Statement was over. Holding it firmly in her hand, the screen filled with Wynn Davison's face, the Republic's press liaison. Tala had watched the woman report the National Statement every week for ten years. She knew her face nearly as well as she knew her own reflection. She was confident and poised, and she was gorgeous, with long locks of the darkest brown hair and the palest blue eyes that always seemed to gleam. Arguably, Wynn Davison and Thias were the most visible faces of the Republic. Even more so than President Royer, who seemed to like to have an air of mystery around him, as far as the public went.

"Good evening, people of the Republic of Columbia," Wynn said, her mouth curved into a small smile. Her voice echoed from behind Tala as it also played on the TV built into her bed and down the hall from the TV in the living room, all of which automatically powered on for the Statement. "I'm Wynn Davison, and this is your weekly National Statement.

"In Republic news, preparations for President Royer II's upcoming birthday celebration are in full swing, and the Republic of Columbia is excited to host this event, with many world leaders expected to attend. You'll have your opportunity to see our finest citizens and guests as they arrive on the gold carpet from the comforts of your home as we livestream the welcome event.

"In response to the ongoing water crisis inside our largest cities, Columbia City, Michigan City, Alexandria, and Providence, new water restrictions will be implemented. The daily water allotment for all rural households outside these cities' limits is now being decreased by one gallon. This small reduction is expected to decrease the deficit within our most populated areas, allowing over forty million gallons to be redirected. These new restrictions are effective immediately. All city and county officials around the country have updated the programming of our water dispensary systems," she said, then pursed her lips together, a small, kind smile on her mouth, wrinkles in the corners of her eyes.

Tala thought about the districts throughout the city that notoriously ran out of water daily, before their allotment was even used. She knew it was a growing concern and had been an ongoing issue. People never knew when they would run out. Thankfully, this had never happened to her or anyone she knew.

"And lastly," Wynn said as she straightened her body, her smile fading into something sober, "Director Alexander has confirmed that a raid was executed this afternoon throughout the Washington Terrace district of the Walhurst peninsula. Four computer hackers, all identified to have ties with the Unified Rebels, were arrested, and another nine suspected sympathizers have been taken into custody." Wynn's face was replaced by video footage taken of the raid showing Bishop directing agents as they carried seized computers and electronics out of a pod. A crowd had gathered in the background, a few crying as they watched the scene unfold. "This has been an ongoing Militia Forces investigation. No other information related to this case will be disclosed at this time," she continued.

"As usual, citizens are encouraged to contact Militia Forces to report any suspicious activity," Wynn said, her face returning to the screen. "A reminder that reports can be made anonymously, and all are strictly confidential," she said and gave a slight pause. "This is Wynn Davison wishing everyone a good evening." She gave a wide smile and a small nod of her head to the cameras. Then the screen went black, the broadcast ending.

Tala took a breath, her mind quickly bringing her back to the case file on her palm pad, the Statement being instantly buried in the back of her mind.

She stared at her palm pad with rising trepidation, smoothing her thumb across its glassy surface. Swiping her finger, she unlocked the device and stared at the blue icon labeled *Case File 10RCJ236MRP*. Tala's heart pounded heavily, and with an uneven exhale, she tapped the file.

CONFIDENTIAL
Case File 10RCJ236MRP
Security Clearance: Level 9

ORDER OF ASSASSINATION

Subject(s): Jameson Alexander, Brit Alexander, Tala Alexander
Statute 475A of Republic of Columbia Declaration of Policy and Aims
Charges: Government Obstruction; Treason against the Republic of Columbia
Penalty: Death by assassination

Tala's stomach dropped, her blood running cold. The word *assassination* glared back at her. Her chest tightened as she took in a labored breath. She blinked hard, her brain stuttering. It was as if time stood still, that word hanging in the air: assassination. A million questions surged all at once in her mind, and she looked away from the screen. Gripping her palm pad, her hands were turning clammy.

Assassination.

She closed her eyes, taking a slow and steady breath. *Keep reading,* she told herself. She had to continue. She had wanted the truth. This was the truth.

She turned back to the file, steeling herself.

Case Summary: Brit Alexander (biochemist): suspect for security breach at Stanger Research Lab, secure government facility, resulting in the escape of fourteen test subjects scheduled for termination. Test subjects still at large. Per statute 475A, article 47, the accused of government security breaches are suspect to termination pending government review. Due to the delicate security information breached in this case, a unanimous vote (excluding Director of Militia Forces Jameson Alexander) ruled in favor of assassination. Covert execution to be conducted by Militia Forces. Subjects to be included: Brit Alexander, accused; Jameson Alexander, sympathizer; minor: Tala Alexander (15 years), collateral.

Plan of Action:

A) Subjects will be unknowingly sedated through pentobarbital, administered via a beverage prepared by Thias Alexander.
B) Once subjects are incapacitated, an MF tactical operations team will covertly firebomb the house under the cover of night.
    a. Thias Alexander will be removed from the home before being set on fire.
        i. Thias Alexander is endorsed to accede to the position of director of Militia Forces, per Statute 10784T of the Republic of Columbia Declaration of Policy and Aims.
    b. Ruled cause of the fire will be a gas leak.

Signed: Viktor Royer II, President of Republic of Columbia
      Mikel Murdo, Chief Justice

With her heart in her throat, Tala continued to scroll to the second document in the file.

CONFIDENTIAL
Case File 10RCJ236MRP
Security Clearance: Level 9

<u>**MISSION STATUS REPORT**</u>
Subject(s): Jameson Alexander, Brit Alexander, Tala Alexander
Statute 475A of Republic of Columbia Declaration of Policy and Aims
Charges: Government Obstruction; Treason against the Republic of
Columbia
Penalty: Death by assassination
Status: Partial Completion

    A)   Brit Alexander: *terminated*
    B)   Jameson Alexander: *terminated*
    C)   Tala Alexander: *incomplete/failed termination*
           a.   Assassination order rescinded/dismissal of further action
                  i.   Issued by Director of Militia Forces Thias
                         Alexander
                 ii.   Minor custody to be assumed by nearest kin:
                         Thias Alexander

Amendment approved unanimously.
Signed: Viktor Royer II, President of Republic of Columbia
       Mikel Murdo, Chief Justice
       Thias Alexander, Director of Militia Forces

Tala stared, mouth agape, her mind unable to string two thoughts together. Thias's name glared back at her. She knew the signature, yet her brain struggled to catch up with what her eyes registered. She read the file again, her mind knowing the words but unable to comprehend them. It was all wrong. Every thought in her head seemed to be in conflict with each other.

But it was there in her hand. Undisputable.

It never was a gas leak. "Assassination," she said aloud, the word tasting bitter on her tongue. They had been murdered, by their own people, their own country. The country they built. And they had tried to murder her.

Sedated? It was no wonder she had been groggy, unable to wake her mind that night. Why her memories were still a blur. They told her she was tired from being woken from her sleep, that the smoke inhalation, chemical asphyxiants, and low oxygen, had caused her disorientation. And maybe that was true, but she was meant to never wake up.

And Thias was part of it. He had been with them on their last night together not because they were family, but because he was complicit in their murder. Slowly, the pieces began to fit together, falling into place. She closed her eyes, feeling the sting of tears gathering.

Thias was suddenly a stranger to her, and she couldn't understand what could possibly have been his motivation to kill his own family. All these years, she had taken him at his word; he had looked her in the eye and lied to her. His betrayal was almost tangible, burning into her soul.

An urge to vomit came over Tala, and she inhaled deeply through her nose, pushing it away.

Her emotions were overwhelming her: anger, sadness, shock, hatred, and devastation all woven together. She couldn't have separated them from each other if she tried. She had been so naïve and chastised herself for her ignorance. Her whole life she had been contented to follow everyone's lead. Her mind was a swirling vortex of clashing thoughts and emotion. Nothing felt real anymore.

She slid from her bed to her knees, her head falling into her hands. She willed herself to cry, desperate for a release, but the tears that had gathered had since dried, anger following in their wake.

There was a stagnant ache deep in her chest. *Treason. Assassination. Termination.* The words played on a reel in her mind.

Tala could hear the whispers of Thias in her head, and she recoiled. Her sudden hatred was now a raging river that flowed through her, no end in sight, swiftly taking anything that had been good in their relationship with it.

Her breath shuddered and a chill ran through her.

Tala rose to her feet. Crossing her bedroom in only a few strides, she went to the small jewelry box on her dresser. Inside were her mother's pearl earrings, one of the few things recovered from the safe after the fire. But it wasn't the pearls she reached for. She grasped the thin gold chain between her fingers. Pulling it out of the box, the pendant dangled from the bottom. She eyed it carefully.

She reached for the pendant, taking the delicate triangle of the Republic in her hands. She smoothed her thumb over it. The upright triangle that didn't connect at the bottom: the social hierarchy of the Republic, with the government at the very tip.

"But why is it broken on the bottom?" she had asked her father once, so long ago she couldn't quite remember when.

"Because human nature is flawed," he'd said matter-of-factly. *"So we look to our leaders, the greatest authority, for truth and knowledge. The bottom of the triangle will always be broken, it will always be disconnected because of human imperfection. But our people, our country, it is all held together by our leaders just as the top point holds the triangle together."*

Tala took a breath as she slammed the necklace onto the dresser. That authority murdered her family. Had tried to murder her. They had taken everything from her. She dedicated her life in service to the Republic, but now she could see it for what it truly was. It was broken. It was corrupt. It was a lie. And Thias was a part of it all.

What she couldn't understand was why she had been spared.

She felt foolish. She had trusted them, never thinking otherwise, and her loyalty and altruism had been used against her. She had been made, strategically conditioned and trained, to defend her homeland. And now, she realized, she had believed in a false hero.

There were so many thoughts in her head, emotions in her heart that she couldn't pin even one of them down. Her shoulders sagged, the ache so deep inside her. *Thias*, she thought, his name hanging in her mind. She wasn't just a creation of the Republic, she was who he had made her to be. And she had come to see herself solely as others expected her to be. There was never a time in her life when she had been without her brother. She trusted him. She loved him. The truth was going to change her. She had been made different already. But how did someone unlearn everything they had been taught? All she had ever been was the Tala Thias wanted her to be. If she stripped that away, what was left of her?

Tala sat on her floor, hunched over and propped against her bed in the quiet stillness of her room, hugging her knees to her chest. The thoughts that had overwhelmed her had briefly quieted as time slowly ticked by. She was unsure how long she'd been sitting there. Her anger had drained through her body, and now she was simply numb, an empty shell, and her eyes stared unfocused into a mindless void.

The light pattering of rain on her windows registered in her ears, bringing her back. She blinked away the fog. With her mind clearing, she thought of her mother, a biochemist for Stanger Research Lab, according to the file. She knew it wasn't a coincidence that the name Stanger had also been on Kane's adoption record.

Tala pulled herself upright and reached for her palm pad, opening the file again.

Brit Alexander (biochemist): suspect for security breach at Stanger Research Lab, secure government facility, resulting in the escape of fourteen test subjects scheduled for termination. Test subjects still at large.

"Yes, this was something that had been done to me… medical research."

Kane's words played back in her head, and her body gave a small tremble, now understanding. It was her mother. She was the one who had hurt him.

When she discovered her parents' case had been sealed, she knew there was information that she didn't know. That there was more to the story than she had been told. But she had never imagined she'd fall into such a black hole. How far into the darkness did it all go?

Tala felt suddenly lost. She had been led into a place unknown and was uncertain where to go. In what direction did she take the first step? She was alone. In the span of one night, she had lost Thias, she had lost her parents all over again. All she had was herself, and even that woman she didn't know.

Amid the sound of the rain, Tala heard a faint ting on the glass of her balcony door. She looked up to see it had grown dark. Kane's face was lit up by the soft glow of light in her bedroom, the rain glistening off his face. She rose to her feet, making her way to the door. She opened it, feeling the chilly air rush into her bedroom, sending goosebumps up her arms.

"How did you…" she asked as she made her way to the balcony railing, hidden mostly by wilting plants and a small tree, and peered over the edge to the ground below.

"When I was here yesterday," he said, standing in the cold and wet darkness, "I figured out which balcony is yours."

"You climbed all the way up here?" she asked. She turned, mouth agape, and met his gaze. She felt her face getting wet from the rain and stepped back into her bedroom.

"It's easier than it looks," he said with a smirk. "Just can't be afraid of heights."

"What if someone had seen you?" she asked, still stunned.

"It's dark. And I was fast. No one saw a thing, and there aren't security cameras on any of the balconies," he said, still standing outside, seemingly unfazed by the drizzle coming down on him.

She gave a slow nod, torn between her grief and her relief at seeing him.

Tala saw his eyes narrow as he studied her, and she knew he could read the emotion on her face. Looking at him now, she felt something stir inside her.

He took a small step closer to her, though still not moving to come inside. "Something's happened," he said cautiously.

Tala was quiet; she felt vulnerable with his eyes on her. But she didn't shy away, she didn't back down, instead she stood a little taller.

"Want to talk about it?" he asked quietly.

"I do. Mostly because it involves you," she admitted, finally saying aloud what was hanging in her mind. "Come in," she said, motioning with her hand.

He entered her bedroom slowly, reluctantly, and she closed the door behind him. She couldn't quite decide on his reticence. Although Mila wasn't home, and likely wouldn't be for some time, she still closed her bedroom door.

He shed his wet leather jacket, hanging it from her balcony door handle. Tala motioned to him to sit beside her on the edge of her bed.

"I did something today," she began, diving right in before she lost her nerve. "I illegally gained access to a case file. To my parents' case file." She saw a quick flicker in his eyes. "And I learned that my mother worked for a place called Stanger Research Lab."

He held her gaze, giving nothing away, and so she continued. "I also found a public adoption record for Kane Ryan of Bedley, signed by both Ismet Ryan and the single name Stanger. That's you," she whispered, suddenly feeling like she had invaded something personal and private. He hadn't known she went digging for him, but his expression didn't change with her revelation.

"Kane," she said softly. "I don't have the same skills as you. I'm not a human lie detector, but I ask you to be honest with me. I can't handle another lie."

His jaw was set in a hard line, and his gaze did not waver. Tala swallowed hard, and he gave a slow nod of his head.

She knew the answer to her question, but she had to ask it anyway. She had to hear him say it aloud. This moment, she knew, was going to reveal everything about Kane and what was building between them, two strangers that had come together in the most unlikely way.

"It was my mother who did this. She was part of the organization that experimented on you. Wasn't she?"

"Yes," he said quietly with a sad, reluctant nod. "Yes, she was."

Despite already knowing it, the truth still hit her like a blow to the chest, knocking the breath from her lungs, and her gaze dropped from his. It wasn't just Thias's lies that weighed on her, they were her mother's too. She had been her best friend, and Tala had been so lost after her death. But she didn't know this version of her. It was in her death, eleven years later, that Tala was finally discovering who she truly was.

"But Tala," Kane's voice was low and quiet, raspy. "She wasn't what you're thinking."

"Then tell me, who was she? Because clearly, she wasn't what I thought she was," she said, choking on rising emotion.

Kane sighed, his shoulders dropping, and he placed his hands in his lap. "I was thirteen when I was taken away. My father, who was a cruel bastard, couldn't care for me. And one day, a pair of government agents showed up at our house. They needed kids for an advanced military program the Republic was building, super-soldiers, and he was all too willing to let me go. They gave him a stipend, and he gave them me. My brother, Addox, stayed behind," he said, his eyes lingering on his folded hands.

"There were twenty-four of us," he said. "We were all young. Eleven to seventeen years old. And I wasn't there for even a week before the experiments started."

Tala felt a tightening in her chest as she listened to him, hanging on his every word.

"In the beginning, they were small biopsies from all over my body, inside and out. Then it was viruses they would expose us to so that they could test different medications. I would sometimes go weeks at a time so sick that I felt like I was on my deathbed. Other times, I would go weeks feeling fine. We had a doctor," he said, "whose job was to monitor us on a regular basis. She was the one to follow up with us. It was her job to track our vitals, symptoms, and side effects, and to report back our condition.

"The first time I saw her, I remember thinking that she reminded me of my mother. Her hair was straight and short, unlike my mother's, which was always long with wild curls, but they were both blonds, soft and golden like the sun. And with eyes that were blue like Lake Michigan on a clear day. Her voice was kind, and she never showed impatience with me."

"My mother," Tala whispered, conjuring her image in her mind.

"I was in that facility for four years," Kane said, clearing his throat, "and she was the only one who ever cared. Our happiness and safety were always her priority. She was the one who showed me *The Wizard of Oz*," he said with a nostalgic grin. "Toward the end, though, things got worse. I was sick more days than not. So were all of the others. It was the last procedure," he said with a grimace.

Tala saw his struggle on his face as he finally turned to meet her gaze. She reached for his hand. She wanted to know him, wanted to understand him. "I died during that procedure," he said, his voice cracking just enough for her to hear. "When I was brought back, I was what I am now. They turned me, all of us, into monsters. We could do things that no normal human could. And it was all so that the Republic could have an unrivaled military that could never be beaten." His eyes dulled and his shoulders sagged.

"But in succeeding in their experiments, they ultimately failed because they had built something they couldn't control. And one night, I was woken from a dead sleep," he said as he shook his head. "I was so confused. But your mother just quietly ushered all of us to the doors. All twenty-four. As we made our way to the basement down a back stairwell, I heard the alarm sound. It was loud and piercing as it screamed into the quiet night. Once I was outside the facility, I just ran. I blurred as quickly as I could, and I never looked back."

Tala was at a loss for words, and she knew her horror was written across her face. There was a beat of silence between them. His voice was steady when he spoke, but it was in his eyes that she saw his pain, his fears untold. He didn't want to be pitied, he wanted to be accepted.

He was letting her in. He was exposing his vulnerability and putting his trust in her.

She raised her hand and gently ran her thumb across his face, down his cheek, and over the coarse scruff along his jaw. He didn't flinch at her touch, and his eyes didn't waver. His dark eyes pierced through her, bringing in a wave of calm, and in that moment, she was certain.

"It was you," she finally said, her voice barely a whisper. "The fire."

He gave a solemn nod.

"How? Why?" she stammered, emotion rising in her again.

"I had nowhere to go. I was just a seventeen-year-old boy, a freak, with no home. With no family," he said, his voice strained as he looked away. "Your mom was the only person I could think of. For a week, unknowingly to any of you, I slept on the furniture on your back patio. It was the only place I felt safe," he said. "Then one night, I woke to some half dozen men, all dressed in black with their faces covered, and I helplessly watched as they launched fire grenades through your windows. I hid in a big tree in your yard. They were gone almost as quickly as they had come. And within only a minute or two, the entire house was engulfed in flames. I raced inside and got to you first. But I couldn't get to the others."

"Kane," she said, his name lingering on her tongue, "you are not a monster, or a freak, as you say," she said adamantly. "You saved my life. Twice," she added. "I wouldn't be here if it wasn't for you."

Tala thought of her mother, the woman who had cared for all those children. She understood why Kane would feel a connection to her, and she couldn't fault him for it. She was the closest thing he had to a mother after his own died, and in her, he found comfort during a horrific time in his life.

A part of Tala wanted to be forgiving, but she would never be able to overlook what she'd chosen to be a part of. She now understood an entirely different side to her. She may have been the mother she remembered, but she was not the person she'd known.

Who had each of them been when they had laughed together? How quickly love could turn to hate in a moment so brief, at the first taste of poison. Would the truth contaminate all their good moments, her memories of happiness?

Throughout the years, Tala could often feel her mother in the sun, the rain, the very air she breathed. But in that moment, she was nowhere to be found. She was gone. And Tala wasn't sure if in finding the truth it was her mother who left her, or she who left her mother.

"The fire was the work of the Republic," she said quietly.

Kane silently held her gaze.

"The penalty for helping you escape. And Thias knew about it. He was part of it. I saw the file and his signature with my own eyes." Tala blinked, feeling the sting of tears as she looked away. Kane's hand smoothed down her back, and she felt comfort in his touch. "Who am I without all these people? How do I move forward? And where do I go?" she asked, emotion rising once again in her voice.

"The truth has a way of uncovering more than just a lie," he said. "It lets you see everything in a different light. It can help bring perspective. As for who you are, your heart knows. Your head may not, but trust your heart, it knows the way. I know one thing for certain," he said, his voice calm and steady, "and that is that you will be okay. You're a survivor."

She took a deep, shaky breath. In exposing their deepest vulnerabilities to each other, there was a depth to the honesty between them. He was now the single person who knew her best. With Kane beside her, Tala felt her anger ebb. She closed her eyes, letting her old life wash over her in her mind. She swallowed hard her emotion as she felt a light deep inside suddenly extinguish.

EIGHT

14 years earlier

Kane kept to himself. He preferred isolation over conversation. And he was completely content when he was left alone. There were twenty-three others like him, and while they shared the commons, they were separated by gender in their dorms. Kane had a top bunk in the corner near a window. And although it was often cold and drafty in the winter months, he liked being able to look outside. Even if he only ever saw the parking lot.

He'd been sick for the last week, another trial run for a new antibiotic, or so he was told, and was finally beginning to feel like himself again. He sat in his bed, propped up against the wall, a book in his lap. Every day seemed to be like the last, and he frequently lost track of time, track of the day, track of the month. But Dr. A's office had a calendar on the wall, and his weekly psychological and physical evaluations were a good way to orient himself. But all it really did was show him how long he'd been in the facility, the days droning on with no end in sight. So when he looked at that calendar, he often just wondered what the point of it was. There was no light at the end of the tunnel for him. The calendar was a measure of his past more than of his future.

Every day, they were required to participate in educational lessons, excused only if they were too sick. At first, Kane wasn't sure why, but when cognitive testing began, he had a better understanding of why the doctors had wanted them to maintain sharp intellection. It was in that compulsory schooling that he had found an escape through books. In Bedley, he avoided them at all costs, scoffing at them in school. He had never seen the point of them. But now, they were an escape for him, if only a mental one. He didn't like all books, but anything on history he ravenously ate up. There were so many events that had taken place throughout all of world history, so many people that influenced change in every culture and time period, and all of it fascinated him.

Reading now about a giant ocean liner, an unsinkable ship, and its perilous first and last voyage, he paused to think about how he would respond had he been the captain. Would he have fought to be the first onto a lifeboat, or would he have valiantly gone down with it?

"Nose in a book again?" Cyrus sneered, strolling into the dormitory, his lackeys, Dexter and Reid, in tow. They were a tight group of boys, a year older than Kane, who liked to wreak havoc around their living quarters when they got bored. They liked shouting caustic taunts and criticism at the others. They played pranks and liked to cause trouble. Kane didn't know much about any of them, he didn't care, but he assumed that like him, like most of the group, these boys grew up in an economically disadvantaged family or town. They reminded him of Zak and his crew back in Bedley. He was typically good at avoiding Cyrus, but he knew those days were numbered.

"You're like the girls… a pussy," Cyrus said with a mocking laugh. They'd been on him for a solid week now, taking jabs where they could.

"*Are you a pussy, Kane?*" His father's words rang back in his head and rage began spreading through him, rapidly multiplying with each laugh of the three boys. Kane was a powder keg ready to blow, and this was the last straw. He swiftly jumped off his bed. Catching Cyrus off guard, he shoved him hard into the bunk beside his. Kane heard the loud crack of his head against the metal frame.

"Son of a bitch!" Cyrus yelled.

"He's actually challenging you!" Reid jeered.

Kane knew his chances were slim. There were three of them, and they were his size or larger, not to mention he was still on the mend from being sick. But he also wasn't going to back down. His ability and willingness to fight were his only armor.

Regaining his footing, Cyrus gave a hard swing, his fist meeting Kane's jaw.

Kane didn't give a second thought and charged at Cyrus, sending him careening into Dexter while Reid punched Kane in the abdomen, knocking the wind out of him. Kane's shoulders slouched as he struggled for breath.

Reid and Dexter seized Kane, each holding him in an arm lock. He felt the sharp pinch in his shoulders.

"You think you stand a chance against us?" Cyrus taunted in a fit of laughter as he rubbed at the back of his head.

Kane was silent as he straightened his body, glaring back at him. He thought briefly of the ocean liner he was reading about, and he realized this was his moment of truth. He was willing to go down with the ship.

With Kane unable to defend himself, Cyrus socked him hard in the ribs. Pain exploded throughout his chest. He flinched and grimaced, but he didn't make a sound. Kane clenched his jaw, breathing heavily as he waited for the sharp pain to pass. His eyes met Cyrus's again, holding them steady.

"Still haven't had enough," Cyrus said snidely, Reid and Dexter laughing haughtily in his ears.

Kane gnashed his teeth, taking labored breaths through his nose. For a brief second, Kane felt Dexter loosen his grip. Kane smashed his heel down onto his foot. Dexter yelled out and released his hold. With an arm now free, Kane turned, slamming his elbow into the side of Reid's face.

As Reid released his grip, Cyrus jabbed him in the jaw again. Kane tasted blood in his mouth. He took an unsteady swing but stumbled over his footing. Cyrus punched him a third time, sending him spinning.

Kane staggered backward as he brought his hand to his bleeding lip. He charged at Cyrus, the two of them falling hard to the tile floor. Kane pinned him to the floor and slugged him across the face.

Dexter kicked him hard in the side, pain expanding through his rib cage, and despite himself, he cried out.

"Hey! Hey! Hey!" a woman's voice shrieked in the background, and Kane knew right away that it was Dr. A. He rolled to the ground, panting as he clutched his hand to his side.

"Break it up! All of you!" she demanded.

Kane rose to his feet, Cyrus doing the same, and the four boys hung their heads as Dr. Alexander pointed a knowing finger at them.

"All of you," she said, leveling her voice, "will be on bathroom detail for a week."

The boys were silent, and Kane dared to raise his head to look at her.

"You three," she said, pointing at Cyrus and the other two, "to the commons. Kane, to my office," she said curtly. Turning on her heel, she made her way toward the door, and Kane, his shoulders slumped, lumbered after her.

He followed her to her office, which generally he enjoyed going to. It had a sizeable, plush couch he could sink into and a bookshelf, floor to ceiling, filled mostly with medical books. But there were also others in the mix, even some which had been banned by the Republic. She seemed indifferent about owning any of them, and she always let him read whatever he wanted. She had a passion for rare books from before the war. There were so many to choose from.

"Take a seat," she said gently, motioning to the couch rather than to the hard chairs beside her desk.

"I'm sorry, Dr. A," he mumbled. She reminded him so much of his mother, and it often felt that when he disappointed her, he was simultaneously disappointing his mother. Then he would chastise himself for thinking his mother could be anywhere where he could disappoint her. There was a time after her death when he thought she had become a star in the nighttime sky, there to guide him. But here he was, imprisoned in a medical lab, and he realized those thoughts were naïve and just plain stupid. She was nowhere.

"I expect behavior like this from those other boys, but I'm surprised by yours," Dr. Alexander said, her voice soft and kind as she took a seat beside him, handing him a tissue.

Pressing it against his bloody lip, he felt it sting. He looked up, her bright blue eyes looking at him with compassion.

"Someone had to stand up to them," he asserted.

Dr. Alexander nodded as she folded her hands in her lap. "I find that your aggression is more defensive than it is offensive," she said. "It's reactionary. I think you've been in a perpetual stage of fight or flight for so much of your life, and this is how you respond. But Kane," she said calmly, "not all warriors are fighters. It's important to find a way to channel your anger in other ways so that you can walk away from these situations."

Kane shook his head. "You don't get it."

"Then enlighten me."

"I had to do it," he mumbled. "Some fights just have to take place," he said as he looked away. He folded his arms across his chest, only to feel a surge of pain in his rib cage that was enough to take his breath away. He dropped them to his sides.

"We all have roles to play in life, ways that we can contribute that are unique to us," she said. "And it's our responsibility to both ourselves and the society that we fit in to find what that contribution is."

"I don't have much control over the society I'm in at the moment," he said spitefully.

"Kane," she said gently, her voice steady, "you are playing an important role, more than you know, for the greater good. And that includes all of society. Here," she said, rising to her feet and crossing her office in only a few strides. She opened her desk drawer and pulled out a small chip, then returned to his side on the couch.

"Watch this," she said, handing it to him. "It's called *The Wizard of Oz*."

"I'm not sure what this is," he said in confusion.

"It's a movie. It was popular long before the war, and I stumbled upon this copy by happy accident," she said with a light voice. "It has been very popular with my daughter, Tala. She's only a couple of years younger than you."

"What is it?" he asked, turning it over in his hands.

"It's about a group of misfits that stumble upon qualities within themselves that they didn't know were there. They're on a journey, and each one has to play their part if they're ever going to make it to their final destination, the Emerald City," she explained. "I think you could learn something from it."

Kane looked at her and gave her a gracious smile.

"You can watch it now from my tablet if you'd like, right here in my office. And in the future, please feel free to spend your reading time here. You may find you have fewer distractions than in your dormitory," she said with a knowing smirk. "Now, please excuse me while I go deal with the other boys," she said, rising from the couch and making her way to her door.

"Dr. A," he called to her. She paused and looked back at him. "Thank you," he said.

She gave him a warm smile, then slipped out of the office.

Tala opened her eyes, the sun careening in through the windows, and despite its jarring brightness, it was refreshing. She stretched her body and gazed up at the ceiling of her bed. After only a moment of mental solitude, her mind came back to her. As she lay there, the warm sun pouring over her, she wondered what was more heartbreaking, the betrayal of being lied to for so long, or her shattered illusions. She reminded herself why she stole the file in the first place: truth. And now she had it. There were no longer questions that needed to be answered but rather a new reality that needed to be accepted.

There was a small rap outside her bedroom, and Tala sat up, Mila edging her face around the door.

"Oh, good," she said with a smile, "you're awake."

"Just barely," she mumbled through a yawn.

"You, umm… have a visitor," she said with hesitation.

Tala cocked her head in confusion. "Who?"

"It's Chancellor Adams," she said.

"Vaughn?" Tala asked with surprise. His trip was shorter than she'd expected. "Give me a minute, I'll be right out."

"Sure." Mila gave her a nod, then slipped away. Tala heard muffled voices outside her bedroom as she tossed her blankets aside.

She sighed as she glimpsed herself in the mirror. Her eyes had dark bags below them, her hair was frizzy and skewed in all directions. She felt mortified at the idea of Vaughn waiting outside her door, that he would see her like this while he was undoubtedly put together and perfect as ever. She'd never seen him look otherwise.

Feeling irritated by his surprise rather than elated, she ran a brush through her hair and pulled it back, dabbed some makeup under her eyes, then threw on a pair of jeans and a thick sweater.

Tala tried to keep her expression impassive when she finally emerged from her room to see him waiting for her on a stool at her island counter.

His smile was wide, with small wrinkles in the corners of his eyes when he saw her.

"I wasn't expecting you," she said as she approached him, hugging her arms to her body. Mila, she noticed, had made herself absent.

"I got back to the city late last night, and I wanted to see you," he said, still smiling, showing off his perfect teeth, the dimple in his cheek. "So, I brought you coffee," he said, handing her a to-go cup.

"How'd you even know I'm a coffee drinker?" she asked, then took a drink. It was hot and smooth and perfect and exactly what she needed.

"The cups on your desk at Command were a glaring indicator," he said, then laughed.

Tala nodded with a guilty smile.

"I'd say that if there was someone who deserved the luxury of a nice coffee, it's you," he said with a coy smile. "And I came to ask you to dinner tonight." There was a gleam in his eye.

"Okay," she said, hearing the unexpected hesitation in her voice that she hoped he didn't pick up on.

Looking pleased, Vaughn rose to his feet, then leaned in, giving Tala's cheek a soft brush of his lips. "I'll see you tonight," he whispered, and Tala felt herself blush. "I'll send a car at seven," he said as he made his way to the door.

He gave her one last lingering look, then quickly disappeared, leaving her alone in her kitchen. She sighed, then headed back to her bedroom. As she made her bed, Kane pushed his way to the front of her thoughts, and she knew exactly how she wanted to spend her day off.

❖

Emerging from his bedroom in the bomb shelter, Kane was caught off guard to see Tala standing in his pod. He couldn't help but think she was so beautiful, and he felt happiness at the unexpected sight of her. He sucked in a

185

hard breath, telling himself he couldn't go there. Not with Tala. If there was someone he couldn't go there with, it was her.

"I was wondering if you had some time and wanted to maybe…" She shifted her feet, and he could hear the quickening of her heartbeat from across the room. "Maybe spend the day together?" she asked as her eyes met his.

Taking him by surprise, he nodded as he crossed the room, only half aware of Max as he sat in the corner on his computer. "Sure."

"Maybe without all the heavy topics of conversation," she suggested, and he smiled.

Max knew his story. And no one else. Until now. He had known the day would come with Tala when he would have to choose to either lie and continue hiding or to lay bare his truth. The depth of their friendship, or whatever was growing between them, would be a reflection of their ability to be honest with each other. When she realized who he was, he knew he could be nothing but honest with her, despite the risk to himself. She was living a life paved with lies and betrayal, and he wouldn't lay another deceitful brick. He had been terrified. How could he not be? But his story had washed over her like a wave in a storm surge, and she had been sturdy and calm, she was not afraid. She had looked at him, exposed and vulnerable, with acceptance and compassion. That moment changed everything. He only ever let people see what he wanted them to, but Tala had experienced who he really was.

They pushed their way through the crowded sidewalk at a brisk pace, making their way to the nearest subtrain. "You met Mila through her brother?" he asked as he looked over at her. It was small talk, but he wanted to know her better. He wanted to know everything he could about her.

It was an unusually warm fall day, and she wanted to spend it at the beach. Despite himself, he couldn't turn down the opportunity to be with her. He also couldn't remember the last time he'd felt this kind of happiness. Maybe never.

Tala nodded. "I met Maverick when I was in the academy. Admittedly, I hated him at first," she said with a laugh under her breath as they walked quickly, descending below street level to the subtrain platform. "He was so hard on me during drills, but it just made me push harder, which was the point, I guess. In the end, we were close. He was my best friend," she said.

He watched her smile fade, a faraway look on her face. "Are you still close?" he asked with hesitation. He knew about Ronin, but she had never mentioned Maverick before.

Tala took a slow breath as they stepped onto the crowded train. "He graduated in the class ahead of me. Six months before I did. He was the one who got my pod. We had plans to live together, to work at Command together," she said with a pause. "But he was killed while on assignment before all of that."

"Tala," he said gently.

"I don't know many details of his death," she said, and he could hear the traces of emotion in her voice. "Files for agents killed in action are classified above my clearance. But Thias told me once, I think to give me some closure, that he'd gone missing and that his body later washed up on shore in the South Columbia Bay. They had to use dental records to identify him," she added.

"I'm so sorry. I had no idea." His words sounded as feeble as they felt.

Kane heard the sadness in her voice, he could hear it in her heartbeat, and he let silence settle between them as they raced through the underground. She stood so near him in the packed train that it made his pulse quicken. He was on alert, carefully watching the people around them, but no one seemed to pay any attention to them.

When they finally emerged from the subtrain in Walhurst, they were met with a warm sun and a cool breeze, a hint of salt hanging in the air, the rush of the ocean in the distance.

She turned toward him, life returning in her eyes. "When Maverick was killed, to honor him, his immediate family were made Preferred citizens, upgraded from Standard. It allowed Mila to be eligible for a teaching position at Heritage Academy, the youth private school in southern Stoughbour. So suddenly, I had a half-empty pod, and she was moving from Baxtham, so it seemed right for her to move in with me."

Together, they rounded a corner, the wide expanse of the ocean coming into view. The blue sky meeting the blue water that stretched endlessly before them. There were few people on the beach this time of year, and its near desertion put Kane at ease being in public with Tala, even after having been on the train together.

"The one good thing to come out of all that was Mila. She's my very best friend. Sometimes a little wild compared to me," she said with a chuckle, the sadness in her voice fading. "She's always moving between boyfriends, but I think after she lost Mav it just became easier to keep people at arm's length. At least where men are concerned," she said. She took a deep breath, exhaling slowly, her shoulders falling.

"Sorry," she said suddenly as she glanced up at him. "I know I said no heavy conversation. I just wanted to share him with you. I don't usually tell that story," she said, her eyes meeting his. They were a light, crystal blue, clear as the day and completely surrendering. "And I've fully monopolized our conversation."

The truth was that he was entirely content listening to her, and he hung on her every word.

He looked at her with a small grin on the corners of his mouth and shrugged. "I'd rather listen than talk," he said. "So, it worked out. I'm glad you told me."

She held his gaze and smiled.

"I like this," he said after a moment. "Real conversation. No secrets or conspiracies. Besides, I haven't been to the beach in ages. It's nice to get out," he said as he gestured out over the water.

She smiled. "I thought the problems of the world, or at least the Republic, could wait a couple of hours," she said.

He nodded. "I couldn't agree more."

Kane shoved his hands deep into his pockets as they stepped onto the pier, his shoes scuffing across the uneven wooden planks with each step.

Tala was quiet, and he looked at her, her face filled with joy as she looked out over the vast ocean. In that moment, she looked less burdened. Her blond hair whipped around her face in the wind, her eyes were wide and full of wonder, her mouth curved into a small smile. And while she couldn't tear her eyes away from the view, he couldn't tear his away from her.

It was unnerving to him how much she made him feel things he had long since given up on. He felt himself losing himself in her, and nothing scared him more.

"Have you ever seen anything so beautiful?" she asked as they came to the end of the pier, the sound of cawing seagulls, and the roar of the waves crashing into the pillars below filling the air around them.

"No," he whispered.

Tala turned and gazed up at him, her eyes settling on his, and his breath caught. She was real, and he was real. For the first time, he had no walls around himself, which was both exhilarating and terrifying in equal measure.

"You're happy today," he said.

She shrugged. "I've decided that I've let people steer me and use me for too long. It's time I take control for myself. And today, with you, the ocean, the sky, the sun, I choose to be happy. For as long as I can be."

She turned toward the water, her face catching the sun, and she sighed.

"Don't get me wrong," she said quietly, her voice almost a whisper on the wind, but he had no trouble hearing her. She took a step and leaned into him, and his heart began to race. "Everything isn't all right. But somehow, this will pass," she affirmed with conviction. "I wanted the truth, and now I have it. I'm finding that grief isn't just a single place I've been, but rather a road I've traveled all these years. With every step, it changes. And I think that even in learning who my mother really was, my brother, this road doesn't end. It just takes on different scenery as I move along."

She looked up at him, her eyes full of contentment. And despite himself, he slipped an arm around her, pulling her closer. He let out a shaky, uneven breath and wondered at what point she had become so important to him. It was like a summer rain, watching each drop fall from the clouds. At first, it's nothing but wet pavement. Then suddenly, the gutters are like swollen rivers, the downspouts like waterfalls, every drop unknowingly adding up.

❖

Back in Stoughbour, as Tala emerged from the subtrain near her pod, Kane beside her, she slowed her pace, if only to drag out their afternoon a little longer. It had been a perfect day. The most perfect in a long time, and she was reluctant to bring it to a close.

"So, what is it you have going on tonight?" he asked, his foot kicking loose gravel on the sidewalk, the sleeve of his jacket brushing along her arm.

"I umm…" she stuttered, not wanting to say too much, feeling almost guilty after they had just spent the whole day together. "I'm having dinner with Vaughn."

If Kane had a reaction, he didn't show it, staying in quiet stride beside her on the busy sidewalk.

Silence settled between them, and she stole a glance in his direction as they stopped in front of her building. With his jaw set and his lips pressed tightly together, he looked serious, but when he turned to her, his eyes meeting hers, she saw their warm depth. She found herself wondering what he was thinking. Did he think of her as often as she thought of him?

"Thank you for today," she said, not looking away. She felt a surge of fluttering in her belly, and before she could stop herself, she reached up and ran her thumb gently across his jaw, his scruff coarse to the touch.

"Don't be a stranger," she said with a smirk. But he was a stranger, and yet he wasn't at the same time.

The corner of his mouth curled, and she dropped her hand.

"Tala?" a voice called from behind her.

She spun on her heel to find Ronin standing only feet away from her. He looked at Kane with bewilderment and confusion.

Tala felt a pang of instant panic. She glanced back at Kane, who was already on his way down the street, his back to them. He had quickly put distance between them, then disappeared into the throng of pedestrians.

"Who was that?" Ronin asked with a curious smirk.

"Oh, umm, him?" she said nervously, taking a long, slow breath. "No idea. Just literally tripped over him."

His face showed that he was completely unconvinced. "You looked like you knew each other," he persisted. "Are you seeing someone? I thought you and the chancellor were—"

"No and no," she said firmly.

"So, you're not seeing anyone? Including Vaughn?" he pressed.

"I don't know what Vaughn and I are, but I am certainly not seeing that man. I don't even know who he is. Just some guy on the street," she said as she averted her gaze.

She knew he was studying her, and it felt as though his eyes were burning into her, cutting through her lie. The moment she had touched Kane's face, she had felt a bolt of energy and excitement strike her, and if any of it had registered on her face, Ronin wouldn't be quick to let it go.

"So, what're you doing here?" she asked, brushing her hair off her shoulder.

He lifted a white bag. "Wine. I came for that drink."

"Ahh," she said, her memory returning to her. "Well, I have to get ready because I'm going out with Vaughn, but we can drink while I do that. Besides," she said as she turned toward her building, relieved to not have to look at him, "you can help me decide what to wear. You know even you're better at that than I am."

"Too true," he said with a laugh, coming up beside her. He jerked his head, flipping his hair out of his eyes, then followed her up to her pod.

Ronin, familiar with Tala's kitchen, went to the cupboard to grab wine glasses.

"Mila here?" he asked while he gave a quick scan of the pod.

"I don't think so," she said, shaking her head. "Her niece was having a birthday party."

"Always the family girl," he said while he poured two glasses of wine, then handed one to her. She took a sip of the light, sweet white wine.

"Mmm," she said.

"You really didn't know that guy?" he asked again with scrutiny. "It's just that I saw you touch his face."

"Only because I tripped so hard, I went careening into him," she said, turning away from him and heading down the hall to her bedroom. It was easier to lie when she wasn't looking him in the face. Here she was, bent on learning the truth for her own life, and she was lying to one of the people closest to her. She hated herself for her hypocrisy. Ronin deserved more.

"Well, it's a shame," he called after her. "He might not be your type, but that guy was good looking."

Tala smiled to herself. *Yes, yes, he is.*

"Come back here," she called from her bedroom. "I need help."

Ronin appeared in her doorway a moment later. "Not sure I'm much of a substitute for Mila, but I'll do my best," he said as he headed to her closet. "How dressy are you supposed to be?"

She shrugged. "He didn't say. But our last few times together were Thias-dressy. As in, heels for me," she said, hating the idea of another evening in them. They made her feel uncomfortable, like she was floundering with every step.

"For someone who doesn't like to dress up, you sure have quite the collection," he said as he began pulling dresses out, studying each one carefully.

She sighed as she sat on her bed. "Only because Thias insists on that kind of attire. *All* the time," she emphasized.

Ronin turned toward her with a lopsided smirk on his face, his hair brushing over his brow. "You sound like you resent him a little for it."

"I do," she said. "And now there's Vaughn, who is the exact same."

"Vaughn's a real catch. Brains, looks, and position. I'd say you should find his interest in you incredibly flattering."

"What's that supposed to mean?"

"I didn't mean it like that," he said quickly. "This one." He pulled a black dress from her closet.

She groaned as she snatched it from his hands and stepped into the bathroom to change. The dress was fitted, accenting the curves of her body, hanging off her shoulders, and she felt exposed. The skirt was short but lengthened as it wrapped around to the back. She had worn it only one other time, for Thias's birthday last year.

This isn't me, she thought as she gazed at her reflection in the mirror. She smoothed her hands over the satin material and reluctantly stepped out of the bathroom.

"Yes," Ronin said with a pleased smile. "A hundred yeses. If a woman showed up to date me in that dress, I'm pretty sure I'd propose on the spot."

"Well, I hope he doesn't do that. I'm going to have to borrow Mila's coat again," she said, slipping into a pair of black pumps. "I have nothing."

His eyes narrowed. "Maybe that's something you should consider investing in," he said and smirked. "You're the princess of the Republic, I think an evening coat would be a requirement."

"Don't call me that," she said with a warning glare, and he laughed.

She finished her makeup, added some loose curls to her hair, then stared back at her reflection, shaking her head. She looked pretty, that much she was willing to admit, but it still wasn't her.

Stepping into the living room, Ronin, who'd turned on the TV, watching a show comfortably from her couch, gave her an approving nod. "If he doesn't swoon over you in that, he never will."

"Guess we'll find out," she said. Her palm pad vibrated in her hand, a notice across the screen that her car had arrived. "Time to go." She finished the last of the wine in her glass, then set it on the counter.

Ronin smiled as he followed her to the door. "Knock him dead, Tal."

Tala was dropped off in front of Vaughn's upscale building, an angular tower of glass and steel. He sent her a message, instructing her to go to the third floor, then gave her a code to access the south elevator to take to the forty-seventh floor. In her heels, she teetered up a wide staircase made of sleek marble, then rode the elevator which opened to Vaughn's pod. He appeared from around the corner, and when he saw her, his eyes lit up. She felt them wander up and down her body, and she blushed.

"You look incredible," he said, reaching for her hand. He gently pulled her through the elevator doorway and kissed her.

"Come in," he said, a moment later. "I'm glad you're here." He gave her a relaxed, yet confident grin. It struck her that he'd never appeared nervous or unsure of himself. There was nothing awkward about him.

Tala stepped into the pod, and even though she'd been there once before, she was still struck by its luxurious beauty. The entry opened to a large room with a high vaulted ceiling, a second level balcony overlooking them. The whole room had been large enough to host a party the year before with at least fifty guests. Two staircases on each side of the great room, lined with a glass paneled railing, led to the second level. The focal point of it all, however, was a solid glass waterfall reaching up to the ceiling, the sound of the trickle of water faint.

A wall of windows looking over an outdoor wrap-around balcony offered a panoramic view of the city, dazzling lights as far as the eye could see. On the far end was a living room with black leather sofas seated around a chiseled limestone fireplace, a small fire lit within. In the lavish pod, she felt out of place, even if she did look the part.

"Your place is lovely," she said as she turned to him. He was studying her carefully. A look of delight played in his eyes.

"It's better with you here," he said. "Your brother pointed out that you'd been here before, security for a party last year. I'm sorry I didn't realize. I typically don't pay much attention to those who work behind the scenes. I hope you like seafood, the caterer should be here soon. But first," he said as he made his way to the kitchen island and reached for two glasses of wine that had already been poured. He handed her one, then motioned toward the living room. She took a seat on the soft, leather sofa, Vaughn sitting close beside her, and she caught the subtle scent of patchouli on him. It reminded her of Thias.

"I have something for you," he said as he set his glass on the sleek coffee table beside hers, then reached for a small gray box with a purple ribbon tied around it.

"What's this?" she asked as he set it in her hands.

He shrugged dismissively. "Just something I saw that made me think of you."

Tala hesitantly untied the ribbon, and lifting off the top of the box, she found a silver double-knotted bangle, a large oval diamond in the center of the knot. She gasped in surprise.

"Vaughn," she said as she looked up at him, "this is too much."

"Nonsense."

"It's beautiful," she said as she lifted it out of the box.

"Which is why it belongs on your wrist," he said as he gently took it from her. Taking her hand in his, which was soft and warm, he slipped the bracelet on, then looked up at her. His eyes met hers, and she saw something hungry in them as he gazed at her, still holding her hand.

Unsure what to think of the gift, Tala felt uneasy and was relieved when the elevator opened, the caterer entering the room, pushing a cart with their dinner.

"Ah," Vaughn said as he released her hand and stood. He grabbed his wine glass, taking a large drink, then made his way to the dining table, Tala close behind.

As the caterer set their table, Vaughn gently pulled out her chair and Tala sat, then he took the seat across from her.

"Will there be anything else, Chancellor?" the man asked when he finished.

"That'll be all," he said curtly.

He gave a small bow of his head, then left as quickly as he had come.

"This all looks delicious," Tala said as she looked down at her plate. She felt her hunger deep in her belly.

"Well, I'm glad. I'm very particular about food. I plan all my menus carefully. For tonight I've chosen one of my favorites, Chilean sea bass, whipped potatoes and champagne truffle sauce with roasted Brussel sprouts, a fennel salad, and lastly, a ten-layer carrot cake with pineapple syrup," he said proudly. He raised his glass of wine. "A toast."

Tala raised hers above her plate.

"To you and me. And every small step we take into our future," he said with a grin, then took a drink.

He certainly was sure of himself, she thought, and he appeared to be certain of her, as well.

"Your trip was a success?" she asked, then took a bite of her food.

He shrugged. "Not really. More of a waste of time. A meeting with the DeSoto vice president and Governor Barrington from the Central Colonies. There's tension over trade agreements," he said. "But you already knew that from the small part of our meeting that you were privy to the other day."

Tala nodded. "You mentioned having debriefed the perp I arrested with the drugs and explosives," she said, treading lightly, careful with everything she said.

"That's right," he said. "But only the first interrogation. Thias was in charge of the interrogations in the days that followed."

Lie.

Her chest tightened. There was a look in his eyes that she didn't quite trust. "Was it ever determined that he was a Unified Rebel?" she asked.

"That much was clear by the ink that covered him," he said flatly as he ate.

Tala's mind raced as she tried to remember if she had noticed anything on him when she arrested him, but her mind was coming up blank.

"He was just pushing drugs, and the explosives were for another Rebel attempt at hijacking imported goods coming into the port," he said dismissively.

His explanation was plausible, with the exception of the blatant lie he told her. And it didn't explain the hidden cache of guns or the fabricated evidence on her attackers.

"The firearms," she said slowly, "whatever came of those?"

"Haven't heard anything. But I only just got back late last night," he said, not looking up from his plate.

Tala nodded, her mind turning the information over in her head. Did his meeting with Barrington have anything to do with the weapons case? It was suspected that the Rebels had strongholds in the Colonies, though the Republic was unable to confirm that with any certainty. They were everywhere and nowhere, it seemed. There was still the possibility that the guns were being smuggled by the Rebels, just like everyone assumed. But her gut told her there was a different story. There were too many loose ends with that theory, and not all of the dots connected.

"You seem deep in thought," he observed.

Tala took a breath. "Sorry, my mind is just on a case."

He smirked at her. "A loyal agent never truly takes a day off."

"Something like that," she said. She considered her next words carefully. "Can I ask you another question?"

He looked up at her and smiled. "Of course."

"Do you know anything about those hackers that were arrested yesterday? I mean, I haven't been to Command since it happened. I saw Agent Bishop was on the scene from the video that aired on the Statement last night."

"Oh, that one's a mess. I don't know many details," he said. "There was a glitch on Julio Martinez's palm pad. Something to do with his conference calling application. Then a few days later, Eli Valdi reported the same problem."

"The cabinet members?" she asked.

He nodded. "I guess the tech department thought it wasn't a coincidence, so they launched an investigation."

Tala listened intently as he spoke.

"They found malware in their application. Months ago, all the cabinet members and Representative Hudson updated their conference calling applications, per the recommendation of tech services."

"Malware? Someone planted a virus?" Who was smart enough to pull something like that off with government officials? Who was brave enough?

"It gets worse," he said soberly. "And I'm only telling you this because you're MF. That virus compromised their banking credentials. The hackers were able to get into Columbia Central Bank and Federal Treasury accounts. Someone has been slowly withdrawing money to an offshore account. The account was closed almost as quickly as the raid happened, but not before withdrawing all the funds that had been hemorrhaged. We weren't able to trace anything."

"How were they able to find the hackers in the first place?" she asked.

Vaughn let out a low laugh. "We have people on the inside. Agents who've been undercover for years. And our tech department is exceptionally good at what they do."

"But how'd they get the malware into the application in the first place?"

Vaughn's smile faded into something serious, but he said nothing, and then it dawned on Tala. "You think there's a mole?" she asked.

"It's possible," he said. He pursed his lips, his brow furrowing.

"And you think it's the Rebels? What's their agenda?"

He shrugged a shoulder. "Personally, and I have nothing to back this up, I think they're ramping up to something. They've never done anything this sophisticated before. They're usually just annoying, wreaking havoc for the sake of it. But there's been a lot of Rebel activity in the country recently. And no one ever knows what their endgame is. Or if they've ever had one to begin with. Of course they're no match for us. Not even close." There was something menacing in his eyes. "Regardless, they're a risk to our country. The Rebels and their schisies are going to regret it if they ever come up against us."

Tala swallowed hard. He wore the same savage expression on his face that Thias often did. Thias's vision for the future was dominance. His desires for control and power were unceasing, and she was seeing that now in Vaughn. She shifted awkwardly in her chair, her appetite suddenly gone.

"Well, I think that's enough talk about that," he said, his voice shifting back to jovial.

She thought back to Thias's words over a week earlier. *"There is unrest building..."*

And what had the president said in the meeting with the dignitaries… that there were *"growing tensions with the DeSoto government…"*

Although she'd never heard of DeSoto and the UR working together, she couldn't help but wonder if everything was related, that maybe somehow the pieces all fit together. Or maybe one thing had nothing to do with the next. Her mind was busy processing everything Vaughn had revealed to her, the information bouncing around in her brain.

"Are you finished?" he asked, interrupting her thoughts.

Tala glanced down at her unfinished dessert, then back up at Vaughn and nodded, giving him a small smile.

"Great. Let's move to the living room. My housekeeper will handle this."

Tala took a seat on a sofa, she had three to choose from, and could feel the subtle heat from the fireplace on her skin. Vaughn's proximity to her when he sat didn't go amiss.

He reached his arm behind her, resting it along the back of the couch, the tips of his fingers brushing across her bare shoulder, and she felt herself quiver.

"You're nervous," he said quietly as he leaned into her and softly kissed her neck. His other hand reached around her, cupping her cheek, and he turned her face toward him. Tala sucked in a breath as he pressed his mouth against hers. At first, it was soft and tender, then he pressed harder, pulling her into him, and she kissed him back. He tasted like their wine and the syrup from their dessert, and he kissed her deeper yet.

Tala slipped her arms around him as he embraced her, his hand trailing up her back and running through her hair. His lips left her mouth and roamed to her jaw, down her neck, and along her collarbone. She closed her eyes, willing her nerves to settle. But she seemed to only grow tenser with every kiss and was unsure of where to stop him.

He was a good kisser, and she found delight in the taste of him, the smell of his cologne and shampoo when she breathed, but there was something about him that made her anxious.

Vaughn's lips brushed across the top of her exposed shoulder, then he looked up, his eyes meeting hers, and in one look, she was certain that he would swallow her whole if she let him.

He brought his mouth to hers again, pressing his body against her, holding her firmly in his arms. She brought her hand to his face and brushed her thumb along his lips, separating them from hers. He sighed into her, and she couldn't tell if it was in pleasure or disappointment.

When she pulled back, he relaxed his grasp on her. She once again saw the hungry look in his eyes. He smiled, his perfect and smooth smile, the dimple in his cheek.

He was gorgeous and confident and suave, but like Thias, she was certain he was good at showing the sides of himself that he wanted people to see to get what he wanted. And she felt sure that when he looked at her, he saw a pretty woman in a pretty dress and thought he could be just one more person to make her what he wanted.

She'd glimpsed a different side of him though, and that image hung in the back of her mind for a reason. The same reason both his lie and the look in his eyes now, the one that said she was already his, set her on edge.

If she wasn't going to believe the lies anymore, then she had to be honest with herself too. And this, she thought, was not what she wanted.

❖

Kane made his way through the small bar, which was dimly lit, a thrum of chatter echoing throughout. He spotted him as soon as he walked through the door, seated in a booth in the back corner, the soft glow of a lamp hanging from the ceiling just bright enough to make out his bleached, shaggy hair. His face was still holding on to a tan from the summer months, and he gave a nod to Kane when he spotted him.

Kane slipped into the booth, sliding off his hood. "I was surprised to get a message from you."

He nodded with an easy smile. "Glad you came."

Kane rested his hands on the table, which was tacky to the touch. "It's been a while."

"It has. Tell me what's new."

Kane shrugged. "Same as always."

He chuckled under his breath. "I've got some running you could do if you're looking for some cash. You know how it works. Always easier than training someone new."

"I'm fine for now," Kane said, leaning in closer. "You going to tell me what this is about? I know you're not here to chitchat."

"True," he said. "I came to tell you that you've been spotted."

"Spotted?" Kane asked, taken aback, a spike in his heart rate. "Who?"

"Doesn't matter who. What matters is that you were seen with Tala Alexander," he said. "What could you possibly be doing with her? And how did you two even stumble into each other's lives?"

Kane could hear the accusation in his voice but said nothing.

"I've always thought of you as a smart guy, Kane, but this, this is more than stupid. This is reckless. For someone who lives off the grid, you're risking a lot by associating with her. People may not know to look for you, but she's an Alexander. There are eyes on her."

Kane swallowed hard, running his hand over his head. He could feel the rough stubble and made a mental note to shave. "No one will know who I am," he said in a feeble rebuttal.

"They'll make a point of finding out. You don't exactly look like the typical guy she should be with."

He was right. This is exactly what Kane had feared. All the reasons he'd told himself to stay away came rushing back. But there was something inside of him, in his very chemistry, that felt the need to seek her out.

"You're not just risking yourself. Think about her."

Kane took a deep breath and asked himself what he was willing to put on the line. Himself? Clearly. But Tala? He couldn't do that to her.

"I'm not here to tell you what to do. Merely warn you. I'd like to think we're friends after everything. But you're playing with fire. So don't be surprised if you get burned."

NINE

Tala woke to the buzzing hum of her palm pad as it vibrated across her nightstand. Groggily, she reached out for it, and prying her eyelids open, she saw an alert flashing across the screen. The TV in her bed came to life, and she sat upright, rubbing the sleep away as she watched Thias, streaming live, step up to the familiar podium. She recoiled at the sight of him. Everything she now knew tainted the way she saw him, an acrid taste in her mouth as she watched him on her screen.

"Early this morning," he said with his usual stern expression, his jaw set in a firm line, a small furrow of his brow, "an attack was carried out at the Port of Columbia on an incoming shipment from Mazanada. Two rounds of explosives were detonated. The first, at approximately 7:03, and the second at 7:10. We believe the first explosion, which left three shipping workers injured, was a diversion while the second explosion made it possible for part of the shipment to be hijacked and placed on a getaway boat. Militia Forces coast guard was unable to stop the malefactors. This was a strategic and deliberate attack on the Republic. I would like to stress that while there were injuries, there were no casualties. At this time, no one has claimed responsibility, but due to previous attacks of a similar nature, it is believed it was carried out by Unified Rebels. An investigation is now underway," he said, his voice never wavering, his eyes so focused it was as though his glare could penetrate even through the screen of her palm pad. Tala had seen this face, too many times, and she knew he was raging.

She recalled her conversation with Vaughn the previous night, his suspicions the UR were ramping up to something. While shipping hijackings were nothing new, she couldn't get his warning out of her head.

Thias continued on her screen, reining her thoughts in. "Militia Forces has cleared the area, and at this time, we believe there is no imminent danger or risk to other incoming shipments or the general public. With that said, we are emphasizing vigilance until more details emerge. Our goal, as always, is the safety of all citizens of the Republic of Columbia. Anyone who commits treason against our great nation will be punished to the highest extent of the law. We will have no tolerance for any Rebels within our borders. That is all at this time. I will not be taking any questions," he said with a firm nod of his head as he turned and swiftly exited the stage. The broadcast ended, and her screen went black.

Tala sighed. She knew Command would be in chaos. It had been months since the UR hit one of the shipping ports. Every hit they made was more refined than the last.

She threw herself back into her pillows and groaned. Her palm pad sprang to life again, and Tala was surprised to see Thias calling her.

She took a slow, deep breath, bracing herself as she answered. "Saw your National Statement," she said, smoothing her hand over her unsightly bedhead.

"Shit's hit the fan," he said with a scowl. "Damn Ash Song and her Rebels and schisies. They're a petty inconvenience. They've just made a mess of things. I've only got a second, but I need you to come to dinner tonight."

Tala's brows scrunched. Being with him was the last thing she wanted. "Why? I thought you'd be swamped with this."

"I am," he asserted. "But there's something I need to discuss with you. It's imperative. Dinner. I'll send a car at six. I've got to go," he said hurriedly, and before she could utter a word, he was gone.

There was a quiet knock on Tala's door.

"I thought I heard your voice," Mila said, her face appearing around her door.

Tala smiled at the sight of her.

Mila stepped into the bedroom, making her way to the bed where she took a seat near Tala's feet. "Heard about the bombings. Well, it was hard to miss as the alert blared across all of our screens," she said. After losing Maverick the way she had, Mila was always anxious after any kind of Rebel strike.

Tala sighed, her shoulders sinking.

"Think you'll have to go in?" she asked.

"I haven't heard from my captain. So hopefully not. I'm sure Command is in mayhem," Tala said as she rubbed the last traces of sleep from her eyes.

"Heard you come home last night. But you disappeared into your room before I could come out and ask about your date. Tell me about it. Was Vaughn perfect and dreamy and gorgeous as always?" Mila smiled. Tala knew she was trying to distract herself.

It was true, he was dreamy and gorgeous, on the surface, Tala thought. She considered her words carefully. "I think Vaughn knows exactly what to say and when to say it to get what he wants. He reminds me of Thias."

Mila winced. "That's never good. I mean, to see your brother in the guy you're dating."

"I think I'm going to end it," Tala said.

Mila's eyes grew wide in surprise. "Didn't see that coming. Vaughn doesn't seem the kind of guy to be dumped. Did he do something?"

Tala exhaled a deep breath. "He was pushy," she said. "More aggressive than I wanted." There was no one else she would be that honest with.

"He didn't, like, do something to you, did he?" she asked, her face twisting up.

Tala shook her head. "No, nothing like that. But he clearly wanted things that I didn't. It all just moved so quickly, and I wasn't sure how we'd even gotten to that point. But when his hands were on me, when he kissed me, I couldn't help but be on edge." Tala could see Thias's disappointment already. He was insistent that she settle down with someone. And Vaughn was everything he wanted for her.

"Well, I'd say it's better to figure all this out early on," Mila said. "Before anyone's heart gets broken."

"I'm just not sure how to tell him," she admitted.

Mila's mouth turned down. "Don't know what to tell you about that one. I just straight-up tell the guys I end things with. But I have the feeling Vaughn needs to be handled a little more delicately."

Tala nodded, and she felt anxiety in her chest all over again. He wouldn't take it well, of that she was certain.

"Let's get things off your mind and go out tonight for drinks," Mila said with an eager smile. "I'll cancel my date. We'll invite Ronin too."

"Can't," Tala said. Mila's smile quickly fell. "I have to be at Thias's for dinner. He insisted. But," she said with a smirk, "in his haste, he never told me what I have to wear."

"Which means you'll wear pants," Mila said dully.

"I could use a new pair."

"Shopping?" she asked, her eyes brightening. "Oh, yes please."

The black sedan pulled into Thias's drive right on time, and he stood waiting for her, opening her door once it came to a stop. Her heart couldn't help but hammer in her chest at the sight of him, and she felt the simmer of anger in her body.

Tala slid out of the backseat, and Thias gave her a look up and down. "Pants, really?" he said in obvious disappointment.

"You didn't say otherwise," she said with a defiant smirk.

"Well, at least you still look nice," he conceded.

Tala smiled to herself, reveling in her victory. She had chosen a white pant suit with cropped pants and sleeves, a nude, lace top, and heels to match. There was something empowering about having chosen something for herself, even if it was only an outfit.

Tala felt Thias's hand brush gently across her back as he guided her up the path to the door.

"The kids are down and are looking forward to seeing you," he said.

Tala smiled. He rarely had Jax and Millie, who were four and two, around when he hosted dinners. He parented like their father had. He was satisfied with himself as a parent by being able to provide for his children. What he lacked in affection was always made up for in opportunity and privilege.

She was met with squeals of delight when she went into the house, and she felt her anger ebb at the sight of those innocent, sweet faces. Tala dropped to her knees as the children ran to hug her. Thias stood over them and gave a low chuckle.

"Goodness," Tala said as she looked them over, smoothing Jax's shirt. "How have you gotten so big?" she exclaimed and ran a finger through Millie's silky, dark hair. Both kids looked like Thias, Millie's dark hair being the only exception.

"Don't bombard her," Nina fussed as she came up to them and gently pulled the children off her.

Tala laughed as she stood, and looking across the room, she was startled to see Vaughn standing near the kitchen island, an amused smile on his face. "Oh," she said in surprise.

"I hope that's a good *oh*," he said as he approached.

Her eyes flickered between him and Thias for a moment, who was also smiling in amusement. She couldn't help but feel like the joke was all on her.

"Of course it is," she said, forcing a grin, then let out a slow, steady exhale.

"A drink," Thias said as he snapped his fingers to get the attention of their server who nodded in understanding, then quickly scurried out of sight.

Vaughn reached for her hand, and bringing it to his mouth, gave her a soft kiss on her knuckle. Knowing Thias was watching, she felt heat rush to her face as she shifted uneasily.

"Come children," the nanny said as she made her way down the stairs to the great room.

Jax reached for Tala's hand, pulling her down to his level. He sweetly kissed her cheek.

"Aww," she said as she tapped the tip of his nose. "Thanks, sweetie."

He smiled at her, so much like her father's when he was young, she thought. His blond hair sweeping across his forehead. The nanny scooped up Millie and took Jax by the hand.

"It's time for your dinner," she said with a smile at Jax, then disappeared upstairs with the children.

The server appeared beside Tala, silently handing her a glass of wine, then quickly returned to the kitchen.

"Come in, make yourselves comfortable," Thias said as he waved them away from the entryway. He pulled his palm pad from his pocket and gave it a few taps, turning on soft piano music and dimming the lights. The ambiance was meant to have a relaxing effect throughout the room, but anxiety still coursed through Tala like an electrical current.

Tala crossed the water feature in the floor and took a seat on the sofa, Vaughn sitting close beside her, his thigh brushing against hers. He reached for her, finding her bare wrist, and she felt her cheeks redden knowing what he was looking for.

"You're not wearing it," he said quietly, leaning into her. "Do you not like it?"

"Oh, I love it," she said encouragingly, her eyes meeting his. "I… I just didn't think about it."

"I bought it so that you would wear it," he said. His smile faded and his lips pursed.

"I'm sorry," she said, feeling defensive, taken aback by his harsh expression. "I don't typically wear much jewelry, so really, it didn't even cross my mind."

He stared at her, an imperious look in his eyes, and Tala moved uncomfortably away from him.

"I'll do better. Promise," she said to placate him, knowing this was the wrong place to upset him or argue about something as trivial as a bangle.

Vaughn's firm glare lasted another moment before his eyes finally softened, his jaw slackening. "I just want to see it on you. Next time."

"What are you two so deeply in conversation about?" Thias asked as he took a seat in a chair near them.

"Oh, it's nothing," Vaughn said with a haughty laugh.

"The bombing today," Tala said, changing the subject, "it was the Rebels? The Statement said there were injuries."

"Just minor ones. Everyone's been released from the hospital. And yes," he said with exhaustion in his voice, "it was undoubtedly the Rebels. UR leaders, Ash Song and Jasper Colson, released a statement this afternoon from somewhere in Pacifica claiming responsibility for it. President Walker is too lenient on them out there, and they are entirely out of my jurisdiction."

"They seem to be causing more and more problems these days," she said.

Thias shrugged. "They do this. There is a flurry of activity from them and then it dies down for a while. They're just a complication, nothing more. Enough of this talk, I get plenty of it everywhere else in my life," he said as he straightened. "Are you two planning to be at President Royer's upcoming birthday party together?" he asked with a smirk, his eyes, an icy blue, meeting Tala's.

"I hadn't officially asked," Vaughn said with a low chuckle. "But I assumed so." His gaze fell on her, and her chest tightened. She adjusted her body again to put more distance between them.

"Oh, umm… yeah," she said, her heart sinking.

"Are we discussing the president's birthday?" Nina asked as she took a seat on the opposite sofa. "It's his fiftieth, and they are pulling out all the stops," she said, her eyes lighting up. "Tala, you must let me take you to get a gown. I know how that's not your thing."

Tala felt her body tense as she forced a smile across her face. "That's generous, Nina."

"We're Alexander women, we must represent," she said, giving Tala a knowing nod.

"Well said," Thias said as he stood. "It looks like dinner is ready."

Dinner was monopolized with conversation about the attack on the port, and both Thias and Vaughn lamented over having to work with Pacifica's President Walker who they described as insolent and weak. She could feel Vaughn's eyes on her while they ate and was careful to keep her gaze averted. She didn't want to do anything to encourage him.

The Rebels, she learned, had managed to seize and get away with a cargo container filled with electronics, for what, they didn't know. And to make matters worse, Mazanada, where the shipment had come from, was accusing the Republic of lax security, threatening to withdraw all shipments bound for the country. Tala had never known the Republic to ever have lax security for anything.

"We're teetering on an international crisis here," Vaughn said sternly. "I've been on the phone or in meetings all day. So, to get your invitation tonight was a welcomed relief."

"I don't think we need to go that far. Not in front of the ladies anyway," Thias said curtly, the corner of his mouth curling into a severe frown.

Tala glanced in Vaughn's direction. His body stiffening, and she noticed for the first time a vein running down the side of his neck that seemed more pronounced with his tension. "Of course," he said, his voice tight and low.

"Well, I think that finishes dinner," Nina said in a hurried breath. "Who would like more wine?" She turned and waved her finger at the server, who quickly approached the table with a bottle, topping off each glass. "Anyone care to sit out on the veranda? It's an unusually warm evening."

"I need to first have a word with Tala," Thias said, rising from his chair. "My office," he said coolly, his eyes meeting hers.

Tala felt a flutter in her chest. "Of course," she said, not letting her gaze fall.

He turned and headed down a hallway leading off the living room, Tala close behind. He entered a security code on the digital panel outside the door, then stepped into the office. It was a spacious room with a large, interactive desk in the middle, two chairs opposite the desk.

"Have a seat," he said, gesturing toward the chairs in front of his desk, his eyes meeting hers, his expression giving nothing away.

Tala felt her pulse quicken as she sat, tucking one ankle behind the other, sitting tall. The gnawing in her belly told her something was off.

Thias circled his desk, taking a seat in his white leather chair opposite her. Folding his hands in his lap, he leaned back, looking comfortable. He said nothing, his eyes holding her gaze.

She refused to look away.

He continued to sit in silence, impassive, watching her. With every passing minute, anxiety settled deeper into her bones.

"Are you going to tell me what this is about?" she finally asked.

A smile curled at the corner of his mouth as he sat up. Resting his arms on the desk, he leaned forward, as if he were pressing himself into her space, and she readjusted in the chair.

"There's been a breach on an MF server," he said matter-of-factly. "The records and archives server to be specific. An unknown user accessed a classified file and downloaded it offsite. Unfortunately, that's where we lost it. Tech services wasn't able to trace it any further. Someone covered their tracks well."

"And how does this have anything to do with me?" she asked coolly, though she felt her chest constricting.

"It has everything to do with you," he said.

Tala slipped her hands between her legs to keep them from shaking.

"See, it wasn't just any case that was accessed, it was the one on mom's and dad's deaths. It was the fire," he said. "What I don't know is who would want to see that file after all these years. And why."

"A good question," she said, keeping her voice level. She knew he was scrutinizing every move she made, every breath she took, looking for any tell that would give her away.

"Security Section has opened an investigation," he continued. "And since you're included in that file, they'll question you about it."

"I don't know anything about that file," she said. She could feel his glare cutting through her lie.

He was quiet for a moment, his hands coming together, forming a steeple with his fingers. "There's more to that case than you've been told. And I think maybe it's time to finally tell you the truth. Just in case your curiosity was to ever get the best of you."

Tala felt her mouth go dry. "What're you talking about?"

"I'm talking about the fire. See, the official cause was determined to be a gas leak. That's what was released to the public," he said.

"Are you saying it wasn't?" she asked.

His eyes narrowed, their intensity flaring like a fire. "Actually, it was a cover. Truth is, it was arson. It was an assassination."

"What?" she gasped, her mouth falling open. This was it. Her performance had to be on-point. She had to sell her reaction. "What do you mean assassination? That's absurd. Who would…" she let her sentence fall away.

"The Republic."

Tala's eyes widened. "I don't understand."

"See, mom was accused of treason and was deemed a threat to the country," he said with nearly no emotion, indifferent to his revelation. "She compromised a high-level government research project."

"No. No…" she said, shaking her head. "Mom was a biochemist. She worked on medicine. Thias, this makes no sense."

"I can't give you details of the research project. And that information isn't disclosed in the case file. But mom was guilty. And dad, well, he'd have been sympathetic to her," he said. "Their marriage was a liability."

"Sympathetic? He was a government leader!" she exclaimed, her voice high.

"It's not as simple as that," he said calmly. "Mom's assassination would've compromised his leadership role. You really think he'd have gone back to work for the people who killed her?"

"You mean murdered!" she yelled. "And what about us? We were in that house." Her anger, her heartbreak, it all began to seep into the cracks of her resolve, a pit opening in her stomach as she thought about the part he played in all of it. "You had something to do with this, didn't you?" she asked, her voice breaking. "There's a reason you showed up on the lawn after the house exploded. You weren't in the house to begin with, were you?"

"I had no choice," he said.

"No choice? Are you kidding me? And what about me? Where do I fit into this story? Was I supposed to be killed too?" Her emotions tore through her, and she no longer knew what was real and what was for show.

"You were collateral damage. You weren't supposed to make it out of that house," he said, his eyes softening. "And it almost killed me, the thought of losing you. But what was I going to do? Royer came to me. I was going to be the next director of Militia Forces. I was going to have a position. I did what I had to do for my country."

Speechless, Tala stood, looking away from him. That's what this came down to? Position? She knew she shouldn't be surprised it was all about his power, but she was nonetheless.

"But you made it out. And so I petitioned to take custody of you, to rescind the order on you, and they relented. At that point, I had officially assumed the position. I had power, and I used it to keep you alive," he said. "Tala, look at me," he demanded sharply.

She took a breath, steeling herself as she turned toward him. Her hatred was visceral, burning through her veins as she met his gaze.

"I couldn't let them hurt you."

"You mean murder me," she said. "You think you're some kind of hero now? How, how can I ever trust you after this?"

He rose to his feet and circled his desk, approaching her. There was tension in his shoulders, in his face, his jaw ticking.

"For eleven years, you've looked me in the eye and lied to me," she said, her voice shaking. Despite herself, tears pooled in her eyes. "I hate you. I hate you for all of it," she said bitterly.

"I was protecting you!" he yelled, his voice loud and thunderous, sending a chill down her spine. "You were fifteen years old. The last thing you needed to know was the truth. You never would've understood." He took a step closer to her, and she struggled to take a breath.

"Don't try to justify what you did. You murdered them! You tried to murder me," she said, shoving him, pushing him away. She couldn't put enough distance between them.

"It wasn't my story to tell," he said sternly.

"But it was," she said, quickly wiping at a tear as it fell down her cheek. "There was no one else to tell it. You've known since the beginning, and I hate you for it."

"You need to get over it," he snapped. "I already told you I did what I had to do to protect you, and I won't let you hate me for that. I'm all the family you've got left."

"And you made sure of that," she said, tipping her head, her eyes narrowing.

"In time, you'll understand," he said.

She would never understand. And she would never forgive him. This would forever be a chasm between them, dividing them, and they would never traverse it.

"I'm sorry you had to learn the truth at all," he said.

Her breath caught in her throat as she stared at him. "Why are you telling me this? After all this time?" she asked, composing herself.

"In light of the breach, I wanted to put it on record that you know what's in the file, that I revealed to you the confidential information contained in it. Because Security Section is going to give you a lie detection evaluation, and they will ask you about the case. And when they do, you'll be able to tell them you know the details, that I told you what was in that file."

Her mind spun with confusion, his words circling and expanding in her head. "I don't understand," she said.

"Oh, I think you do," he said. The look in his eyes set her on edge, making her heart race. "Look, Tala, I know this isn't easy information to absorb. But mom was a traitor, and her actions came with a price. I'm sorry if you think you can't trust me anymore. But if you believe nothing else, believe this. Everything I ever do is for the good of the Republic. Mom betrayed both of us, and this was not easy for me either. I sealed that file, and I kept this secret to protect you. And you can't fault me for that," he said sternly, his mouth setting in a hard line.

Tala glared at him, her anger seething. "Actually, I can." She turned quickly on her heel and hurried from his office. It wasn't until she heard the door close behind her that she finally took a breath, her body shaking.

She made her way back to the great room, catching the inquisitive looks of Vaughn and Nina as she rounded the corner. Without a word to either of them, she headed for the door, not giving a second glance behind her as she left.

Tala gave an apprehensive knock on the growingly familiar white door, glancing around as three cars drove past her down the darkened street. The savory smell of food wafted in the air, and she heard a scuffle behind the door. It opened a moment later, Max standing before her.

"Tala," he exclaimed as he nudged his glasses, his brows raised. "Of course it's you," he said with a half-smile that she wasn't sure was entirely genuine, then he stepped aside to let her in.

She glanced around the pod, then across the room, she saw Kane as he appeared from the hatch in the floor, and he looked at her in surprise.

"Hi," he said with a smile, his face brightening. "I wasn't expecting you," he said, catching her gaze.

She felt herself blush as she shifted on her heels. "I came from Thias's." She could still hear the emotion in her voice.

Kane nodded as Max crossed the room between them, taking a seat on the sofa.

"That's why you're all dressed up," he said. "You look… nice." The corner of his mouth curved up.

She was sure that he could hear her racing heart. And simply the sight of Kane was doing nothing to calm it. "Come in," he said, motioning toward the living room.

Tala took a seat opposite Max, Kane sliding onto the armrest of the same couch but keeping some distance between them. "Something happen?" he asked, getting right to the point.

"Can't I just stop by?" she asked with a nervous laugh that she knew he saw through.

"Sure, you can. But you're upset about something," he said, eyeing her carefully.

She sighed in resignation. "There's no getting anything past you," she said as she sunk back into the sofa. "I've had a weird day," she admitted.

"Let me guess," Max said. "Everyone is all stressed out about that stupid bombing in the port this morning," he said with an amused chuckle.

Tala cocked her head. "Well, yes, people are stressed about that," she said. "That wasn't what I had in mind, but now I'm curious. Are you suggesting it wasn't a big deal?" she asked.

Max glanced at Kane who eyed him sternly.

"Now who's the human lie detector? Tell me," she demanded.

"Well," Max stammered, "we don't think it was a big deal. People are overreacting."

"We?" she asked, glancing up at Kane.

"Tala, it doesn't matter," Kane said. "Let's talk about what you came here for."

"Are you saying it was no big deal that the Rebels attacked our port, again, and stole from the Republic, again?" she asked as she rose to her feet. Her emotions were riding high already, and this was going to push her over the edge. "Are you?" she repeated.

"It was a shipment from Mazanada," Max said. "It was probably just coffee or something, and most citizens can't afford to drink it anyway, so who cares about some stuffy coffee drinkers?"

"Is this how you feel?" she asked, looking back to Kane.

"Look," Kane said calmly, "I don't condone their approach, but when the Rebels take something, there's usually a reason behind it. Outside of the city, there are always stories about how they help people. They do good things for our people. I hardly think they're the terrorist organization they're made out to be. But this isn't what you came here for," he insisted.

"The Republic takes care of its citizens," she said defensively as she stood. *She* helped take care of their people. "And they would be able to do a better job if the Rebels weren't stealing from them," she asserted, her voice getting louder.

Max sat unmoving, wide-eyed.

Kane ran his hand over his head. "They take care of the people on top," he said. "It's a caste system, Tala. The Rebels are just trying to give others a chance too."

Tala stared breathless at him. "You know there were people who were hurt in that bombing, right?" she said bitterly as she crossed her arms.

"I said I didn't condone their approach. Just that, maybe, I understood why they do what they do," he said.

"This was a mistake," she said through clenched teeth as she headed toward the door. "I shouldn't have come."

"Tala, wait," he called after her.

"The Republic isn't perfect," she snapped, as she turned back toward him. "No one knows that better than me. But the system is designed to support people as they need it. My family helped create the system for that very reason."

"No," Kane said with the shake of his head. "It supports people based on whether they deserve it. The Rebels do the opposite."

"With the Republic's resources! Doling out help to the people with the very stuff they stole in the first place doesn't makes them heroes," she exclaimed. "I don't understand why you'd defend them. My job, what I put myself on the line for, is to protect my people. And I've never let anyone's citizenship status stop me from helping someone. So, when you accuse the Republic, you're accusing me too," she said, reaching for the door. "I'm leaving. And don't you dare follow me."

"Tala—" Kane called, but his voice was cut off as she slammed the door behind her.

She was fuming, her anger boiling inside her as she made her way back down the narrow street. A block away, she pulled out her palm pad, powered it on again, then called the first person who came to mind.

"Tala?" Ronin asked, his face on the screen. "Where are you?"

She quickly glanced around to make sure there weren't any discernable buildings in sight that would give away her whereabouts in Oxwick. Being there would certainly raise questions. "I'm headed home. Wondering if you want to meet me for a drink?"

"Of course I do," he said happily.

"Meet at the Met Lounge in twenty," she said, then ended her call. She stopped on the street corner and took a breath, willing her racing heart to slow. She closed her eyes for a moment, focusing on her breathing and pushing all the chaos in her mind aside.

After a few minutes, feeling calmer and more in control, Tala opened her eyes, then headed for the subtrain.

Ronin's face lit up when he spotted Tala making her way across the crowded, upscale bar, where she always had a standing reservation. It was her go-to place with Mila and Ronin. Crystal chandeliers hung from the ceiling, and a man dressed smartly in a pressed maroon suit played on a grand piano in the center of the room. The buzz of conversation filled Tala's ears, and she caught the glimpses of people as they watched her walk past. She was definitely recognized by the crowd in the Met Lounge.

"Wow, you look nice," he said, standing to greet her. "A dirty martini," he called over his shoulder to the bartender who knew exactly what she liked.

Tala took a seat on the plush leather stool beside him. "I was at Thias's," she said.

"And you're clearly upset," he said. "Or pissed. Or both."

"And I don't want to talk about it," she said. She was fairly sure she wasn't allowed to anyway, the truth about her parents or Kane.

Ronin nodded silently as her drink was set in front of Tala.

"Here you go, Miss Alexander," the bartender said with a friendly smile.

Tala offered him a weak and forced grin, then reached for her glass and took a large drink.

"How was your date with the chancellor last night?" Ronin asked.

"I don't want to talk about that either."

"Oh boy. You're in a mood," he said with a low chuckle. "Better drink up so the happier version of you comes out."

Tala frowned, then took another drink. "Can I ask you a question?" she asked, squaring her body to him. There was something about his familiarity that was relaxing to her. Maybe the vodka and music were helping too.

"Of course," he said.

"The citizenship classes," she paused, "would you liken them to a caste system?"

Ronin's eyes narrowed as he considered her question. "No, I wouldn't," he said after a moment. "A caste system doesn't allow you to move up or down, but rather keeps you stagnant in the place you're in. The bulk of our people are Standard citizens. The only reason someone would be Sub-Standard or worse, Nameless, would be because of criminal history, failed education, or illegality in the country," he said. "And likewise, people can become Preferred if they have a distinct or rare skill or talent, or move into prestigious positions of leadership or authority."

Tala contemplated this. Her thoughts aligned with his and she felt justified in her argument. Except for Preferreds, everyone was automatically born a Standard citizen. If someone's classification was reduced, it was of their own doing.

"People will always be defined in relation to things like wealth, education, and position," he said. "The citizenship hierarchy of the Republic being no exception. Why would you ask that anyway?" he asked with a raised brow.

"Oh, just something I overheard," she said dismissively. She thought she had understood Kane. She thought he had understood her. It was baffling to her how he could sympathize with and defend the Rebels. Supporting the UR was a punishable crime in the Republic. Being a schisy was a betrayal to the nation.

"What do you think Command is going to be like tomorrow with all this stuff with the Rebels?" he asked after finishing his drink. He quickly waved down to the bartender for a second.

"I was surprised we weren't called in today," she admitted.

"I was, too, actually."

Tala sighed, her mind still on Kane. Maybe she'd been wrong about him, wrong to put her trust so blindly into someone she was certain just her affiliation with could get her in trouble. But, she reminded herself, he had put his trust in her too. Knowing who he was now, she should be turning him in, not sneaking around with him. She was used to things being black and white, but Kane was all gray area for her.

"Tala?" Ronin called, snapping his fingers. "You in there?"

"Sorry!" she said, straightening. "My mind is elsewhere," she admitted guiltily.

"I can see that," he said with an amused smile.

"What did you say?" she asked, pushing thoughts of Kane away and telling herself to focus on Ronin.

"I asked if you were going to the president's big birthday bash that's coming up?"

She nodded. "Thias wouldn't let me out of it even if I tried."

"But you're an—"

"Alexander," she finished. "Yes, I'm aware. Although my name is more titular than anything."

"Maybe," he said with a shrug. "I think it's more than you think though. Our people relate with you more so than with Thias. You have a good reputation. You do good things for them, Thias just intimidates everyone," he said with a small laugh.

"Thias… intimidating? I had no idea," she said wryly as she nudged him with her shoulder.

"Ahh, there she is," Ronin said. "The happier Tala I know and love."

She eyed him and gave him a sly and knowing smile. He had a way of bringing that out in her. He always had, since the very beginning of their partnership. Of their friendship.

It was only a few minutes before curfew when Tala made it back to her pod, feeling more composed and less emotional. Mila had left her a message that she'd gone to bed with a headache, so she made sure to stay quiet as she made her way through their pod. Though once Mila was asleep, there was little that could wake her. She tossed her palm pad onto her bed, then slipped off her heels, letting out a low groan. She turned and glanced at herself in the mirror. Despite her roller coaster evening, she still looked surprisingly put together. She opened the drawer of the small gray box on her dresser and pulled out the bangle from Vaughn. She sighed as she turned it over in her hands, the large diamond glistening in the lamplight. It really was too much, and now that she wanted to end things, it was awkward to have it.

A small tap on her balcony door made her jump, and she knew who it was before even turning around. She wasn't entirely sure she wanted to see him. She closed her eyes and took a slow breath, then crossed her bedroom and opened the door to him. Kane's hands were shoved into the pockets of his jacket, his shoulders hunched forward.

"Can we talk?" he asked sheepishly.

Tala was exhausted, emotionally drained, and wasn't sure how to feel at the sight of him. While she still felt irritated, their earlier conversation fresh in her mind, she also couldn't bring herself to turn him away.

"You look like you were just sent to the principal's office," she said.

"No," he said with a shake of his head. "I never cared about that. But I do care about this right now." He lifted his gaze, his eyes meeting hers. "Tala, I'm sorry. I didn't mean to upset you or insinuate that you didn't care about your people. I know you've made the Republic your life's work."

Looking into his eyes, she studied him, seeing his regret, and she felt her anger toward him fade. "Come in," she said after a moment, stepping aside to let him into the room.

He lingered in the doorway for a second, then averting his eyes, he stepped inside, Tala closing the door behind him.

"We can't get into any kind of argument here," she said, glancing at the closed door to the hallway. "Mila's asleep."

"Well, that works out well because I didn't come here to fight. Only grovel," he said with a coy smile.

Despite herself, she felt a small smile tug at the corner of her mouth. "Sit," she said, nodding toward her bed while she took a seat. His presence seemed to fill her bedroom.

"Does this mean you forgive me?" he asked.

She shrugged. "Haven't decided yet."

"You came over tonight for a reason, and if you still want to talk about it, I'm here to listen," he said quietly in his deep voice.

Tala looked intently at him, at his eyes nearly dark as night, the ones that had haunted her for so many years, and she saw a small fleck of gold in his irises that she'd never noticed before. Kane gave little away with his facial expressions, but his eyes, they showed deep emotion, and there was something about the way he looked at her that disarmed her, that made her pulse quicken, that made her feel like she was the only thing that mattered when they looked at her. They commanded her gaze, and she felt a flutter deep inside.

"It's Thias," she said, with an unsteady voice. "Tonight, after dinner, he told me the truth about the fire, about my parents' deaths."

His brow raised as he tilted his head to the side. "Out of the blue? I don't… why would he do that?"

She gave a small shake of her head. "Because he knows there was a breach and the file was accessed. And I'm pretty sure he knows it was me."

"Tala, that's bad," he said. "That's a serious offense, and Max—"

"He knows nothing about Max. And the thing is, I don't think he's going to report me," she said calmly, although her mind was swimming in confusion. "He told me I was going to be given a lie detection evaluation by Security Section, but—"

"Tala!"

"No, Kane, he said he put it on record that he revealed to me what's in the file. There's no way I could beat that test. So, when I'm asked, I can now honestly say I know what's in that case file without being at risk for criminal charges."

"So, he's letting you off the hook? He's covering for you, giving you an out," he said, his eyes narrowing.

"I think so," she whispered. "I just don't know why."

Kane was quiet. She felt him studying her, and she looked away.

"And last night, Vaughn said something to me," she said. She cringed that she even had to mention his name. There was something that felt wrong talking about him with Kane, bringing his name into the space between them, and she felt him shift beside her. "When I probed him about Masters, he said Thias had interviewed him for days. Just like my captain said.

"He also gave me some of the details of the case with those hackers who were arrested a few days ago," she said, then launched into a recital of that conversation, Kane listening intently.

"It sounds like your relationship with the chancellor is revealing all kinds of information," he said, his eyes not meeting hers.

"Yes, but the thing is," she said with a loud sigh. "Maybe I shouldn't be talking to you about this."

His gaze met hers. "Tala, it's okay," he said, nodding encouragingly.

"I'm ending it. Not that anything has really started," she added quickly. "But I can't let it go any further. I can't be with someone I know is lying to me."

Kane was quiet for a moment, studying her carefully, his expression unreadable.

"Tala," he finally said. "He clearly trusts you enough to give you information you're technically not privy to. You were taken off Masters's case. You shouldn't know anything about his death."

"But they're lies," she countered. "And I'm just not interested in him."

He paused. "But even in the lies, we learn things. And if there's a chance you can get more information, then I think… I think," he stammered, his expression hardening, "you should continue seeing him. For the sake of your case."

Tala saw a flicker in his eyes.

She looked away, dropping her head into her hands.

"What is it?" he asked. "What else is going through your head?"

She couldn't bring her eyes to meet his, her heart pounding hard. "I don't know how to fake a relationship with him. He's… he's…" Embarrassed, the words wouldn't form on her tongue.

"Hey," he said, reaching for her chin, gently turning her head toward him. "He's what?" he asked, his eyes filled with genuine concern.

"He's pushy," she whispered, using the same word she had with Mila. She felt her cheeks flush.

Kane dropped his hand, his brows furrowed, and she could see him registering her words.

He sighed. "You mean he wants things from you."

"He gave me a bracelet, completely over the top, and tonight he got so weird when he noticed I wasn't wearing it. He feels so… territorial," she admitted. She closed her eyes and took a slow breath. Steeling herself, she met his gaze. "But maybe you're right. Maybe I should see what kind of information I can get out of him first. He clearly trusts me enough to divulge information," she conceded.

He shook his head. "No. No, I would never ask you to put yourself in a position like that, with a guy like that," he said adamantly.

"I can do it," she said asserted. "I can," she repeated, more to herself than to him. "Just for a little longer."

His eyes filled with worry and concern, and she offered him a reassuring smile.

"Trust me," she whispered.

"If anything happened to you, I—"

"I'll be fine. I can do this," she said. Without thinking, she brought her hand to his face. His skin was soft and warm, the scruff on his chin and jaw was rough, and she brushed her thumb over it. In the quiet that settled between them, her heart pounded with fervor, and she felt her cheeks flush. But this time it wasn't out of embarrassment. Despite her nerves, her body felt charged and alive. She couldn't bring herself to look away from him. And his eyes never wavered from hers.

"Tala," he murmured, his voice low and deep.

Before she could stop herself, she leaned into him and pressed her lips against his. They hung there for a brief second, then she felt him lean into her, kissing her back.

The room disappeared around them, and in that moment, Tala was aware of only two things, her racing heart and the feeling of his lips on hers. His hand slid up her arm, then he pulled her closer, and she let out a slow exhale.

When they separated, Tala felt warm all over, her lips and fingers tingling, and she gave him a small smile.

Kane was quiet, but the corners of his mouth turned up, and she saw a gleam in his eyes.

TEN

"You're playing with fire. So, don't be surprised if you get burned."

That had been his warning.

Fire, he thought to himself between pull-ups as he dangled from the bar suspended from his ceiling. He pulled himself up, his chin touching the bar. Wasn't that what had started this all those years ago? Because he saved her from a fire?

He had tossed and turned all night, unable to get Tala out of his head. He pulled himself up again, exhaling a deep, low grunt, not from fatigue but frustration.

Just like that, he could feel her lips on his all over again. He had seen it in her eyes, heard it in her heart, the way it quickened, the hitch in her breath, and the next thing he knew, her mouth was on his, and he felt life breathed into the very depths of him. He'd never experienced anything like that before and knew he never would again. It was like that moment had been written into the fabric of time and the universe had conspired to make it possible.

"Hey man, what're you doing down here?" Max asked, his head emerging through the open hatch. "You're up early. I can hear you all the way up here," he said as he descended the ladder. "Things not go well with Tala last night?" he asked, reaching the bottom. Max had been asleep when he got home, and Kane had been careful not to wake him.

"No," Kane said, releasing his grip on the bar, dropping to the floor. Despite his many, many pull-ups, he had barely broken a sweat.

"That bad?" he asked with a grimace.

"I meant no, things didn't go bad," he said as he took a seat at the foot of his bed, wiping at the light sweat with the bottom of his shirt.

"Ahh, so you two worked it out," Max said with a small chuckle.

Kane gave him a sober look, and Max's smile quickly faded. "I don't understand. What's the problem?"

He sighed and ran his hand across his head, smooth again from a fresh shave. "I've gotten in way too deep," he admitted and frowned.

Max hmphed and rolled his eyes. "I could've told you that the night you two killed that gang out by the docks." Max eyed him scrupulously. "But that's not what you're talking about. There's more going on between you two than just this case."

Kane's shoulders dropped and he threw his head back. "No," he said on an exhale. "Yes," he said, his eyes meeting Max's. "Maybe. Damn it, I don't know!" he cursed as he stood. "This can't happen," he said, turning to Max. "I'm nobody. I was a nobody before, and now I'm a genetically enhanced nobody. I have nothing, which means I have nothing to give her. She's an Alexander," he reasoned with himself. "And Thias's sister. And MF. She should be arresting me, not…" he said, letting his sentence fall away.

Kane began pacing. "Every time I'm with her, there're a million reasons to walk away racing through my head, each one telling me to put as much distance as possible between us. But as soon as I leave her, the only thing I can think about is how and when I'm going to see her again. But being with me puts her at risk." He paused, glancing at Max, who stood contentedly listening, leaning against the ladder. "I'm a Nameless. Technically a fugitive. I'm the very last person she should be with," Kane said as his shoulders hung in defeat. "And it's not even just that she's a Preferred, but she's—"

"An Alexander," Max said with a nod. "Yeah, you've said that. But here's the thing, Kane. That's just a name. She's not her grandfather, not her father, and she's certainly not her brother. She's Tala. And Tala sees you. Not as some boy from the sticks with a deadbeat pops, not as some man with freakish super-human skills, she sees *you*. And she still chooses to show up," he said. "Have you told her any of this?"

"No," Kane mumbled.

Max gave his glasses a nudge. "Well, I think you should. You'll have a better sense of direction for yourself when you know where she's at."

Kane was quiet as he eyed him across the room and gave a weak smile. Max was looking rather sure of himself and his advice. And Kane knew he was right.

"You've never been in a position like this before," Max said. "Where the truth is all out there. She still comes back. I think that says something about you and something about her. You've brought your guard down with her, and now you have to decide if you're going to really let her in or not. And I'm thinking you're going to need to figure it out quickly, because she'll be back. She has a way of showing up here. And in the most conspicuous ways. Maybe mention that," he said as he scrunched up his nose. "Now," he said, standing up straighter, "I've got a job to get to. Try to stay out of trouble. And don't do anything dumb." He cast Kane a sideways glance.

Kane sighed. "Yeah, trouble and dumb? I think I'm way past both of those."

"Tell her where you're at. You've been open about everything else," he said.

"Yeah," he said, his mind still spinning.

Max eyed him carefully. "Just be honest. See where it goes."

"That's the problem, Max, it can't go anywhere. As much as I want it to, it can't. And that's the end to this story," he said taking a seat on the bed again.

"Maybe," he said with a shrug. "But maybe not. Now, enough pep talk, I really do have to go. Just think about what I said." With a nod, he quickly climbed back up the ladder and through the hatch.

Kane watched him disappear and heard him leave the pod two minutes later. Alone again, Tala filled his mind. With a sigh, he got down on the floor and started push-ups. Up and down, Tala. Up and down, her smile. Up and down, her laugh. Up and down, her perfect blue eyes. He tried to push through his frustration, but it was nearly impossible with her presence taking up every corner of his brain. Up and down. Tala.

Never in his life had he ever met anyone like her. He had put up defenses against everyone, but she had managed to walk past them all. In his head, the answer was simple, let her go. But his heart couldn't do it, he couldn't walk away.

❖

"Having a better day?" Ronin asked as Tala took a seat at her desk, opposite him, her coffee in hand. Still charged from the night before, she didn't need the caffeine, but drank it anyway.

"Maybe," she said, giving him a coy smile. She looked around the rotunda, which seemed more chaotic than usual that morning.

"Something happen between when I left you last night and this morning? I mean, I didn't think I left you in that good of a mood," he said and chuckled. "Unless maybe I am that good. Tell me. Is it the chancellor?" he asked, leaning in closer.

She shook her head. "There's nothing to tell. Just having a better day."

His eyes narrowed, and Tala let out a small laugh as she averted her gaze.

"Ah, Alexander," Kole said as he approached from behind, and Tala swiveled around on her chair. "You're needed in security room three for questioning on a case. Please secure your duty belt and weapon in your desk."

She had been warned this was coming, but her heart couldn't help but beat quicker.

"Oh," Kole added quickly, "the report came back this morning on the firearms from the warehouse. Turns out they're all registered to DeSoto. Every single one," he said.

Tala cocked her head in surprise. "But…" she stammered. She stopped herself, feeling Ronin's eyes on her. Clenching her jaw, she bit back her urge to argue.

"Do we have any leads as to why they were in the Republic?" Ronin asked, turning toward Kole.

"Director Alexander is handling this case, so I'm not sure of the details," Kole said.

"Any chance there's a connection between DeSoto and the Unified Rebels?" he asked.

Kole's usual furrow deepened. "As I just said, I don't have any of that information," he said curtly. "Alexander, the security room. Security Section shouldn't have to wait for you," he said crossly.

Ronin's head snapped in her direction as Kole briskly walked away, and Tala rose to her feet, balling her clammy fists. She couldn't think about the guns now.

"Security Section?" he asked, his eyes wide with alarm.

"I'm sure it's nothing," she said as she gave him a small smile, if only to placate herself. Accessing that file wasn't the only secret she was hiding.

Tala's hands trembled as she entered the security room. She shoved them deep into her pockets to steady them. Two agents, one tall and slender with a full head of thick gray hair, the other stocky with wire-framed glasses and a thin mustache, were waiting for her.

"Agent Alexander, thanks for coming," the stocky man said in a croaky voice. "I'm Agent Gellar and this is Agent Mayes," he said as he nodded toward the other agent.

"We're Security Section," Mayes said as he adjusted his tie and cleared his throat. "Today we'll be conducting a lie detection evaluation on you regarding an on-going security investigation. Are you aware of the investigation?" he asked.

"Only that there is one," she said.

"Okay then," he said with a nod. "Please take a seat." He motioned toward a solo chair in the center of the room.

Tala sat, her body letting out a small shiver from the chill in the room. It smelled like it had been recently sanitized, the bite of ammonia lingering in the air.

"Today we'll be asking you a series of questions as well as presenting you with audio stimuli to determine your knowledge in relation to our investigation. We'll ask controlled questions, and both relevant and irrelevant questions, all of which will help calibrate your responses to help determine if you have concealed any information or have unauthorized knowledge of the case," Gellar said matter-of-factly.

Mayes approached Tala with a headband attached with spider-like legs, each leg with a different color node on the tip. "This," he said as he slipped it over her head and tightened it in the back, catching some of her hair in the buckle, "is an optical brain scanner. It will show us the parts of your brain that light up when asked a question and when exposed to specific words or phrases."

"Okay," she said, trying to hide the shake in her voice. She cast a furtive glance at Gellar, who sat at a desk in the corner of the room, near a wall of two-way mirrors. He paid no attention to her as his fingers manipulated the computer desktop.

Mayes held up two black straps. "If you could lift your arms, please," he said.

Tala's mind was in a frenzy as she thought through her responses to the evaluation, but she'd never had one before and didn't have a clue what they would ask her. As instructed, she lifted her hands above her head. He reached around her, wrapping one of the straps around her torso, over her diaphragm. Once it was firmly secured, he motioned for her to drop her arms. "Just one more," he said as he wrapped a second around the top of her chest, just below her collarbone. "These, along with the cushion in your seat, will monitor body movement, heart rate, and breathing rhythms.

The straps felt restrictive as Tala tried to take a deep breath. Her nerves were making her insides quake, and despite the cold, she felt her hands growing sweaty at her sides.

Mayes slipped a cuff around her bicep and small sensors onto the tips of her fingers

"And what are these?" she asked, trying to distract her mind from her ever-growing anxiety.

"To measure blood pressure and perspiration levels," he said.

The way her heart pounded and her body began to perspire, Tala was suddenly sure she would fail the test even before it began. "You're certainly thorough," she mused with a feeble smile. She absentmindedly bounced her foot, the sole of her boot squeaking on the tile floor.

"We take matters like this very seriously," Gellar said as he looked up at her for the first time in minutes.

Tala's mouth went dry, and she swallowed hard. "Of course. I wasn't implying otherwise."

She needed something to distract her, to relax her. An image of Kane flashed in her mind, and she quickly pushed it away. He seemed to only stir a more visceral reaction in her, which was not what she needed at that moment. Her mother, she thought. Her mind took her back to the first time she showed her *The Wizard of Oz*. Given everything she'd recently learned, she was unsure why that was the thought she conjured, but sharing that movie together was a favorite memory. In that moment, she needed a happy memory, and that one seemed to still be untainted.

"It's from before the war," she had said as they curled up on the couch together, sharing a thick, fuzzy blanket while it snowed outside. *"It survived because it's a beloved classic. And even after all this time, it can be applied to our lives."*

"Lastly," Mayes said as he moved a camera with a wide lens directly in front of her face, only inches from her nose, "this is a dual infrared scanner, monitoring pupil dilation in addition to mapping the thermal imaging in your face."

She took an unsteady breath as she glanced to the side, watching as Gellar pulled up a 3D image that emanated from the surface of the desk, six graphs manifesting in the air.

Mayes crossed the room, mumbling something quietly to Gellar.

Tala's chest was tight, and not just from the straps encased around her. The pounding of her heart filled her ears, drowning out the whispers between the agents. Thinking up any kind of lie during the test would be futile. She could never beat it, and she instantly felt gratitude toward Thias. She hated that. She didn't want to be indebted to him in any way.

Despite herself, she thought of Kane again. She had to protect him, no matter what. She was suddenly indifferent to any consequences for herself. She would accept her fate. But she would not give him up. Max neither. Seeing the depths of her selfishness, she chastised herself for involving them at all. This was her mess. She felt a guilty tug on her heart.

"We'll begin with our control questions," Gellar said, catching her gaze from the corner of her eye.

Tala nodded, taking a constricted breath.

"You're out of the woods, you're out of the dark, you're out of the night," she sang silently to herself.

"Please answer the following questions truthfully, using yes or no responses. Keep your eyes ahead of you, looking into the camera, and refrain from moving your body," Gellar said dully. "Number one. Your name is Tala Alexander, you're twenty-six."

"Yes," she said. She was surprised how strong the urge was to nod with her response.

"You're the only child of Jameson and Brit Alexander."

"No."

"You are currently sitting in a chair in Militia Forces Command Headquarters."

"Yes."

"You are the younger sister of Director Thias Alexander."

Tala's breath caught at the mention of his name, then she slowly exhaled. "Yes," she said after a brief pause.

"You have blue eyes."

"Yes."

"Now you will answer the following questions with a lie. Again, refrain from moving," Gellar said. From the corner of her eye, she could just make out Mayes as he leaned against the wall, his arms folded across his chest.

"You live at 2020 Market Street," he said.

"Yes," she said, the lie rolling off her tongue.

"Your MF captain is Mason Kole."

"No."

"Your MF partner is Ronin Ashby."

"No."

"You have served the Militia Forces for four years."

"Yes."

"Eight multiplied by two totals thirty-two."

"Yes."

"Good," Gellar said, no inflection in his voice. "Now we will ask a series of questions or make statements that are both relevant and irrelevant to our case. Please answer truthfully to all of them, once again using yes or no responses."

"We must be over the rainbow," she continued in her mind, letting the words wash over her.

"We are here today to investigate a breach on one of our servers. The compromised case file is number 10RCJ236MRP. Are you familiar with this case?"

"Yes," she said with a steady breath.

"Are you aware this file is regarding the deaths of Jameson and Brit Alexander?"

"Yes."

"Did Director Alexander reveal the contents of the file to you?"

"Yes."

"Have you ever willfully broken chain of command or a direct order from MF authority?"

"Toto, I have a feeling we're not in Kansas anymore."

Tala's head turned slightly as she looked across the room at Gellar. "No."

Gellar looked over from the graphs in front of him, his eyes meeting hers. "Please refrain from any movement."

"Did the details of the case file reveal that Jameson and Brit Alexander were killed in a coordinated government assassination?"

Tala felt her heart begin to pound harder in her chest. How, she wondered, was she supposed to stay calm when she was so emotionally connected to the case? No one was calm when learning their parents had been murdered.

"Yes." Tala felt a tickle on the side of her face, and the urge to scratch was hard to suppress.

"In the wake of your parents' deaths, you were raised by Thias Alexander."

"Yes."

"Do you currently or have you ever had level nine security clearance?"

"No," she said quickly, hearing the crack in her voice, albeit miniscule.

"Hold on to your breath, hold on to your heart, hold on to your hope."

She took a small breath, letting her shoulders fall.

"You had a personal relationship, of any kind, with former MF agent Maverick Sanders."

"Yes."

"Agent Sanders was killed in a vehicular accident while on-duty."

"No." She thought about how Thias had revealed information to her about his death. Information she was not supposed to know. Though the details he gave her were still few. She was sure he was immune to any ramifications for doing so.

"Did you personally access the case file under investigation?" Gellar asked.

Tala swallowed hard and closed her eyes, her dread filling her up. She felt a tightening around her throat.

"No," she said after a moment.

"Did Thias reveal to you that you were originally targeted in the assassination of your parents?"

Tala felt a flare of anger as she thought about how he had slipped all of them a drug. How he escaped the house before it was set on fire. How he petitioned to spare her afterward. How, in his head, he thought he was her champion for this.

"Yes."

"Were you ever aware that your mother was working on a classified government research project?"

Tala wasn't sure the answer to this question. Did they mean before Thias had told her the truth? Then yes, she was. But Thias did tell her, so technically she had known before they started the test. She couldn't help but feel like this question was meant to entrap her.

"Yes," she finally answered.

"You recently discovered a hidden collection of firearms in a warehouse in Ganbury."

"Yes," she said, answering more confidently. Though this wasn't a safe topic for her either, as far as she knew, no one had any suspicions of her.

"Have you ever worked in collusion with another government or group entity against the Republic of Columbia?"

"No." Unless she included working for herself. Though she wasn't working against the Republic. Quite the opposite.

"Have you ever been approached by someone to perform any act that violates the Republic's Declaration of Policy and Aims?"

"No."

"Have you discussed the details of this case with any other agent except for Director Thias Alexander?"

"No," she said, though her pulse spiked with the question. But Kane was not an agent, she reasoned with herself.

"Okay," Gellar said. Tala's head turned ever-so-slightly as he adjusted his glasses on his face. "Now we will simply provide you with a list of words or phrases that may or may not relate to this case. Simply look at the camera ahead of you. Do not speak and refrain as best as possible from moving during this part of the evaluation. Let's begin."

"Case file 10RCJ236MRP. Level nine security clearance. Stoughbour." He spoke slowly, giving a small pause between each phrase. "Illegal access. Assassination."

"Put 'em up, put 'em up. Which one of you first? I'll fight you both together if you want."

"Brit Alexander. Unified Rebels. Double-agent. Forgery. Captain Kole. Arson. Republic of Columbia. Accident. Thias Alexander."

Despite herself, Tala felt her jaw clench.

"Loyalty. Security risk. Agent Ashby. Terrorist. Treason. Columbia City. Maverick Sanders. Walhurst. President Royer II. Militia Forces. DeSoto.

Brother. Parents. Murder. Mila Sanders. Confidential information. Jameson Alexander. Walhurst. Agent."

Gellar went quiet, and Tala fought to keep her body still. It ached in her arms and legs as she restrained herself. She willed her eyes to stay forward, focusing hard on the camera, feeling tears gather in the corners.

"Agent, you may relax," Mayes said as he approached her. He pushed away the infrared camera, and Tala felt herself take a breath. She looked at Gellar, who continued to manipulate the computer and graphs in front of his face. Then suddenly they disappeared, and he rose to his feet, abruptly leaving the room, a tablet in his hand.

Tala was quiet as Mayes removed the equipment from her body. She sighed with relief when the straps around her chest and torso were finally released. Once he slid the headband off her head, she let her eyes meet his.

"When will I find out the results?" she asked.

"They'll be immediate. Someone will be in shortly," he said, then turned away. "Please wait here," he said with a glance over his shoulder, then he, too, left the room.

Alone, Tala hugged her arms to her body. It was over. What was done was done, and despite her lack of confidence in herself, she was sure of one thing. She had protected Kane. She was confident that none of her responses jeopardized him.

Tala tried to shake her anxiety away as she stood up from the chair. Slowly, she walked the perimeter of the room. She paused to stare at her reflection in the two-way mirror and gently pressed her fingertips to the glass, leaving small prints behind when she pulled her hand away.

The door of the security room opened, and Tala turned quickly to see Thias, a tablet in his hands. She was unable to read the expression on his face, and she felt a flutter inside.

He stared at her, his blue eyes steady on her, and she shifted her body. Squaring herself to him, she took a deep breath, bracing herself for the impact. She expected an agent to enter at any moment to arrest her.

"It appears you harbor some animosity where I'm concerned," he said, faintly amused. He seemed to fill the doorway as he stood in it, unmoving.

"Can you blame me?" she asked, not looking away. She would not back down, no matter the results. "Were you watching?" she asked, glancing behind her at the two-way mirror.

"Of course," he said. "I know you think I betrayed you, and you're angry with me. But," he said with a shake of his head, "your heartache is with our mother. You can't fault me for trying to protect you." He raised a brow and fell quiet for a moment. She could feel his glare cutting through her. "As for your test, you passed."

Tala's relief crashed over her like a tidal wave. The release of tension brought tears to her eyes, and she quickly blinked them away.

"You're welcome," he said flatly. She saw a flicker in his eyes as he looked at her.

Tala felt a pit in her stomach as she wondered what he wasn't saying. There had to be something in those results because the truth was she had lied. She suddenly felt uneasy, not sure what he wanted from her. Did he want forgiveness? He never seemed the type to need such grace from anyone in his life. Did he want gratitude? He'd certainly thrive on that, which would only elevate him, feeding his ego. She refused to give him either.

Lifting her chin, she made her way toward him. All she wanted now was to get out of that room. He lingered in the doorway for a moment, holding her gaze. She felt her pulse quicken, then he silently stepped aside, letting her brush past him. She took a breath of relief once she reached the end of the hall. Tears gathered in her eyes once more, but this time she was unable to blink them away. She turned and headed immediately for the restroom, passing by the rotunda without so much as a glance at anyone.

♦♦♦

"Are you going to tell me what that was all about?" Ronin exclaimed when Tala made it back to her desk, the buzz of the rotunda loud and alive.

"Just a case that's being investigated," she said, her heart rate still not back to normal. "It's no big deal." She pulled her duty belt from her desk and secured it around her waist again.

"I beg to differ. It's a very big deal for an agent to be brought in by Security Section," he insisted. "Did they administer a lie detection evaluation?"

She nodded. "And I passed. There's nothing to worry about," she said, but she still felt his eyes on her.

A loud, blaring alarm erupted from her palm pad, an alert from emergency dispatch flashing across her screen. When a call came into dispatch, if no MF agents were near the emergency location, an agent team was automatically assigned to the call. This time it was her and Ronin.

REPORTED SHOOTING. HUDSON HEIGHTS, OXWICK. AGENTS RESPOND.

Kole emerged hastily from his office. "Bishop, Kassis, you're backup!" he yelled across the rotunda.

Tala was on her feet in the blink of an eye, Ronin beside her. They sprinted across the rotunda toward the parking garage. Their agency car was parked closest to the doors, and they swiftly climbed in and took off, Tala catching a glimpse of Bishop and Kassis as they rushed past. They sped through the garage, their sirens on the car wailing loudly. The traffic and pedestrians outside quickly parted to let them through.

Their autonomous car sped through the streets of Stoughbour as they made their way toward the Oxwick bridge, triggering censors in traffic lights and surrounding vehicles to create a clear route for them. It maneuvered smoothly around corners, its blaring sirens warning pedestrians of its rapid approach.

Tala pulled out her palm pad. "Shooter, white male, dark hair, about six feet, dark shirt, dark jeans, red cap," she said, reading the details aloud. "Confirmed victims with multiple injuries, casualties unknown. Neck ink on the suspect. Seen fleeing the Hudson Heights district, Highland and Harvey streets in Oxwick." Her heart dropped. Max's pod was on Harvey, near Highland, in the Hudson Heights district.

"We need to go faster," she said breathlessly as they exited the bridge that spanned the East River. She knew their car was already going as quickly as it safely would, and for a fleeting second, she considered taking manual control of it. She was desperate for more details to come across her palm pad, anything about the victims, but nothing came.

Less than two minutes later, their car arrived on the scene, coming to a stop on Harvey, and they rushed from their car to the nearby victims. Two women, hysterical and crying, huddled together in a store doorway, one clutching her shoulder with an obvious gunshot wound.

Tala knelt beside her, prying her hand off the wound for a better look. "No exit wound, and the blood has already begun to clot," she said to Ronin, which meant an artery hadn't been hit. "You need to put pressure on it," she said, turning back to the victim.

"Which way did the suspect go?" Ronin asked just as Bishop and Kassis's car pulled up beside theirs.

"That way," the woman with the gunshot wound cried, pointing down Harvey with a shaky hand. "That way," she repeated.

Kassis rushed to the aid of the two women, calling for medical support on his palm pad, the emergency kit from his car in his hands. "I've got this. Go," he said as he dropped to his knees beside the woman.

Ronin, Tala, and Bishop drew their plasma guns and proceeded down the narrow street, which was heavily shaded from the tall buildings on both sides. Tala looked up, rows of fire escape balconies and ladders lined the exterior walls of the antiquated buildings that flanked them.

Tala repeated aloud the description of the perpetrator as the three of them eased their way cautiously down the street, their eyes swiftly scanning the extensive web above them.

She glanced ahead, spotting the white door to Max's pod, and swallowed hard. Tala caught sudden movement from the corner of her eye, a man high above on an escape balcony, his red cap standing out even from street level.

"Visual of a possible suspect," she said quietly. "Three stories up, to the left."

Bishop and Ronin looked up.

"Affirmative. I see him," Ronin whispered and gave a nod of his head.

A sudden gunshot rang out, and the three of them dove for cover in a nearby doorway. More shots, bullets ricocheting off the concrete ground and brick building. Crawling on her knees across the pavement, Tala inched out of the doorway, peering above her, and she caught a glimpse of the suspect as he ascended a ladder to the fourth story.

"Help me!" she yelled as she jumped to her feet, holstering her gun. She reached for the ladder hanging above her, just out of her reach. Ronin came up quickly from behind, hoisting her high enough to grab the bottom rung. Reaching for the next rung, then the third, she pulled her dangling body up, then quickly began climbing, Ronin catching the ladder below her. It was old and rusted and creaked under the weight of both of them.

Gunshots rang out for a second time. Tala faltered, the sharp corner of a rail slicing through the sleeve of her jacket, cutting her shoulder. Instinctively, she threw an arm over her head to shield herself while she clung to the ladder. She caught her breath, and with a reprieve in the gunshots, she continued her climb as quickly as her hands could grab each rung. She looked up, setting her sights on the suspect who was somewhere between the fifth and sixth stories. She watched as he reached for a rung above him. In an instant, it snapped, and he dropped to the fifth-floor balcony, making a clatter on the rickety, iron platform.

Tala climbed faster, her heart pounding with adrenaline, and she could hear Ronin somewhere behind her. The suspect got off two more shots, and when they ceased, Tala was confident he was out of bullets. Breathless, she forged ahead, climbing higher yet.

As she approached the fifth-story balcony, her fingers grabbing hold of the top rung, the suspect stomped hard, smashing them beneath his shoe, and she cried out. Gritting her teeth, she lurched herself forward, catching his pant leg, and with a firm tug, he fell onto his back, giving her enough time to swing her body over the top of the ladder and onto the platform, which shook unsteadily.

The suspect stumbled back to his feet and charged at Tala, pushing her backward into the railing, knocking the wind out of her. She swung her arm hard, her fist striking his face, and he faltered. With a second blow, he dropped to his knees, and Tala kicked the gun from his grasp. Reaching for his wrist, she wrenched his arm behind him.

"It's over," she spat in his ear as Ronin appeared at her side, handing her a restraint cuff. She slipped it over his hands, tightening it around his wrists, then pulled him to his feet as Ronin reached for the gun in the corner.

"We've got a crowd," he said, nodding over the balcony, and Tala saw the dozens that had gathered below.

"Come on," she said as she pushed their suspect toward Ronin, Bishop finally making it to the top.

"Nice of you to join us," Tala said.

"Oh, suck it," he snarled, his forehead puckered.

"Let's go," Ronin said as he pushed the suspect toward the ladder. "He'll follow you down," he said with a nod to Bishop.

Ronin carefully guided the suspect, his hands bound in front of him, down the fire escape ladders to street level, Tala following behind them, her fingers throbbing with the grab of every rung.

Dropping from the last ladder, her feet hitting the concrete, she glanced up, and her eyes flared as she saw Kane standing in the crowd, a smirk on the corner of his mouth. She felt her heart jump as their eyes met for a brief second. Then she quickly turned away, hiding the grin on her face, and saw that Ronin was watching her. His eyes shifted as he glanced toward the crowd. When he looked back at her, his eyes narrowed. She knew he'd seen Kane, and she knew he recognized him. Ronin never forgot a face.

Ronin gave the suspect a hard push toward Bishop. "Get him out of here," he said, then turned to Tala. "I saw that," he said bluntly once Bishop was out of earshot.

"Saw what?" she asked, not meeting his eyes as she assessed the gash on her shoulder, her torn sleeve stained with blood. She clutched it with her opposite hand, wincing as she applied pressure.

"Oh, come on, Tala. I'm not stupid. You know exactly what I'm talking about," he countered. "That guy down there, it's the same guy I saw outside your pod the other day."

"I don't know who you're talking about," she said, glancing down the street, relieved Kane was no longer there. "It's a city of twelve million people. I highly doubt it's the same guy," she asserted.

Ronin studied her, sizing her up. "Tala, you can talk to me," he said gently with pleading eyes.

"There's nothing to talk about," she affirmed, meeting his gaze. She raised her chin and stood taller. "I don't know who you're talking about."

She told herself that she lied because he would never understand the truth. But in her heart, she knew that every lie was a conscious decision she made, every one chipping away at the foundation of their friendship. She was free to choose to lie, but she wasn't free to choose the consequences of each one she told, and in that moment, she feared that the price of her lies would be the cost of their friendship. Her heart sank, and she took a deep breath, then turned her back to him and made her way to their car.

ELEVEN

Tala stood in front of her full-length mirror and stared back at herself. Another dress. Another pair of heels. She sighed as she ran her fingers through her hair, her long, blond locks falling down her back and over her shoulders.

She was startled by the soft tap on her balcony door, and she smiled as Kane's silhouette appeared behind the glass. She opened the door, and he gave her a brief scan up and down. A smile curled on the corner of his mouth, and she felt a flutter inside her. There was something about the way he looked at her that made her feel empowered, that made her feel like more than just a girl in a dress.

"Wow," he said. "You, you look…really nice." His eyes met hers, and she felt another flurry in her belly, goosebumps raising across her arms and down her back. "Vaughn? Or Thias? Or both?" he asked as he took a seat on the edge of her bed.

"Vaughn," she said quietly. She saw a flicker in his eyes, and her stomach sank.

"It's like being on a mission," he said after a moment as he glanced down to his hands in his lap.

Tala nodded. Vaughn had come to Command not long after she'd gotten back from her call that afternoon, and when he asked her to his pod for dinner, she was quick to suggest a restaurant instead. She would have more control in a public setting. He'd seemed disappointed at first, but then quickly perked up, his charming side returning.

"I got word today on the firearms," she said. "My captain said the report came back that they were from DeSoto."

"Not all of them," he said, finally looking up.

"Maybe it was just the one I took that was the Republic's," she suggested, more hopefully than realistically. Even as it came out of her mouth, she could hear how ridiculous she sounded.

"But it wasn't," he said, flatly. "And you know it."

"I also don't believe they were able to recover the serial numbers from all of them. I saw them. There was nothing left of most of them. But Kole didn't have many details," she said, then paused. "Ronin suggested the UR could have some connection with DeSoto. That they could be working together."

He shook his head. "I don't think so. Both the UR and DeSoto are being setup for something. I just don't know what," he said confidently. "The UR and DeSoto don't work together. They never have, Tala."

"Don't forget the bombing at the port. That was the Rebels, if that has anything to do with all of this," she added. "Maybe you're right about the UR and DeSoto in the past, but do you think there's any chance they could be working together now?" she asked.

The expression on his face still told her no. Kane was quiet while her mind raced through the possibilities: the Republic and DeSoto, DeSoto and the UR, the Republic and the UR. All of it seemed unlikely and equally baffling, and she sighed with frustration.

"Maybe I can probe Vaughn for information," she said hopefully. After all, that was why she had agreed to dinner, to keep up the pretense of a relationship.

"I don't know much about DeSoto, and I highly doubt the Rebels are involved in this thing with the guns, but I'll ask around," he said, averting his gaze.

Tala cocked her head curiously just as there was a knock on her bedroom door.

Kane jerked quickly to his feet, his eyes wide, and swiftly moved across the room to the wall beside the door, his fists balled tightly.

She saw the alarm on his face and quietly held up her hand as she made her way to the door, opening it just enough to see Mila standing on the other side.

"Oh, look at you!" she exclaimed, giving the door a nudge to open it wider. "Just seeing if you're ready. Do you need anything?" she asked, her eyes glinting with happiness.

Tala smiled. "Well, I don't need a coat anymore," she said with a laugh. "I'm good if you think so." She turned her body just slightly to give Mila a full view of the dress. Unlike so many of the others, this one was long-sleeved, covering her bandaged shoulder.

"I know so," she said with an approving nod.

Tala's palm pad vibrated from her bed, and she glanced over her shoulder at it, knowing it meant Vaughn was there. She sighed, her shoulders slumping.

"You okay?" Mila asked with scrutiny.

"Yeah," she said with a half-smile. "I'm good. I'll be right out."

When Mila left, Tala eased her door closed and looked at Kane, a hint of panic still in his eyes.

"It's okay," she whispered. She didn't want to leave him. She wanted to kiss him. She wanted to press herself into him. She wanted to feel his arms around her. Her eyes lingered on him as he made his way to her balcony door.

"Have fun tonight," he whispered, his small smile not quite meeting his eyes.

Tala pressed her lips together as she nodded. He opened the door, slipped out, and as fast as he had come, he was gone.

Standing in the entrance at Madison Park Bistro, Vaughn slipped Tala's coat off and handed it to the coat check. She finally broke down and bought one for herself when she and Mila had gone shopping. She was unsure why she'd put it off for so long. It had taken Mila ten-times longer to decide on it than it had taken Tala to nod in approval.

He placed his hand gently on the small of her back as they made their way through the crowded restaurant, turning heads with every table they passed. They were seated in a corner, beneath a large mural of a tempestuous sea, their banquette table dressed in white linen with crystal glasses and small lights in the center designed to look like soft, flickering candles. They looked so real one would hardly believe otherwise.

Tala looked out at the bustling restaurant, recognizing many faces she was familiar with, even if she didn't know them personally. Archer Wight, dean for Oliphant University, Columbia City's most prestigious private school. The Associate City Representative Kavan Parker and his comely wife, Adira, who was notorious around the city, known for her expensive, often unrealistic, taste in everything from clothing and jewelry to artwork, food and wine. She was known to throw the most lavish parties. And then there was Beck Rivera, the Republic's Medical and Health Services director, whom she recognized from many of Thias's dinner parties, seated beside his wife, Farah, whom Tala had always liked.

She swallowed unsteadily as she took in the room. This was a see-and-be-seen crowd. Vaughn's intentions were becoming clearer and clearer.

"This is lovely," she said, feeling the sudden tension in her shoulders. Word would spread quickly that she and Vaughn had been spotted together, something she wasn't entirely ready for. She tried to stay out of the Republic's spotlight for a reason.

"I'm glad you like it. It's one of my favorites," he said and gave her his ever-charming smile.

Sitting across from her, he reached for her hand, cupping it in his, his thumb brushing across the bracelet on her wrist, the bangle he'd given her. He seemed pleased. "Tell me about your day," he said with a raised brow, his soft, chestnut brown eyes on her.

She lifted her shoulder, shrugging, feeling a dull ache from her injury. "Just another day," she said.

"Heard there was a shooting in Oxwick," he said as he ran his free hand through his thick, dark hair. "The Christian-Moore merlot. The bottle," he said when their server, a short, thin man in a deep navy tuxedo appeared beside them. He gave a nod of his head. "Of course, Chancellor. May I get an appetizer for you to begin with?"

Vaughn released Tala's hand and adjusted his tie. "We'll start with the salmon rillette and the Asian tuna tartare," he said, glancing up.

Their server gave another nod, then swiftly left. Vaughn turned back to Tala, his eyes poring over her, a smile curling on the corner of his mouth. Tala felt her pulse quicken.

"Ordering for me again," she said with a coy smile.

He gave a low chuckle. "I told you, I'm very particular about food. And I'm confident you'll like this."

"Okay," she said as she inclined her head. From the corner of her eye, she saw the furtive glances from people at nearby tables.

"Now, where were we?" he asked. "Oxwick."

She nodded. "Yes, Oxwick. There's not much to tell. Two women were robbed by a man as they left a pharmacy. But we apprehended him without incident."

He was quiet for a moment, studying her, and Tala shifted in her chair. "Rumor has it that it was you who apprehended him," he said.

"My, word travels quickly to you. I was just doing my job."

"And you do it superbly," he said.

Their server reappeared, setting two wine glasses on the table, then poured a small amount in Vaughn's. Bringing it to his nose, Vaughn inhaled deeply, then after giving it a small swirl, he took a drink.

"Oh, yes," he said with delight.

Their server gave a small smile, almost in relief, and he poured more into Vaughn's glass, then Tala's. "Would you like more time to look at the menu?" he asked.

"Yes," Vaughn said flatly.

Their server gave a small bow before hurrying away. People often did the same with Thias. And her, when she was recognized.

"Here," Vaughn said, handing a menu to her. "I recommend the langoustine with the hiramasa or the lobster."

She smiled at him as she opened her menu. "I appreciate the suggestion."

He sat back in his seat, his eyes intently on her, and he grinned, showing off the dimple in his cheek. "I have to ask," he said as he folded his hands on the table, not bothering to so much as glance at the menu. "Do you ever see yourself stepping down from your MF position? To have a family? You're great at what you do, and your reputation certainly precedes you, but surely, it's not something you will pursue long-term. Not once you're married."

Tala eyed him carefully, suppressing her irritation. Now he sounded like Thias. "I like what I do. I've worked hard to get where I am," she said. She wasn't an agent to simply bide her time until a husband came along. "I guess I would have to see how my future unfolds. I can't say either way at this time." She felt the most non-comital approach would be the best for the situation. But the truth was that she'd never step down from MF unless it was what she wanted.

He nodded. "I respect that."

"Can I ask," she said, carefully considering her words, "how are things with DeSoto?"

He sighed, his shoulders dropping, a tension line forming across his forehead. "I certainly have my work cut out for me with all of that. Mazanada is still threatening to pull out from our trade agreements. To them, it looks like we can't keep the Rebels in check. It's making us look weak," he said, his jaw clenching. "And now with this gun crisis…" he added, letting his sentence trail, a vacant look in his eyes.

"What about the guns?" she prodded gently.

"You didn't hear?" he asked, seeming to snap back to reality.

"That they're from DeSoto?"

He nodded. "We suspect they're working with the Unified Rebels. Smuggling the guns to the Colonies through the Republic. We speculate the Rebels have strongholds there. Even if their governors vehemently deny any knowledge of them."

Tala cocked her head in confusion. Although their entire southern border spanned DeSoto, they extended farther west than the Republic, past the Mississippi River, where the Republic ended. DeSoto also bordered the Central Colonies and Pacifica. Surely, she thought, it would be easier to go straight from DeSoto into the Colonies and bypass the Republic altogether. There was too much risk going through the Republic.

"I'll tell you this," he said, his eyes narrowing, a flash of fury in them as his pupils flared and he leaned in closer to her. "President Royer is clear. If DeSoto ever posed a serious risk to the Republic, we would hit them hard, the full weight of our strength bearing down on them."

Vaughn's menacing look as he spoke was unmistakable, she'd seen it in Thias before. Tala's thoughts began to spin.

"Are you saying you think they're planning something?" she asked, keeping her voice low.

He was silent as he pensively studied her. She felt herself grow uneasy with his gaze fixed on her.

The silence between them lingered for another moment, then his face softened and his shoulders relaxed, and Tala let out a slow exhale.

"I've probably said too much already," he said dismissively with a wave of his hand. "Even if you are MF. And an Alexander," he added. "I think our evening deserves a lighter conversation." He lifted his glass toward her. "To you, the most beautiful woman in the Republic." His brow arched, and he gave her his usual suave and charming smile.

Suppressing her urge to roll her eyes, she gave him a flirtatious smile in return, lifted her glass and let it gently clink the side of his, then took a drink.

Stepping out of the restaurant, Tala felt the cold drizzling rain on her face, the smell of the wet concrete in the air. She quickly ducked into the backseat of Vaughn's J.D. Bradley, Vaughn sliding in after her.

As the car pulled into traffic, he slipped his arm behind her, pulling her closely, and although she felt her body stiffen, she let herself lean into him.

Without preamble, he pressed his lips to her neck, sending a chill down her spine. She turned her face to him, her mouth finding his. He tasted like wine and red meat, and he slipped his arms around her, sliding his hands into her hair.

When she pulled back, she saw an eagerness flash in his eyes, and she swallowed hard, her mouth going dry.

The corner of his mouth pulled into a smirk, then he leaned in and pressed his lips against her neck again. He made his way up to her earlobe, then to her lips, and she closed her eyes, sliding her hand down his arm, cold and damp from the rain.

"Come to my pod," he said breathlessly between kisses.

Tala felt her stomach drop, her heart pounding hard and fast. She ran her fingers along his smooth jaw, her thumb lingering on the dimple in his cheek. "It's been a long day," she whispered in a hushed breath. "But I've had a lovely evening," she said as she pressed her lips lightly against his.

He sighed, pulling his fingers through her long hair, letting them skim down her back. "That's fine," he said crossly after a minute. "I have things I should work on anyway." He pulled back from her, and she welcomed the space between them.

The car pulled up to her building, Vaughn not masking the disappointment on his face, and he leaned in for another kiss.

"We'll talk soon," he said while she opened the door.

She pursed her lips and smiled. The cold rain was falling steadily now, and after she slipped from the car, she hurried to her doors, glancing over her shoulder once she reached cover. She watched in relief as his car drove away.

Eleven years earlier

Kane rested on a padded, inclined table, his ankles and wrists secured tightly to it by thick metal cuffs, and a small pillow rested under his head. An IV ran into one arm, and there were nodules on his chest, legs, and temples that connected to wires which fed into a panel with a digital screen. He watched the jagged line bounce up and down from his heartbeat. But he paid no attention to the other numbers, neither knowing nor caring what any of them meant. He looked away, his eyes gazing up at the bright, white lights overhead, and he sighed as he drummed his fingers on the table.

He was no longer afraid.

There was no point in it. They were going to do to him what they wanted, regardless of how he felt. Being afraid gave them power over him, and he refused to give that to them. His response was the only thing he had any control over, and he was determined not to forfeit that.

The door opened and there was the sound of shuffling feet on the floor, but he didn't break his gaze at the ceiling.

"How're we doing today?" He recognized Dr. Murphy's voice as he approached him, but Kane was silent, tuning him out, intent on focusing his eyes up above him. Dr. Murphy gave a low laugh. "You're the stoic one in the group," he said. "I like that about you."

Kane said nothing, still drumming his fingers.

"Right then," Dr. Murphy said. "Today will be a difficult one," he said to Kane as he checked the IV line.

This was enough to catch his attention, and Kane redirected his gaze toward the doctor. In the background, he saw the nurse readying a tray of vials. So many vials.

"You going to kill me or what?" Kane asked coolly.

"Actually, yes," Dr. Murphy conceded.

Kane's eyes flared, and his chest tightened. He had been waiting for this day. But he suddenly wasn't sure he was ready for it.

"This is what we've been building up to all these years," Dr. Murphy said. "And it's very exciting that we've reached this point. If we're successful, the Republic will never have to fear another an enemy. Ever. We're making history."

"So, the others, the ones who haven't been back to the living quarters," Kane said, the reality dawning on him, "did it work on them?"

"Actually, yes. They all pulled through. And they're being monitored elsewhere, separate from the rest of you who have yet to go through the procedure," he said.

"What's up with the metal cuffs?" Kane asked as his body stiffened, resisting the restraints.

"Ah, titanium steel alloy. They're going to help us keep control of your body."

"Seems a bit extreme," Kane scoffed.

"Not in the slightest, actually," Dr. Murphy said with a haughty laugh. "You're about to become one of the Republic's greatest weapons."

"You really think that if this works, whatever it is, that after all of this, I would be someone who would defend the Republic?" he spat.

"That's the point of all of this, Kane."

"The Republic can kiss my ass," he said as he directed his gaze back to the ceiling.

Dr. Murphy laughed again. "It's that very obstinance that is going to make you exceptional when we're done with you."

"Let's just get this over with," he said as he steadied his breathing. Their machines and all their sensors would pick up his increasing nerves, and he reminded himself that he wasn't going to give them that satisfaction.

From the corner of his eye, Kane watched as the nurse brought the tray to Dr. Murphy, each vial lined neatly in a row, a syringe for each one, and he swallowed hard.

"Okay," Dr. Murphy said. "We'll take these one at a time. And unfortunately, I can't give you anything for the pain. There's too high of a risk of possible drug interactions," he said flatly, with no emotion, as he reached for the first syringe and vial. Carefully he pulled the chalky yellow liquid into the chamber, then stuck the needle into the IV and pushed the plunger down.

The unknown liquid was cold, icy as it spread through Kane's arm, into his shoulder and chest, then filled the rest of his body with a biting chill that made him shudder. His surroundings began to grow fuzzy as dizziness washed over him and he swallowed hard, a bitter, metallic taste in his mouth.

As Dr. Murphy injected a second solution, this one clear and tinted light blue, a warm sensation quickly drove away the icy cold in his veins. It started as only a warm tingle, but quickly intensified, and he felt his pulse quicken. He balled his fists and took deep breaths as his body grew hotter and hotter.

With the injection of a third liquid, Kane felt his chest constrict, a painful heaviness settling on him. Focusing on his breathing, he slowly inhaled long, deep breaths. But in only seconds, the pressure began to build, and he felt his racing pulse pounding in his head. Each breath became more labored as the pressure in his chest intensified, and from the corner of his eye, he watched a fourth injection go in.

The room began spinning, a sudden and overwhelming urge to vomit coming over him, and he swallowed back the bile rising in his mouth.

Agonizing pain surged through him, and Kane gnashed his teeth, his hands clenched into tight fists, and he struggled for air. The pressure in his chest was unbearable, the searing pain suffocating him as he struggled for breath.

From somewhere in the distance, he heard a faint yelling, a low, guttural growl that quickly turned into a piercing shriek and he realized then it was coming from himself. Tears gathering in his eyes spilled over, running down the sides of his face and filling his ears. He opened his mouth, gasping for air. Torturous pain gripped his lungs, tightening its grasp, slowly strangling him, and his body began convulsing, held down by the cuffs that restrained him.

He fought the restraints as he attempted to claw at his chest, if only to tear apart his flesh to release the pressure, the heavy, debilitating pressure that only seemed to penetrate deeper and deeper with every passing second.

The lights in the ceiling began to dim, the world growing darker and darker. The stabbing pain was excruciating as it tore through his body, and he closed his eyes, the unbearable agony pulling him deeper into the burning threshes of hell, and he longed to meet death, if only as a welcome friend.

◆◆◆

Kane woke to the steady, rhythmic sound of a heartbeat. He winced as he opened his eyes, the bright lights instantly burning them.

"The light sensitivity will pass," a woman said, her voice gentle.

He struggled to bring her into focus. With the lights above, she looked ethereal, and as the fog began to dissipate, he realized it was Dr. A. She wore her white lab coat, her blond hair flipped out at the bottom, and she smiled kindly down at him.

"You gave us all a little scare," she said softly as she pulled at his eyelids. "Pupil dilation looks good," she called over her shoulder.

"Can you tell me what you hear?" she asked him, coming more and more into focus.

"Umm," he mumbled, his throat dry and scratchy. He heard a light, rhythmic thumping and struggled to pinpoint what it was; it was both strange and familiar. As she leaned closer to him, he realized it was her heartbeat that he was hearing. He looked up at her in startled confusion. She was coming more and more into focus with each passing second, and he was seeing her with clarity that he never had before, the flakes of her dry skin on her forehead, the soft, white down above her top, chapped lip.

"Can you feel this?" she asked as she ran something along the bottoms of his feet.

He nodded as he looked around the room, noticing then a woman near the door in the back, a tablet in her hand. Her eyes were wide and her face blanched. He realized he could make out her heartbeat as well. Dr. A's was steady while the other woman's was quick and erratic.

"Doc, what's going on?" he asked, hearing the panic in his voice.

"Your senses," she said casually, "they're heightened. Am I right?"

He nodded as he picked up the subtle scent of vanilla on her skin, mixed with a hint of almond in her hair. He'd never noticed that before.

"I'm going to prop your head up a bit," she said. "I want you to tell me if you can read the letters on the wall."

Kane blinked as he gazed across the room at the chart on the wall opposite him. He read the letters out loud, rattling them off quickly. Dr. Alexander let out a small laugh.

"What's so funny?" he asked, his head snapping in her direction.

"I'm just amazed," she said jovially. "I have twenty-twenty vision and I can only manage the first two rows. But you, you can see all five with ease."

"Why? How?" he stammered.

"It's all part of the new and improved you."

His grogginess had completely dissipated, the room and everything around him in full focus. He felt aware of everything: the slight layer of fine dust on the tabletop near him, residual fingerprints on the surface of the equipment around him, the small spots of vomit and blood on his shirt, a thin strand of brown hair left behind on the ruffled blanket at his side.

"You're looking more alert," Dr. Alexander said, and he nodded. "Let's try to stand."

With the restraints no longer holding him down, Kane slid off the table with ease.

"Think you could do a light jog?" she asked as she motioned toward a treadmill along the far wall to his right.

"Sure," he said with hesitation.

Kane stepped onto the deck of the treadmill, and she turned it on, its hum loud in his ears, and he winced at the sudden sound. He started out in a slow jog, then watched as Dr. Alexander began to increase the speed.

"Tell me if it gets to be too much," she said.

He watched the numbers on the panel in front of him, climbing higher with each step, yet his feet had no trouble keeping up. His heart rate and breath stayed steady and nearly unchanged even as his pace continued to quicken.

"What's going on?" he gasped when the treadmill hit thirty miles per hour. He continued to run with the machine, feeling only minor fatigue.

"You'll get used to all of it soon. Your body will adjust to the overdrive your senses are in," she said. "In a day or two, we'll test your speed out in the yard. Some of the others are up to fifty miles-per-hour or so. You'll continue to improve over the next week. You can get off the treadmill," she said. "Reached top speed in two minutes," she said over her shoulder to the other woman.

Kane's mind struggled to process what was happening. He followed Dr. Alexander back to the medical table, and she motioned for him to sit.

Now," she said as she grabbed a scalpel from the counter. "I hate to have to do this, but there really is no other way." She approached him quickly, then grabbing his arm, she sliced the blade across his skin, cutting him deeply, blood running down his arm in an instant.

"What the hell?" he yelled as he pulled his arm away. Clutching it to his chest, feeling the warm blood soaking through his shirt. His arm began to tingle in a way it never had before. A sensation of pins and needles spread through it and into his shoulder, growing warm, the stinging pain rapidly dulling. Dr. Alexander stood quietly beside him, watching him carefully, an amused smile on her face.

"Here," she said after a minute, handing him a damp towel. "Please wipe the blood off."

Kane furrowed his brow and apprehensively took the towel. Wiping the blood from his arm, his jaw fell. He stared gapingly at the cut that was now only a faint pink line, like he had been scratched by a dull tree branch rather than cut by a sharp blade.

"Roughly a minute and a half," she called over her shoulder, and like all the other times, the woman quickly tapped the screen of the tablet. "You'll need your rest after this. Between healing itself and your physical exertions just now, your body will need to recover."

"What the hell's going on?" he demanded, his voice loud and booming as it echoed through the room. The woman in the corner gave a small jump, her heart rate spiking. He could make out the beads of perspiration forming along her hairline.

"Kane, calm down," Dr. Alexander said softly, her voice soothing. "It's all a part of the improved you. All of you will make this transition."

"Transition?" he asked with confusion.

"Your heightened senses. Your speed and dexterity. Your physical strength. Your healing capabilities. You and the others are going to change the Republic. With skills like these, you will be our country's first line of defense," she said.

"Super-soldiers," he said, the reality dawning on him, and his heart dropped.

"You'll make us the most powerful nation the world has ever seen. No one would ever stand a chance against us. You'll make us unstoppable. This kind of power ensures prevailing peace," she said.

Kane fell silent. His eyes lingered on her, then he dropped his gaze to his unsteady hands. He felt it inside of him just then. It started out small, taking root deep inside, and began to grow. At first, he was unsure of what it was. But it continued to spread through him, surging through his veins and filling every crevice of his body. He closed his eyes, his shoulders dropping, and in that moment, he realized what it was.

Fear.

❖

Tala sat at her desk, her mind everywhere other than on her work. Her shoulders slouched over as she looked down at her computer through glazed eyes. Her thoughts were running wild. DeSoto, she knew, was not moving guns to the Central Colonies. She wasn't sure of much, but of this she was.

Not only was it too risky to go through the Republic, but going north to Columbia City was over eight hundred miles out of the way. They weren't coming from the south just to go west. So why say they were? And how, if at all, did the UR fit into the equation? Kane seemed to think there was no connection, but Tala couldn't completely rule out the possibility. She was wracked with confusion and frustration, both giving her a headache.

Her palm pad buzzed in her pocket, bringing her thoughts back. She looked at it to see a message from Mila.

Made reservations for us at The Stone Table for dinner. Girl time. See you at seven.

Tala quickly replied to her, looking forward to the reprieve from the chaotic charade her life seemed to have become.

"Tala," Ronin said as he approached her from behind, and she glanced up at him. "Can we talk?" he asked, his eyes fixed soberly on her. He looked tired, like he hadn't slept.

"Sure," she said uneasily as she stood from her desk.

Without a word, Ronin turned and headed for the interrogation rooms. He took the first vacant one and closed the door behind her, sealing them off from the rest of Command.

He was slow to meet her gaze, his eyelids drooping as he rubbed his temples. He paced the room, circling the table and chairs in the middle before finally looking up at her.

"The other day," he said, his eyes meeting hers, "I found you leaving the Records Department. And you told me you had pulled old cases to compare to that string of burglaries we just wrapped up," he said matter-of-factly.

She nodded, her hands growing warm and clammy, and she felt heat go to her cheeks.

"I pulled those cases. And I know you didn't look at them," he said assertively, his eyes boring into her the way he did when he interviewed a suspect.

Tala's breath hitched as she screwed up her face. "Why would you say that?" She cringed on the inside. She should've really pulled them, at least to fortify her lie. She had been so focused on everything else that she was getting sloppy in her everyday work.

"The similarities in those cases and the recent ones are so alarmingly obvious. You're a good agent, and they wouldn't have gotten past you. That's how I know you didn't look at them. So, I want to know," he said, his voice rising, "why would you lie to me? And what were you doing in Records if you weren't working our active case?"

"Are you accusing me of something?" she asked sharply.

Ronin sighed as he crossed his arms. "You've been acting off for weeks now." He pointed his finger firmly at her. "I've heard rumors around Command that there was a breach on one of the servers, and then you mysteriously are called in by Security Section, and—"

"I told you I was cleared," she asserted, her body stiffening.

"Cleared from what? What is it that you needed to be cleared from in the first place?" he demanded.

Tala was silent and swallowed the bitter taste of anger rising in her. "It's classified."

He eyed her skeptically. "That's convenient."

Tala shifted on her feet. This, she thought, was what all her lies had brought her to. Anger and guilt seethed inside her, her gut twisting into knots.

Ronin pushed his hair out of his eyes. "How about how you've been unable to let things go after our recent cases have been closed?" he argued. "You've been bordering on insubordination more than once recently. And what about that guy? First, I see him with you outside your pod, and then yesterday he was at our crime scene. And don't placate me and tell me it wasn't him or that it was some coincidence. I know it was the same guy. Don't insult my intelligence by telling me otherwise. What I don't understand is why you'd have to lie about him in the first place," he said with a frown, a deep crease across his forehead.

He was right about all of it. And still, she stood there, unable to say anything. This was her chance to make it right between them. After this, their relationship would forever be altered by all the lies. In that moment, her heart broke.

Ronin slammed his fist on the table. "We've been partners for years! We've been friends. And you're really just going to stand there with nothing to say? Or is your silence just so you don't have to lie to my face again?" he spat.

"Ronin," she said quietly, her mind was chaotic and full as she searched desperately for the right words to say to him. He was one of the most important people in her life, and now she was making strangers of them. Everything had changed since the first warehouse arrest. She was already putting Kane and Max at risk, she couldn't do it to Ronin too. Someday, she promised herself, she would make it right.

"What're you up to, Tala?" he asked, his voice commanding and filled with anger.

"You know me, Ronin," she said, finding her voice. "I would never do anything to put my country at risk or to those I love at risk. And that includes you," she said firmly, standing a little taller. That, for once, was the truth.

His eyes narrowed, his brow furrowed, then his arms dropped to his sides. "Wrong answer," he said. His glare lingered on her for another moment, then he turned on his heel and left the room, the door slamming behind him.

With a heavy heart, Tala gave a knock on the white door, then she waited. The sound of approaching footsteps startled her, and she turned to see a gaunt man walking down the narrow street, a cigarette dangling between his lips, smoke curling from the tip. He eyed her carefully and clicked his tongue.

She looked away and exhaled deeply, her breath shuddering. Tala knocked again, harder, and a moment later, she heard muffled sounds from inside. The door opened to Max as he stood in the doorway, barely filling it. His dark hair, shaggy on top, was combed back away from his forehead, and the blue printed t-shirt he wore was taut across his belly. Tala stood nearly eye-level with him, and she offered a feeble smile. In the background, she could still hear the sound of the stranger's footsteps as they slid lazily across the pavement.

"Why am I not surprised to see you back here?" he said. "And in your MF uniform, no less. Are you trying to draw attention here?" His eyes darted in both directions down the street, lingering briefly on the man. Max quickly moved aside and waved her in.

"Is he here?" she asked as she stepped inside the pod. Her eyes snapped to the kitchen where Kane stood beside the counter. It was like her senses could feel him, find him, even before her mind had a chance to act. She felt her shoulders fall in relief at the very sight of him.

"You need to be more careful when you come here," Max lectured as he closed and locked the front door. "You're awfully conspicuous when you show up here like that, your gun and all just out there in the open for anyone to see."

"I'm sorry," she said as she turned toward him.

"Sorry hasn't kept him safe for nine years. Sorry won't cut it if you attract MF attention to us," he said breathlessly as he nudged his glasses.

"Max," Kane said in a low voice.

"Unbelievable. You're just as reckless as she is," he said shrilly.

"You're right," Tala said.

Max looked between Tala and Kane, then he sighed in defeat. "She's all yours," he said with a nod toward Kane, then he made his way across the room and took a seat on one of the couches.

Kane approached her slowly. "You spared me a climb up all those balconies tonight," he said with a smirk, and she couldn't help but give him a small smile through pursed lips. Her eyes wandered over to Max, and she knew he was right. There would be nothing inconspicuous about her standing outside their door in full uniform. But she had to see Kane.

"Can we talk?" she asked, her voice unsteady as she looked back to Kane.

He nodded, then pointed toward the hatch in the floor. "Down there."

"Is it okay if I take this off?" she asked as she motioned to her duty belt and gun. Tala glanced at Max.

"I'm not touching that thing!" he exclaimed, throwing his hands up. "I wouldn't know the first thing to do with it. I'd most likely shoot myself."

Despite herself, Tala let out a small laugh. "There's a trigger lock, but I think leaving it alone is best."

"Yeah," he said with a nod, a chunk of hair falling around his face. "I think so too."

Tala unclipped the belt, double-checked the safety, then set it on the table. She followed Kane to the shelter below. As she descended the ladder, it dawned on her that pods with bomb shelters were registered with the government. This one, she knew, must not be and was suddenly curious how Max had found it. It certainly was the ideal way to hide someone.

Kane took a seat on his bed, resting his elbows on his thighs as he looked across the room at her. "You look like you had a stressful day," he said, and she sighed.

"It's Ronin," she said quietly as she propped herself against the wall. "All my lies are catching up to me."

"I knew he recognized me," he said, his shoulders slumping. "If it weren't for me, you'd have less to lie about," he said. Tala saw the regret on his face.

She shook her head. "No, I'd still have plenty to lie about. You're the good in all of it," she said as she met his gaze, silence settling over them for a moment. "He knows I'm covering something up."

"Think he'll be a problem?" he asked.

"He doesn't have anything on me legally speaking. Reporting me for acting strangely or seeing me with a guy certainly would be dismissed by my captain without further inquiry."

Kane was quiet for a moment. "You said yesterday that people suspected a connection between DeSoto and the Rebels," he said. His voice was deep with a small rasp.

She nodded. "Ronin suggested that. And then Vaughn voiced the same theory," she said. "But I'm still unconvinced."

"There's no validity to it," he said bluntly as he rubbed his thumb across his jaw.

"Why do you say that?"

He sighed and shrugged. "I asked around," he said, holding her gaze.

Tala studied him carefully. "Do you have any ink?" she blurted out, surprising even herself.

Kane's expression turned serious, and he went quiet.

"In the beginning," she said as she crossed her arms, "you were adamant that my attackers weren't Rebels. And I agreed with you. But then you were so sympathetic to the bombing and heist at the port, and now you tell me you've been asking around about a connection with DeSoto. Most people don't admit to knowing any of the Rebels, and the UR doesn't particularly advertise their members or agenda. Which stands to reason that you would have to know someone in their organization. Specifically, someone that's high enough up to be knowledgeable of any possible connection with the DeSoto government," she said, her gaze not wavering.

He remained quiet as he looked at her, tension in his shoulders and jaw.

Tala crossed the room and sat beside him on the bed. "Look, you don't have to tell me," she said as she put her hand on his arm. He turned, squaring his body to her. "Just… just don't lie to me," she said, hearing the emotion in her voice. "Please."

"I've never lied to you," he said quietly, his voice steady. "And I never would. That's not who we are." He reached out and tucked a lock of her hair behind her ear, his thumb brushing along her cheek.

His touch was like an electrical shock, and Tala felt her pulse quicken.

He exhaled loudly. "Tala, I was seventeen when I got out of that lab. And I had nobody. The Republic would've killed me if they found me. I couldn't go home. I slept on the streets and ate whatever food I could scrounge up or steal," he said, his voice quiet but firm, with no apology in it. "I made friends with some people, and in exchange for some favors, I had a place to sleep that wasn't behind a trash dumpster. And I had real food to eat."

"Exchange for what?" she asked, hoping she sounded more sympathetic than accusatory. Right then, she didn't want to be Tala the Militia Forces agent.

He sighed and dropped his head in his hands, and his shoulders slumped. "I don't want this to change how you look at me," he said quietly.

She reached for his hands, taking them in hers, and he lifted his head, his eyes meeting hers. She gave him an assuring nod. "It's okay."

"I passed along information and weapons. I helped move people a few times. Stole a truck once. But mostly I was just a lookout for MF while they conducted business," he said as he rose to his feet, his hands letting go of hers. "People don't usually mess with me. But I was never really a full-fledged member. I did what I had to do to get by until, by some miracle, I found Max. I still know people though," he said. "And I've done a few small things here and there over the years. But I keep Max in mind. He is risking enough having me living with him. But the UR have their rules. And I was no exception." He went quiet as he looked at her, and she swallowed a rising lump in her throat. Then with one hand, he tugged at the back of his collar, pulling his shirt off in one swift move, revealing black ink covering his chest, across his heart, nearly reaching his collarbone, and stretching down the side of his torso to his hip.

Tala's breath caught as she stood. She approached him slowly, and she felt his eyes on her, but she couldn't pull hers from the ink on his body. She reached out and brushed her fingers along his smooth skin, running across the lines of the ink, feeling the warmth of his body beneath her touch. She traced the black lines around his chest and down his side, then lifted her eyes to meet his.

They were dark, filled with both fear and exhilaration.

"A phoenix," she whispered.

He nodded silently.

"You died," she said, her heart pounding so loudly it drowned out all of her other thoughts, "yet here you are. Risen from your ashes."

Her words hung in the air between them, and Tala felt the world stand still. She felt vulnerable with his eyes on her, but it didn't scare her. Everything divided them, yet it felt like it was destiny that had brought them together. She slid her hand around his neck and pulled herself to him, his skin warm and soft. His arms slipped around her, pulling her closer. Leaning forward, he pressed his mouth to hers. Warmth spread through her as she kissed him back, letting herself melt into him.

The chaos in her mind stilled, and everything became clear to her. She knew that he was what she had been looking for all along. And that maybe she had already been his, even before she knew him.

When they finally pulled apart, she saw a thrill in his eyes, and she craved more of him. He could kiss her once for every star in the nighttime sky and it still wouldn't be enough. She smiled as she brushed her thumb along his jaw, his facial hair coarse beneath her touch. As he gazed down at her, a smile curled on the corner of his mouth. She knew she would never own her heart ever again.

Tala hated that she'd had to leave him. She wanted only to stay, to get lost in him, but Mila would be counting on her, and she couldn't risk damaging any more relationships in her life. She was desperate to hang on to as much of the good in her life as she could.

Just before reaching the subtrain platform, she powered on her palm pad, only to be met with an alert from Command.

Body recovered from the East River. Positive identification. Victim is MF Agent and Jerez Island Prison Warden Rhonda Mills.

Tala's heart sank as she reread the alert. Mills, who had tipped her off in the very beginning of everything, was dead?

TWELVE

Command was in a frenzy the following morning when Tala stepped through the front doors. It wasn't every day that one of their own was killed. Her thoughts circled round and round in her head, one particular memory standing out.

"Tala, you were good," Mills said with an approving nod, her dark hair pulled into a pony so tight it tugged at the corners of her eyes and along her temples.

"Top five," Tala said breathlessly in the humid afternoon air, the hot sun bearing down on her. She had a sharp cramp in her side, and her arms and legs quivered unsteadily from fatigue as she glanced over her shoulder at the obstacle course, the Warrior Course, she'd just completed. Adrenaline was still surging through her veins. She glanced down at herself, her standard cadet uniform, thick pants of twilled fabric and a cotton tee that was now wetter than it was dry, dirt staining its dull mossy color.

"You need to be better," Maverick said, more matter-of-fact than smug. He stood a full head taller than Tala, and even though it was late in the day, she could see his face was still smooth and clean-shaven. It wasn't that he was ever rude or condescending with Tala, but she couldn't help but feel he had unrealistic expectations of her, which only irritated her.

"What?" she gasped with a ragged breath. With her adrenaline beginning to wear off, her arms hung sluggishly at her sides, their dead weight growing heavy.

"He's right," Mills said, her arms crossing her body. "You're a woman in a man's world here. Nothing will ever be good enough unless you're first."

"And you're an Alexander," Maverick added. "You'll have to prove to everyone you deserve your spot," he said.

Her eyes narrowed as she scrutinized him. He was clean, dry, and put together, while she was uncomfortable in her dirty and wet uniform. She envied him. His sandy brown hair, she noticed, was recently trimmed, short on the sides and just long enough on the top to comb to the side. The standard-issue haircut for cadets. As his eyes met hers, she saw something she hadn't before, but she couldn't quite pinpoint what it was. Respect?

"Every morning," Mills said, "before the morning alarm, run the course."

Tala's heart fell. The barbed wire crawl, the Tyrolean traverse, the twenty-foot inverted wall she had to safely get her human-like dummy over, the tire drag, the Tower — an over 50-foot wall to repel down — the ape hanger… she felt anticipated pain and fatigue run through her body.

"I'll run it with you," Maverick said. "Every day."

"What?" Her eyes darted to him in surprise. He had the highest marksmanship scores, the fastest explosive disablement and Warrior Course times. He was the best in the academy and certainly didn't need the practice. Maverick Sanders was a name whispered throughout the ranks, with cadets and trainers alike.

He nodded as he shrugged his shoulder. "I'll be right there until you're better than me," he said, a smirk curling on the corner of his mouth. "Because I know you deserve to be here. And we'll show everyone else."

"I agree," Mills said with a serene face. "I completely agree."

Ronin, hunched over their desk, didn't so much as look up at her as she sat down across from him. She studied him, his small and subtle movements as he worked at his computer. His brown hair flopped over his forehead, his lean yet sinewy body, the tension in his face, his slow and steady breaths. It now seemed he was just as much a stranger to her as he was familiar.

As she watched him, she couldn't help but feel that maybe he was failing her as much as she was failing him. She had changed and she wouldn't deny that. The lies, the secrets, they made everything different. But at her core, she was still the same person. She was still loyal and committed to her people and those she loved. He was so quick to accuse her rather than understand her.

Each lie she told him, each doubt he had in her, killed a piece of their friendship, and Tala wasn't sure how much could die before there was nothing left to revive.

"Hey, princess," Bishop said as he approached. "Heard your old pal from the academy was a snitch."

"What?" she asked, her head snapping in his direction.

"You didn't hear?" he jeered. "When they pulled her from the river, shot, by the way, they found ink on her. Looks like she was doing double-duty." He laughed.

Tala's eyes narrowed.

"It's true," Ronin said, finally looking up from his computer. "I overheard Kole."

"Maybe you're with the Rebels too, and that's how you got through the academy," Bishop charged.

"You only wish that so you don't look so pathetic coming in behind me all the time," she said. She heard a small snicker come from Ronin, though he still didn't look at her.

"You think you're untouchable," Bishop snapped, holding up a finger. "But your day is coming, and I will best you."

"Are you threatening me?" she asked.

"I'm warning you," he said coolly, his hands in his pockets.

"Bishop," Captain Kole called from across the rotunda as he approached them. "Director Alexander is reassigning you and Kassis to the Quarry Square security detail team. They're still clearing the cordoned-off area around the park. You'll need to get your new assignment details from team leads Weston and Tippin. Review their security plans and get started on it immediately. The president's Annual Address is in five days and we're already behind. This is the top priority," he said. He turned to Tala. "Alexander, you're wanted in my office. The director is waiting for you."

Tala glanced up, but Kole's office blinds were closed, and she swallowed hard. "Yes, Captain," she said, standing. She let her shoulder catch Bishop as she passed, and he let out a loud disgruntled breath.

Tala's throat was tight as she steeled herself before stepping into the office. She hadn't seen or spoken to Thias since her lie detection evaluation. There was nothing he could say to her to make things right between them. She was steadfast in her anger. Taking a deep breath, she opened the door, Thias looking up as she shuffled into the office.

"I know I'm not your favorite person right now," he said, his eyes not unkind but not friendly either. "But I need to ask you some questions." He motioned to an empty chair beside Kole's desk.

Tala hesitantly took the seat and folded her arms across her chest. She was there under protest. But as her boss, there was nothing she could do to completely avoid him.

"I presume you've heard about Agent Mills," he said.

She nodded. "How could I not? I got the alert on my palm pad last night," she paused. "Is it true, you found ink on her?"

"It is," he said flatly as he took Kole's chair. He leaned forward, resting his hands on the desk, his fingers intertwined with each other.

"And she was shot? That's how she died? Who shot her?" she asked.

Thias nodded. "Those details are unclear. There is an open investigation. One," he said sternly as he lifted a finger, "you are not allowed to be a part of. I know the personal connection you had with Mills from the academy, and I don't need any interference from you. She was the prison warden, which means she could've compromised a lot of criminal cases and detainments if it's determined she was working against the Republic."

She cocked her head to the side. "So, if I'm not allowed to have any part in this, what am I doing in here?

"I wanted to ask you if you had any idea about Mills. Any suspicions? I know you had a reliable informant at the prison, and you would have inevitably had contact with Mills on several occasions."

"*Had* an informant? How'd you know my informant is dead? And how'd you know who he was in the first place? It's called a Confidential Informant for a reason," she said.

The corner of his mouth curled into a cold smile. "Oh, dear sister," he said in near mockery, "there is very little that goes on in this country, especially where security is concerned, that I don't know about."

Tala's anger was once again taking root, and she clenched a fist.

"Back to Mills," he said flatly.

"No," she said honestly. "I never had any indication she was working with the Unified Rebels or anyone else."

Thias was quiet as he studied her, a flicker of something in his eyes.

"If you don't believe me, you can do another lie detection evaluation. I don't know a thing," she said, biting back her attitude.

He gave a slow nod of his head. "I believe you," he said after a moment.

"Was there anything else?" she asked impatiently.

"Actually, yes," he said. "I wanted to know how you're taking the information about our parents. About the fire. I'm asking you here because I didn't think you'd accept an invitation to the house," he said.

"I'm not sure how I'm supposed to answer that," she said, caught off guard. She didn't want to talk to him about any of it.

He shrugged. "Truthfully. What you found in that file had to come as a shock to you."

She took note of his word choice… what she found. She had to tread lightly with every word she said. "It did," she said, holding his gaze. "How do you think I should be taking it?" she asked harshly. "It's a lot to wrap my head around." Which was true.

"I can see that," he said as he leaned back in the chair. "And how are things with Vaughn?"

"Is this a social call?" she snapped. "I have a job to do."

Thias laughed. "If you don't want to do this here, we can certainly set something up."

She sighed in defeat. She'd never get away from him. "Fine. What'd you have in mind? I know you have something. This was likely your plan all along. Irritate me until you got your way."

He chuckled. "Dinner," he said. "The four of us."

"At a restaurant," she added. "You choose."

"Anything else? We seem to always have dinner," he said with amusement.

Tala cringed. He was enjoying this too much, and all she wanted was to get away from him.

"Fine. The theater. Or the symphony." Anything to minimize interaction with him and Vaughn.

"I'll get a suite," he said with a nod. "I know how much you enjoy the symphony."

"May I go now?" she asked as she rose to her feet.

"I'll let you know our reservation."

Nine years earlier

"Did you memorize her description?" Avery asked as he held out a palm pad showing the image of a small woman, jet black hair and narrow, thin eyes. Avery's dark hooded sweatshirt was pulled over his head, covering most of his awful, blue-tinted hair, its long sleeves concealing the armful of ink Kane knew he had.

Kane nodded.

"She goes by Ivy. She'll give you the book and you'll slip it in your sack, just like any other student at the university. Here," he said, giving a palm pad to Kane. "This one's good for twenty-four hours and has a student ID on it for you. Remember your code phrase, 'It's too cold to read outside today.' She'll be coming from the subtrain from Baxtham at 4 o'clock. Keep your encounter brief but casual."

"Don't draw attention. I know," Kane said with an eye roll. "This isn't my first time."

Avery eyed him carefully. "No, it's not," he said. "But it's important this handoff is made."

He learned long ago not to ask questions when he ran jobs for the Rebels. He was given just enough information to get his missions done and no more. And he liked it that way. Nothing personal. "I'll make the drop with the package at the bookstore at five," Kane said flatly.

Avery nodded. "Your window is short. Willa will only be alone in the shop for fifteen minutes."

Kane grabbed the messenger bag and looped his arm and head through it, letting it hang to the side off his hip. "You'll hear from me when the job's done," he said as he rose from his seat at the table in the far back corner of the small, nearly empty pub. He gave one last glance at Avery, then left.

Stepping onto the busy street in the Old Town district in Walhurst, Kane could see his breath in the cold, icy air. He pulled his leather jacket tighter, the jacket Avery had gotten him just two days earlier, which Kane was certain had been stolen. Avery wasn't the kind of guy with access to leather. But then Kane wasn't either. Like with everything else, he didn't want any details on how he got it. The point was that he'd have a jacket for the winter months. That was all that mattered to him. He had barely survived last year, which had been a particularly brutal winter, even for the northeast.

He ambled down the street, blending in like any other Republic citizen, even though he had no citizenship at all. He knew he'd be arrested and detained the moment he was caught, then worse once he was identified. But he was confident he wouldn't be caught. He had an edge on every MF agent in the city. In the country, for that matter. All thanks to the Republic. And it was a thrill. Being arrested simply wasn't a concern for him. Not when he had more important matters to consider, like what his next meal would be or where he would sleep that night. Avery, of course, had no idea what Kane was capable of but liked using him because he got the job done. Kane had yet to fail any task. As long as he kept up the errands for Avery, he knew he'd at least have his couch to sleep on. It wasn't much, old, tattered, and sagging in the middle, often giving Kane a backache by morning. But, he reminded himself, it was better than the spot behind the dumpster on Grantham Avenue.

Kane spotted the clock tower from the Columbia Institute of Technology above the nearby treetops. He shoved his hands deep into his pockets, shielding them from the biting cold. While people and students hustled by in all directions, their faces tucked behind scarves or in their jackets, he took a seat on a bench with a good view of the subtrain exit. He shivered, then glanced at the time on the palm pad. He often got palm pads loaded with false information, just in case an issue was to arise with the authorities. But in the two years he'd been running for the UR, he'd never had to use even one. And he wasn't intending to start.

He shoved the palm pad back into his pocket, then pulled the collar of his jacket higher.

Damn it was cold.

A wave of people began emerging from the subtrain exit, and Kane stood, alert as he scanned the crowd. People spilled from the exit in droves, and Kane carefully scanned each one of them. Then finally, he spotted her. Small, looking exactly like she had in the photo, and in a heavy coat and mittens that practically swallowed her up. She looked far warmer than he was, and no one he'd ever suspect as a Rebel. She looked younger than him, with a round face and rosy cheeks.

He waited for her to cross the street, then jogged to catch up to her as she headed toward the university.

"It's too cold to read outside today," he said as he fell in stride beside her, keeping his eyes averted.

She stopped and turned toward him, studying him with a cocked eyebrow. "Phoenix, I presume."

"I'm looking for a good book," he said with a smirk as Ivy reached into her bag and pulled out an old, tattered book, its cover peeling on the edges. The *Iliad*. His gaze lingered on its title, which stirred curiosity in him. He reached for it and took it carefully in his hands, staring down at it.

"It's just a book," she said, eyeing him carefully. "You can handle this, right?"

Kane's eyes narrowed as he looked at her. "Of course I can," he scoffed. "But really, there's no such thing as *just* a book. Now, I think it's time to move on," he said with a jerk of his head, then slipped the book under the flap of his bag. Without another word, he turned on his heel and began heading down the busy street. He didn't get more than a few steps before abruptly halting, his heart nearly stopping in his chest while his brain struggled to catch up, processing what was before his eyes. It couldn't be.

But there he was. Not much taller than when he'd left him all those years ago, his face still hidden behind thick-framed glasses. His hair was longer, not buzzed short like it had been when they were kids. And he looked a little fuller in the mid-section, which was a pleasant surprise. He hurried down the sidewalk, his head down, his jacket zipped up to his chin, a large backpack strapped to his back.

Max.

Forgetting entirely about Ivy and the book in his bag, Kane took off at a brisk pace, weaving through the heavy crowd, following Max through the open mall in front of the university entrance. When he reached him, he paused, afraid to say his name. What did he know? What did he think?

Before Kane could decide anything, Max came to a stop, pulling his palm pad from his pocket, and when he turned and looked up, his mouth dropped.

"What?" Max said on a heavy exhale, his eyes growing wide.

Kane pressed his mouth in a firm line and gave him a nod. Before he could say anything, Max charged at him, the two of them colliding as he wrapped his arms around him, and they both laughed.

"I…I…" Max stumbled over his words when he finally stepped back and looked Kane up and down. "Man, what happened to you? Where've you been?"

"We can't talk here," Kane said, lowering his voice.

Max's brows knit together in confusion as his head turned, as if on a swivel, looking around. "Why not?"

"I can explain later," he said steadily. "Can you meet me at 5:30 on the other side of Walhurst?"

Max nodded eagerly. "Of course! Where?"

Kane gave a quick look around, then reached for Max's palm pad and quickly typed in an address. "Mention to no one that you've seen me," he said sternly as he handed it back to him.

Max's eyes were wide, his mouth gaped open. "But I don—"

"No one," he repeated firmly. "I'll see you soon."

Kane made the drop like planned and didn't linger in the bookstore like he usually did. For maybe the first time. His mind was a flurry of thoughts. What would Max say? Could he still be trusted after all these years? Could Kane tell him the truth? Would he scare him and send him running?

Kane's hands shook with nerves as he made his way down side streets until he finally made it to the pub where he often met Avery. No one there would give them a second glance. It tended to be a no-questions kind of place.

Once inside the dimly lit pub that smelled of stale cigarettes, liquor, and mold, Kane took a seat in the far back with a clear view of the entrance. Then he waited.

Right at 5:30, as if he'd been standing outside just to walk in exactly on time, Max walked through the front doors. He spotted Kane in the corner, and even from across the room, his joy was unmistakable. He eagerly made his way across the pub and took a seat across the small table from Kane.

"I… I just can't wrap my head around this," Max exclaimed.

Kane couldn't help but smile, something he felt he rarely did anymore. "I can't believe it's you," he said, folding his hands and resting them on the table. They simply stared in silence at each other, and Kane could hear Max's excitement simply by the sound of his racing heart.

Finally, Max leaned in closer, the light in his eyes dimming. "What kind of trouble are you in?" he asked quietly as his eyes darted furtively around the room.

"What makes you think I'm in trouble?" Kane asked with a low, throaty laugh.

"You mean, other than because you said at the university that it wasn't safe to talk? Or maybe it's because you were always in trouble. Since the day I met you," Max said with a knowing grin.

"Damn. It's such a long story," Kane said, wracking his brain trying to find the beginning.

"I have to ask," Max said, leaning in farther. "Did you leave on your own? Bedley?"

Kane threw his head back in a loud exhale. "That deadbeat of mine sold me off to be a lab rat. He didn't want me to be his problem anymore."

Max's face went sober. "I knew it," he said, cursing under his breath. "I knew you wouldn't just leave. Your dad's dead," he said flatly, his gaze not dropping from Kane's.

"Really?" he asked, feeling a flicker of pleasure.

He nodded. "Couple years ago now. The house burned down. MF found his scorched body with a bullet to the head. They said it was murder-arson, the case unsolved. Rumor has it you came back and finished him. It's not like no one knew what an asshole he was," Max said.

"I can tell you it wasn't me. But I'm not sorry to hear about it," he said. "What about Addox?"

Max shrugged. "Don't know. After your pops died, Addox just left. No one knows what happened to him. But it makes sense he wouldn't stay in the same town where he lost everyone else. Probably in some small town along the shores of one of the lakes. Fishing was his whole life. It was all he knew."

"He was always so sensitive. And a coward," Kane said as he looked away, the image of his brother coming to mind. So quiet and timid, the brown freckles on his light skin and brown hair that could never be cut in a straight line. He and Kane never looked much like brothers. And their personalities couldn't have been any different either.

Max shrugged his shoulders. "What'd they do to you?"

Kane was quiet as he met Max's gaze. He could see the guilt in his friend's eyes, like he really thought he could've done something for him.

"It was the government, wasn't it?" Max said in a hushed voice.

"The program has been shut down," Kane said matter-of-factly. He wasn't going to be made a victim.

"Program? Let me guess," he said without irony, giving his glasses a nudge as they slid down his nose, "you're not supposed to exist."

"Bingo."

"What'd they do to you?" Max's head dipped low.

Kane shook his head. "You wouldn't believe me if I told you."

"Try me."

"Not here," he said.

"You can trust me," Max said with a nod.

Kane listened to the steady beat of Max's heart, his breathing. He watched his pupils, even through the dim light, and he sighed. Same Max he remembered.

"I know," he said after a minute. "I'll show you. Just not here."

"So, what do you do? Where are you living?" Max asked.

Kane shrugged. "All over. I stay with people when I can. Otherwise, there's a dumpster I've gotten familiar with. But it's a bitch in the winter like this," he said with a laugh. "Don't," he said, seeing the look on Max's face. "Don't pity me. As far as I'm concerned, I'm one of the lucky ones. I got away. Not everyone could say that."

"So, you have nothing. That's what you're saying," Max said.

"It's not as bad as it sounds. I get to live on my terms, which is a first," he said.

"In the shadows," Max asserted. "Have you ever thought about going somewhere else? The Colonies? Or farther west to Pacifica or Tahari?"

"Not sure there's much more for me in any of those places than there is here. Except for maybe warmer winters. At least here I've got friends," he said with a shrug.

"Yeah, so many friends if you sleep behind a damn dumpster."

"Enough about me. What're you doing here, in the city? You're a long way from Bedley," Kane said with a smile.

"I got into a program. Full scholarship. An accelerated tech program at the university," he said.

"They got you for your brains, huh? Finally," Kane said with a chuckle.

"Promoted my citizenship too. Which means I have money I can send back to my family," he said with another nudge of his glasses. "I'm moving up in the world."

"So, it's a government program."

Max nodded. "There's not much I can't build, code, or hack," he said. "And like I said, I can support my family. And now you," he said, his eyes meeting Kane's from behind his thick frames.

"Ah, Max—"

"If you think I'm letting you go back to someone's couch or behind a dumpster, you're out of your mind. This isn't negotiable."

Kane swallowed hard, surprised by the emotion rising in him. He gave Max a small smile as he ran his hand through the thick curls on his head. "I don't know what to say," he said after a moment.

"I'm in some lame pod now, and you will actually have to be on my couch. But there're buildings in the east neighborhoods, ones that survived the war, and I know many have bomb shelters. I heard some guys in one of my classes talking about them. I'll find us one that hasn't been registered with the government," he said confidently.

"Pods go so fast. How do you think you could pull that off?" Kane asked skeptically.

"I just said there isn't much I can't hack, didn't I? I'll get us one," he said with a gleam in his eye. "You'll just have to suck it up on the couch a little longer."

Kane leaned back against the chair and sighed. It was pointless to argue with him, and the truth was, he didn't want to. This was a chance he never thought he'd have. After all these years, he'd have a home again. He'd have a family again. That's what Max had always been.

After changing into jeans and a comfortable t-shirt, Tala collapsed onto her couch. With Mila not home yet, it was quiet in her pod, and the sun cast long shadows through the windows. Her body was wracked with exhaustion.

For weeks she had been running long days and late nights, and it was catching up with her.

But even as she tried to simply catch her breath, her mind was busy. In addition to everything else, she now had Mills to consider. Had she really been a Rebel? She'd never come across to Tala as anything other than a loyal agent to the Republic. But then again, she had revealed information to her that was highly confidential. Tala didn't know what to think about anything anymore. The sound of her thoughts was deafening. And her mind was moving so fast Tala feared the chaos was going to consume her whole.

But despite all the madness, there was one good thing. One that brought a smile to her heart and peace to her soul. Kane. There he was, strong and steadfast in the middle of the storm. An anchor.

She had been taught, trained in opposition to the Rebels and their cause. They threatened the Republic. The idea that Kane had been a part of them, however, didn't frighten her. It didn't push her away. She wondered what it meant now that she only wanted to run to him rather than from him.

She found him magnetic, and he filled her brain, even more than all the secrets and lies. She had never seen him coming, and he was unlike anyone she had ever imagined. Their many differences had every reason to divide them, yet he seemed to understand her better than anyone ever had. He was an experience unlike anything she'd ever known. It wasn't just the recent upheavals in her life that were changing her, Kane was changing her.

He was beautiful, not just to look at, but his soul was beautiful. He knew heartbreak and defeat, he knew struggle and loss, yet he had not been hardened. His compassion ran deep. He was strong and soft. Confident and humble. Honest and kind. And when he looked at Tala, she believed he truly saw her, not as he wanted her to be, but as she was and who she was becoming.

He had come to her from the unexpected and changed the very axis her world rotated on.

Tala felt her eyes grow heavy, her breathing slowing, and with Kane's face lingering in her mind, she closed her eyes and let herself drift off.

Tala was jolted awake by a steady knocking on her door. She struggled for a moment to gather her bearings, clearing the fog from her mind. Remembering she was in her living room, she sat up, wiping the sleep from her eyes. She stood from the couch and unsteadily made her way to the door. Her heart dropped in disappointment when she opened it to find it was Vaughn who stood on the other side. Not that Kane ever used the door to her pod.

He met her with his charismatic smile and that dimple that somehow only elevated his charm. In his hands were both flowers and a bottle of wine.

"I tried calling," he said as he leaned in and kissed her cheek.

"I, uh, fell asleep," she mumbled groggily as he brushed past her into her pod. "I wasn't expecting you." She quickly ran her fingers through her hair, smoothing it down.

"I know," he said as he set the bottle down, then turned toward her. "But I wanted to see you. For some time for just the two of us."

"Oh," she said under her breath as she cringed inwardly.

"And these are for you," he said as he handed her the bouquet of succulent red roses, rich in perfume, that she knew would have cost a fortune this time of year.

She took them and offered him a gracious smile. "They're beautiful."

He shrugged. "How about some wine? I've had a very long day. And I assume you have as well if you were sleeping." He laughed, a gleam in his eyes.

Tala nodded and quickly poured two glasses of wine. She handed one to Vaughn as he made himself comfortable on her couch, unbuttoning his suit coat and loosening his tie.

"Will you excuse me for just a moment?" she asked, setting her glass down on the coffee table.

He nodded. "I'm not going anywhere," he said with a smirk, and she felt a knot tighten in her stomach.

She gave him a half-smile, then hurried to her bedroom where she pulled out her palm pad and sent a quick message to Mila.

Need you to come home within 30 min. No later. Pretend I never sent you this message, and do not volunteer to leave and give me any privacy once you get here. No questions, please. Can you do this? I'll owe you forever.

Tala took a seat on her bed, taking long, slow breaths as she waited for a response. It had grown dark, she noticed, and she glanced at the time. It was after nine, and she'd slept away her evening.

She heard a soft thud outside her bedroom and went to the balcony door. She was both relieved and disappointed when she didn't see Kane. Tala's palm pad vibrated in her hand.

Yes. I can do that.

She sighed in relief. She glanced at her reflection in the mirror, wiping her fingers beneath her eyes and giving her hair a quick tousle, then headed back into the living room. She wasn't bent on impressing Vaughn, but she didn't want to look like a mess either.

Tala took a seat near Vaughn on the sofa, careful to keep some space between them, and reached for her wine glass. His eyes caught hers as he adjusted his body, moving closer, pressing his leg against hers.

"So," he said as he slipped an arm behind her, a playful smirk on the corner of his mouth. "I've never seen you so… comfortable," he said with a wave over her body.

Tala glanced down at herself. It was true. Other than the one time he'd shown up early in the morning, he'd only ever seen her dressed up or in uniform, and she felt some resentment that he seemed to find her less appealing this way. This was who she was. She wasn't like Thias. She liked things simple rather than luxurious, even if it was how she'd been raised.

"This is what you get from me after I've had a long day," she said bitterly.

"Oh, no need to get defensive," he said with a low chuckle. "Just an observation." He took a drink of his wine, then set it on the table and looked at her.

She knew what he wanted, and she felt herself squirm. She took a large drink of her wine, feeling the tart flavor explode in her mouth. He reached for her glass, taking it from her hands, then set it beside his on the coffee table. He pulled her close, brushing his thumb against the side of her face, and Tala steeled herself.

He pressed his mouth to hers, and she hesitated for a moment before kissing him back.

"You okay?" he asked as he pulled away, his eyes narrowing.

"Of course," she said. He'd caught her off guard, and he was perceptive of her reticence. She was grateful she wouldn't have to hold him off for long. Her mind raced as she tried to formulate a plan… she had to manage him… but she'd been so consumed with so many other things and now she couldn't think up one thing to do, and she felt her panic rising inside her.

Take it slow, she told herself and reached over, sliding her fingers through his hair, soft and thick, and he smiled. Leaning into her, he kissed her again, and she kissed him back.

Tala could taste the wine on his lips, and she could smell the hint of a lingering cologne on him after a long day. His hands settled on her waist, and in a quick and swift move, he pulled her onto his lap, a leg on each side of him, and she caught her breath in surprise.

He pressed his mouth to hers with fervor, and she felt her pulse quicken. He was commanding when he kissed her, holding on to her like she was something he owned, something he had a right to. His hands crept up and down her back, and a moment later, his fingers slipped under the hem of her shirt, his hand pressing against her bare skin. Her mouth went dry, and she felt her breath shake as she exhaled. His lips moved along her jaw and to her neck, and his hands slid farther up her back.

"You know," she said quietly, afraid he would hear the quiver in her voice. He pulled away to look at her, his hands slipping out from under her shirt. His gaze lingered on hers, and she felt his eyes penetrating her.

"Are you okay?" he asked as his brows furrowed.

"I just," she said, stammering, trying to buy herself time. "I hate to bring work up," she said quietly.

"But?" he asked impatiently, his arms secured around her, holding her firmly on his lap.

"It's just that Agent Mills, she was a friend. And now I find out—"

"She's a traitor," he said flatly.

She nodded. "I'm nervous," she said, this time letting her voice quiver. "There's so much happening," she whispered.

Wrinkles formed in the corners of his eyes as he smiled, his face softening, and he fingered a strand of hair around her face. "I know," he said with a nod. "But you can rest easy. Things are being handled."

"Handled?" she asked, unable to mask her surprise.

He nodded. "Just know that things are being taken care of," he said with a look that she couldn't quite pin down. She started to grow uneasy. "I'd never let anything happen to you," he said steadily with assurance.

Tala swallowed and gave a small nod of her head. This was what he liked, an insecure Tala that he could be the hero for. But she didn't want a hero. She never had.

He leaned in to kiss her again, and her breath hitched when his hand slipped beneath her shirt for a second time. His warm fingers brushed along her back, and goosebumps raised across her body.

He pulled her against him and kissed her deeply, letting out a deep groan. Tala, not knowing where to put her hands, let her fingers glide through his hair again, her nails sliding down the back of his neck and over the tense muscles in his shoulders. His lips moved along her jaw and to her neck, lingering near her ear, and he groaned for a second time. He found her mouth again as his hands roamed higher up her back.

There was a jiggle at the door, and a second later, Mila came barging into the room. Tala hoped the relief that washed over her wasn't so apparently written across her face.

"Oh!" Mila gasped. "I'm so sorry. I had no idea you were here, Chancellor." Her wide eyes carefully met Tala's.

Tala pulled back from him, and as his grip finally loosened, she slid easily off his lap. His eyes flared as he cleared his throat and straightened his tie. There was tension in his face, a tic in his jaw.

Mila made her way to the sofa and took a seat on the armrest. "I'm sorry I'm so late tonight," she said with a small smile that Tala was sure Vaughn didn't pick up on.

Tala sat up straighter. "I didn't realize what time it is," she said, playing along with her act. Vaughn reached for his glass, finishing his wine in three large swallows before setting it back down.

"And this is why I live alone," he muttered as he adjusted his suit coat and smoothed his shirt. He stood up and pulled Tala up beside him. "I think I'll call it a night."

Tala nodded, then looked at Mila. With her face turned away from Vaughn, she mouthed a thank you to her. Mila grinned at her with amusement in her eyes.

Vaughn hastily made his way across the room, Tala following behind him. At the door, he turned toward her, his gaze lingering on her for a moment. His frustration was palpable. Then he leaned in and kissed her cheek. "We'll talk soon," he said, a weak smile on the corner of his mouth. Then he opened the door and left in a hurry. Tala listened to the fading sound of his footsteps, then when she could hear them no more, she closed the door. She sighed in relief and turned to Mila, who looked at her with a conspiratorial and curious grin.

"Still haven't had the heart to break things off?" she mused.

"It's complicated," Tala admitted as she made her way back to the sofa, collapsing onto the soft cushions.

Mila nodded. "Clearly." She reached for Tala's wine glass and took a large swig. "Though you didn't exactly look like a girl who wanted to break up."

"Like I said, it's complicated. But thank you for intervening," she said. "I really owe you."

She waved her hand dismissively. "Nah. I was on my way home when you messaged me anyway. I would've interrupted either way."

Tala took the glass back and finished the wine, then brought both hers and Vaughn's to the kitchen sink. She glanced at her palm pad. It was nearly ten. "Do you mind if I step out for a little bit?" she asked.

"Of course not," Mila said as she slid her shoes off. "Is the rest of that wine off limits?"

"It's all yours," she called over her shoulder as she made her way down the hall. Tala stepped into her bedroom for a moment. Grabbing her black zip-up jacket, she gave her empty balcony another disappointing glance.

"I'll be back by curfew," she said as she headed through the living room toward the door.

"Hope you have more fun with your secret boyfriend," Mila said from the couch as she turned on the TV.

Tala went still. "What?" she asked in a raspy breath as she glanced over her shoulder.

"I'm kidding," Mila said with a laugh. "Unless there's something you want to tell me."

Tala shook her head. "No. Nothing to tell."

Mila eyed her carefully, and Tala let out a nervous laugh, then quickly stepped into the hall, pulling the door closed behind her. As she set off for the elevators, Kane's face came to mind, and she felt her heart flutter. She couldn't help but smile.

Powering off her palm pad, Tala walked at a hurried pace from the subtrain toward Kane's. It was a brisk night, and she could see her breath dancing in the freezing air. She burrowed her hands into the deep pockets of her jacket, her body shivering as she pushed her way down the crowded sidewalk.

She felt an eagerness to see Kane again. While her mind was often muddling through her case, Kane was always in her thoughts. It was him that seemed to ground her in the chaos. Her thoughts were divided and fragmented, and as much as she wanted it to not be true, she was beginning to suspect Thias played at least a small part in all of it. Everything at Command seemed to be elevated to him, then either quickly dismissed or classified out of reach. He was at the top of all of it. But he was not one to give anything away. He was smart and guarded. Vaughn was different. He inadvertently gave her information, tiny crumbs. And after his most recent comments, she was confident that something was coming. And Thias knew about it. She was almost sure of it. He had said it himself, little happened in the Republic that he didn't know about.

His biggest mistake, though, would be underestimating her. He had built her to be his puppet, to bend at his will, but in attempting to mold her to his likeness, he had overlooked one thing, the power of her mind. He had influenced her thoughts and behaviors for so long, and she had ignorantly allowed him to do so, but she wasn't that person anymore. She had set forth to uncover the truth, and in the process, was uncovering a new side to herself, one that was unhindered by manipulated facts and masterfully created lies.

Her face cold and her breath labored, Tala was relieved when the white door to Max's pod came into view. She walked so quickly she was nearing a jog, her shoes shuffling along the pavement. She knocked hard on the door, her hand stiff and near frozen, and she bounced eagerly on the balls of her feet.

"Tala?" Max asked when he opened the door. He tipped his head and screwed up his face. "What're you doing here?"

"I came to see Kane," she said, thinking it was obvious.

"Uh, he left here an hour ago. Said he was going to your pod," Max said. "I take it you weren't home."

"Oh," she said under her breath, her heart dropping. An hour ago, she'd been home. She'd been with Vaughn.

Max moved aside. "You can wait for him if you want."

Tala had a feeling that would be futile, and she sighed in frustration. "No," she said with a shake of her head. "You can tell him I stopped by though. And," she said with a pause, "please tell him it wasn't what it sounded like."

"What wasn't?" he asked with a raised brow.

"He'll know. Just please tell him. It's important." Filled with regret, Tala shoved her hands back into her coat, turned, then retreated down the dark street, back toward the subtrain.

THIRTEEN

Light piano music could be heard over the thrum of conversation and the soft ambient sounds of the restaurant. The air was thick with the savory smells of food wafting through the room. Servers dressed in lush, dark green suits with black bowties gracefully and swiftly moved about, catering to the needs of every patron.

They were seated in a private alcove off the smallest of the five dining rooms, reserved for the most elite. Heavy, velvet drapes swept around the small archway creating an intimate atmosphere for their party of four. The black and gold Art Deco was contrasted by plush purple seating, and the tables of the open dining room were set in concentric circles around a three-tiered golden fountain.

Tala reached for her martini, the chandelier above refracting rays of light, catching the crystal of her glass. Thias was in a jovial mood, laughing and telling stories, and Tala was sure to smile on cue, to nod on cue, to laugh on cue, and as Vaughn slid his hand under the table, his fingers dragging across her thigh, she reluctantly slipped her hand into his. It was easier than having his hand creeping up her leg.

The low chatter around her lulled Tala into a trance, and while she was sitting in one of the finest restaurants in the Republic, her mind was far away.

"Tala?"

She faintly registered the sound of her name and looked up to see Thias, Nina, and Vaughn staring wide-eyed at her.

"Sorry," she said with a tepid smile. "I think the alcohol has gone to my head."

"Your cheeks are red," Nina said.

"Oh," she said, bringing her hand to her face, feeling the warmth beneath her touch. "I'm fine," she said with a dismissive wave.

"I asked what you thought of the symphony," Thias said, his eyes studying her as he lifted his scotch to his mouth.

Tala had watched the conductor as he stood behind the lectern, his baton in hand while he moved it through the air with precise rhythm, summoning the sound from each instrument. Their tunes melded together to create the most beautiful music. It wavered between gentle and tender, booming and intense, and Tala felt the energy of every note pulse through her.

"I loved it," she said. "It's been so long since I've been. I'm glad you were able to get a suite so last minute," she said, and Vaughn gave her hand a small squeeze.

"That's never a problem for me," he said with a chuckle. "You loved it growing up." His smile didn't quite meet his eyes as he gazed across the table at her. "It seemed to really play with your emotions tonight, though. You looked on the verge of tears a few times."

"Oh, good music does that to me too," Nina said as she leaned into Thias, and he gently ran his hand down her bare arm.

"Truly, I enjoyed it," Tala said honestly. An opportunity to tell even a small truth in her life was a welcomed relief, even if it meant pleasing her brother.

"That makes two of us," Vaughn said as he pulled her hand out from under the table and gently kissed the top of it, smiling as he gazed up at her.

"I see you two have been spotted around the city," Nina said. "I saw on my daily newsfeed on my palm pad this morning that you were seen together at Madison Park Bistro a few nights ago. Rumor is you're dating," she said with a coy smile. "Adira Parker asked me about you two, but I said nothing.

You know how she can be when something starts going around. She can be such a gossip." Nina let out a breathy laugh, then took a drink of her martini.

"Maybe it's time to confirm the rumors," Thias said, tipping his head to the side, his eyes meeting Tala's.

"I think that's a great idea," Vaughn said. "Would you agree it's appropriate to officially make it public?" he asked, squaring his body to Tala.

She felt her mouth go dry, and she adjusted in her seat, pulling her hand back from his grip. "I uh… yeah," she stammered. "I didn't realize there were rumors."

Nina laughed. "Well, only good ones. Everyone who's anyone around the city, I'm sure, has heard them, so coming out will hardly be a big deal. How about the president's birthday party tomorrow evening? It'll be a national spectacle. The media will be there, and you're both sure to be spotlighted, especially if you're together."

Tala cringed inwardly as reality dawned on her, hitting her with the weight of a ton of bricks. Vaughn had taken her to Madison Park with this in mind. He knew what people would say. He was the type to operate with plan and purpose. A pit opened in her stomach. She'd been played. Again. She'd let herself be manipulated. Again. Once again, she was simply a puppet at the hands of its master. But she couldn't care less about how the Republic responded to her and Vaughn, it was Kane she thought of in that moment. She had yet to see him since Vaughn was at her pod two nights before, and her heart sank at the thought of him hearing the news. Even if he knew it was a charade, there was something about it that felt dishonest to him.

"I think that's as good a time as any," she said, forcing a smile, heat once again creeping into her cheeks. She leaned toward him, kissing his cheek, his face smooth as her lips brushed over it. She saw the corner of Thias's mouth curl into a small grin.

"Tala," Nina said as she reached across the table, grabbing her hand in eagerness, "are you all set for tomorrow evening? Gown and all?"

Tala pursed her lips and smiled, marveling that what Tala might wear to a party could be her biggest concern. "I am. Thanks to my podmate." She wasn't about to admit that she'd only bought her gown earlier that day, under the careful direction of Mila.

"Excellent. And I assume you have a stylist and makeup artist. It would be so last minute to book someone now," she said. "Anyone good anyway."

"I have that taken care of as well." She nodded, and Vaughn leaned into her, breathing in her hair.

"You will undoubtedly be the most beautiful woman there," he said under his breath, then reached for her wrist, his fingers running over the dangling bangle.

"Only the best for you," she said, then reached for her martini, taking a large gulp to finish it.

"Well, I hate to bring this evening to a close," Thias said, "but I've been getting repeated messages for the last hour, and I don't think I can overlook them any longer. Vaughn, we're being requested for a meeting with Chief Justice Murdo."

"So late?" Nina asked, her face falling.

Thias cast her a sideways glance, his lips pursed.

"I only mean that it will be a long day for you. But we're all so fortunate you work as hard as you do for all of us," she added quickly.

Thias let out a low grumble as he stood and pulled out Nina's chair.

Vaughn sighed as he rose to his feet, adjusting his suit coat and smoothing his tie. "At least let me drive you home before my job swallows me whole by the end of the night," he said as he stepped closer to Tala, resting his hand on the small of her back.

She nodded and gave a small smile. "Yes, thank you." She felt only relief he had work to get back to. Lacing her fingers through his, they followed Thias and Nina through a larger dining room toward the front entrance.

Agent Grant appeared in the lobby as they were met by waitstaff with their coats, and Vaughn gently helped Tala into hers.

"Director, Chancellor," the restaurant manager said as he came from around a corner, "my deepest apologies. It appears there's been a small fender-bender right in front of the restaurant. I really don't know why people insist on manually driving these days. Your cars have been brought just down the street, right around the corner," he said with a twitch in his jaw.

Thias gave the man a hardened look, then glanced out the door. "Fine," he said flatly, then reached for Nina's hand.

Tala hooked her arm through Vaughn's, and they followed them out into the night. Two vehicles sat parked in front of the doors, one with a crunched rear fender, the other with a crunched front fender, an MF prowler parked behind them. Traffic whirred past in a rush, the air biting at Tala's bare legs, and she instinctively leaned in closer to Vaughn for warmth. She could hear muffled conversation ahead of them from Thias and Nina, though she couldn't make out anything they said. Approaching the corner, Tala's heel caught an uneven edge in the sidewalk, and she stumbled, falling hard into Vaughn.

"Whoa," he said with a laugh. "You weren't kidding when you said the alcohol went to your head tonight."

Tala let out a nervous laugh, steadying herself. As she turned the corner, her body collided face first with another pedestrian on the street, and when she looked up, her heart fell. Kane.

His mouth gaped, and his eyes flared. "I'm sorry. So sorry," he mumbled hurriedly, and for a moment, he seemed unable to look away from her.

Tala was frozen as she stared back at him. His eyes quickly darted to Vaughn, then back to her, and she saw the panic on his face. He abruptly dropped his gaze to the ground and took a wide step around them to pass.

She turned as she watched him hurry down the street in the opposite direction. He glanced over his shoulder once, then continued on his way.

"Tala?" Vaughn asked, and her head jerked toward him.

"I'm such a klutz," she said with a nervous laugh as she steadied herself.

"Do you know him?" he asked, his eyes shifting away from her as he watched Kane walk briskly away from them.

"Know him?" she scoffed. "Don't be ridiculous."

Vaughn looked at her for a long moment, then slid his hand along her back, nudging her along. "He looked like he knew you," he said.

"That doesn't mean I know him." She gave a low chuckle. "I'm both MF and an Alexander. The chances of him knowing who I am are far greater than they are of me knowing him."

"Touché," he said as his car came into view.

"I had a nice night," she said when he slid into the backseat after her.

"Nice?" he said with a cocked eyebrow.

"Okay, really nice. I love the symphony. I always have," she said nostalgically.

"It's unfortunate I can't take credit for it," he said. "But regardless, it's always an honor to have you on my arm. My very own princess," he said, eyeing her with a smile that showed off the dimple in his cheek.

She recoiled, irritation flaring inside. She swallowed hard as she forced a wide grin across her face.

He leaned in to kiss her, and she wasn't sure what she hated more, carrying on with him, acting innocent and pathetic, or letting him physically touch her.

Their drive to her pod was a short one, and Vaughn, reluctant to let her go, slid his arms around her waist, pulling her close.

"I hate to say goodnight," he whispered, his breath hot on her cheek.

"But duty calls," she said, pushing against him.

He kissed her, his hands running through her hair, then with a heavy sigh, he released his grasp on her.

Tala slipped quickly out of the car and stood along the curb, watching in relief as it drove away, disappearing halfway down the block with all the other traffic.

Her pod was dark, and she glanced at the time on her palm pad. It was nearly eleven, and Mila's door was closed. She quietly made her way to her bedroom, desperately hoping to find Kane waiting for her, although something told her she wouldn't. She opened the door to her balcony, the cold air rushing over her, and with a shiver, she stepped out onto it. It was lined with browning plants and a small tree that had now dropped almost all of its leaves. Her heart sank when she found it empty. As she turned to go back in, something white fluttering in the breeze across the floor caught her eye, a folded piece of paper, and she bent down to pick it up.

I hope I didn't blow anything for you tonight. I really wasn't expecting to run into you. Literally. I think we might be taking too many risks. Time for us to take a break. I'll be in touch in a few days.

-K

Her eyes closed as she crumpled the paper into a ball, then shoved it into the pocket of her coat as she made her way back inside. She crossed the expanse of her entire pod in half as many strides as usual, and the next thing she knew, she was back on the street, her heels clacking with every hurried step toward the subtrain.

Her anger was palpable. Everything in her life seemed to be falling apart, but Kane was her constant. His presence, simply by being, fortified her. And now he was giving up on her.

She took a seat in the back corner of the train and, ignoring a few furtive glances and a couple of blatant stares, she focused her attention ahead. Every muscle in her body was tense, every nerve firing with an abandoned fury that she was sure she was about to lose control of.

She held the crumpled ball of paper in her clenched hand, still shoved in her pocket. She could feel his words bleeding into her grasp.

When she exited the subtrain platform, she walked briskly down the sidewalk, her heels tapping along with each step. Tala could see her breath with every exhale into the cold night, and as she rounded onto Harvey Street, she side-stepped a patch of ice that had formed at the base of a leaking water pipe.

She reached Max's and gave three loud raps on the door. She noticed the bangle on her wrist, its diamond center so conspicuous, and slipped it off, tucking it safely in her pocket. She heard a scuffle inside, then Max appeared a moment later.

"A little late for a social call," he said with a lopsided grin and a nasal laugh.

"Where is he?" she snapped.

"Oh, you're mad," he said, his eyes widening, his smile falling quickly away.

Tala pushed past him and spotted Kane as he rose from the couch.

"Tala," he said.

"Do come in," Max mumbled as he closed the door.

"What the hell is this?" she asked as she threw the balled-up note at Kane, hitting him squarely in the chest, then dropping to the floor.

"I think it's pretty self-explanatory," he said. "We can talk about this tomorrow."

"No, we're talking about this now," she insisted, her voice booming through the quiet pod.

"Maybe if you're going to have it out with each other, you could do it in Kane's room," Max interjected.

"It's twenty after eleven, Tala. We can talk tomorrow," Kane said as he buried his hands into the pockets of his jeans.

"I'm not leaving," she said firmly as she crossed her arms.

"You know…" Max said feebly, "the bomb shelter, where no one would hear you yelling, instead of right here where the four-pod radius can hear you."

Tala snapped her head in his direction and narrowed her eyes.

"Or you know," Max said, his voice unsteady as he shifted his feet, "right here's fine too."

Tala met Kane's gaze, her body stiffening as she stood resolutely in place.

"Fine." He sighed. "Let's talk." He turned toward the hatch in the floor.

Tala slipped out of her coat, draping it over the back of a chair, then stepped out of her heels. With her bare feet on the cold floor, she followed Kane across the room, and he motioned for her to climb down the ladder first.

The shelter, with its concrete floor and walls, was cool, sending a chill across her arms and legs. She silently watched him climb down the ladder after her, pulling the hatch closed behind him. Skipping the last four rungs, he dropped to the floor with a thud.

"Look," he started before she could say anything, "I really hope I didn't mess things up for you tonight," he said as he turned toward her. "Mrs. Knox asked me to do her a favor. I had no idea you'd be in that part of the city tonight," he said.

"It's fine," she said, her anger ebbing. "I handled Vaughn. You don't need to worry about that." The look in his eyes seemed both sad and angry. "I didn't come here to talk about Vaughn," she said, leveling her voice. "I'm here about your note."

He let out a sigh of frustration as he ran his hand over his head. "I know I'm the one who encouraged this charade with the chancellor, but I can't stand seeing him with you," he admitted, his eyes unable to meet hers. "I've been selfish. I put you in danger every time we see each other. Do you know what would happen if someone found out who I was, or what I am, and that you've been spending time with me? And yet I still take every opportunity to be with you." His shoulders slouched, and there was sorrow on his face.

"You don't think I haven't been doing the same?" she said, hearing the rising emotion in her voice. "When you don't show up on my balcony, then I'm here, at your doorstep. You are my first thought in the morning and my last at night."

He was quiet, his eyes finally meeting hers.

"If you've been selfish, then so have I," she said.

"Tonight, when I saw you together, you were laughing, and he slipped his arm around you, and all I could think, other than how badly I wanted to punch him in the face, was that I could never give you that. And I know it's not Vaughn you want, but Tala," he paused, "I have nothing to give you."

She crossed the room, approaching him cautiously.

"This is impossible," he said on a slow exhale. She was now close enough to feel the heat from his body.

She shook her head. "It might not be easy, but it's not impossible," she said.

"Not in a million years could I give you the life you have, the life you deserve. I'm a nobody. A monster," he said, his voice cracking just slightly. "I have nothing to give you, and you deserve the whole world."

She saw pain in his eyes. He'd referred to himself as a monster before and it tugged at her. "You are not nobody. And you are absolutely not a monster," she emphasized firmly. "You say I deserve the world, but what I don't think you realize is that you, you've become my *whole* world," she said, swallowing hard. Their sheer closeness made her heart race, and she reached up, pressing her hand against his cheek, feeling the scruff on his face against her palm. Time seemed to stand still for them, and everything became clear. She hadn't planned for him. But here he was, so close she could feel his breath on her face. Before him, she didn't know what she wanted, but she knew now that it was unequivocally him. It didn't matter how complicated it was. And she would choose him every time in a million lifetimes.

"I love you," she said, the words out of her mouth and hanging in the air between them. She didn't look away from him. She held his gaze, looking into his dark eyes, catching the tiny fleck of gold in them.

He didn't say a word, didn't make a sound. It was a moment of charged silence. But the look in his eyes said it all, and she knew what was about to happen.

He reached out, sliding his hand into her thick, blond hair, then leaned in, pulling her to him. He drew a deep and steady breath, then pressed his lips to hers.

It was a kiss she felt in her entire body, her toes, her fingers, her beating heart, a kiss she felt in her soul.

He wrapped his arms around her. Electrified by his touch, she pressed herself against him, and yet she still didn't feel close enough. She wanted to give him every part of her. She wanted him to know every part of her. She was certain that there was a piece of him in every fiber in her.

Her hands moved down his body, her fingers tingling at the touch of him, and slipped under the hem of his shirt. She glided them across his back, firm and strong, and with a swift tug, he pulled the shirt off.

His hands settled on her hips, his mouth moving slowly along her jawline to her ear, and she sucked in a breath, craving more of him. His lips moved down her neck, and her head fell back. She breathed in the heady scent of him; he was intoxicating.

Tala took a small step back and looked at him, her eyes wandering over him. She felt an ache deep inside, and she turned, holding his gaze over her shoulder. He reached up, tugging at the zipper of her dress, slowly dragging it down her back, his fingers grazing her skin. Tala let the dress slide off her shoulders, down her arms, then fall to the floor. She watched as he looked her over, drinking her in. Warmth spread through her.

She reached for his hand as she took small steps backward toward his bed, and when she felt the mattress against the back of her legs, she slid onto it. She pulled him to her, pressing her body firmly against his, his hands sliding around her waist, embracing her in his grasp. She arched her back as he kissed her neck. A split second before his lips touched hers, electricity ran through her veins. He was her destiny.

He stopped to look at her, his eyes alive and full. "Tala," he whispered, "there's something you need to know." He paused, and she could feel his pounding heart beneath her hand as she pressed it to his chest, his black ink wrapping around his pec and down his side. "I am so completely in love with you."

A smile tugged on the corner of her mouth, and she kissed him, deeply, thoroughly, losing herself in him. He made her heart race and stand still at the same time. He made her forget to breathe. He made the world disappear.

His body was taut under the touch of her hands as they gripped him. Slowly, she lay down, sinking into the mattress as Kane hovered above her. He smiled and let out a small laugh, then pressed his mouth to hers. Her toes curling, Tala closed her eyes as he cradled her in his arms.

She had fallen fully and completely.

Kane pulled Tala tighter as he listened to the sound of her slow, rhythmic breathing while she slept, her chest rising and falling beneath his arms, their bodies entwined together. His heart fell in beat with hers. He buried his face in her hair, her long, blond locks that were splayed across his pillow smelling of sweet lavender. She had fallen asleep long ago, but his mind was full, and sleep was the last thing he wanted to do in that moment. He was content simply holding her while she slept.

He had once dreamed of the stars. Then over the years, they'd gone dark for him, and he had given up on those dreams. But Tala, she was an entire galaxy. For so long, he had resented fate for the life he had, but looking back, he couldn't help but think that every one of those steps in his journey had led him to her, that none of it had been random after all. And she was worth all of it.

He was sure he had never done anything in his life worthy of her, yet here she was. He craved her like the oxygen in his lungs. He felt her in every corner of his body. She was the dream he'd never let himself have. Holding her felt like the most natural thing in the world. He loved her, and he would love her until the day he died. And if there was life after that, he would love her then too.

As opposite as two lives could be, their convergence was not only unexpected, it was extraordinary. But they had been made for each other, and he was certain there was no force strong enough to change the arc of their trajectory.

Tala stirred, and he leaned over, gently kissing her neck, and her eyes fluttered open. She turned toward him, a wide smile spreading across her face.

"How long have I been asleep?" she asked quietly, a small rasp in her voice.

"A while," he said and kissed the corner of her mouth.

"I think I missed the last train," she mumbled, then let out a small laugh.

"Yeah, I'm pretty sure you did." He could listen to her laugh forever.

Tala rolled over to face him, then ran her hand over his bare head, down the back of his neck and along his jawline. "You're beautiful," she whispered.

"Then I'm in good company," he said, studying her in the dim light. She was captivating. "You know," he said softly, "we just made things very complicated."

She shook her head. "No," she said flatly. "This is the one thing that makes complete sense."

He smiled, his heart leaping in his chest. He brushed his fingers along her arm, so soft and pale beside his brown skin. He looked into her eyes, a radiant blue beneath long lashes. She was beautiful. Breathtaking. But she was more than that. She was strong and fierce, determined and loyal. He had watched her change and grow into her own, and that, he thought, was the most beautiful part of her.

"You're smiling," she whispered, her lips grazing across his.

He nodded. "Just thinking about you."

"Anything you want to share?" she asked with a coy grin as she slid her hand up his arm. Goosebumps raised across his body from her touch.

"It's just," he paused, gathering his thoughts, "I thought this was impossible. You and me. But right now, I can't help but think that what's meant to be will always find a way. With you, that's where I'm meant to be."

A spark flared in her eyes, and she pulled herself nearer to him, her hot breath on his face. "I may never let go of you," she whispered. She looked up at him through heavy eyelids, then pressed her lips to his neck.

His breath caught. Everything about her thrilled him. Her very touch set him on fire, and all of his senses were in overdrive. But her heartbeat, he not only heard it, he felt it. He kissed her, hard, with everything in him, and the world fell away. It was only them. When the sun came up, the world would go on, and they would go on with it. But in that moment, it was just them, and he was going to love her so completely.

FOURTEEN

Tala opened her eyes, groggy from a deep sleep. Glancing around the room, it took her a moment to register her surroundings, and she smiled. She was used to the sunlight beaming in on her in the morning, and the windowless bomb shelter made it difficult to guess the time. She gently rolled over, her body only inches from Kane. He looked peaceful, and she wanted to shuffle closer to him, to feel his body against hers, to kiss his face, his cheeks, eyes, lips. She resisted the urge to run her hand over him and instead, contentedly watched him, listened to him. The rhythmic rise and fall of his chest with every slow breath. She wanted to memorize everything about him. She was sure she had never been this happy. There was no fanfare in her epiphany but rather a tranquil sense of comfort that washed over her.

She'd been consumed by secrets and lies, unsure of what was real and what was not, questioning nearly everything. She was in a constant state of conflict. But in the midst of it all, she had found something in herself she knew she wouldn't have otherwise. And Kane had everything to do with it. He was the first person to see below the surface to the true Tala, buried deep below the legacy of her name, false illusions, and high expectations. He didn't change her by loving her, but rather, she had changed by loving him.

He stirred, letting out a small groan, then his eyes opened. Slowly at first, blinking closed, then fluttering open again. The corner of his mouth curled into a smile.

"I thought maybe I dreamed you," he said in a hoarse whisper.

She leaned into him and kissed him.

"Tonight's the big party, huh?" he asked lazily.

Tala nodded.

"I'll watch for you on my TV, just so I can see how beautiful you are."

"No, don't do that," she said hurriedly, remembering the plan for the broadcast. "Vaughn and I are supposed to go public." Her stomach churned with the thought.

"Then I'll watch and laugh to myself because it'll be my arms you'll be in tonight and not his," he said with a smirk.

"I can't carry on with it," she said. "I can't do this to you."

"Tala, you have to. You've come too far. I'll be fine. I'm not excited about it, but I'll be fine," he assured her. He brushed a stray strand of hair away from her face, tucking it behind her ear. "I know where we stand. I don't doubt."

She sighed as she sat up, and she felt his hand glide down her bare back, his fingers electrifying her with his touch. "How do you even know what time it is down here?" she asked.

He rolled over, reaching across the bed to a small nightstand, grabbing a black device Tala hadn't noticed.

"This is how," he said with a chuckle. "A clock."

It was much later than she anticipated, and her heart fell, her perfect night coming to an end. She crawled out of bed and slipped back into her dress from the night before. Glancing over her shoulder, Kane watching her with a grin on his face, she smiled.

Tala threw herself back onto the bed, and holding his face between her hands, she kissed him, slow and deep. He wrapped his arms firmly around her like he would never let her go. And she was perfectly okay with that.

◆◆◆

Tala stepped into her pod and abruptly came to a halt when she saw Mila sitting at the island counter, a steaming cup of coffee in her hands.

"Well, well," she said with an amused smirk at the sight of her. "Look who's making the walk of shame, showing up the next morning in the same dress from the night before. I was wondering where you were this morning."

Tala sighed, and her shoulders sank, though she couldn't completely hide her smile.

"I know it's not Vaughn," Mila said flatly but without judgment. "You want to tell me about him?"

Tala stepped into the kitchen, setting her palm pad on the counter. "It's complicated," she conceded. There was no point in denying anything.

Mila nodded. "I'd say it would have to be if you're still seeing the chancellor, even if he sets your teeth on edge."

"Is it that obvious?"

"No," Mila said. "But I know you."

Tala nodded. Mila, she knew, would never give her away. She hated that she couldn't tell her about Kane. She wanted to yell from the rooftops about him.

"Can I give you some advice?"

"Please," Tala said as she leaned against the counter, slipping off her heels.

"The truth will come out, eventually, and it's my opinion that it's better to be in control of it rather than letting it be in control of you. Right now, you're trying to appease everyone else, your brother especially, I suspect. But at some point, you're going to have to make a decision. I'd much rather it be Vaughn you end things with than whoever your mystery man is. Anyone who can make a woman smile like you were when you walked through that door is not worth letting go of, least of all over someone like the chancellor."

Tala looked away, her eyes wandering to the blue sky out the window. Mila was right. Just a little bit longer, she thought to herself. She wouldn't let it last a moment longer than she needed it to. Kane deserved that. She deserved that.

"Now, let's move past this conversation and start getting you ready for this evening. We've got lots to do," Mila said eagerly with a clap of her hands. "First things first, shower."

Grateful, Tala smiled as she grabbed her palm pad and headed toward her bedroom. "Yes, ma'am," she called over her shoulder. She was at Mila's mercy now.

Tala sat patiently in front of her mirror while Mila went to work on her. She curled her hair, then pulled it back into a delicate side chignon, painted her nails a soft shade of nude that wouldn't clash with her dress, then carefully applied her makeup, accenting her long lashes with bold mascara, finishing her off with a fair pink gloss on her lips. Unlike the time she had made the National Statement, she felt truly beautiful. But it wasn't the makeover that made her feel this way, it was knowing there was someone who saw her, someone who valued what was inside more than what was outside. Vaughn's vision of her went only skin deep.

As the shadows across her bedroom lengthened, the day drawing into the evening, Tala slipped into her gown, a long, sweeping dress that trailed behind her when she walked, the bright color of a fresh summer lemon. It was fitted in the bodice and hugged her hips, showing the gentle curve of her body. The neck was cut high, with a thin, black lace overlay across her chest and over her shoulders, and had a full-circle open back.

"Wow," Mila said on a loud exhale as she stepped back. "I know you hate being called a princess, but if ever there was one, it would be you."

In this one instance, she took it as a compliment. Tala glanced over her shoulder and smiled. The only person she wanted to see her like this was Kane. She cared about no one else. And as she would hang on Vaughn's arm on the purple carpet, in front of all those people, she would smile inside knowing Kane was watching her from afar.

Tala slipped on the bangle and a pair of earrings to complement it, then stepped into her shoes and let out a sigh of approval.

"Do you know who's all expected to be there tonight?" Mila asked as they made their way into the living room.

Tala shrugged. "All Republic leaders, I assume. Maybe those from the Central Colonies and the Great Lakes Federation."

"High rollers and donors undoubtedly," Mila added. "It's a shame I didn't get an invitation. I'm sure there'll be one or two good-looking men there," she swooned with a laugh.

Tala's palm pad vibrated. Vaughn was downstairs. "Right on time," she said, slightly crestfallen, bracing herself for her night ahead.

"Good luck and have fun!" Mila exclaimed. "I'll watch you on the broadcast."

Tala made her way to the street to find Vaughn standing beside his black sedan, a red rose in his hand. His face lit with a smile at the sight of her.

"You are stunning," he said as he leaned in and kissed her softly.

"You clean up well," she said as she adjusted his bowtie. He wore a slim fitted, black tuxedo with a satin lapel and a black shirt, his hair perfectly coiffed. Handsome and exactly as she expected.

He let out a low laugh. "This, my darling, is for you," he said as he handed her the rose.

She accepted it, bringing it to her nose, inhaling its sweet aroma.

"Let's not be late," he said as he opened the door to the car.

They rode to the Larabee Institute of Art in silence, Vaughn distracted by his palm pad, and she was thankful she didn't have to make conversation. Despite herself, her mind was on Kane, and she reminded herself she couldn't afford to be distracted around Vaughn. If she had to be with him, she had to be intentional with everything. He would know if her mind was elsewhere.

Along the shore of the East River, the sun inching toward the horizon, dropping below the city skyline, the museum came into view. It was a looming stone building with a towering colonnade running the length of it. A high-relief frieze adorned the top façade, and large golden banners draped down the front of the building, flanking the arched entranceway, each with the triangle of the Republic.

A heavy crowd of spectators gathered, lining the street while guests dressed in lavish gowns and tuxedos, a couture exhibit on display, posed for photos, some giving interviews to the media, all making their way toward the entrance. And security was heavy, a dense presence of MF all around, and likely just as many out of sight.

Their car joined a long line, waiting its turn to pull in front of the museum, and Vaughn leaned into her, inhaling as he pressed his lips just below her ear.

"Are you ready for this?" he asked as he tucked away his palm pad.

"Of course," she said as she leaned closer, catching his cologne.

"Your brother was so persistent about putting us together, and I really didn't think anything would come of it, but I'm so glad I was wrong," he said with a smile.

Tala tipped her head. "Why didn't you think it would work?"

"I don't know," he said with a casual shrug. "I had only ever thought of you as Militia Forces. Despite your name. But I see now that you're so much more than that."

Tala's anger flared. "And by so much more, you mean high heels and pretty dresses?" The words were off her tongue before she could stop them.

But Vaughn only laughed. "Of course not," he said. "Just that I've learned you're softer, more delicate than I thought."

She pressed her lips in a straight line as she bit back her words. They were caustic and harsh, and the last thing she needed was to start a fight.

"Oh, relax," he said with a wave of his hand. "It's a compliment."

She swallowed hard and gave a nod as their car moved forward, finally pulling in front of the museum.

"Now, let's make this the most wonderful night. We get to share our happiness with the country," he said, then pulled her in for a deep kiss.

Tala stepped out of the car, followed by Vaughn, the cool evening air biting at her bare skin, and she let out a small shiver. She took his arm as he escorted her across the purple carpeted walkway, roped off from the crowd. He waved and nodded at the gawkers with his suave smile, perfect teeth, and that dimple. He was far more comfortable in front of an audience than Tala whose mouth had gone dry at the sight of it all. It felt surreal to be there. Despite the notoriety of her name, she wasn't used to anything more glamorous than a dinner party. She had nothing to do with politics or the running of the country. She tried to avoid the elite class of people in Thias's circle. Without even having entered the museum, Tala knew this party was on an entirely different level than anything else. As Nina said, all the stops had been pulled out for this one night, President Royer II's fiftieth birthday.

Bright lights shone down on them as Tala waved. She heard her name called from somewhere in the distance, whispers of her and Vaughn together spreading rapidly through the crowd, all eyes on them. Tala bit at the inside of her cheek to ground herself. Kane came to mind, and she took a slow breath. These people didn't matter, she told herself. Somewhere across the city, it was Kane who was watching her. Suddenly, she cared about nothing and no one else.

Vaughn nudged her along, and they stepped in front of a camera beside Wynn Davison, dressed in a sweeping silver gown, bright-eyed like she was every week for the National Statement.

"Chancellor Adams," she said with a knowing smile, her voice rising above the thrum of the crowd.

"Always a pleasure, Wynn," he said with his charming smile and a small laugh as he pulled Tala closer.

"As chancellor of International Affairs," she said, "this must be a big night for you, the Republic hosting so many dignitaries and world leaders."

Vaughn nodded. "Of course it's a big night," he said. "We're honored to have so many people here, especially those who traveled from overseas. I believe it speaks to the leadership of our country to have the global respect that we do," he said, dragging his fingers along Tala's exposed back.

"And Tala Alexander," Wynn said cheerfully, "let me begin with how beautiful you look in this gorgeous gown. Truly the princess of the Republic of Columbia."

"Thank you," Tala said as she plastered a gracious smile across her face.

"Of course, we're all familiar with your name, we've heard it frequently in the news recently. And I must say that we are a safer city because we have you to defend our citizens. You're known to always go above and beyond. A champion of the people."

She wanted to roll her eyes.

"I'm just doing my job," she said. "Our people are everything to me. And our teams of agents work together to make this a safe city for everyone." Her cheeks were beginning to feel sore from smiling.

"We've heard rumors for a few weeks now that there may be something going on between you two. Either of you care to comment?" Wynn asked with a gleam in her eye.

Tala gave a small laugh, and Vaughn pulled her closer yet, a firm grasp around her like she was something he owned. It made it all the worse, what she was about to do.

"You know the age-old saying," he said, "a true gentleman doesn't kiss and tell. But I can say with confidence that this one here knows how to captivate a man," he said with a low chuckle as he brought his free hand to his chest and adjusted his lapel.

"Miss Alexander, do you have anything to add?" Wynn asked, trying to mask her disappointment with Vaughn's response.

Of course he was going to make her say it. Tala felt a tug in her heart as she thought of Kane. Then Thias's face came to mind. She knew what she had to do.

Tala forced the biggest smile across her face that she could manage. "Well, he may not kiss and tell, but I'll happily confirm the rumors. The chancellor and I have been seeing each other. But it's all very new, and I'm just eager to see where things go from here," she said. He leaned into her, brushing his lips across her cheek.

Wynn looked more than pleased. "Thank you both," she said. "I wish you a wonderful evening."

"Come," he whispered as he gave her a nudge, and they stepped away from Wynn. Tala paused, falling briefly behind Vaughn. Knowing the camera was still on her, she glanced over her shoulder, giving it one last look, this one only for Kane.

"I can't wait to show you off," he said as he smiled, tugging at her hand.

Tala and Vaughn joined the line of guests waiting to get through security. Militia Forces agents, most of them unfamiliar to Tala, used facial recognition on each guest, then ushered them through a body detector before granting them access to the museum.

Stepping inside the Larabee was like being transported to another world, leaving Tala stunned to silence. They entered through a marble archway and proceeded up a long corridor of stairs of lavish red carpeting. More archways adorned them on both sides, each one supported by tall stone columns dressed in golden lighting. At the top of the stairs, a large great hall opened before them. Its vaulted ceiling was four stories high, with white marble columns that stretched the height of the room. Enormous golden and crystal chandeliers hung from above, throwing gem-like sparkles across the crowd below.

Round tables of white linens and golden-backed chairs filled the room, with tall golden vases, white roses spilling over the tops, standing in the middle of each one. Across the room, an orchestra played on a large stage surrounded by layers of hundreds of luminous lights that flickered like candles perched on golden pedestals. There was a large space in front of the orchestra where people were dancing, golden light streaming over the mosaic floor. The perimeter of the hall was lined with arched doorways that led off to other areas of the museum. Polished, stark white marble statues stood between each doorway, an MF agent positioned like a sentry beside each one.

Conversation and laughter carried through the room above the smooth sound of the orchestra. Tala looked out over the sea of tuxedos and lavish gowns. There were sweeping silks and satins, colorful feathers and fringes, metallic sheens, shimmering beads and jewel embellishments, rich velvets, colorful tulle, and fine lace. This was elegance and high society.

"Wow," Tala whispered on an exhale. She felt Vaughn's gaze on her.

"It's incredible, isn't it?" he asked with an amused smirk. "As someone who has lived in the city her whole life, I'm surprised you've never been here."

"I've never had a reason to come," she admitted.

"Let me introduce you around," he said as he slid his hand onto the small of her back and guided her carefully between tables.

Gloved servers dressed in burgundy velvet suits with bowties to match floated around the room with trays of crystal flutes of golden champagne. Vaughn grabbed two from a woman as she slowly passed, handing one to Tala.

She took a sip, sweet bubbles on her tongue as Vaughn continued across the room.

Tala's eyes couldn't help but wander, a few familiar faces catching her attention. Kavan Parker looked deep in conversation with a tall, broad-looking man dressed in a black suit with a thick fur collar. The man had a woman on his arm, beautiful and slender in an emerald gown, with the most gorgeous copper-red hair. Kavan's wife, Adira, stood beside them looking bored and impatient, and she quickly exchanged her empty flute of champagne for a full one as a server passed by.

Near the orchestra, Tala recognized the Republic's regional representatives, Aiden Gray, Marshall Turner, and Vance Donovan, their wives laughing amongst the three of themselves, each in dresses that swept the floor at their feet.

"Ahh," a short man with jet black hair said when he saw Vaughn and Tala approaching, his face lighting up with a smile. "Chancellor Adams, so good to see you," he exclaimed as he gave a small bow of his head, Vaughn returning the same gesture.

"Ambassador, I'd like to introduce you to Tala Alexander," Vaughn said proudly, glancing at her.

"Alexander? Founding father?" the man asked.

"The very," she said with a smile.

"This is Ambassador Liu from the Reformed People's Republic of China," Vaughn said.

"A pleasure, Ambassador," she said, tipping her head.

"I have to say," said the ambassador, "I have plans tomorrow for a tour of the museum's recent collection from ancient China's Song Dynasty. I am very much looking forward to it."

"I hear it's an impressive exhibit," Vaughn said.

"Miss Alexander," Ambassador Liu said as he turned toward her, standing an entire head beneath her, "how familiar are you with Chinese history and culture?"

"Oh," she said as she gave a furtive glance at Vaughn. "Honestly, I'm not familiar at all," she said apologetically.

He laughed, joined by Vaughn, and she wondered why that was humorous. "Well, with this new collection, perhaps it's a good time to learn."

"Absolutely," she said with another smile and another bow of her head. From across the room, Thias caught her gaze. She gave Vaughn a small nudge with her elbow.

He followed her line of sight. "Ambassador, I'm being called away," he said.

"Of course, of course," he exclaimed. "Miss Alexander," he said as he took her hand, giving her a small bow and a kiss on her knuckle, "it was my pleasure to make your acquaintance. And do enjoy that exhibit," he said with an eager nod and smile.

"Certainly," she said as Vaughn gave a tug of her arm, gently pulling her away.

"He traveled far for this," she said quietly when they were out of earshot.

"We have close relations with Reformed China," he said matter-of-factly, but Tala was already aware of this. They were one of the Republic's most powerful allies. "We also work closely with the private sector in China, specifically with the ambassador."

"My, my," Thias said with a grin as he approached. He reached for Tala's hands, taking them gently in his, and he leaned into her. "Stunning," he said, and she felt herself blush.

"I could say the same about you," Tala said, turning to Nina, who was draped in an azure blue, silk gown, a deep plunging neckline and a high slit up her thigh. Her black hair was pulled tightly into a sleek bun. She was punctuated with bright red lips and an oversized diamond necklace with dangling earrings to match. "You're gorgeous," Tala said as she leaned into her, giving her a small kiss on her cheek.

"I must say, Tala," she said with a grin, "few could pull off a yellow like this." She waved her hand over Tala's dress. "It's a bold choice, and you pull it off superbly."

"I heard about your announcement," Thias said and cleared his throat. "Nicely done."

"Already?" Tala said in surprise.

"Of course already. As I frequently tell you, dear sister, there is rarely anything that happens around here without my knowledge, especially where my own sister is concerned," he said. "How quickly you forget," he chortled.

Both Nina and Vaughn laughed with him.

"Pacifica's President Walker is here," Thias said as he turned toward Vaughn, his voice laced with irritation. "And disappointingly, only two Central Colonies governors are in attendance. Governors Fulton and Barrington are around here somewhere," he said.

"I suggest a wide berth around Walker. If only to avoid a public quarrel," Vaughn said cautiously.

Thias cast him a sideways look.

Sudden applause rang out from across the room, interrupting their conversation. It was infectious as it quickly spread through the crowd. Tala turned, spying President Royer as he made his entrance. She was surprised to see him in a white tuxedo; he rarely strayed from his straight-fit topcoat. His hair, an equal blend of gray and white, was parted on the side, hanging over the tops of his ears, and he wore the same serene expression he always did, not harsh but not welcoming either. He had a way of looking at someone through his squinty, small eyes, a curl at the corners of his mouth that was neither a scowl nor smile that could put anyone on edge. He was impossible to read, his voice never fluctuating with emotion.

President Royer swiftly made his way to the center of the stage where the orchestra played, and the music faded to silence, the audience falling quiet as they dipped into a bow.

"Good evening," he said into a microphone in a dilatory voice that reverberated through the room. "I want to begin by expressing my gratitude for your presence on this night," he said, his expression giving nothing away. "Please enjoy the music, dancing, and good company. And with that said, dinner is ready to be served."

The room once again erupted in heavy applause as he stepped down from the stage, disappearing in the crowd.

"We're at the president's table," Thias said as he slipped his hand behind Nina, ushering her in front of him toward their table.

"Us, as well?" Tala asked Vaughn as she looked over her shoulder, her eyes wide.

"Of course us, as well," he said with a laugh as he offered his arm.

Tala hesitated a moment, then took it, and they followed Thias across the room. In all her life, the only time she had been in any real proximity to Royer was while serving as security. She reminded herself who she was with. Both Thias and Vaughn served in the second and fourth highest positions in the Republic, of course they would be close to President Royer.

Tala felt unsure of herself as they arrived at their table. Chief Justice Murdo and his wife, Esme, were already seated, as well as Ambassador Liu and a small Chinese woman beside him in an elaborate red gown and golden headdress.

Tala took her seat beside the Great Lakes Federation's Vice President Kate Chamberlain, whom she only recognized but didn't know. The Federation's President Winston Hugo sat on Kate's other side, and he smiled kindly at Tala. From across the table, she could feel Thias's eyes on her, but when she met his gaze, he simply tipped his head to her, then turned to Nina.

The last to join the table were President Royer and his son, Alec. His wife had passed away years before, when Alec was just a small child. He was a teenage boy now, and with no mother, his only family left was a distant and cold father. Tala felt a tug at her heart as she looked at him, understanding too well what his life must be like.

"Hello, friends," President Royer said. He cleared his throat and looked around the table, offering everyone the closest thing to a smile that Tala had ever seen from him.

Moments later, servers appeared, placing plates of cacio e pepe frico in front of them, a delicate cracker of baked cheese made into crisps. Tala was hungry but was also anxious to eat in front of the table of esteemed strangers, though she was no stranger to table etiquette. She waited for the others to begin before reaching for her food.

"We have a new face with us tonight," President Royer said after finishing a bite, his eyes settling on Tala.

She felt her pulse quicken under his gaze, her hands growing clammy, and she quickly swallowed her food.

"Mr. President," Vaughn said eagerly, "this is Tala Alexander."

"I know the face," he said. "Our very own princess. It's a wonder we've never met, your name holds such prominence. Then again, you don't hold any political position, so why would we have met?" he asked, his tiny eyes fixed on her, and she adjusted nervously in her chair.

"It's an honor to be here," she said steadily, careful not to fully meet his gaze. She felt the eyes of the table on her and knew her cheeks were pink. Despite herself, she took a small breath in relief when Vaughn reached for her hand beneath the table.

She steeled herself and looked at Thias, a smirk on the corner of his mouth, his eyes wrinkling.

Tala stayed quiet the remainder of their meal, preferring to listen to rather than participate in the conversation, trying her best to enjoy the revelry around her. Everyone spoke mostly of trivial matters during dinner, making a joke here or there. But even when the table laughed, President Royer wore his unchanging expression. After the appetizer was cleared, they were served their first main course of lobster with wild herbs and golden saffron radish that played with the color theme of the room, complemented with edible gold flakes for garnishing. Their second main dish of baby lamb chops and almond pesto, and branzino in a caper brown butter was one of the most amazing things Tala had ever eaten. It was rich and savory, full of flavor.

"How is your dinner?" Vaughn asked in a hushed voice, leaning toward her as their plates were cleared.

"It's incredible," she whispered.

"I think he's the only person more particular about his food than I am," he said with a nod toward the president who was conversing with Ambassador Liu.

Tala smiled as their dessert was served, chocolate-dipped cape berries and gold-dusted truffles which she would have devoured had she not been in the presence of such esteemed guests.

Their final plates had been cleared for several minutes before President Royer finally rose from his chair, and Tala felt herself breathe a sigh of relief when he stepped away from the table.

Slowly, the others stood, dispersing happily around the room. Tala was caught off guard as someone abruptly took the open seat beside her. She turned to see that it was the same woman she'd spotted earlier, with the unforgettable copper-red hair. It was even more gorgeous close-up, the lightly curled, shoulder-length locks that were as vibrant as a blazing fire. She had pale skin, high cheekbones, and light green eyes that took Tala by surprise. Never in her life had she met someone with true green eyes, and she found them striking.

"You're Tala Alexander," the woman said, her voice soft and smooth.

"Yes," Tala said with uncertainty. A glance to her other side showed the man in the black suit with the fur collar had taken the seat beside Vaughn, and the two were laughing haughtily about something.

"I've always wanted to meet you," the woman said with a smile. "I'm Victoria Barrington. That's my husband," she said with a nod.

"Governor Barrington?" Tala asked, the name drawing a ring of familiarity. Elias Barrington was from the Central Colonies, someone Thias had spoken of often over the years. He had been in power since before her parents' deaths.

"The very one," she said with a small laugh. "I'm always disappointed when I come to an event in the Republic and never get to meet you. Your brother has always spoken so highly of you. I happened to catch you on the National Statement a while ago," she said, a gleam in her eye as her gaze steadied on Tala. "I knew your father."

"Oh?" Tala said with surprise.

"Elias was just beginning to emerge in the political scene at the time, and Jameson was… kind. Supportive," she said. "Though I only met your mother once."

"How interesting," Tala said feebly, unsure what to say. She wasn't expecting anyone to bring up either of her parents.

"Anyway," Victoria said as she glanced at her husband, "I don't want to hold you up. I just wanted to take this rare opportunity to meet you. You should come to more events."

"I'm not really the political figure in the family," she said with a small chuckle.

"I think you're more important than you give yourself credit for. Have more credibility than you know," Victoria said with a casual shrug of her shoulder, a crinkle in the corner of her eye. "Elias, let's leave them be," she called sweetly to her husband as she rose from the chair. "It was lovely to meet you, Tala."

Tala watched as Elias clasped his hand over Vaughn's and let out a throaty laugh. "The boss has spoken," he said, then rose to his feet. He reached for his wife, and as they began to walk away, Victoria gave a last glance over her shoulder, a smile on the corner of her mouth that Tala couldn't read.

"A dance?" Vaughn asked.

Drawing her eyes away from the backside of Victoria, she turned to Vaughn. Pressing her lips together in a smile, she nodded.

Taking her by the hand, he led her to the dance floor, the lights surrounding the orchestra flickering in the background. He pulled her body to his, wrapping an arm firmly around her waist as he began to move his feet with the music.

She let him lead, guiding her as he wanted, and she thought of Kane. She would have given so much to be in his arms instead. Her mind took her back to the night before, his touch, his kiss, and she felt herself flush.

"Tell me what you're thinking," Vaughn said, his lips brushing along her ear when he spoke, his breath hot on her cheek.

"Just feeling all that champagne," she said.

"Then it probably won't help if I do this." He let go of her waist and spun her into his arms.

Unsteadily, Tala stumbled into him, and he laughed.

"Sorry, I couldn't help it," he said, his eyes lingering on her.

"You need to warn me before you do that," she admonished with a smile.

"We may need to repeat your dance lessons," Thias said as he and Nina glided up beside them. "Shall we show them how it's done?" he asked Nina, and before she responded, he released her, her body spinning gracefully before being wrapped in his arms, coming to a stop with her face a mere inch from his. He leaned in and kissed her.

Tala felt herself smile. This was the side of him that she loved. Maybe, she thought, she had judged him too harshly. He had hidden the horrible truth, but it was possible that deep down, he really believed he'd been protecting her. Her mind began its efforts to reconcile the dichotomy between his horrible choices and his redeeming qualities. He was a complicated good-bad binary narrative.

"Ah," Thias said, his eyes drifting to something behind Tala. "Vaughn," he said curtly and gave a side tilt of his head. "Ladies, please excuse us, we have some business that needs to be addressed."

Nina looked about to protest but then closed her mouth and gave a small smile instead.

Vaughn leaned in and kissed the corner of Tala's mouth, then gave her hand a small squeeze. "Don't wander too far," he said with a smirk. "This shouldn't be too long."

Tala watched as they hustled off the dance floor toward Chief Justice Murdo. The three men then quickly disappeared into the crowd. Tala turned, her gaze meeting Nina's.

"If you don't mind, I'd like to look around," Tala said.

Nina smiled. "Of course you do. I'll be over there if you need me," she said as she pointed to a group of women, including Adira Parker.

Tala slipped off the dance, floor and her eyes scanned the room, the clusters of people, the laughter, the music, it was all so intoxicating. She caught a glimpse of the back of Vaughn before he stepped into an elevator with the president.

The Larabee was so impressive, and she wondered why she'd never come before now. Art was something she had little understanding of, and therefore, virtually no appreciation for. The words from the ambassador echoed in her head.

"Tala?" a voice called from behind her.

She stopped mid-step, the all too familiar voice ringing in her ears, and turned. "Keegan?" she asked, unable to mask her surprise at seeing him, of all people, at the party. She could count on one hand how many times she'd seen him in the last year since they broke up.

He smiled as he nodded. "You look beautiful," he said. "I had a feeling I'd run into you tonight. I saw you with the chancellor."

Tala recoiled on the inside. Things may not have worked out between her and Keegan, but he was ten-times the man Vaughn was. "I'll admit that you're one of the last people I thought I'd see tonight," she said.

"I've been promoted in my position. I'm now overseeing an engineering team in ballistics. I actually put together a presentation your brother sat in for. Upper management insisted on representation tonight, and I drew the lucky stick."

"I've only ever known you to be ambitious and enterprising, so I'm glad things have worked out," she said. She gave a glance around the room, catching a glimpse of Nina laughing with a woman in a nearly sheer and shimmering grown.

Keegan let out a chuckle as he slid his hands into his pockets. "Well, I don't want to interrupt your evening. You looked like a woman on a mission just now, but I wanted to seize the opportunity to say hello, tell you look beautiful. Though that was never debatable," he said with a smirk.

Tala smiled. Keegan was a charmer like Vaughn, though always far more genuine. "It was good to see you."

Keegan gave her one last smile, his thin lips pressed together, his eyes sloping as they hung on to her for another moment, then he turned and headed toward the bar. When Tala was certain he wouldn't look back at her, she continued her way across the room.

Casually, she approached an arched doorway that led off from the great hall. The MF agent standing guard was unfamiliar to her, and she gave a quick look around.

"Excuse me," she said in a small voice, hoping she wouldn't be recognized. "There's a man at the bar who is clearly drunk and making a bit of a scene."

The agent's eyes shifted briefly between her and the bar, which was mostly obstructed across the room by the crowd.

"Black tux, brown hair, glasses," she added vaguely when his eyes lingered on her.

Tala's gaze didn't waver. After a moment, the agent nodded, then quickly left his post as he headed through the crowd, and Tala, with one last glimpse over her shoulder, slipped through the archway and into a dimly lit hallway. Out of sight from the hall, she slipped her heels off, knowing they would be loud on the marble floor. Clutching them in her left hand, her right picking up the train of her dress, she set off around a corner and into the darkness. She followed the corridors, winding around corners and passing open doorways to smaller galleries, most too faintly lit to see any of the art in them.

Coming to a staircase, she took a quick peek over her shoulder, then ascended it to the next floor to be met by more corridors. No longer able to hear the party, Tala let herself wander, her bare feet carrying her aimlessly. She came to a large gallery, lit just enough to see the large paintings that lined the walls and hung from partitions throughout the room.

Tala stopped at a painting, unsure of what she was looking at. It was a landscape, which was clear enough, with water in the background and cliffs to the side. She brought her hand to her chin and tilted her head as she studied it in the dim lighting. Clocks. Lifeless, dilapidated clocks, on a table, on a branch. And she screwed up her face in confusion. Taking a breath, she moved to the next painting.

She studied it for a moment, taking in all the pieces of it, the shape of a tall woman, almost skeletal, with thin fabric draped over her, and confusingly, with drawers opening from her leg as if she were a dresser. And bizarrely, in the background was a giraffe on fire.

"Yes, I'm certain that things are set, and we can proceed," an unexpected voice carried through the silence from outside the gallery.

Tala's body stiffened, her eyes widening, and she quickly moved behind one of the partitions to hide herself from the open doorway. She heard the sound of approaching feet shuffling across the floor.

"Has the money been transferred?" a male voice asked. Tala immediately recognized it as President Royer's.

"The first half. The other half once the job's complete."

Tala's breath hitched, and her pulsed quickened. It was a voice she'd know from anywhere, and it sent a chill down her spine. Thias.

"And we're sure there is no chance of someone talking?" the president said in his slow, monotone voice.

She stood frozen. With only a small wall partition separating her from a conversation she was certain she wasn't supposed to be privy to, she was afraid to move even a finger.

"The inmates will all receive their cyanide tablet with the rest of their gear tonight when they convene at the safehouse," Thias said assuredly.

Inmates? Cyanide? Tala took a small breath as she strained to listen harder.

"They'll most likely be killed by MF, but anyone captured is clear on their instructions," said another voice that Tala couldn't quite pinpoint. Chief Justice Murdo, she wondered. She'd just seen him leave the party with Thias.

"And there have been no more issues with their weapons?" Royer asked.

"No, Mr. President," Thias said sternly.

"Your first men acted hastily," Royer said in an eerily calm voice. "Nearly compromising our larger agenda."

"The matter has been taken care of," Thias said.

"Good, good," President Royer said. "Where are we with the trade negotiations?"

"We have officially withdrawn from all talks with DeSoto," Vaughn said firmly. Tala's mouth went suddenly dry. "It's been made clear with our allies that tension is high due to a lack of cooperation from President Pierce. That much is at least true," he added.

"It's imperative that there is no room for misinterpretation. Our action must be considered a reaction and not an instigation," President Royer said, his voice carrying through the quiet gallery.

"Understood, Mr. President," Thias said.

"I'm counting on you, Alexander, to carry this out swiftly and effectively. Now, if you gentlemen will please excuse me, I have guests that shouldn't be neglected," he said.

Their conversation fell quiet, and Tala heard the soft tapping of multiple shoes on the marble floor, footsteps dissipating in the distance.

Minutes passed in silence, and her body relaxed. She breathed a sigh of relief, then stepped out from behind the partition. She turned toward the doorway knowing she had been gone long enough. Any longer and it was likely to be noticed by someone.

"Well?" Vaughn asked suddenly in a hushed voice.

Tala froze mid-step, her chest instantly restricting. Her eyes darted to the open doorway before her, exposing her to anyone who walked past. She quickly dashed back behind the partition, her heart in her throat.

"We've come to an agreement on payment," Thias said matter-of-factly.

Tala's heart raced, and she clasped her hand over her mouth to quiet her breathing.

"Have you disclosed the target to him?" Vaughn asked.

"Not yet. I got word from him just as I was arriving at the party. I'll send him the details from my home computer later tonight," Thias said. "Nothing from my government devices or accounts."

Tala braced herself behind the small wall.

"It's a pity, really," Vaughn said, "after so long."

"I've been preparing for just this for years, and nothing is going to stand in my way," Thias said, his voice deep and serious. "Someone has to be willing to make the tough decisions."

"I agree," Vaughn said. "And what about Tala?"

She inhaled sharply at the mention of her name, straining to hear above the deafening pounding of her heart.

"She'll be safe," Thias said flatly. "I'll make sure of that."

"Good. You're sure she knows nothing?" Vaughn asked.

"She thinks she's the hero. She'll fall in line when the time comes. She always does," Thias said.

"I'll keep that in mind when it comes to our relationship," Vaughn said. "Now, if you don't mind, I've got a lovely date that I would like to get back to."

Thias chuckled. "I told you she'd be good for you. You doubted me. But I told you. I just had to get her out of that damn uniform."

"That certainly helped. I'm not too proud to admit I was wrong." Vaughn laughed, his voice echoing through the quiet gallery, and Tala felt a surge of anger.

Their voices fell quiet, and Tala listened as their footfalls faded away. She sat in silence for several long minutes to be sure they were gone.

Slowly, she stepped out from behind the partition, gripping her heels tightly in her hand, and carefully made her way across the room toward the doorway. She peered around the corner to find the corridor empty, and she exhaled with a sigh of relief. Her bare feet on the cold floor, she set off to find her way back to the party, cautious with every step she took, every corner she came to.

Every turn she made led to more hallways, more gallery rooms, more staircases, but never to the great hall. She began to feel panic setting in as she realized she had been gone far too long. The last thing she needed was to be caught roaming the museum. She doubted she'd get the same impunity as Thias.

Her stomach in knots, she continued to wind her way through the labyrinth of the museum. Then she heard it. The sound of the orchestra. She followed the music, letting it guide her. Echoes of conversation and laughter grew louder, and she soon saw the flicker of the lights from the party as an archway leading back to the hall came into view.

Tala took a deep breath and slipped her heels on, then let herself stumble through the doorway, the MF agent standing nearby grabbing her swiftly and firmly by the arm.

"Miss," the agent said in a harsh, yet quiet tone as not to draw attention to them.

Tala looked up into the familiar eyes of Agent Lexa, whom she'd gone through the academy with.

"Tala?" he asked, his face screwed up in confusion and surprise as he recognized her. "What're you doing?"

"Oh, I uh… I was looking for a bathroom. The ladies was full, and I think I had a little too much champagne," she said with a giggly laugh. "I needed something immediately, if you know what I mean."

He studied her for a moment.

"All is good now," she said assuredly.

Agent Lexa gave her a small smile. "You're going to get me into trouble."

"Well, you can search me if it would make you feel better," she said with a wide grin as she bit the corner of her lip.

"Go on," he said with a tip of his head. "No more champagne for you though."

"Got it. Good to see you," she called over her shoulder as she sauntered back into the hall. She spotted Vaughn across the room, standing with two men she didn't know, and she set off for him.

"There you are," she exclaimed as she came up from behind him and looped her arm through his.

"There *you* are," he asserted as he looked at her. "Please excuse us," he said, waving a finger at the other men. They each nodded before walking off. "Where've you been?" he asked sternly, his eyes meeting hers.

She ran her hand gently across his forearm. "I was in the restroom," she said sheepishly.

"Is everything okay?" he asked impatiently.

She leaned in closer, pressing herself slightly against him. "I'm fine," she said. "Nothing a little water couldn't help."

He frowned, assessing her. Then his eyes softened as his fingers found hers. "I was looking for you."

"Well, here I am," she said with a coy smile. She leaned in closer, then kissed him, letting it go deeper with each passing second until finally, she pulled away.

He smiled as he looked back at her. "Another dance?" he asked with a gleam in his eye.

"Absolutely," she said, and she let him lead her to the dance floor.

It was late, after city curfew, when Vaughn dropped Tala off at her pod, much to his reluctance. She didn't know how much longer she could keep holding him off. She saw his eagerness with every goodbye at the end of the night. She would end it before it came to that.

She was exhausted, her feet sore from the heels, and she let out a small groan as she slipped them off. Her pod was quiet, Mila asleep, and she made her way through the darkness to her bedroom. Flipping on a lamp, she sat on the edge of her bed. Despite her physical exhaustion, her mind was full. Full of the conversations she had overheard. Who was being targeted, and what was Thias keeping her safe from? It made sense that he would be at the center of everything after all. Until now, she'd never let her mind fully go there, but her gut had already known.

There was a small rap on her balcony door, and Tala felt a leap of excitement in her chest as she rose from the bed and went to open it.

There stood Kane, in the darkness, his hands buried in the pockets of his jacket that hung open, unzipped despite the cold. A smile curled on the corner of his mouth as he stepped into the room.

"Wow," he said with wonder in his eyes as they swept over her. "You were gorgeous on the broadcast tonight, but in person… you're breathtaking," he said as he pulled her to him and kissed her, his lips soft and warm. "How was it?"

"Incredible," she said. "But this, this is my favorite part of the night," she said as she reached up and kissed him again, slipping her arms around him. She pressed herself against him and kissed him deeper, pushing away her thoughts and reveling in the brief reprieve from her mind. She would kiss him for as long as either of them could stand it, and then she would let her mind return to the real world.

She leaned into him, and he supported her body against his. In his strong and steady arms, she was safe. She was loved. And there would never be a better place.

She wasn't sure how long she'd kissed him for, but even after they pulled apart, she could taste him on her lips. Then reality came back to her, bulldozing to the front of her mind, and her shoulders slumped. She took a breath.

"Something did happen tonight," she said soberly. All she wanted was to get lost in him, but she had to tell him about the cryptic conversations she'd heard.

"What?" he asked with hesitation as Tala led him to her bed where she took a seat, pulling him down beside her. "Vaughn?" he asked with tension in his jaw.

"No. Not like that anyway," she said, shaking her head. "I overheard a conversation, two actually, and I know I was absolutely not supposed to hear either."

"Okay," he said with uncertainty, his brows knitted together.

Tala told him how she had wandered the museum, the gallery she had roamed through, then launched into a running recital of both conversations she'd overheard. Kane's face hardened as he listened.

When she finished, he turned, his eyes dropping to the floor, and he ran his hand over his head.

"This is serious," he said after a moment.

She nodded. "Very."

He was quiet, and she knew his mind was racing, processing the information.

"You're not going to like what I'm about to suggest," he said, looking up.

"Okay," she said with hesitation as she raised a brow.

"It won't be easy. And it will be risky," he cautioned.

"Out with it," she said.

"You need to get into Thias's home computer," he said.

"Whoa," she gasped as she rose to her feet. "That's next to impossible."

"Do you have any better suggestions? You said you overheard him say he was sending information from his home computer. We need to see what that information is. Then we can decide how to proceed," he said adamantly.

"Kane, you're crazy. His house, it's a fortress. His security measures are high, practically impossible to get around. Technological security is tight. So much so that it supersedes the need for almost all manpower." She took a deep breath and turned away from him. "No. No, it can't be done."

Kane was quiet as he rose from the bed and went to her side, slipping his arms around her from behind and resting his chin on her shoulder. She could feel his breath on the side of her face.

"So, we don't do it then," he said.

She turned toward him, her brows furrowed in confusion. "But," she said with a pause.

"I'm not going to be just another person in your life who tells you what to do," he said firmly. "I won't make you do this. You can walk away from all of it if that's what you want."

Unexpected tears pricked the back of her eyes, and Tala swallowed hard. When, she wondered, did she fall so far away from her brother? If she did this, there was no going back.

She thought of everything up to that point: the men who attacked her, the hidden guns, the fabricated evidence, Mills's death. Suddenly she felt dizzy.

She turned in his arms to face him. "When did I become this person? When did I start challenging everything? When did I become someone who defies orders? What am I even trying to stop… who am I even trying to save? I don't know who I am anymore," she said, her words tumbling out of her mouth, her voice shaking.

"You're Tala," Kane asserted softly. "Uninhibited Tala."

"You," she said gently as her eyes met his, "you helped bring me to this point."

He shook his head. "No, I really didn't. But I did watch you come into your own. You got here by making your own choices. You say you don't know who you are, but you're the one who went back to the docks, you took that gun, you stole that case file. You trusted your gut and didn't blindly follow orders. And not because you're defiant, but because you're loyal to those you love, to your people. The motivation behind all of that, that's what defines you, Tala. That's the real you. And I love you for it," he said. "For who you are, for the person you will become, and I refuse to be another person to tell you who you have to be," he said as he brushed his fingers along the side of her cheek, his eyes soft as they looked into hers.

Tala took a breath as his words settled into her. "You're right. It's my job to find the answers and tell the truth, to protect everyone along the way. This is why I became an agent. If it means that I have to do this, that I have to break into that computer, then that's what I'll do." She shook her head firmly. "I won't walk away now. That's not who I am," she said.

The corner of Kane's mouth curled into a smile, his eyes crinkling. "No, I don't believe it is," he said. He leaned in and kissed her, softly, tenderly.

"This was your bright idea," she said with a small, breathy laugh. "How am I going to do this?"

"Not you. We. You, me, and Max."

She tipped her head to the side. "You really think Max will help?"

He nodded. "Reluctantly and under protest. But yes. We won't be able to do it without him."

"Should I call him?" she asked.

"No. Absolutely not," he said firmly. "We can't leave a trail connecting you two any more than there already is. I'll leave here early in the morning, catch him before he goes to work. You'll meet me at my pod an hour later, leaving your palm pad here. I know how to get an unserviced one and I'll have Max hack it. We'll forward all your calls and messages to that one while yours stays here. Then we'll put together a plan, the three of us," he said.

Feeling suddenly overwhelmed, she let out an uneven breath, then nodded. "Okay," she said. "Okay."

He pulled her to him, burying his face in her hair. "It's going to be okay. Somehow, it will be okay," he said.

Tala was afraid to speak, wanting more than anything to believe that.

"Come," he said, releasing her. He took her by the hand and led her to the center of her bedroom.

"What?" she asked in confusion.

He slipped his arms around her waist. "We're going to dance."

"You know how to dance?" she asked, cocking a brow.

He chuckled. "Nope. But there's no way I'm going to miss this opportunity when you look like this. The world's problems will still be there tomorrow. But tonight, it's just you and I."

Tala took a slow breath, letting herself melt into him as their bodies began to sway to music only they could hear. She closed her eyes, letting the moment swallow her up, consuming her whole.

After a while, she opened her eyes and looked up at him, and she smiled. "Definitely the best part of my entire night."

"Mine too," he said, then he kissed her forehead, his lips lingering on her skin.

An alarm blared loudly from Tala's palm pad, startling her. For a second, her gaze caught Kane's, then she let go of him and crossed the room, snatching the palm pad off her dresser. It was an alert from Command.

Jerez Island prison break. Twenty-six inmates unaccounted for. Reports of MF agent injuries. Standby for further information.

Her heart dropped as she read the message aloud, and then again. She looked up at Kane and knew there was fear in her eyes.

"Inmates," she whispered, recalling the conversation from the museum. "It's begun."

He pressed his mouth in a straight line, his eyes steady on hers, and he gave a small nod.

"What have we gotten ourselves into?" she mumbled under her breath.

Kane pulled her tightly into his arms, and she buried her face in his chest. Her whole life, she had blindly trusted everyone else, and now it was time she trusted herself. She had to get into that computer.

FIFTEEN

Tala wound her way down the busy streets of Oxwick, people everywhere going about their lives, indifferent and unaware of her presence, a hood pulled low to cover her hair. She could've been seen more than a dozen times on the way to Kane's before, but today it felt there was more at stake. She needed to draw as little attention to herself as she could.

She gave the door a hard knock, then waited nervously.

Cars drove by and people passed her on the narrow street outside Kane's, and she was careful not to make eye contact with anyone.

Tala knocked again, harder this time.

It opened, Kane standing in front of her.

"You really think you're less recognizable with your hood up?" he asked in amusement.

"It was worth a shot," she said as she stepped inside, and Kane closed the door behind her.

"Oh, look. It's my favorite person," Max said dryly, looking up from his desk, a bright light suspended above him. "You've created a lot of work for me ever since you entered my life."

"I'm sorry," she said as she screwed up her face. "For what it's worth, I am incredibly grateful," she added.

"Yet you keep asking for more," he said. "However, it does seem like we've got something serious on our hands. Which, let me state for the record, is the only reason I agreed to get involved."

"That's fair," she said as she slipped off her hood.

"You left your palm pad behind?" Max asked.

"Yes," she affirmed. "It's in a drawer in my bed."

Kane handed her a different one, used, a little scratched, a small crack in the screen.

"It's already programed," he said. "Max also managed to hack the service provider, deleting the calls logged between you two."

Tala nodded, never having considered that. For an MF agent, she was very sloppy about her own life. The little things were easy to miss. The little things were the downfall almost every time. "So, are we going to brainstorm? Make a plan?" she asked as she looked between the two of them. "This will be no easy task." Her mind raced over Thias's security system. With Thias away, his security detail Grant would also be away. It was the technology that she had to beat.

"I've already got a plan," Max said. He adjusted his glasses, then combed his shaggy hair back with his fingers.

"It didn't take guy-genius long to come up with an idea," Kane said.

"You're going to have to get into your brother's office. Twice," Max said as he reached for something on his desk.

"Twice?" Tala gasped as she crossed the room toward him. A pit formed deep in her belly. Once was pushing it, but twice made her head hurt.

"First, to plant these little bugs," Max said, holding out his hand to show her three tiny, smaller than the tip of her pinkie finger, bugs. One was milky white, the other two nearly translucent. She could faintly make out threads of wire through their epoxy coating.

"What are they?" she asked.

"They don't look like much," Max said. "But these little babies are going to be our best friends. You'll place them inside the house so that I can access the security system."

"How do they work?" she asked curiously as she peered down at them.

"Well, these two," he said, pointing at the two translucent ones, "are for the digital security panels. One goes on any panel. The other on the security panel outside Thias's office. The transmitter in them will override the main processor, allowing us to override the firewall. Then we'll change the password so we can get in. When the system is overridden, I'll also be able to tap into surveillance in the house and on the estate. When we're done and you're out, Thias will get a notice for a routine security update and be prompted for a new password. He'll have no idea it was because we changed it," he said.

"And this one," he said, pointing to the milky white bug, "is for his interactive desk. Not only will it allow us to override the password, but it will also infect it with a virus, activating the mic in the desk. We'll be able to hear anything said from inside that office. If I had more time, I could get it to also transfer files from the computer, but since we don't know what we're looking for, it doesn't have the capacity to transmit that volume of data.

"Keep in mind, they're small, but not invisible. I'll put an adhesive on the back, but you'll need to place them as inconspicuously as possible," he said.

Tala was impressed, but her stomach churned, and her throat felt tight. This was risky, and she was unsure of herself.

"You make it sound so simple," she said.

"Well, it's anything but. Not only do I have to build these little guys, but I have to program them. But I told you once that there's nothing I can't do when it comes to tech," he said with a small, high-pitched chuckle. "There's a reason I was recruited by the government. You think they take a boy from the sticks and make him a Preferred over minor talent?"

"So, I've got to plant the bugs, then go back and get into his office on my own," she said.

Max nodded. "I haven't worked out the logistics of how you're going to do any of that. I figured I'd leave it up to you," he said. "But for now, you two need to leave me to work on these. By the sound of things, we don't have a ton of time."

Kane and Tala looked at each other.

"Well," he said with a shrug, shuffling his feet. "Anything you want to do?"

"You mean potentially on the last day of my life?" she said with a nervous laugh.

"I won't let anything happen to you," he said firmly.

"You can't promise that," she said soberly. She saw sadness in his eyes.

"Tala…" he started.

"No," she said, putting up her hand. "I don't want to get emotional. Come with me," she said. "We're going somewhere."

"Where?" he asked as he reached for his jacket while they headed toward the door.

"The beach," she said. "Max, call me if something comes up," she called over her shoulder, then stepped into the brisk morning air and pulled her hood back up. It was better than nothing.

On the cusp of winter, it was cold at the beach, the wind blowing hard off the water. The ocean was filled with large swells that crashed loudly as they broke close to shore. Tala clenched her jaw to keep her teeth from chattering and slipped her arm through Kane's.

"Think that's a good idea after your big announcement last night?" he asked as he looked at her, his body stiff.

"There's no one here," she said as she motioned around them, the beach empty except for two people farther down the shoreline, at least half a mile away.

He offered a half-smile and gave her a small kiss on the forehead.

Tala's feet sank into the sand, small grains spilling over the top her shoes, but she didn't care. Instead, she let the wind blow off her hood, her hair whipping freely behind her with each step. Her heart was heavy.

"What's the point of all of this?" she asked quietly after several minutes of silence. Although her voice was carried away on the breeze, she knew Kane heard her.

"The point of what?" he asked.

"Of trying to stop whatever is about to happen. Who am I ultimately protecting? This all started because I was trying to protect the Republic. And now I find out it's the Republic that's at the center of all of it," she said. "I've given everything I have to protect my home, and it's my very country that has turned against me," she said, choking on rising emotion. "More than once too. When I do this," she said firmly, steeling herself, "I can't come back from it. What do I do then? Where do I go?"

"We'll figure that out. Together. I won't leave you," he said, slipping his arm over her shoulders, pulling her closer. Tala felt warmer wedged against him.

"When did Thias become this person? Or is this who he's always been, and I was just too blind to ever see it?" Her ignorance made her feel foolish. From her hunger to be loved by him, she had wholly consumed everything he'd fed her: the truth and the lies. And now, looking back, she wasn't sure which was which.

"You can't fault yourself for believing in your brother and for always hoping for the best when it came to him," he said. "Sure, he's not what you thought, but I'm certain he loves you. In some weird, cold way. He's done too much to keep you safe to make me think otherwise."

She shook her head. "There's too much deceit. That's not love."

"You're aware now. Stronger, braver," he said as he turned to face her.

Tala stopped walking, the cold wind biting her face, and she looked up at him. "I'd have no one without you. You're the only person I trust."

"You have Mila," he said encouragingly.

"But I can't be honest with her about all of this. I'd only be putting her at risk. I could never do that."

There was compassion in his eyes. The way he looked at her made her feel stronger. He looked at her to truly see her, which allowed her to let her guard down, and in doing so, she revealed to herself who she was. She had a fire that burned inside, a need to do what was right. The unknown of what lay ahead terrified her, but it wasn't in her to back down, and so she would do it scared.

She squeezed her eyes shut as she tucked her head down, pressing it into Kane's chest. She wasn't sure what she was stopping or who she hoped to save, but the truth was worth something.

"I know how to get into Thias's office," she said as clarity washed over her, and she took a step back, looking up at him. "I might have a workable plan."

He cocked his head.

"Since he told me about my parents' file, I've kept my distance, and he knows I'm hurt. But if I go to him upset and overwhelmed by the truth, he won't want to have that conversation with Nina around. He'll take me into his office," she said with a nod of her head, wondering why she hadn't thought of it right away.

"Make the call," he said.

Tala didn't care that she was dressed in jeans and a sweater, or that her hair, knotted from the wind at the beach, was pulled into a loose ponytail. Her brother's opinion no longer mattered. There would be no going back after she broke into his office, but there was already no going back. She had uncovered enough of the truth to know she had to find a way to walk away from him. As hard as that would be, it would be harder to stay.

Where would she go, and what would she do? She knew nothing outside of Columbia City. She knew nothing outside of Thias. Fear bubbled up with those thoughts, and her hand trembled as she reached out and gave a loud knock on Thias's door. He had been strong enough to look her in the face and lie, and this was her true test. Could she do the same?

Thias opened the door and gave her a quick look up and down. "No matter how hard I try," he said with a shake of his head, "you still show up in jeans."

Tala looked down at herself and shrugged. "This is what you get."

"Come in," he said with resignation as he moved aside.

Tala stepped into the house, her anxiety coursing through her, and she fingered the small bugs in her pocket. Although she could hear Nina with the kids, they were nowhere to be seen.

"I was surprised to hear from you. You wanted to talk?" he asked as he turned his back to her and headed toward the sofa across the room.

She glanced at the digital security panel on the wall beside the front door. But she hesitated, unsure if it would be the most inconspicuous place to put a bug.

"Mind if I get some water?" she asked as she spied the panel on the side of the kitchen island.

"Help yourself," he called over his shoulder as he pulled out his palm pad.

Tala's heart was racing, pounding in her head, as she made her way to the kitchen, her hands shaking even in her pockets. Carefully, she slid out the first bug, feeling it over in her hand. It was small, smooth, and round. Its translucence would help it blend in.

Thias paid her no attention as she grabbed a glass from the cupboard and filled it with water. She took a deep breath, steeled herself, then rounded the corner of the island. Her eyes carefully trained on him, his back still to her, she sucked in a sharp breath, then she stuck the bug on the side of the panel.

She desperately hoped it wouldn't be spotted by someone: Nina, the kids, the staff. Twenty-four hours. That's all she needed.

She drank the water quickly, then set the empty glass in the sink. Taking a slow breath, shoving her hand back into her pocket for the second bug, she made her way toward Thias.

"Take a seat," he said, looking up from his palm pad. He motioned toward the sofa as she approached.

"Can we go somewhere private?" she asked timidly, feeling the remaining bugs with her fingertips.

"Nina's upstairs. We can talk here," he insisted.

Tala bit hard at the inside of her cheek until she tasted blood. With tears pooling in her eyes, she turned toward him. "It's ju… just…" she said, letting herself trip on her words. "I don't want any of them to see me get emotional," she said quietly.

Thias turned to look at her, sliding his palm pad back into his pocket. He studied her for a moment, his head tilted to the side. Finally, he rose to his feet and gently put his hand on her shoulder. "Let's go to my office," he said. Tala turned away to hide her relief.

She followed behind him, pulling the second bug from her pocket. She stuck it to the very tip of her finger as they wound down the hallway.

She stood closely behind him, and he was careful to stand between her and his digital security panel while he entered his password. The door unlocked with a click, then slid open. As Thias stepped through the doorway, Tala reached over, quickly sticking the bug around the side of the panel, more confident this one wouldn't be so easily seen, then for emphasis, she let out a loud, tearful sniffle.

Thias made his way around the desk and took a seat in his high-back chair. Tala dabbed at her eyes as she reached into her pocket for the last of the bugs, then stuck it to the tip of her finger. She leaned forward, letting the desk hide her hands, and heaved an unsteady sigh.

"So," he said, "you're clearly upset. Let's talk. What's going on?" he asked as he leaned forward, lacing his fingers together and resting his arms on the desk. His face was serious but there was something softer in his eyes.

Tala slouched, letting her shoulders look heavy. She let her eyes fill with tears again as she slowly met his gaze. He wanted her small, he wanted her naïve, it was what made him feel powerful. Like Vaughn, he looked past her. They mistook her for fragile and vulnerable.

"Everything," she said, her words quivering when she spoke, "is coming to a head, the truth about mom and dad. And even you," she whispered.

"I wondered when this moment would come," he said.

"All these years," she continued quietly, timidly, "I've had this idea in my head. And none of it is real." She let a tear fall and quickly wiped it from her cheek. This was a balancing act. She had to be emotional enough for him to listen to her, yet he would be annoyed and impatient with too much hysteria. "And I know," she added, "that you were trying to protect me. I see that now."

"Look," he said coolly, "mom betrayed all of us. And it wasn't easy for me to learn the truth either. Imagine what it was like for me. Royer came to me, to prepare me and ready me for what was to come. Then suddenly, I was in the second highest position in the Republic and all eyes were on me, wondering how I was going to respond. I did what had to be done for our country," he said firmly. "Sometimes we have to find a way to make the tough choices."

"Someone has to be willing to make the tough decisions." His words from the party replayed in her mind.

"I bore the brunt of it for both of us. You just weren't ready for the truth," he said. "You were always sensitive. And the academy may have toughened you up some, but I still see that fifteen-year-old girl who lost her parents. This is what I feared all along," he said. "I didn't want to break you like this, but the truth needed to come out, didn't it?" he said, eyeing her carefully.

A flash of anger flared inside her. It was true that the truth had broken her heart. But it hadn't broken her.

"I'm surprised you're coming to me about this," he said after a moment.

"I'm not legally allowed to discuss this with anyone else," she said, careful to keep the anger out of her tone. "And you are my brother."

"Still, it's nice to know you trust me again," he said.

He thought she was softening to him. And maybe for a brief time she had been. Until the truth had been laid bare before her. Undisputable. Despite the act, she wasn't there to bond with him, to seek his comfort, to forgive him. He was now just a job. Nothing else.

Tala's eyes met his, steel blue, his gaze steady and serious. "I guess I'm just lucky to have someone who will go to such measures with me in mind," she said, the words bitter in her mouth. "Me and the country."

"It's my job to protect all of you," he said.

He saw her as weak. He saw her as someone who needed to be protected and saved, and he believed himself to be that person. He would never change; he believed his own version of the truth too much to ever see anything else. Maybe he loved her, as a brother, but if he did, he loved her for who he wanted her to be and not for who she really was. For too many years, she had looked for her worth in him. But she had searched in vain. Somewhere along the way she had lost him, or he had lost her. The truth now lit up the dark space between them and they were on opposite sides of the battlefield. She felt a sting in her chest as she realized they would never come back together.

Looking at him now, she knew this was as close as they'd ever be. Yet even that moment was built on pretense. There was a time when she had clung to illusions, ideas that things could be different between them. But it was time to let go of those. They were just that, illusions and ideas. It was time to walk away. And yet, she wondered if a part of her would always hang on to him. This was her head at war with her heart.

She slid to the edge of her chair, letting her bottom lip quiver. She took a deep breath, exhaling slowly as she leaned forward and stuck the bug to the side of his desk.

Tala lay in the quiet darkness of her bedroom. She had sent a simple message to Max from the hacked palm pad when she left Thias's to let him know the stage was set, but she couldn't bring herself to talk with anyone. Even Kane. She felt simultaneously overwhelmed and numb. She wasn't sure what was worse, being the deceived or being the deceiver.

A flicker of doubt crept into her mind, and for a moment, she wanted to take it all back, everything. This was a burden like no other. It was heavy on her chest and suffocating her. She felt dizzy. She wasn't strong. She wasn't brave. She had been naïve. She had trusted him because she had loved him; she still loved him. And she wondered if it said more about her that she could love him even after all the lies, or more about him that he could lie to her while claiming to love her.

She took a shaky, deep breath, feeling a warm tear run down the side of her face. She wiped at it, smearing the dampness across her cheek. She was beginning to crack. Her world, everything she had ever known, was falling apart, and she didn't know where to turn next. Aside from Kane, she was alone, standing on the precipice of the unknown, and she feared she would take him down with her. Kane couldn't be her casualty.

She had just found him. Even if it was the only way to protect him, how could she say goodbye? The thought made her ache.

She had to let go of Thias, but was there also a way to let go of Kane if it came to that? Without him, she had nothing. And although she knew it was selfish, she wanted to hold on to him the tightest. He had been nothing to her, then fate brought them together and he suddenly became everything.

She was drowning in an ocean of uncertainty, and yet the stakes were higher than ever before. If failing her mission meant she had to walk away from Kane, then she had no choice but to succeed. She wasn't willing to say goodbye to him. She would find a way. She would find the truth.

SIXTEEN

The bugs Tala planted at Thias's were working exactly as Max had designed. The one on the house security panel had allowed them access to surveillance while the one on Thias's computer activated his mic, transmitting all audio from his office directly to Max's computer.

Kane sat at Max's desk, the volume turned low as he listened in on Thias. He'd been listening for hours and all that he'd overheard other than him tapping away on his computer was an uninteresting conversation between him and Nina.

It was late. Max had gone to bed long ago, and when Kane went to Tala's, he'd found her asleep too. She'd left her balcony door unlocked, but seeing her asleep, listening to her slow and steady breathing, he didn't have the heart to wake her. He hoped she was in a peaceful place. She was no doubt wracked with exhaustion and heartache. She tried to hide it, but it was in her eyes.

All of Thias's lies had planted seeds of doubt in everything she knew. And the problem with half-truths and half-lies was that one could never know which was which.

Tala had given her family the best of her. She loved them fiercely, and for that, her grief ran deep. He feared that all the deceit would harden something in her. They didn't deserve to have that kind of power, she deserved better.

Kane understood betrayal. And even after all these years, he still lived with his hatred for his father. But despite everything, he had still known real love: his mother's adoration, Max's unwavering support, and now Tala. What he felt for her ran the deepest. It seeped into the very fibers of his being. She was his game-changer. She brought something to him that he never could've imagined, and he would never regret loving her so fully.

Hearing nothing but the occasional muffled noises of body movement, a sigh here and there, and still more computer tapping, Kane yawned, stretching his arms above his head, then leaned back in the chair, letting his head fall backward.

Just as he closed his eyes, a loud ringing sounded through the computer. A call coming to Thias's palm pad. Kane sat upright, straightening his body, and glanced at the time. It was after one in the morning.

"Did you get my orders?" Thias asked the unknown caller, his voice tight.

Even Kane, with his unrivaled hearing, could only make out inaudible sounds from the other voice on the phone. He tapped the computer, turning up the volume as loud as it would go.

"Yes, I'm sure," Thias said sternly. His voice was full of edge. "Operation Amazon is a go. The president signed off on the order. We need to deploy all four units to the DeSoto border, as well as two squadrons for air support. We're getting reports of DeSoto nationals as far north as Bristol and as far west as Duram City. And we need to be prepared to close the borders, not just the southern border, but the western as well," he said with authority.

Kane strained to make out anything from the caller.

"No!" Thias barked. "I'm not just talking surveillance. If there's one thing we need out there, it's live bodies. We need to respond swiftly if intel suggests a problem. We will only know victory. At all costs," he asserted. "This conversation is over. Just do your job," Thias spat. Then there was silence.

Kane slumped back in the chair, hearing nothing more than Thias's heavy breathing, then more tapping at the computer.

He was curious, wondering why troops were being deployed to the south. Between this development and the Republic's withdrawal from their trade talks, he was certain something with DeSoto was going to happen. What he couldn't understand was why and how DeSoto could possibly tie into their agenda.

"I know it's late," Thias suddenly said, and Kane perked up once again. Thias was on another call. His voice was low, calmer than it had been with the previous one. "Are we set for the Annual Address?" He paused, and once again, Kane strained to hear the second voice on the call, but it was too muffled to make out anything.

"I couldn't care less about them," Thias said dully. "They're all worthless. Simply a means to an end. We've talked about this," he said with a pause. "It's vital that no one is taken alive. We put down anyone who stands in the way. In forty-eight hours, everything will be different," he said, almost jovially, catching Kane off guard. "Kole has his orders. He'll make sure his agents follow protocol."

Thias went quiet, the inaudible sound of Thias's caller mocking Kane.

"I already told you, she knows nothing," Thias said after a moment. "She will have strict orders. I know her," he said flatly. "She'll follow them."

Kane's breath caught in the back of his throat.

"I've got things to finalize for tomorrow. See you then."

Silence.

Kane's fist flexed. In his gut, he knew Thias was talking about Tala. Dark storm clouds of worry and dread were gathering inside him at the thought of her being mixed up in whatever he was planning. He wouldn't let him take her down. And if ever there was a person to fight for, it was her. If ever there was a time to fight, it was now.

Kane heard the breathy, guttural sound of a chuckle through the speakers, and it made the hair on the back of his neck stand. He wondered how far Thias would go to get what he wanted, and if Tala would be able to go just as far to stop him. He swallowed hard, then reached for Max's palm pad. There was only one way he knew to keep her safe. Without hesitation, he made the call.

Tala gave a hard knock on the door, and a moment later, Max's tired, bleary-eyed face appeared. He looked her up and down, then let out an audible sigh.

"Your uniform again?" he said, his shoulders slumped as he stepped to the side to let her pass. "You're supposed to be inconspicuous. And your palm pad?"

"Sorry," she said as she stepped inside. "Powered off." She pulled it from her pocket to show him the battery separated from the phone. "I have to be to Command in a little bit. But I needed to stop by to see if you got anything from the bugs. Were you able to tap into the central system? I fell asleep last night before I could connect with Kane."

"Yes," Kane said as he appeared, coming up through the floor.

"He was up most of the night listening to your brother in his office," Max said as he wandered into the kitchen, his feet shuffling lazily across the floor. "Apparently, the man doesn't sleep."

Even from across the room, Tala could see he was tired.

"You need to get into that computer. Today. There's no waiting," Kane said.

She could hear the urgency and gravity in his voice. "What did you overhear?"

"A couple of conversations. Troops are being mobilized to the southern border. Some kind of orders to kill detained people. I don't know who, but he made it clear that whoever they are, they're not to be taken alive. And," he said, pausing.

She saw his hesitation.

"And what?" she asked.

"He mentioned having special orders for someone. I'm pretty sure he was talking about you."

Her heart fell. Of course Thias had a place for her in all of it. He'd practically said as much at the museum.

"So," Max said, then popped two Vitality pills into his mouth and took a swig of water. "What's your plan to get into his office?"

Tala's eyes flashed between him and Kane, her mind racing. This had been on her mind all morning. It woke her several times in the night. "I think my only option is to go to his house and time it with when Nina has her weekly hair appointment. She's a creature of habit and likes her indulgences. I have to convince her to then let me stay alone in the house, on the pretense of waiting for Thias to come home."

"Is that really your best idea?" Kane asked. "The whole premise of that has too many holes. Why would Thias come home in the middle of the day? What would you have to talk to him in the middle of your workday about? Would you normally show up unannounced?" he asked, driving his point home. "And this is all assuming she has this appointment."

"Do you have a better idea?" she asked with more attitude than she had intended. "It's not like I can be there when he is. And the only way in is to be invited."

Kane stared quietly at her.

"It might be her only option," Max said quietly. He turned to Tala. "You need someone to let you into the house. And then you need a reason for them to leave you alone. I don't see another way around this. We're out of time," he said bluntly, looking briefly at Kane.

Tala nodded as she looked back at Kane. "He's right. It's now or never. I'll make this work."

Kane said nothing, his lips pursed.

"Hopefully my little toy can help," Max said, walking across the room to his desk where he grabbed a small box and brought it to Tala. "I got this from the technology research lab at work."

He opened it to show a tiny bead attached to a short, thin wire.

"What is it?" she asked, looking up at him.

"It's a comm earpiece," he said casually. "I can hear you and you can hear me."

"Seriously?" she said as she reached for it and carefully set it in the palm of her hand, studying it closely. It was about the size of a pencil eraser, maybe smaller. Nothing like they used at Command.

"It has an adhesive on it and sits just inside your ear canal," he said. "We'll be able to communicate the entire time you're in the house."

"Can the security system pick up its transmission?" she asked.

Max was quiet.

"Hopefully, with Max's access to the security system, we can thwart any alarm or notification before it gets sent out. That is, if it's picked up at all," Kane interjected. "It's a risk we're going to have to take."

Risk. He meant a risk she would have to take. A wave of nausea came over Tala, and she felt lightheaded. She knew she was about to attempt the impossible. What she didn't know was what would happen if she was caught.

"Tala?" Kane asked as he moved to her side.

Slowly, she turned and met his gaze, but when she opened her mouth, nothing came out. She'd done more missions for Militia Forces than she could count. But this was unlike any other. This was against Thias, her director, her brother.

"You okay, Tala?" Max asked. "You're not talking and you're white as a ghost."

She was frozen. Paralyzed. Her chest restricting, choking the air from her lungs. Her racing heart was pounding in her head. It was deafening.

"Tala?" Kane whispered, slipping an arm around her.

She swallowed hard, her gaze dropping to the floor. She was afraid. There was no other way to describe what she was feeling. She was certain this was the first time in her life that something truly terrified her.

She exhaled slowly.

"Tala, look at me," Kane said, his voice low and commanding, and slowly she lifted her eyes to him. His were soft, dark, and familiar.

"You can do this," he said with conviction. "You're braver than you know. You're trained for this. Forget that it's Thias. Just go in there and do what you know how to do."

She gave a small nod, knowing he was right. *Brave.* She wanted to be brave. This was her chance. She told herself she wasn't the small, insignificant woman Thias thought she was, and now was her chance to prove that to herself.

Slowly, she felt herself coming back together, grounded with Kane beside her, and she nodded again, firmly. "Yes," she finally said.

"Here," Max said, his hand outstretched, holding a palm pad even more beat up than the last. "Keep this on you and call me when you're ready. Put in the earpiece, and I'll tap into you. I'll be in your head the whole time," he said gently, kindly. "You won't be alone."

"Okay," she whispered as she looked at him gratefully, then took the palm pad.

"I'll give you two a moment," he said, then turned and briskly walked away, disappearing down the hallway.

Tala looked up at Kane. "What if I can't do this?" she asked, cringing at the tremor in her voice.

"But you can," he said assuredly.

"What if I fail?" she asked.

"Don't think about that. Just focus on what you have to do."

She took a breath. "I'm sorry about last night. I should've come to you."

He shook his head. "No, it's okay. You were asleep when I checked in. I'm glad you got some rest," he said. "You needed it."

"What comes next? I mean, if I pull this off, what happens after that? I don't even know if uncovering the truth will change anything. Where will I go? I have nothing outside this city," she said, hating her desperation.

"We'll figure that out," he said calmly as he ran his fingers down her arm.

She let out a loud sigh, her shoulders slouching forward. "I've got to go," she said quietly, her voice thick. "I've been assigned to a final sweep around Quarry Square. I'll get away this afternoon and go to Thias's. I'll come to you when the job's done."

"Tala," he said as he squared himself to her, grabbing her by the shoulders. "I believe in you. If there is someone who can do this, it's you."

She swallowed hard. "I guess we're going to find out if that's true," she said. She leaned into him, pressing her mouth to his, her lips lingering against his. When she pulled away, she took another deep breath, steeling herself. "I'll see you soon."

Command was busy and alive, teeming with agents brought in from all over the city, and Tala sat quietly at her desk, waiting to receive her orders.

"Ronin," she said, leaning forward to get his attention over the cacophony that filled the rotunda.

He silently looked up at her, his hair flopped to the side, his lips pursed.

"Can we talk?" she asked.

"Depends. Are you going to tell me the truth? You going to tell me who the guy is?" he asked flatly.

Tala was quiet, unsure how to answer. She had already lied so much.

"That's what I thought," he said curtly, then rose from his chair and abruptly walked away.

Her heart sank. She had lied, and he had given up on her. Where did that leave them?

"All right, everyone quiet down," Captain Kole yelled above the noise, and it quickly tapered into silence. "If you've been assigned to Quarry Square, I need you all to make your way to the briefing room. There you will find the details of your team and the building around the park you are responsible for. Each one was evacuated and cleared three days ago, and this is merely a final sweep. Our K-9 units will meet you on scene. Everyone will have a radiation sensor for electromagnetic and nuclear detection. I want every floor cleared," he commanded.

The mass of agents moved toward the hallway, Tala buried in the middle, Ronin just ahead of her. He kept his distance in the briefing room, where they received their detailed assignments. She wasn't surprised to be assigned to the same team as him. After all, they were still partners. But she wasn't familiar with the other four agents she was teamed with, knowing only that they came from Baxtham, just across the Columbia River. Each grabbed their gear and made their way to the parking garage where large vans waited to take them across town.

Though there was a bite in the air, the sun was warm on Tala's face when she climbed out of the van. The breeze was hardly strong enough to shake the leaves in the trees, and she took a deep breath. She watched as a throng of agents spread out, flooding the park, each team heading to their assigned building. It struck Tala as curious that no one was approaching the Prescot building, the tallest of all of them with over fifty floors, looking over the north side of the park, where the stage had already been set up.

"Who's got the Prescot?" she asked the agent beside her as they crossed the grassy park toward the Cambridge building on the east side.

"It's already been cleared," he said.

"When? By who?" she asked as she glanced at it over her shoulder.

"Director Alexander had a special ops team clear it," he said. "Hey, isn't that your brother? You're Tala Alexander," he said with familiarity registering on his face.

Tala nodded. "Yeah, he's my brother," she mumbled.

She caught Ronin's gaze, his look cold and distant. He lingered for a moment, then turned and opened the door to the Cambridge building, holding it for each agent, and Tala tensely passed by him, feeling his eyes on her.

The team divided into three pairs, each pair alternating every third floor. Ronin was quick to choose a different partner, leaving Tala with Agent Willis, a tall, brawny man with a cropped haircut and a neck that nearly disappeared into his shoulders.

"Isn't Ashby your partner?" he asked, his voice deep and throaty as he tapped the hilt of his gun secured in his duty belt.

"He is," she said flatly as she looked away from him. "But a break is nice every now and then."

"Saw you on the broadcast the other night," he said. She could hear the mockery in his voice.

"It was a good party," she said breezily.

"Must be nice, getting to attend things like that. Why even do Militia Forces? It's not something you'd expect to see a princess do," he said with a haughty laugh.

Tala stopped hard in her tracks and turned toward him. "I'm not a damn princess. And I do this job because I want to. And because I'm good at it. And there's a reason I've got a desk at Command while you sit back in the dusty offices in Baxtham," she snapped. "Now, take the offices on the right side of the hallway, and I'll take the left. Unless, of course, you think you need my help," she said, her eyes meetings his, daring him to challenge her.

Willis's eyes narrowed, and she saw a tic in his neck. "Certainly didn't see this side of you the other night," he said, then turned into a vacant office.

Tala went from office to office, scanning each one thoroughly with her radiation sensor, and by the ninth floor, she was met by the K-9 unit.

"Looks like you've got the meathead," Agent Kay from Command said with a knowing smirk as he nodded through the open door to Agent Willis across the hall.

Tala rolled her eyes. "And he's as dumb as you would imagine."

He laughed, giving the dog a jerk of the leash. "Well," he said, "I've got a lot of floors to finish."

"Hey," Tala called after him as he started to make his way down the hall. He stopped and turned toward her. "The Prescot building, I heard it was cleared by special ops. Do you know anything about that?"

He shrugged. "I heard there might be a security risk, so Director Alexander assembled a special team to go through it. Don't think they found anything. But better to be extra cautious."

"Thanks," she said with a nod.

"No prob," he said, then turned and resumed his direction down the hall, the dog pulling hard on the leash as it led the way.

Tala cleared each office in silence, working quickly while carefully watching the time. After she cleared her final floor, she caught the elevator to the ground level where she was met by Ronin in the lobby.

"Tell me something," he said quietly as she headed for the entrance. She stopped and turned toward him. They were alone. "When did I become someone you lie to? And why is it that you need to lie in the first place? You've changed, and I don't even recognize you anymore. What are you messed up in?" he asked, his eyes full of emotion as he gave his head a shake.

"Have I really changed?" she asked, meeting his gaze, standing up straighter. "Or have you overlooked who I really am? If you think I could be involved in something I shouldn't be, then you didn't know me as well as we both thought," she said.

He was quiet, studying her carefully.

"Whatever," she said with the wave of her hand. "I've got to go." She turned on her heel, and leaving Ronin alone in the lobby, she left the building.

Tala stood outside the gate on the edge of the property, and she could make out Thias's house through the trees, the light breeze catching on her skin, sending a shiver down her spine. This was it. Strangely, it felt as if everything, all her training, all her missions, had been preparing her for just this. She felt her determination alive in her veins, and she wasn't going to back down.

"You there?" she asked after slipping the bead into her ear canal and giving it a small tap.

"I'm here," Max said, as promised, in his usual high-pitched voice.

Every nerve in her body was ablaze with adrenaline. Kane was right, even if it was Thias, it was still just another mission.

She steeled herself as she pulled the hacked palm pad out of her pocket and typed her message to Thias.

I'm at your house. Told you were here. Came to talk.

She hit send. Max was prepared to intercept the message to delay its delivery, just long enough to get Nina to let her into the house. Putting the palm pad back into her pocket, she turned and pressed on the security pad at the entrance of the closed gate. A moment later, Nina's face appeared on the screen.

"Tala?" she said in surprise.

"Can you let me in?" Tala asked calmly, casually.

"Umm, sure," Nina said. The gate buzzed a few seconds later, then slowly began to retract, and Tala made her way on foot up the driveway.

Nina met her at the door, confusion on her face.

"What're you doing here?" she asked.

"I came to talk with Thias. I was told he was home," Tala said.

"No," Nina said with an apprehensive shake of her head, her brows furrowing.

"Oh," Tala said flatly, letting her shoulders drop. "He must be on his way then. I was told he left his office. I sent him a message to let him know I'm here. I just haven't heard back from him yet. Mind if I just wait inside?"

"Umm, okay," Nina said, still confused. "But I don't think he's coming home. It's a busy day for him with the Annual Address tomorrow."

Tala breezed past her and made her way into the quiet house. She was relieved to find Nina alone. "That's just what I was told. I really do need to speak with him. You don't mind if I wait here until I hear back from him, do you?" she asked as she turned, her eyes meeting Nina's. "Hopefully, he'll respond soon."

"I'll message him," Nina said after closing the door. She made her way to the kitchen where she grabbed her palm pad from the counter and quickly sent a message to Thias which, Tala knew, would be delayed because Max was jamming the frequency around the house.

"Can I get you anything?" Nina asked as she shifted her feet.

"Water would be great," Tala said as she took a seat at the counter.

Nina took a bottle from the fridge and handed it to her. Tala opened it, then took a swig, the water cold on her teeth.

"Okay," Max said, his voice playing in her ear. "Sit still for the next sixty seconds. Make only small movements," he instructed, "and I'll put the security footage on a loop."

"I'm surprised," Nina said, "that you aren't busy preparing for tomorrow."

"Oh, I was busy all morning and early this afternoon. I was assigned to a security sweep through one of the buildings around Quarry Square," Tala said, then gave her a small smile as she slowly leaned forward, resting her elbows on the counter.

Nina glanced down at her palm pad. "It's not like him not to respond to me right away," she said as she looked back up.

"I haven't heard from him yet either," she said.

"A few more seconds," Max said.

"Where are the kids?" Tala asked.

"They're about to wrap up school. I'm going to have to go pick them up in a few minutes," she said, glancing down at her palm pad again. "Nanny has an appointment, so I have to drive today. I'm missing my weekly hair appointment. It's rather inconvenient."

"Oh, I can imagine," Tala said, relieved Nina still had a reason to leave.

"Maybe you could come back later? After I've spoken to Thias. I don't think he's on his way home," she insisted.

"I'm sorry, Nina. I hope I'm not putting you out, but it's important that I speak with him," she asserted. "I have no problem waiting here while you run to get the kids. I'd love to see them," she said with a smile.

Nina was quiet as she studied Tala, her deep brown eyes full of hesitation.

"I love seeing those little monsters," Tala added, then let out a chuckle.

"I… I guess that would be fine. I'll keep trying to reach Thias," Nina said. "Just wait here. Cassandra, our housekeeper, should be here soon." Nina's palm pad buzzed, and Tala's body went rigid as Nina glanced down at the screen. "My alarm," she said. "I have to go, but I won't be long."

"You're good," Max said in her ear. "Security is looped."

Tala nodded. "See you soon," she said and gave her a reassuring smile. She pulled her palm pad from her pocket, pretending to busy herself, hoping Nina wouldn't notice the different device in its state of disrepair, unlike her actual palm pad.

Nina turned away from Tala, then headed for the door. A moment later, she was gone.

"Sit tight," Max said. "I'll let you know when you're in the clear."

Tala felt her pulse quicken, and she took a long, slow breath to steady herself. She took another swig of water.

"I've got to let your message to Thias go out," he said. "As soon as she leaves the property, I won't be able to jam her signal without jamming half the block," he said in a hurried breath.

Tala felt heat in her cheeks, and she gave a small nod of her head knowing he was watching her through the security footage. Kane too.

"You're good to go," he said a few seconds later.

Tala shot off the stool and headed across the room, then wound her way down the hallway to the office. When she reached the door, she took a deep breath.

"Password," she said as she stared at the security panel.

"Your birthday," Max said. She could hear the tension in his voice, and she willed herself to breathe while she quickly typed the numbers in.

ACCESS DENIED

The panel blinked red, and her chest tightened. "That didn't work," she snapped.

"Oh boy. Hold on," Max said.

"Hold on?" she repeated incredulously.

"Try it again," he said.

She quickly typed in the numbers for a second time and watched as the panel lit up green, the door sliding open. Tala quickly stepped inside and made her way around the desk, and pulling out Thias's chair, she took a seat.

"Okay. What's next?" she asked as she swiped her hand across the desk surface to wake up the computer. Her heart was beating quicker with every passing moment.

"It's asking for a passcode, right?" he asked.

"Yes," she confirmed

"You need to type in seven zeroes," he said. "There's a failsafe in his system. You will have two separate passcodes to put in or the alarm will trigger, and it'll lock down."

Tala typed frantically on the desk, a second passcode prompting after the first.

"It's your birthday again," Max said.

Tala typed it in and as she pressed *enter*, she held her breath, her body rigid. A second later, she was at Thias's home screen, his files organized in neat rows.

"What am I looking for?" she asked.

"I've no idea!" Max exclaimed. "This was your intel!"

Tala's heart sank. "I don't know either. He failed to mention in the conversation I overheard how he labels the files in his computer!"

"Just tell us what you're looking at," Max said, his voice leveling.

"Everything seems to have a code name," she said. Her body was growing hot all over as she scanned the file names. Her eyes flared when she spotted her father's name, and she tapped the file. It opened to what looked like a scanned document, and she immediately recognized her father's handwriting.

I look at my son and see the future of our great nation, stronger than any that have come before it. The vision of my father inspires me on a daily basis to be the best leader that I can be. People will always be broken, plagued by imperfection, but the Republic of Columbia can hold us all together, can protect us, and lead us into prosperity.

Our leaders are exceptional because they are willing to make the hard choices. It is what sets us apart. They are willing to fight for our credibility, for our place in the world, for our place in history. The Republic of Columbia is the future.

"Tala," Max snapped in her ear, bringing her back. "Tell me what you're looking at."

"I… I think it's a journal entry. Or something. It's my dad's," she said.

"I'm sure it's a great read, but that'll have to be for another day," he said impatiently.

"Right." She closed the file, returning to the home screen. She scanned the files for anything to stand out to her.

"Read them aloud," Max repeated.

"Rawhide, Timberwolf, Palmer, Amazon, Ramrod—"

"Amazon!" Max interrupted. "Kane says Amazon."

Tala tapped the file with her finger, her eyes scanning rapidly through the document.

"They're Militia Forces orders," she said. "Deploying troops to the southern border. Lots of them." Her eyes raced over every line, her heart pounding. She was running out of time. She quickly closed the file.

"You're going to have to guess," Max said. Tala heard the deflation in his voice, and she realized she was going to fail. There just wasn't enough time.

She tapped Timberwolf, her eyes skimming as quickly as her mind could keep up with her. Details of a fighter-flight exercise. She returned to the home screen. She sucked in a deep breath, closing her eyes, steadying her racing heart. When she opened them, she reached her hand out and tapped Ramrod.

The words at the very top caught her attention: *Inmate Roster*.

A row of photos appeared before her eyes, all inmates registered to Jerez Island, their names beside each one.

"I may have found something," she said, her eyes scanning the document. She started counting as she continued to scroll.

Thirty.

"How many inmates escaped from Jerez two days ago?" she asked hurriedly.

"Kane says twenty-six," Max said.

Tala's throat went dry as she approached the end of the photos, suddenly staring at the faces of her four attackers from the warehouse, the four men she and Kane had killed.

A name accompanied each photo, along with a prison release date. She knew immediately that they were not the names that the men had been IDed with by Command after their deaths.

"That makes thirty," she whispered, more to herself than to Max.

"What?"

She was quiet as she read farther down. Every name was listed alphabetically, a long string of numbers beside each one, then followed by a dollar amount.

"Has the money been transferred?"

"The first half. The other half when the job's complete."

"The inmates will all receive their cyanide tablet with the rest of their gear…"

"They're bank accounts," she mumbled. Her mind was buzzing as she continued to scroll, stopping when she came to a map of Quarry Square, red Xs positioned throughout the park, and quickly she began to count.

"Tala, what are you seeing?" Max demanded with impatience in her ear.

"I… I think it's the inmates that escaped. Money transfers to them," she said, still counting.

Thirty.

"You're making no sense," Max said.

"The rest of their gear."

"They'll most likely be killed by MF."

Reality dawned on her. "It's a massacre," she said breathlessly, her heart dropping. "I think they're planning a shooting at the Annual Address tomorrow. The map is right here. The guns…" she stammered, "they were for the inmates that escaped." A wave of nausea came over her as she pictured all those people that would be at the park tomorrow.

"Tala," Max said, "you need to get out of there. Nina will be back anytime," he said anxiously.

Tala ignored his warning and returned to the home screen, scanning it one last time. One word suddenly stood out to her. A name. One from before her time as an agent. And she wasn't even sure how her mind registered it. But there it was. *Palmer.*

With an unsteady finger, she tapped the file.

The document was a single page, her eyes sweeping over it quickly yet carefully. The blood suddenly drained from her body.

"Oh, god," she gasped.

"Tala! You've got to get out of there," Max yelled in her ear. "Someone's there. They entered from a side door. The sensor in the security system just lit up," Max said so rapidly that each word could hardly be distinguished from the next.

Panic filled Tala, the air in her lungs suddenly feeling solid. She quickly closed the file, then swept her hand across the desktop to lock the terminal. She hurried to her feet and carefully slid the chair back into place. Thias would notice if anything was amiss. She bolted to the door, her heart pounding heavily and rapidly, and quickly left the office.

When she heard the door lock behind her, she took a small breath and swiftly began to make her way back down the hallway, back to the great room. As she rounded the corner, she was met by a small, round woman, dressed in gray, a wrap over her head to cover her hair. Tala's heart all but stopped in her chest. Cassandra.

"Miss?" the woman asked with a raised brow, blocking Tala in the hallway.

"Oh," Tala said, steadying her voice. "Mrs. Alexander went to get the kids from school," she said as she shoved her hands in her pockets to keep them from shaking. "I'm just waiting for them to get back."

"Is there something you need?" Cassandra asked as she took a small peek around Tala, glancing down the hallway.

"Oh, no," Tala said with a dismissive wave. "I lost an earring last night when I was here, and so I was just retracing my steps."

Cassandra's face gave nothing away. "If I find it when I clean, I will let the missus know," she said with a gentle nod.

"That would be great," Tala said as she plastered a smile across her face. Her heart rate was just beginning to slow. "It's just a small pearl."

The front door opened, Tala's head jerking to the side, Jax racing into the house in a fit of laughter. Nina appeared after him, Millie on her hip, her head of dark, long hair resting on Nina's shoulder with heavy eyes.

Tala brushed quickly past Cassandra and ran to scoop Jax up into her arms.

"Hi!" she exclaimed. She kissed him on the forehead before putting him back down.

"Everything okay?" Nina asked, glancing between Tala and the housekeeper.

"Look, look," Jax said eagerly as he slipped his backpack off his shoulders.

"What have you got?" Tala asked as she dropped to one knee. She glanced up at Nina, who was studying her intently. "Oh, I was just telling your housekeeper I lost an earring last night when I was with Thias," Tala said, turning back at Jax to avoid Nina's scrutiny.

"An earring? You didn't mention that," Nina said coolly.

It wasn't even a good lie, as she rarely wore jewelry, but it was all she could manage at the moment. "I completely spaced it," she said with a chuckle. "Things have been crazy lately, my mind has a million things on it," she said with a breathy laugh.

"I made this!" Jax announced happily as he pulled a painting from his pack.

"Wow!" Tala said with a wide smile as she pulled him into her arms, pointing her finger at his creation. "That is a great painting."

He smiled proudly.

"I heard back from Thias," Nina said, sleepy Millie still on her hip. "He's been in meetings all day. He is most definitely not coming home until late."

"Oh," Tala said as she looked up at her. "Wonder why my captain said he would be here," she said, screwing up her face.

"He didn't message you?" she asked.

Tala reached for her palm pad, pulling it out of her pocket and seeing that Thias had responded to her. "I guess he did. I was talking to my partner, I didn't even see his message come through," she said with a shrug.

"I know you wanted to see the children," Nina said. "But I really should put Millie down."

"That's fine," Tala said as she stood. "If Thias won't be coming home, I really should get back to Command."

"What is it you came to speak with him about?" Nina asked, her eyes still not leaving Tala.

"It was just a follow-up from our conversation last night," she said.

Nina didn't respond.

"Did he tell you about our conversation?" Tala asked, her smile falling away as she cocked her head to the side.

"No," she said flatly. "He said that was between you two."

Tala gave her a small smile. "Probably best. I'll get going," she said.

"Would you like me to call you a car?" Nina asked, then gave Tala a hesitant smile.

"The subtrain isn't far," Tala said as she put her palm pad back in her pocket.

"You know, it would be easier if you had a car service to rely on," Nina said. "I can't imagine riding in those filthy subtrain cars."

Tala gave her a small laugh. "I'll pass on the car service. I don't mind the subtrain."

"Someday, Tala," she said curtly, "you're going to need to step into your role as an Alexander. And they don't ride the subtrain."

Tala let her eyes meet Nina's. "So I've been told," she said, then pressed her lips together. "I better go," she finally said after a moment.

"I'll make sure your brother gets in touch with you," Nina said as she ran her hand down Millie's back.

"Thank you," Tala said. She leaned down and kissed Jax's head through his thick blond hair. "I'll see you soon, buddy."

He reached out and hugged her leg. "Bye, bye," he said with a squeeze. Tala felt a tug at her heart as she wondered if this truly was goodbye.

Tala felt tears prick the back of her eyes and quickly turned, blinking them away, then headed for the front door, Nina following closely on her heels.

With a glance over her shoulder, Tala forced a smile. "See you soon," she said, then opened the door.

Tala quickly stepped outside, and when the door finally closed, she let out a large exhale. Briskly, she made her way down the driveway, and after leaving the property, she turned to go north, away from the bay, to the nearest subtrain.

Her heart began to pound as she quickened her pace.

"Tala?" Max's voice finally played in her ear.

"I'm here. I'm on my way," she said breathlessly.

"Tala," he asserted, "what else did you find? I know you found something."

Tala took a deep breath. "Yeah, I found something," she said as she looked around. "Not only do I think they're going to open fire on the crowd tomorrow at the address, which, for the record, I think the president is in on, but—" she paused as she slowed her pace and came to a stop, catching her breath. She gave another glance around. Not even a car in sight.

"But what? What else was there?" he asked anxiously.

She closed her eyes and pinched the bridge of her nose. "Thias is going to assassinate President Royer."

SEVENTEEN

Tala sat silently in the back corner of the subtrain, her shock was almost paralyzing, and she struggled to even catch her breath. The words she'd read played back to her in her head, circling round in her brain, yet her mind struggled to catch up. She shuddered, feeling the eyes of other passengers on her, but she kept her gaze averted and withdrew farther into the corner.

Taking a slow, labored breath, Tala pulled her arms around herself. She bit hard at the inside of her cheek, feeling the numbness in her body begin to recede, leaving in its wake palpable grief and anger. Her fury burned through her veins, yet the ache she felt was so deep it spread into her bones.

She was standing on the edge of an abyss with nowhere to go. There were going to be twenty-six men hiding among the crowd at Quarry Square, armed with guns, guns she tried to take away. How would she ever be able to stop all of them? She was just one person. And then there was the president, who was going to be in the sights of the Militia Forces' most notorious sniper: Palmer. Was he even worth saving?

She considered going to the media. But she had no proof of anything. It was state-run, and no one would take her word over Thias's. And an accusation of that magnitude would likely have her dead before she stepped foot out the front doors.

Thias, Royer, even Vaughn, they had all the power and there was no one to hold them accountable. Tala was disposable, even to her brother.

She had trusted him, she had loved him. After her parents' death, she had made him her whole world. After her loss, he'd been her anchor when she was drifting in a storm of pain and loss. But she had been a fool. She had put too much into him, and now she stood to lose it all. There was no way out. There was a time when she would've taken a bullet for him only to now find that he was the one holding the gun all along.

She finally had the truth but no real answers. What she had found was bigger than her. Bigger than anything she could do. She was powerless. She had taken an oath to protect her people, her country, and now she was going to fail them all. She needed an army. The world, as she knew it, was about to crumble.

Tala exited the subtrain, stepping into the cold, the late afternoon sun about to be eclipsed by the buildings around her, and walked the last two blocks to her pod which was empty. Mila wouldn't be home from work for at least an hour. She stepped into her room, and changing out of her uniform, she slipped into a pair of jeans and a fitted t-shirt, then let her hair down. After grabbing her jacket, she made her way down to the street, then set off for the subtrain.

She pulled her hood up and found a seat on the train, keeping her head down and avoided eye contact with everyone around her. She was on edge, uncertain of what would finally push her over.

All this time, it was all the lies that had been wearing her thin, but in the end, it was the truth that broke her. Was it finally time to just let go? To walk away from everything? That thought was almost the hardest one to swallow. When had she become someone who gives up? When had she become someone who didn't try?

A chill ran through her, Thias's face lingering in her mind. It felt like he had become an enemy in only a single moment. But the truth, she now understood, was that he had made himself her enemy long ago. They were now strangers. Strangers with a million memories between them. But strangers no less.

All that was left was to finally decide. Would she stay and fight a battle she was sure to lose, or would she surrender, sure to lose herself?

Going to Max's had become second nature, and she didn't remember actually walking, but she found herself at his door anyway. She reached out and knocked hard. The seconds that ticked by seemed to stand still and she banged a second time, Max's face finally appearing a moment later.

"Hi," he said somberly, and Tala saw the pity in his eyes as he gazed at her through his glasses.

"Don't do that," she snapped.

"Do what?" he asked, affronted as she pushed past him into his pod.

"Look at me like that. Like I've been defeated. Like I'm broken," she said, even though she did feel defeated. She did feel broken. But it was one thing to feel those things for herself, it was another to see the confirmation in someone else.

"Excuse me for thinking you needed a little sympathy right now," he said with a shake of his head as he closed the door and locked it.

Tala stopped and turned toward him. "I'm sorry," she said quietly.

He shrugged his shoulder. "It's fine. Truth is, I didn't know what to say. What do you say when you're looking at betrayal and government conspiracy in the face? This is new territory for me," he said with an uncomfortable smirk, and despite herself, Tala gave him a weak grin.

"Where's Kane?" she asked.

"Here," he said, coming up from his bedroom, his eyes finding hers. He climbed through the hatch and made his way across the room to her.

"What do I do?" she asked, her voice cracking. "I can't save anyone. But I can't stay here and pretend I know nothing. And I have nowhere to go," she said, tears pricking the back of her eyes as she bit on her lip to keep it from trembling.

He reached for her and pulled her into him, wrapping his arms around her. Her face pressed against his solid chest, she took a deep, unsteady breath. He made her feel safe. There was something about being in his arms that seemed to divide her burdens.

"Tell me what you found," he said quietly as he held her.

"It was a money transfer. Palmer," she said, her voice uneven as she recalled what she'd seen. "He was a sniper for the Republic long ago. I… I don't even know his full name. Or if that's his real name. But he's a legend in the MF. Thias paid him a ton of money, and the memo with the instructions was clear. The target is Royer."

"Did it say when?" Max asked with trepidation.

"It was dated for tomorrow. There was a time on the instructions. 1:15 PM. Then it said PB-F32," she said, recalling the document. "I don't know what it means. The address starts tomorrow at one. There will be a short introduction and by 1:15, the president will likely be at the podium."

"Did it say where he would shoot from?" Kane asked, his hand sliding down her arm, and she pulled back.

"No," she said, shaking her head. "There are buildings all around that park. And they've all been cleared. There are armed MF that will be on duty, stationed at all those buildings and in the park all night and tomorrow until the address is over," she said.

"Well, they have to have some kind of plan," Max said.

"You think?" she said as she turned toward him.

"Hey, watch yourself. I've done a lot for you in the last twenty-four hours," he said with furrowed brows.

Tala turned back to Kane. "Tell me what to do," she said desperately.

"What time is it right now?" he asked as he glanced across the room at Max.

"Almost five. Why?"

Kane sighed as he turned back to Tala. "Just wait," he said calmly.

"Wait? What am I waiting for?" she asked.

"The photos of the inmates," he said, "would you be able to ID any of them at the park tomorrow?"

She shook her head. "Probably not. I didn't get to look at them long enough to memorize any details. There were a lot of them. I didn't recognize any of them either. Those men will be dressed to fit in. They're not going to do anything to draw attention to themselves. I don't even know how they plan on getting that many guys with guns into a secured perimeter," she exclaimed, then turned quickly toward Max. "And yes, they've clearly got some kind of plan. I just don't know what."

Max threw his hands in the air, his eyes wide, and Tala turned back to Kane.

"I can't defend anyone against that many shooters," she said quietly, her eyes meeting his. "No one would believe me. I don't know who I would even trust to go to about this. Definitely not Kole. Not even Ronin. I can't protect anyone."

There was a knock on the door, and Tala's body went rigid as her eyes darted across the room at Max, who looked as caught off guard as she was.

"Did someone follow you?" he snapped accusingly.

"Relax, both of you," Kane said as he stepped around Tala toward the door. "I invited him."

"Invited who?" Tala asked as he opened the door to a man, not much older than her, with shoulder-length hair that was bleached and yellow-tinted, with dark roots at the scalp.

Kane stepped aside, and the man sauntered into the room, his eyes meeting Tala's, and he gave a pleased grin.

She adjusted her stance as she studied him, not an air of recognition, and she knew he was studying her just as intently.

"Tala Alexander," he said, his mouth curled into a smile. "Never in a million years did I think this would ever happen."

"What's going on?" she asked as she looked at Kane. "Who is this?"

"Tala, this is—"

"Avery Carver," the man said with a small bow.

Tala's breath hitched as she looked at him, taking him in, his dark, worn jeans, his black hooded sweatshirt, the stud piercing in his chin. She didn't know his face, but she knew his name. "You're a Unified Rebel," she said.

He nodded as he let out a small laugh. "You've heard of me. It's nice to know I've got a good reputation."

"I wouldn't describe it like that," she said. "What's going on?" she demanded as she turned to Kane again. "What's he doing here?"

"I came to talk," Avery said smoothly.

"Talk?" she asked as she looked at him. "I should be arresting you, not talking with you. What're we supposed to talk about?" she asked incredulously. "We're on opposites sides."

"Not as opposite as you think," he said.

She let out a small exhale, uncertainty and unease coursing through her.

"I'm here to talk about how we're going to get you out of the city," he said matter-of-factly. "Out of the country."

Tala looked at Kane with wide eyes, and he gave her a single nod of confirmation. "It's true. That's why he's here. I called him."

"Whoa," she said, her hand coming up in the air. "I'm not going anywhere with him."

"Do you have any better options?" Avery asked.

She stood there silently, glancing between him and Kane. How could he ever think she'd go with a Rebel? This went against everything she knew.

"I don't know all the details of what you've got going on," Avery said calmly, "but I know enough to know you're about to be screwed over by the Republic. And your brother."

Tala remained quiet, her eyes fixed on him.

"And we're willing to get you both out of here, to somewhere safe," he said. "Now, let's sit and chat," he said, striding across the room to the dining table, clearly more comfortable in her presence than she was in his.

Tala stood in stunned silence, and for a moment, she could only look blankly at Kane.

"Is this a conversation I should be a part of?" Max interjected from the kitchen.

"Yes, take a seat," Kane said with a nod toward Max. He slipped his hand onto Tala's back, giving her a small nudge, gently urging her toward the table. "We're all going to have this conversation."

This was all wrong. The UR was an enemy of the Republic, and now she was about to sit at a table with a known Rebel leader.

But Kane trusted him enough to bring him here, she reasoned with herself. And if there was a way out of the country, shouldn't she at least hear him out? But he was a Rebel. Her mind raced with conflicting thoughts.

Tala pulled out a chair and sat, her eyes on Avery, surveying him, taking him in. He didn't look menacing. So many Rebels she'd arrested over the years looked rough and were almost always cocky and defiant. While Avery certainly came across as confident, there was something about him that was… different. She just couldn't pinpoint how.

"You're trying to decide whether or not you can trust me," he said flatly, his gaze holding hers.

"Of course I am," she said.

He gave a small laugh.

"Tell me what you know and what it is that you plan to do about it," she said as she leaned forward, resting her elbows on the table.

"I don't know many details of your situation. And I'd like to keep it that way. I just know that you stumbled into something you weren't supposed to. And whatever it is, it'll make it unsafe for you to be in the city afterward," he said. "You finally see the Republic for what it is. It has betrayed you."

Tala was silent, a knot in the back of her throat.

"Kane contacted me last night telling me your life was in jeopardy. I've worked it out with my superiors, and we've decided it's worth the risk to get you out," he said.

"Who are these people, your superiors? And where would I go?" she asked.

"You can't really expect me to tell you that," he said with a knowing smirk. "Not until after you've committed to the plan. And even then, it will be on a need-to-know basis. This is high risk. For everyone involved."

"First, I have to ask," she said with a pause. "I had a friend who was murdered. And she's been accused of being UR. My partner even confirmed she had ink."

"Mills?" he scoffed. "Oh, no. She wasn't one of us. She was likely just a casualty of whatever this larger plan you've uncovered is. Easier for prisoners to escape when the capable warden is out of the way, I suspect."

"It's bad," she said bluntly. "What's planned. And I won't be able to intervene enough to make any kind of difference. But I won't idly sit by either. I have to do something. Those are my people."

"And I'm here to offer you a chance to truly help your people," Avery said.

Tala's eyes narrowed. "How?" she asked skeptically.

"It's the condition of getting you out."

"I'm listening," she acquiesced, surprising herself.

"We're about more than just wreaking havoc around the Republic and stealing goods. Even though that's all you think of us. We provide for our people. We help financially, we help with food and other resources. We help with health care. And we have a larger vision. But our numbers aren't there yet. We're growing, our reach is expanding even beyond the Republic. But there is fear. Fear of retaliation. Dissidents of the Republic simply disappear and families are left broken. Fear is a real motivator, and it paralyzes people.

It keeps them from taking action. But hope is also a motivator. Hope for safety, opportunity, and for a better life. Those were the principles the Republic was created on, but it has fallen so far away from that. I'm sure this isn't the vision your grandfather had."

Tala gave a slow nod of her head, understanding. "You want a face for your cause. An influencer."

"It wouldn't just be you, of course, but yes," he said, brushing a strand of hair out of his face. "And what better face than one they already know?"

"But who's to say I can create that kind of hope?" she asked.

"People see good in you. Even Thias knows that. Which is why he used you to give that National Statement a while back. He knew your face would assuage people's fear," he asserted. "You, your link to your grandfather, your role as MF, you still represent the ideals of safety, of protection, of the good that people believe in."

Tala drew in a long breath. "What's your ultimate goal? What is it that you need to garner support for?" She leaned back in her chair, folding her arms across her body.

"To bring back the United States," he said, his chin raised.

"Ha!" she exclaimed. "The U.S. has been dead for nearly a hundred years."

But his countenance said he was serious. "It isn't long enough ago that people have forgotten what it stood for. The ideals of democracy aren't dead. People would be allowed to have a voice, and to rise and fall of their own volition.

"The Republic oppresses our people. Everything is state-run," he continued, his voice rising. "Unless you've got some special or unique skill, you never rise above certain classifications. Unless you're a criminal, you stay where you're born."

"A caste system," she said as she glanced at Kane.

"You know nothing but privilege, Tala. And I don't say that to be condescending. We're all born into something. But take Kane here," he said with a nod in his direction. "He lives in the shadows, hiding away. He has no opportunity to ever become anything else. Surely you want more for him."

She felt heat creep into her cheeks, her freedoms and opportunities because of her name and citizenship suddenly feeling conspicuous. Kane was everything to her, and the injustices against him went beyond the experiments done to him.

She had put her faith in her country, believing in its ideals and what it stood for. But now, she realized, a nation was simply just a label, and it was always going to only ever be as good or bad, as strong or weak, as those who led it. What was about to happen wasn't the Republic she had been taught to believe in. It was corrupt and unjust. A country that could plan the massacre of its own people, for reasons she had yet to understand, was broken at its core. Her people deserved better.

"You wanted the truth," Avery said. "You couldn't expect it to be simple. It rarely ever is. Now you must decide what to do with it. Alone, you won't make any kind of difference. From the little that I do know about your situation, I'm certain Thias won't hesitate to take you down if you intervene. I can't help you tomorrow. But I'm giving you the chance for us to fight together, for the bigger picture, to help bring about the change that I think you want. I'm sure you have a thousand reasons to just walk away, to not join us. But I dare you to have a thousand and one reasons to want to make a difference. This is your chance to truly be for your people."

She sighed, her shoulders falling, cracking and fracturing under the weight of the world. Was Avery right? Was this her only chance to do right by her people? But to go with the Rebels would be to swim against the current of her life and all that she'd believed.

"You said you could get us both out?" she asked as she glanced at Kane sitting silently beside her, a somber, pensive look on his face.

"That's right," Avery said, leaning in, his arms on the table. "My superiors agreed to both of you."

"You'd come with me?" she asked. She suddenly felt torn between a rush of relief and a fear of the danger she would inadvertently put him in.

"I won't leave you," he said seriously, his jaw set in a hard line. There was something in the way his eyes fixed on her that said he wouldn't be swayed in his decision. And as wrong as it might be, she knew she wouldn't be able to leave him.

"Where would we go?" she asked, looking back at Avery.

"The Central Colonies. Though I can't say where. But you'll be safe there," he said. "I'll be straight with you though, it's going to be dangerous. And it won't be easy. But if there's anyone who can do it, it's us."

"What if the borders close?" Kane asked. "Thias is deploying troops to the south. He mentioned closing both the southern and western borders."

"That will certainly make things more difficult," Avery said, though he didn't seem fazed with the possibility.

"What if we went north, through the Great Lakes Federation?" Tala asked.

"Not a chance," Avery said, sitting back in his chair. "We don't have routes through there. We don't have the connections there that we do in the Republic. And if we were ever found, we'd be sent straight back to the Republic, into the very hands we're trying to escape. As dangerous as this is, it would be ten times worse to go north."

Tala's head was beginning to throb. "What about Max?"

"I can't go with," Max said quietly, speaking for the first time since they'd all sat down. "Though I'm flattered you thought of me. Getting the two of you out will be hard enough. No one's looking for me," he said. "And I'm already inside the government. I can be an asset from here."

Avery nodded. "And we're prepared to provide protection for him."

She needed to decide. She had to be all in or all out. There was no halfway. Was she strong enough to walk away? Was she strong enough to let go, to go with the people she had been taught to hate?

"When would we leave?" she asked.

"Day after tomorrow. I can't give you details though."

She nodded in understanding.

"Do I have to decide right now?" she asked as she brought her fingers to her temples.

"You have until seven tomorrow night. Kane knows how to contact me. Then you'll have to be to our safehouse by the next morning so that we can execute the plan we're putting together."

"Okay. I got it," she said with a nod.

With their conversation over, Avery didn't linger, leaving Tala with just Kane and Max. Her heart felt heavy as she looked at them both. For years, Max was all that Kane had, and now she was going to separate them.

"There are no right answers," she said quietly into the deafening silence among the three of them. "I stay… I go… it all comes at a price."

"I think what it comes down to is, in the end, which option is worth that cost," Max said.

"I can't simply do nothing," she affirmed, mostly to herself. "If Royer dies, as second in command, Thias would become president. That's how the system is structured. His son, Alec, isn't old enough to succeed him. And as horrible as Royer is, Thias will only be worse. I can't let that happen."

The Republic of Columbia was her home, the one she had sworn to protect. President Royer's choices reflected his character, and despite everything, she couldn't let him be murdered because that was a reflection of her character. If she could protect even one life, then she will have honored the oath she had taken.

♦♦♦

Tala stayed at Kane's until after dark, then the two set off for Stoughbour, to her pod. As she made her way to the subtrain, the hacked palm pad she was still carrying buzzed, and she pulled it from her pocket to see it was Vaughn calling her. He was one of the last people she wanted to talk to, and she quickly dismissed the call.

She hadn't decided to go with the Rebels, but she hadn't decided against it either. Either way, she knew it would be important to have things in order if she had to leave at a moment's notice. Although she still didn't know where she would go. She was likely to be recognized anywhere.

To avoid being seen together, Kane walked in strides half a block behind Tala and rode in a separate subtrain car. Despite the little impact she knew she would make tomorrow, she felt a little more resolved in having made a decision to act. On the way to Kane's, she had only felt broken. But like a bone in the body, maybe she would emerge stronger in the places where she had been broken. She felt her determination taking root somewhere deep inside, fortifying her for what was to come.

The palm pad buzzed in her pocket again as she emerged from the subtrain platform, and her pulse quickened at the sight of Thias on the cracked screen. This was a call she knew she had to take. She braced herself. Declining the video option, she selected audio and answered.

"Hi," she said, trying to keep her voice level.

"I messaged you earlier. You never responded," he said. She realized suddenly that he was right. First, he'd messaged that he wasn't going to be home that afternoon, then again shortly after she left his house, and she'd forgotten to respond both times.

"What did you come over for? And why would you think I'd be home in the middle of the day?" he asked, his voice was loud and tight. Despite the crowd around her, the traffic whirring by, she had no difficulty hearing him.

Hearing his voice, surprisingly, her nervousness began to slip away. She no longer owed him anything. Yesterday, he had been her brother. But today, everything different.

"I had a few more questions about mom, but they don't matter anymore. None of it matters anymore" she said simply, evading part of his questions. She felt her heart pulling away.

"Are you okay?" he asked.

"I'm just tired," she said, which was the truth. She couldn't remember another time in her life when she'd been so incredibly exhausted.

"Has Captain Kole given you your orders for tomorrow?" he asked.

"No."

"I've assigned you to the south side of Quarry Square."

"Why? That's nowhere near the event. My team will be on the west entrance."

"We need security around the entire perimeter, the south side included. That's where I want you."

"Just me? This seems like a punishment," she said, hearing the bite in her tone. "Do you not think I'm capable of crowd control and security?"

"This is an order, Tala. And not from your brother but your director. I'm merely giving you a courtesy heads up," he said sharply.

"Of course," she said quietly. "I've got to go. Tomorrow will be a long day."

"But it'll be a good day," he said with unmistakable pleasure in his voice.

A chill ran through her body, and she quickly tapped the screen and ended the call. She paused on the sidewalk, coming to a stop in the middle of the crowd. People paid her no attention as they moved around her, all oblivious to what was coming. She envied their ignorance. She wanted only one minute's reprieve, a break from the heaviness bearing down on her and the chaotic thoughts that consumed her mind.

With her building just ahead, Tala resumed her walk, slowly, in no hurry. Things were about to get out of control, her life about to implode, and she was going to seize every moment of calm before the wave hit.

"Tala!" a voice boomed through the night. She looked up to see Vaughn leaning against the side of his sedan, dressed sharply in a navy suit. He smiled as he approached her, kissing her lightly on her lips. She took a small step back to put some distance between them.

"What're you doing here?" she asked, not hiding her surprise.

"I just tried calling you. I came to see you," he said with a laugh. "I know I've been busy, but I haven't heard from you since the party, and I just couldn't go another day without seeing your beautiful face. How perfect to find you just now."

Tala pressed her lips together, frowning.

"Let's go out. Dinner, drinks, whatever you want. I'll give you time to change, slip into something beautiful. But let's do something," he said eagerly as he reached out and brushed his thumb across her cheek.

"Not tonight."

"What?" he said with exasperation, his brow furrowing.

"I'm going to stay in tonight," she said. She wasn't about to spend her last night of freedom putting on an act with him. The only person she wanted to be with was Kane, and she felt a tug at her heart knowing he was somewhere in the background watching this encounter.

"Well, then let's go to my place," he said as he took a step closer, closing the gap she had put between them. He reached up, sliding his fingers into her hair, and she suppressed a shudder. "Or we can stay here, I'm okay with that too."

She shook her head and pulled his hand away. "Not tonight," she said steadily as she retreated from him again.

He looked chastened, his jaw clenching, and she saw a flash of fury in his eyes. All at once, he lost his dash of handsomeness and charisma. "You're turning me down?" he asked incredulously.

"Sorry," she said without contrition.

"Wow," he said as he ran his fingers through his hair. "I'm not even sure what to say."

"Good night, Vaughn," she said, then turned on her heel and headed for the doors of her building. She felt his angry eyes on her as she walked away. But like with Thias, she just didn't care.

"Hi," Tala said with surprise when she saw Mila standing in the living room, a suitcase on the floor beside her.

"Oh, I'm so glad I didn't miss you!" she said with her usual bubbly smile, a sparkle of happiness in her eyes that Tala envied.

Tala glanced around the room, then back to Mila. "Where're you going?" she asked.

"To my parents'. My dad managed tickets to the Annual Address tomorrow, and I'm so excited to go. I've never seen President Royer in person before. Unlike other people who dine at his table," she said with a small laugh. She fingered the ends of a long strand of hair hanging past her shoulders.

"No," she said firmly. The color drained from her face. "You can't do that."

"Go to the address?" Mila asked, a look of confusion crossing over her. "Why not?"

Tala's mind raced for something to say. "It's just… just…" she stumbled over her words. "There're going to be more people there tomorrow than previous years. It's going to be a giant congested mess. It won't be any fun," she added. "I know how your family loves to just pop popcorn and sit around the TV together and watch it. That will be so much more fun, I promise," she asserted. If something ever happened to Mila, she could never live with herself. The idea of it opened a pit in her stomach.

"Besides," Tala said, "there are some security concerns."

"Really?" she asked, taken aback, worry instantly filling her eyes.

"Oh, I'm sure it'll be fine," she said calmly. "But it's credible enough that they're bringing in more agents." Tala recoiled at her words. Now she was lying to Mila. It never stopped.

"I don't understand," Mila said, a crease in her forehead as she shuffled on her feet. "Why would they ever risk letting the president out in public if there was a credible threat against him?"

"It's being handled. Just promise me you won't go. It's not worth it."

"Umm, okay," she said, her mouth turning down in disappointment. "If it means that much to you."

"It does," Tala said, nodding eagerly in relief. "It really does."

"Well, then," Mila said, the smile now gone from her face. "You stay safe tomorrow."

"I will," Tala said. Then she lurched forward, throwing her arms around Mila, hugging her tightly, a sting in her chest. "You're my best friend," she whispered, tears that she couldn't control pooling in her eyes.

Mila wrapped her arms around her, hugging her back. "Are you okay?" she asked as Tala buried her face into Mila's thick, brown locks. She fought to blink the tears away.

"I just needed you to know that," she said, then finally pulled away.

"No really, Tala," she said, her gaze on her, her eyes filled with concern. "Are you okay?"

Tala nodded, swallowing her emotion. "I just don't tell you that enough," she said with a small grin as she wiped at her eyes, not giving her tears the chance to break free.

"Well," Mila said with a smile, "for what it's worth, you're my best friend too."

With a heavy heart, Kane sat on Tala's bed, watching in silence as she stuffed her belongings into a duffel. There were little memorabilia. A photo that she took out of a frame of her and Mila and a second of her and Ronin. A pair of pearl earrings from a small jewelry box.

He hated that he couldn't fix this for her.

He watched her movements. She was grace. He studied her face, serene, but not hardened. There was fear inside her, but he knew the lion of her determination roared louder. He looked at her with wonder in his eyes. The storm brewed around her, yet she remained a pillar of strength that would not bend. In the face of evil, she remained uncompromised. She was a quiet warrior, carefully choosing her battles, and when she was called upon, she would fight.

She was about to put everything on the line, and he was afraid. He'd never been one to be scared of what lurked in the shadows. But in this moment, he was filled with dread.

Giving in and giving up wasn't in her nature. It wasn't who she was, and he loved her for that. But the thought of losing her took the very breath from his lungs.

She finished packing, zipping the bag shut, then tossed it to the side. Turning toward him, her eyes met his gaze, and he felt his heart skip a beat. He reached his hand out to her.

She went to him, lacing her fingers through his as she sat across his lap, their faces only inches apart.

Gently, he ran the tips of his fingers along her hairline and down her face and gave her a small smile.

"What're you thinking?" he asked quietly, his voice low and raspy.

"A little bit of everything," she said with a sad smile. "I can't help but think I've created my own heartbreak."

"You can't blame yourself for wanting love and truth from your own family. You expected in return what you so willingly gave to them," he said.

"Maybe," she said, her gaze dropping from his, her shoulders falling forward.

The pained expression on her face was enough to break his heart. He hated his powerlessness. All he knew to do was to hold her in his arms, tell her she could do this, and wish like hell she would be safe.

He knew for certain that holding on to Thias would break her heart, over and over again. But even if she found a way to let go, he wondered if a part of her would grieve him forever.

"I don't want to think about this right now," she said, lifting her chin, her eyes meeting his once again. They were arresting and disarming. "What will be will be. I can't change any of it. I'll just have to take it as it comes. I don't know what tomorrow will bring," she said quietly, and he saw the look of something different pass over her. "I just want this night to be about us," she said. She leaned into him, pressing her lips gently against his. They were sweet and soft, and he craved her like oxygen.

"I want to give you everything I have," she whispered against his mouth.

She stirred his very soul. She was the beginning and the end, and he wanted nothing more than to lose himself in her. His arms slipped around her, and he pulled her into him, then he kissed her with a fervor that shook his body to the very core.

EIGHTEEN

With Kane beside her, Tala breathlessly wound her way through the streets around Quarry Square. She'd long since left her post knowing the assignment was futile. It was an unusually warm day, the sun high in a cloudless sky, and perspiration was building beneath the neckline of her frag jacket.

There were people everywhere, the swollen crowd moving like liquid through the streets and avenues, everyone trying to get through security into the park, and Tala was constantly looking over her shoulder to make sure she hadn't lost Kane.

The stage where the president would make his address came into view, flagpoles lining the back, creating a colorful backdrop. The breeze was just strong enough to lift the flags, their fabric flapping freely, their emblems waving for all to see.

Tala stopped at the northwest security perimeter and watched as people filed, one-by-one, through security checkpoints, where their IDs were checked, and they walked through body scanners. There was no way to tell who was there with murder on their mind. She still wasn't sure how twenty-six men were going to make it past all the MF in the first place, but Thias would have a meticulous plan for just that. Her eyes scanned the perimeter of the park, moving from one towering building surrounding them to the next, and the thousands of windows that overlooked them. Militia Forces agents were positioned at every entrance to each building. The K-9 units roamed randomly through the crowd, and although she couldn't see them, she knew there were snipers hidden somewhere with a bird's eye view below.

"Tala," Kane said above the noise of the crowd. "You're not going to be able to stop anything unless we figure out where *he's* going to be." He was guarded with his words. The last thing they needed was for panic to ensue by mentioning a shooter. She heard the tension in his voice, feeling it herself throughout her body.

Tala's eyes continued to roam frantically over each building, but there were just too many possibilities. She glanced at the time on her palm pad. They had exactly ten minutes before the address would begin, and her mind spun like a whirling dervish. She closed her eyes and took a deep breath to orient herself, bringing her hands to her temples as she sorted through the information she had. She got one shot at this.

The crowd was loud, the sounds of feet shuffling across the pavement, laughter and conversation deafening, the wailing of a child not far away.

Tala reached out to Kane, grabbing hold of his arm, grounding herself. Her mind replayed the images from Thias's computer on a loop. Patiently, she let her mind comb through the files, trusting that something would catch her attention. She was homing in on her training, waiting for the smallest detail to stand out from the rest.

"The Prescot building," she said finally as she opened her eyes and glanced up at Kane. They both turned toward the looming building to the north.

"Why that one?" he asked.

"It was cleared by special ops under orders from Thias," she said, not knowing why she hadn't thought of it until now. The answer seemed so clear. "PB-F32," she repeated, the image staring glaringly back at her in her mind. "Thirty-second floor?"

"What if you're wrong?" he asked.

"Then we're no better off than we are now. But it's my best guess. And that's better than no guess," she said as she reached for his hand, pulling him through the crowd toward the Prescot. Going against the flow, people pushed and shoved, and they quickly became stagnant with nowhere to move. She glanced over her shoulder at Kane, seeing the worry in his eyes.

"Militia Forces coming through!" she yelled above the cacophony of the crowd. The faces around her turned in her direction, and people inched closer together to create a pathway. Tala continued to call out as she pushed through the mass, bumping into people, stepping on feet as she forged on. Kane stayed on her heels, and they eventually stumbled out of the throng and onto the sidewalk in front of the Prescot building as it cast a shadow over the stage.

Two agents stood on alert, flanking the front doors, their plasma guns in their hands rather than holstered in their duty belts. From her position, Tala could see a third agent blocking a side door and knew there was likely a fourth agent on the other side of the building and a fifth along the back.

"I think we need to split up," Kane said.

Tala's head snapped in his direction. "Split up?"

He nodded. "I'm going to try to get to Royer and you can go after the sniper," he said. "Maybe, just maybe, if we both come at this from each end, one of us will be successful."

"Kane, you can't use your—"

"I won't," he interrupted quickly. "Take Ronin for backup. I'll manage on my own."

"Ronin?" she asked, screwing up her face.

Kane turned, pointing to their left, and Tala spotted him, less than fifty yards from them, directing the crowd toward the security checkpoints.

"He won't come with me," she said as she turned back to Kane.

"Make him. I don't want you in that building alone. I know you're more than capable, but you don't know what you're walking into," he said flatly, his jaw set in a hard line. "Come with me," he called over his shoulder as he took off in a light jog around the side of the building, and Tala followed after him.

Together, they stood behind a row of high, manicured shrubs, keeping them out of sight from the agents. Through a small gap in the greenery, Tala spotted the fifth MF pacing along the back of the building, just as she suspected. At least they were predictable.

"I can subdue him," Kane said. "I need a restraint cuff."

Tala quickly reached into her cargo pocket and pulled out the reinforced plastic band and handed it to him.

"What're you going to do?" she asked.

"Choke out," he said matter-of-factly. "I'll cuff him and get him away from the building. But you won't have more than three or four minutes before he regains consciousness and tries to make his way back here to report the breach," he said.

"And what about you?" Her heart was pounding wildly in her chest knowing their moment was fast approaching.

"I can move quickly, remember?" he said with a smirk. "I'll get him far enough away, then look for the president."

"He'll be heavily guarded," she said in protest. She didn't want him to leave her. They were in this together.

He nodded. "Tala, I've got to try."

"I know," she said sadly, understanding better than anyone why he needed to at least try.

"Well, here goes," he said, his eyes lingering on hers.

Tala stood solemnly beside him, not wanting to be the first to walk away.

"Get Ronin and get into that building," he said after a moment.

"And you, don't be seen," she said. Her heart was heavy as she looked up at him, trying to memorize everything about him: the glare of the sun on his shaven head, his thick brows that came to a small point along the top, his wide nose, his deep, dark eyes that she often found herself lost in, the black scruff along his jaw, over his chin and around his mouth. She felt herself choking up and swallowed hard to push away her emotions. She couldn't think about the worst. She had to keep the mission in the forefront of her mind, or she knew she'd fall apart.

"We meet back at Max's."

Tala gave a knowing nod and took in a long breath. "Okay," she said, and before she could talk herself out of it, she turned to find Ronin.

"Tala, wait!" Kane yelled as he reached for her arm. She spun around quickly, face-to-face with him. She could feel his breath on her face, her heart hammering in her chest. "I love you," he whispered, then lowered his head and pressed his mouth to hers.

She kissed him back, pushing every ounce of her fervor into it. A moment later, a moment too soon, he pulled back, and she saw his distress.

"I love you too," she whispered, her voice hardly audible. Her emotion rising, she turned away. She had to go now or she feared she wouldn't go at all. With a glance over her shoulder, he was gone.

Tala jogged down the sidewalk, pushing people aside as she hurried toward Ronin, her heart in her throat.

"Ronin," she called out to him, and he turned toward her, a stern look on his face. "I need your help," she said breathlessly.

"No," he said flatly and looked away.

"You can be mad at me all you want, but this is important, and I need your help," she pleaded.

"What're you talking about? Don't you have orders to be on the other side of the park?" he asked.

She let out a grunt of frustration as she grabbed him by the arm and tugged hard, pulling him off the edge of the curb.

"What the hell?" he snapped as he jerked his arm free.

"I don't have time to argue with you," she said, her eyes meeting his. "There's a sniper. They're going to shoot Royer," she said quietly, leaning into him.

"What?" he asked, his face scrunching up.

"You have to believe me," she said, hearing her desperation. "I swear to you on every good memory we have. If our friendship ever meant anything to you, you'll come with me. Now," she urged.

He was quiet as he studied her, but there was no time, and she took his silence as a yes. She reached for his arm once more, tugging him hard, and this time his body responded. While she jogged briskly toward the Prescot building, he flanked her on the right.

They rounded the back of the building, the agent now gone, and she rushed to the door.

"How do you know this?" Ronin asked. She slipped inside the ajar door, likely thanks to Kane, with him right behind her.

"I broke into Thias's computer," she said as she withdrew her gun from her duty belt. "The elevator," she said, spying it just ahead.

"You broke into his computer?" he asked incredulously. "What does Thias have to do with any of this?"

"He has everything to do with this." She tapped the button on the wall, the elevator doors opening, and she rushed inside, Ronin following her. "We'll take this to the thirty-first floor, then the stairs to the thirty-second," she said. The elevator gave a small jerk, then began to hum as they slowly climbed each floor of the building.

"You know where the shooter is?" he asked.

Her eyes met his, and she gave a slight shake of her head. "I don't know with any certainty. This is my best guess," she admitted.

"And what if you're wrong?"

She quietly pressed her lips together and gave a small shrug of her shoulders.

"So help me, Tala, if you're lying to me," he said harshly.

"I'm not lying to you!" she asserted. She took a breath. "And yes," she said, her eyes meeting his, "it was the same man you saw both times. And yes, I know him." There was an immediate relief in her chest as she said the words aloud. For once, it was the truth coming off her tongue. But she couldn't help but think it would be too little too late.

His eyes narrowed as he looked at her.

"I'm in love with him."

Ronin was quiet, but the anger in his eyes seemed to ebb. A moment later, the elevator came to a stop, the door dinging as it opened. She broke his gaze, cautiously stepping out of it, her gun drawn in front of her.

They stepped into a vacant hallway, and Tala looked around for the stairs.

"The end of the hall. To the left," Ronin said quietly, pointing with the tip of his gun.

Together, they set off in a brisk jog, mindful of every office they passed. The stairwell echoed their every sound as they gingerly made their way higher and higher. Tala's heart raced, tension throughout her body. With her adrenaline coursing through her veins, she focused on her breathing.

On the landing outside the door on the thirty-second floor, Ronin gave a small nod, then swiftly pulled the door open. It squealed loudly, metal on metal, and she cringed.

Alert, her heart pounding, she carefully stepped into the hallway, her head on a swivel as she looked in both directions. One hall led to the west, the other to the south. With the stage on the south side of the building, Tala turned right, Ronin falling in stride on her heels. Her heart skipped a beat at every office door they approached, her stomach in her throat as she peered inside.

Even through closed windows, Tala could hear the roar of the crowd below as a woman's voice rang loudly through the microphone, and Tala's chest tightened. They were running out of time. Her eyes caught Ronin's, his unease mirroring hers.

They continued down the hallway, cautious with every step they took, moving along in unison like they always had on any other mission.

Just ahead, Tala heard a faint thud, and she glanced over her shoulder at Ronin. He nodded to confirm he'd heard it too. As quietly as her feet would take her, she peered into the next office, finding it vacant except for a single man, his back to the door and a bolt action rifle in his hands. Palmer. He stood in front of a wall of windows that overlooked Quarry Square, and Tala spied the small circle cut out of the glass windowpane.

"Don't move," she called out steadily to him, lifting her gun and pointing it at him.

He paused, then slowly turned on his heel, the gun in one hand, ammo in the other, and the corner of his mouth curled up into a menacing smile as he looked back at her.

"Put the gun down," Ronin demanded loudly as he stepped ahead of Tala into the room, his gun also aimed at him.

Palmer was silent, unmoving, his smile making the hair on the back of Tala's neck stand. In the distance, she could still hear the woman's voice over the hum of the crowd below.

"I gave you an order," Ronin said, his voice echoing throughout the vacant office.

Tala stepped farther inside and slowly advanced toward to the sniper. "Put it down," she commanded. "I will shoot."

"No, you won't," a voice called through an open door on the left side of the room. She'd know that voice from anywhere, and her heart stopped, an icy chill running through her.

Thias appeared before her from an adjacent office with two guns, a handgun in one hand, a plasma gun in the other.

"Thias?" she gasped, nearly tripping over his name. She turned, pointing her gun at him.

"I had a feeling I'd see you this afternoon," he said, his voice deep and steady and spiteful. "I found this," he said as he turned his hand over, one of the small bugs stuck to the tip of his finger, and she swallowed hard, her mouth going dry. "And I knew you'd been in my office. That whole story you concocted yesterday when you showed up at my house," he said, taking small steps toward her. He aimed one gun at Ronin, the other at her. "What I don't know is who you've been working with. Because these bugs, I know you didn't make them. I'm guessing it's the same person who helped you hack that server."

Tala's hands quivered, the tip of her gun shaking, and she bit the inside of her cheek until she tasted blood. Beyond the windows, she heard cheers from the crowd. "Why are you doing this?" she asked. She could see Ronin from the corner of her eye, his gun still on Palmer.

"Why?" Thias spat. "Because my country *needs* me. My people need a leader who is willing to make the tough choices. Royer is weak, and the Republic will always be weak with him in power. I'm doing this for my country. I'm doing this for you," he said, a cunning smile on his face. "We have our family honor to uphold. Mom and her choice to commit treason put a stain on our name, and I intend to right her wrongs. I'm protecting you. Everything I've ever done was to protect you, to protect the Republic."

"No!" she yelled and clenched teeth. "You're only protecting yourself. You've told yourself so many lies that you don't even know what the truth is anymore. You aren't protecting me or your people. All you want is power, and I won't let you do this," she said, emotion rising in her voice. She gripped her gun so hard her knuckles were turning white. She'd never fully understood the true depth of Thias's hunger for power until now.

"Palmer, get yourself into position," Thias demanded as he glanced at the sniper, still wearing his menacing smirk. From the corner of her eye, she watched Ronin take a step closer to him.

"There are two of us and two of you, and neither of you is walking out of here," she asserted. "Ronin will shoot him before he has a chance to press that trigger."

"Maybe you should try counting again," an unexpected voice called from behind.

Ronin's head jerked to the side, and Tala looked quickly over her shoulder, watching Bishop as he stepped into the room, his gun aimed directly at Ronin.

"Bishop? What the hell?" Ronin snapped.

He shrugged, a scowl across his face. "I wasn't going to miss this party."

Tala watched as Palmer loaded the rifle, then adjusted his scope.

"You can't do this, Thias," she pleaded. "All those people out there, how can you be so willing to kill them?" She looked breathlessly between Palmer and Thias. "They've done nothing but trust you and your leadership. What do you even get from murdering them?"

"What you mean murdering *them*?" Ronin gasped. "There are more?"

"There're gunmen in the crowd below," she said with a shaky voice. With a glance to the side, she saw his surprise, his mouth agape.

"Tala, I didn't know," he said apologetically. "I should've just…" his voice fell away.

She cringed. It should be her apologizing, not him. She looked back to Thias, her eyes staring down the barrel of his gun.

"That's none of your business," Thias said coolly as he stepped farther into the room.

"You're so calculated," she sneered. "So manipulative in every move you make and in every word you say. But I see who you really are. You're a coward, and you're afraid of never measuring up. I've experienced who you truly are, and sooner or later, the Republic will too. The truth will come out, it will tell its story, and you'll have no way to defend yourself," she said.

Tala watched Bishop from the corner of her eye as he circled her and Ronin, pinning them between himself and Thias, and Ronin shifted his gun. Tala gave him a sidelong glance, his eyes meeting hers. A pit opened in her stomach. She was the one who had put him in this danger, and now she saw no way out of it. They were at a standstill. While her gun was aimed at Thias, he had one aimed at her and one at Ronin. Ronin's gun was pointed at Bishop, and Bishop's was pointed at Ronin.

Thias laughed, a deep, arrogant, and diabolical laugh. "You're trying to figure out how you're going to get out of here. Like I'm going to just let you walk after this."

Tala breathed heavily, her heart pounding so loudly it was nearly drowning out the crowd in the park.

The people below erupted into boisterous shouts and cheers, and a moment later, she heard President Royer's voice carry over the noise.

Palmer stuck plugs in his ears, then calmly lifted the gun. Easing the barrel through the cutout in the window, he dropped to his right knee. He steadied the butt of the gun against his shoulder as he leveled his eyes through the scope, adjusting it again as he put the president in his sights.

Again, Tala's eyes darted frantically between Palmer and Thias. "Thias, don't do this," she begged.

She turned, aiming her gun at Palmer, her mind racing as she looked for a way out. They were outnumbered and outgunned. If she shot Palmer, Bishop would undoubtedly shoot Ronin, and Thias, she was certain, wouldn't hesitate to shoot her. It was a moment of truth finally coming to a head between her and her brother.

Not long before her death, her mother sat on the edge of Tala's bed, running her fingers through Tala's hair after several long days at work. Tala knew something was wrong and when she asked her about it, her mother had sighed and simply said to her, *"Monsters aren't born, Tala."* At the time, she had been confused, not knowing where it had come from or what she meant.

But her mother had been wrong. There were two kinds of monsters, Tala thought to herself. Some are made over time, slowly as memories and experiences harden them and wickedness replaces the spark of innocence in their heart. Others are born with malice and fire in their veins, and they never have the chance to be anything else. It is at the very core of who they are. Tala wondered which was Thias. He was about to show what he really had in him.

Was he willing to kill his own sister?

Palmer glanced at Thias, who gave a nod of his head. He turned back to his scope, hesitated only long enough to suck in a breath, then pressed the trigger. A loud boom reverberated through the room, the acrid smell of gunpowder and propellant wafting through the air. Tala, who was less than ten feet from the shooter, brought a hand to the side of her head, a loud ringing erupting in her ears, drowning out the screams of terror below as sudden gunfire from within the crowd rang out.

As Palmer turned to Thias, a smug smirk on his face, he nodded. "Target is eliminated," he said in a hoarse voice.

Thias approached him, a dark look in his eyes, a victorious smile on his face. In a quick and abrupt movement, he turned the plasma gun and shot him, directly in the heart from only feet away. Palmer dropped to the floor, his blood spattered against the white wall and windowpane behind him.

Tala recoiled, and as Thias turned toward her, she leveled her eyes on him, meeting his cold, hard glare. He tossed the plasma gun to the floor beside Palmer's limp body, then switching the handgun to his other hand, he raised it, aiming it at Tala again. She watched Bishop continue to circle her and Ronin as he approached Thias, and he laughed sadistically.

"Finally, am one step ahead of the princess," he jested.

Tala shuddered, her heart pounding, adrenaline and anger surging through her. The tinnitus in her ears ebbing, she took a slow, deep breath. She saw the look in Thias's eyes and suddenly she knew.

Swiftly, Tala turned on her heel. Two shots rang out, followed immediately by two dull thumps to the floor.

She gasped. "No!" she bellowed as she saw Ronin's body on the floor, clutching his chest, grunting loudly.

She inhaled sharply as she turned back to Thias, her eyes lingering only briefly on Bishop's lifeless body on the floor, her shot to his head bleeding out. Thias reached down and picked back up the plasma gun, then slowly made his way to the doorway, the handgun still fixed on Tala.

She lifted her gun, aiming hers back at him as tears flooded her eyes. How had it come to this? She heard Ronin's low, guttural groans as he recoiled on the ground.

"When MF gets up here," Thias said calmly, his jaw set and a triumphant gleam in his eyes, "they'll find Agent Ashby, shot by an illegal handgun, and they'll know it was a DeSoto insurgent. They'll see the sniper, dead, with a wound to the heart by a plasma gun, and they'll know he was killed by one of our own. Ronin won't be able to dispute my story, and as the Republic's new president, I'll praise him for his ultimate sacrifice. Bishop," he said with a careless shrug, "well, he'll just be a casualty, accused as a traitor. And you," he hissed, as he continued toward the door, "you're going to let me out of here. Hold your friend, Tala," he nodded toward Ronin, who coughed through labored breaths, his hands covered in blood as he clutched his chest where the bullet had penetrated his frag jacket. "Let the last thing he sees be the eyes of someone he loved."

"DeSoto insurgents?" she gasped. "Thias, this is wrong. It's all wrong!"

His head cocked, an eerie calm coming over him. "No, this is how it has to be. I can live with the blood on my hands. This is war. And war isn't about who's right or wrong, but rather who is left in the end. And no one stands a chance against me."

"I trusted you," she said, choking on her emotion, her vision clouding.

"That was your mistake."

"I'll hunt you down," she spat. "I'll make you pay for this. For all of it!" she yelled. "You're dead to me!"

"Your only chance is to run, Tala. Because *I* am going to hunt you. And I'll have an entire army. What will you have?"

Tala felt her chest tighten as she glanced down at Ronin. His loud grunts filled her ears. There was so much blood. She looked back to Thias. "You're nothing but a vicious torch, setting fire wherever you go. But just remember," she said with a warning, "those who play with fire are bound to be burned. And I won't rest until that day comes."

"You think you can defeat me. But you'll never be fully rid of me," he said spitefully. "I am woven into the very core of who you are; we are eternally intertwined. No one knows you better than me, and I will haunt you for the rest of your life," he said, his icy gaze piercing her. Tala glanced down at Ronin, blood now trickling from the corners of his mouth. When she looked up, Thias was gone.

Tala dropped to the floor. "Ronin," she said, her voice shaking. "Ronin, I'm so sorry," she said, more tears welling in her eyes. She moved his hands, soaked in thick, warm blood, away from his chest. Of course Thias would use bullets that could pierce their ballistic armor. Carefully, she unhooked his frag jacket and slid him out of it. He let out a savage scream. Tala pressed her hands firmly on his wound to stop the bleeding. As he coughed, blood spewed from his mouth, and he let out an agonizing groan.

He shook his head. "Tala," he said quietly between erratic breaths.

She reached for her palm pad, fumbling it, his blood sticky on her hands, but wasn't sure who to call. Kane, she thought, she needed Kane. But she had no way to reach him. Surely, he'd come looking for her. If only Ronin could hold on.

But Kane, she knew, wasn't coming. That wasn't their plan.

Max, she thought. But he couldn't help her either. And it wasn't safe for her to call him.

With tears running down her cheeks, she let out a scream. "I need help!" she yelled to no one, then tossed the palm pad to the side and pressed her other hand to Ronin's chest. The overwhelming scent of blood filled her nostrils.

In the distance, Tala could hear the chaos of the crowd below, gunfire still ringing out, but all that mattered to her now was Ronin.

She wanted to apologize to him, to beg his forgiveness for all the lies she'd told.

"Be strong," she said, her bottom lip trembling. "You've got to hold on a little longer. Help is coming," she said, then sniffled hard, her words caught in her throat. He had only ever been honest with her, and despite her good intentions, she couldn't say the same about herself.

He shook his head again. "I'm so sorry," he whispered. "I didn't… didn't believe you," he choked, struggling for breath.

"You didn't know," she asserted, her tears dripping off her chin. "How could you have known?"

"It was like…" he sputtered, "like I woke up one day and didn't know who you were." His labored breaths were growing shallow. "But now," he whispered as tears pooled in his eyes, "I realize I was never looking at the true you, the real Tala." Like a dam giving way, his tears flowed freely down the side of his face as he looked up at her, his eyes full of regret. "And I'm just glad I got to glimpse her in the end," he said, his voice growing weaker with every word he spoke. He blinked hard and coughed. He made gurgling noises with each slow breath, more blood seeping from the corners of his mouth.

"I'm so sorry," she said, her voice shaking. He was slipping away from her and all she could do was watch. She was helpless. And it had been her who led him to his fate. And for what? President Royer was dead, she'd been unable to stop that. And Thias was gone. She'd been unable to keep him. All that was left was a goodbye that she didn't want to say.

"Ronin, just hang in there," she pleaded as she pressed her hands harder to his chest, the thick blood oozing through her fingers. Her eyes met his, soft and brown, his hair flopped to the side like always. In one moment, he was looking back at her, his face grimacing in pain, then his mouth slackened, his chest falling, the life in his eyes suddenly gone.

"No," she gasped, her tears streaming down her face with an uncontrollable force. She reached out, her two fingers searching for a pulse in his neck. "No," she said breathlessly when she found nothing and dropped her head to his chest. Her body heaved as she cried, choking on her tears, then she let out a shrill scream.

"I'm sorry," she cried through heavy, raspy breaths. "I'm so sorry."

She lifted her head and gave him another look. He already didn't look like the Ronin she had known. His skin was pallid and waxy, and his eyes were empty. She reached over and gently closed them, leaving behind bloody fingerprints on his skin. Taking a shaky breath, she leaned across him and kissed his forehead, which was clammy to the touch. "I love you," she whispered, the words seeming to hang on her tongue as she closed her eyes for a moment.

She had failed him. She had failed everyone.

Tala opened her eyes and rose to her feet, then without a second glance, she left the empty room. But it was no longer empty. It had become the final resting place for three people, whose bodies were now nothing more than vacant shells, their lives ended in the blink of an eye.

NINETEEN

Tala was numb, walking aimlessly down the street with no grasp on where she was. It didn't matter. Despite the sunshine, goosebumps raised beneath the long sleeves of her uniform, the blood-soaked fabric clinging to her arms. People ran past her screaming, crying, but she couldn't help them. She couldn't help anyone.

She knew her heart was beating, keeping her alive, yet she couldn't feel it. It was shattered into a million pieces. The air was gone from her lungs, and she was unable to even open her mouth to speak. Her face was tight, covered in her crusted tears and Ronin's dried blood.

Blood that was shed because of her.

She was weak in the knees, her legs threatening to buckle under the weight of her body, and she stumbled on uneven pavement as she rounded a corner, her shoulder colliding into the brick veneer of a building.

She didn't try to stop her fall, her body collapsing to the ground, the loose gravel scraping her palms raw. She coughed and rolled to the side, people rushing frantically past her, hysteria surrounding her. She sat up, propping herself against the building, her bloodied hands shaking as she gently rested them in her lap.

The world was spinning around her, and a wave of nausea washed over her. The urge to vomit rose up inside her but subsided after several deep breaths.

She watched as people continued to run past, some as bloody as she was. Some more so. A disheveled woman cried as she clutched a small child, about Millie's age, to her chest. A man, wild-eyed, dressed in a suit, his white shirt soaked through with dark red blood, spun in circles, his arms outstretched, and he bellowed words Tala couldn't process.

There was weeping all around her, the sound of sirens wailing in the distance, and yet she couldn't move. Closing her eyes, Ronin's face played in her mind. His lopsided grin, his soft brown eyes, and his hair flopped to the side, always falling into his eyes. She heard his laugh, joyful and light.

She took a shaky breath and brought her knees to her chest, hugging them against her body, and she leaned forward, setting her chin atop her knee. Another wave of nausea came over her, and she breathed slowly through her nose until it once again eased.

"Agent," she heard in a desperate plea as a pair of feet appeared beside her.

Tala looked up, a woman's body silhouetted from the sun behind her.

"Miss. Agent. I need your help. My Joey. I can't find my Joey," she cried.

Tala gave the woman a small shake of her head. "I'm sorry," she whispered, so quietly she hadn't even heard her own voice over the chaos around them. Tala's eyes dropped, and she set her chin back onto her knee. A moment later, the woman was gone. With her shoulders hunched over, Tala wondered if it was possible to disappear into herself. She would swallow herself whole if she could.

Tala stared, unblinking ahead, her eyes empty and cold. She wasn't sure how long she had been sitting there. Long enough for the sun to dip low in the sky. Long enough for the panic around her to dissipate. People still flooded past her, but the frenzy was dissipating. Those who were left were stunned and in shock.

411

Her mind went to Kane. Where was Kane?

She felt her heartbeat return as she thought of him. She had to get to Kane.

She took a deep breath, fortifying herself, and stood. Unstable on her feet, she wavered, bracing herself with one hand on the building. She took a moment, steadying herself, then let go of the wall and stepped off the sidewalk. She had to find Kane.

She reached into her pocket and pulled out her palm pad, dried blood smeared across the screen, her fingerprints stamped onto it. She tossed it to the ground and with all the force she could summon, she slammed the heel of her boot down onto it, repeatedly stomping on it, watching it break apart, piece by piece.

The subtrain was teeming with people, everyone trying desperately to get somewhere, to get to someone. Tala held a railing above her to support her standing body in the fast-moving train, her other hand firmly on the butt of her gun. She felt people's eyes on her, not because she was Tala Alexander, but more likely because she was an agent, or because she had dried blood covering her. Her hands, her uniform, her forehead and face from when she had dropped her head to Ronin's chest, from wiping at her tears. She was covered in Ronin.

Ronin, she thought. He was dead. Her chest tightened, and she took a shaky, shallow breath. A headache was taking hold in the back of her head. She looked no one in the eyes, just stared straight ahead, silent and stoic as the train sped through the underbelly of the city.

When they made it to her stop, she pushed fiercely through the mass of people to get out of the train, and weaving through the crowds on the platform, she fought her way topside, where she took in the fresh air in gulps. She let it fill her body.

The crowd along the street was tense. People sobbed. Others walked in stunned silence. It was eerie how quiet it could be with so many people around her. But she understood it. Conversation was idle in a time such as this. People's silence said everything. People had entire conversations in simply one quiet glance.

Tala made her way down Harvey Street, stumbling over her own feet, and she was relieved to finally reach the familiar white door of Max's pod. She didn't bother to knock but rather opened it and let her body fall inside.

"Tala!" Kane yelled, his relief at the sight of her palpable. He rushed to her, blurring across the room like only he could, and pulled her into him, squeezing her hard. With his face buried in her neck, he whispered over and over again, "Oh, thank god, oh, thank god."

When he pulled back to look at her, she saw the terror on his face, in his eyes. "Are you hurt?" he asked as his hand roamed over her body, looking for an injury.

"It's not my blood," she whispered, and she felt the tears prick at the back of her eyes. She swallowed hard as she gave a shake of her throbbing head. Her eyes met his, unable to mask the pain in them. "He's dead," she mumbled in a hoarse voice.

"Who?" he asked with apprehension. "Royer? Thias?"

She felt her eyes well, his name on her lips, but when she opened her mouth, nothing came out. Her shoulders slumped, and she felt the warm tears break free and run down her cheeks.

Kane reached up and wiped at the small drops on her face, drying her cheeks with his hands.

"Who, Tala?" he urged gently.

She swallowed hard and took a shaky breath, her body quivering. "Ronin."

Kane let out a low sigh and pulled her into him. With her face pressed against his chest, her legs gave out, her body collapsing into his. But he was strong and held her up as she clung to him like he was her last lifeline.

She cried, unashamed of her tears. If there was someone worth her tears, it was Ronin. And she deserved every ounce of pain that was tearing through her body.

Her chest heaved, and she gasped for air, choking on her emotion, and Kane only held her tighter.

Like when she had sat on the street, lost in her grief, time disappeared, and Tala had no idea how long he held her. But at some point, the tears dried, and her breathing normalized. She found the strength to stand again. And when she pulled back, meeting his gaze, she was thankful for his silence. She was on edge, and it wouldn't take much to push her over, to plunge her into the darkness.

"How about a shower? Clean you up," he said, his voice gentle in the silence around them.

Looking down at her stained hands, she nodded. She couldn't keep Ronin's blood on her any longer. It was physically painful to have it on her skin, and she wanted to tear it from her body. She followed Kane to the bathroom, and while he started the shower, she sat quietly on the closed toilet seat.

He turned toward her, and reaching around her, he unclipped her duty belt and set it aside. One by one, he removed her shoes, her socks. He loosened her frag jacket and slid it off, also covered in blood, but much harder to see on the black material. He held her hands in his, his thumbs brushing over her ripped up palms.

His eyes met hers as he reached for the hem of her shirt. He gave it a tug and slipped it up, over her head, and she then saw the dried blood on her arms that had seeped through the sleeves of her uniform.

Ronin was all over her, and she fought her returning nausea. She rose and slipped out of her pants. A minute later, she stood under the hot shower of water that ran red as soon as it washed over her skin.

Kane handed her a washcloth and a bar of soap, set a towel on the toilet, then turned for the door. "I'll be right out here if you need anything," he said, and Tala simply nodded from behind the shower curtain, even though he couldn't see her.

Ronin was dead. The words played on repeat. Her heart knew it. Her head needed to process it now.

Death, she thought. How could it hurt so much, it was death? By the very nature of it, it should cease all pain. But the reality of it was that it left crippling, soul-wrenching pain in its wake. There was nothing that made a person more aware that they were alive than when pain like that tore through their heart, and in those moments, all they could crave was death, if only for its release.

Tala took a shuddered breath as she reached for the bar of soap and gently lathered it over her hands, her arms, and the rest of her body. She cleaned her face, scrubbing hard on her skin.

The last of the red-stained water washed down the drain, the last of Ronin disappearing into the abyss, and despite the heat of the water and the steam all around her, Tala shivered. She looked over her body, rinsed cleaned, renewed, and her heart was heavy. Turning the water hotter, she took a deep breath, exhaling slowly. She dropped her head back, letting it run over her, tingling on her scalp, and she quickly shampooed her hair.

Afterward, she lingered under the shower, tears filling her eyes, mixing with the water as it ran down her face. Her body heaved as she stood there, alone. Then she straightened, pushing her emotion down, and turned off the shower. Goosebumps raised over her skin as she reached for the towel Kane left her. Wrapping herself in it, she stepped out of the shower, then sat on the closed toilet, her long, wet strands of hair running down her back and over her shoulders, dripping onto the tile floor.

She took in a long, deep breath, steadier now. She picked absentmindedly at the fibers of the towel, her mind full. She thought of Thias, and despite the pain her in heart, she steeled herself. She would not break because of him. She refused to give him that power. He had already taken Ronin. She wasn't going to let him take any more. There was now only one thing left to do, and in that moment, she was certain. It was time to accept Avery's offer. She had to use her pain as her motivation. If Ronin wasn't going to have died in vain, she was going to have to let her grief arm her, to prepare her to fight for all that had been lost.

Tala rose to her feet and left the small bathroom. She found Kane and Max on the couch, both of them tense, looking on edge. Kane's eyes met hers, and she gave him a bleak smile. At least she had him.

"Let me grab your bag," he said as he hopped to his feet and sprang across the room toward the kitchen where the duffel she packed sat on the floor. He grabbed it by the strap and brought it to her.

"Please, don't ask how I am," she said quietly, her voice rough. "You know how I am. Don't make me put it into words."

He nodded in understanding.

She took the bag from him and made her way back to the bathroom, dressing quickly. She towel-dried her hair and ran a brush through it, and as she went to put it back in the bag, she spotted Ronin's face, smiling back at her.

She reached into the duffel and grabbed the photograph, taken less than a year earlier at an MF awards dinner, and felt a sting in her chest as she looked down at it. Her finger traced over his face, his smiling, happy face, and her breath caught. "I'll do right for you," she whispered as though he could hear her. Her eyes lingered for another moment, then she dropped the photo back into the bag and zipped it shut.

"Tala," Kane called as she made her way down the hallway toward him. "There's going to be a broadcast from Thias," he said when he saw her approaching.

A pit formed in her stomach as she made her way around the couch and took a seat beside him, curling her body into him.

"We don't have to watch this," he whispered into her wet hair.

"We do," she said with a nod.

The TV automatically came to life not even a moment later, commanding the attention of the three of them.

"Good evening, citizens of the Republic of Columbia," Thias said, his face appearing before her, and Tala felt a flash of anger. All those mangled, bloodied people who had rushed past her on the streets, and here he stood before them in his pressed blue suit that complimented his eyes, his blond hair perfectly coiffed, and she cringed.

"I come to you tonight with a heavy heart," he said with sad eyes. "Today, during the Republic of Columbia's Annual Presidential Address, our beloved President Royer II was deliberately and tragically assassinated, struck down by a sniper who was later killed by our Militia Forces. And while the president was killed, a simultaneous deadly act of terror was executed by armed gunmen on the crowd that had gathered at Quarry Square on this would-be joyous occasion. We are still getting reports of casualties as area hospitals have been inundated with people from all over the country who had come for the address today. Preliminary reports estimate the death toll at two hundred fifty-six, and regretfully, it is expected to climb," he paused, bringing his hand briefly to his mouth in a show of emotion. "An online site has been created as a resource for people to locate their loved ones. People can refer to the newly created site for the names of those identified as deceased, injured, or missing. This site will be linked to our government page, available on every device, and will be updated frequently. Please use this resource for locating your loved ones before contacting Militia Forces who are busy at this very minute investigating the tragedy at Quarry Square." Thias was calm and poised as he spoke, his mouth curved downward in a grim frown.

Tala's fists clenched at her sides. All around the city, all around the country, people were hanging on his every word. They had no idea the lie they were buying into.

"Dutifully, it is I who assumes the presidency. And I do so with a humble heart, vowing to all our citizens to be the leader they need during such a trying time. My office has been bombarded with questions as to who would carry out such a horrific plan, and while they are denying responsibility, intel indicates that these senseless attacks were carried out by DeSoto nationals. We have suspects in custody at this time. I consider this an extreme act of aggression made toward the Republic by our southern neighbor, and as your new president, I vow to hit back hard. Harder than we were hit today. Those we have lost will not be in vain, and we will make sure justice is served.

"President Royer was an honorable man who served this great country as a loyal leader and patriot, valuing the principles that this great nation was built upon. My deepest sympathies go out to his family, his son, Alec, as he grieves not only his president but also his beloved father."

Thias straightened and quietly cleared his throat as he lifted his chin high. "Tonight, we are filled with sadness, disbelief, and confusion as we try to find a reason behind this tragedy. We have been shaken, but we will not fall. Rest assured, our Militia Forces is powerful, and they are prepared. They will protect our citizens at all costs. I offer my condolences to all who are grieving and to all whose lives have been irrevocably and tragically shattered. I stand before you tonight honored to be your president. I will also be retaining my position as director of Militia Forces during this delicate and pivotal time until a suitable replacement can be made. I am strong in my resolve that we will come back from this. The determination of our people and our leaders will not rest until we are triumphant. Thank you," he said with a solemn nod of his head. The camera focused on him for another moment, then the broadcast ended, and the screen went black.

Tala turned to Kane, her anger seething. "How did this happen?" she asked in a whisper.

Both Kane and Max were quiet, but their silence felt louder than any conversation ever could.

Thias was president. He was both first and second in command now. Ronin was dead. Royer was dead. Hundreds of her people were dead. It was agonizing the way her failures taunted her, like she hadn't tried at all. They stared her in the eyes. They mocked her.

"I'm going to accept Avery's offer," she said resolutely, her voice strong and steady, the words rolling off her tongue.

Kane's eyes met hers, the corners wrinkling slightly, his mouth curled into a sullen grin. "Always a fighter."

"I can't give up now. I've come too far to see it end like this. And I refuse to let Ronin's death be for nothing," she said, feeling the emotion rising in her chest at the mention of his name, her eyes dropping to her hands as she absentmindedly picked at her scuffed palms. "I just," she said, her words barely a whisper, "I can't believe he's gone."

Kane reached for her, his hand gently lifting her chin until her eyes met his. "His death will always be with you, of course it will. But so will your memories."

Tala took a long, slow breath and nodded, knowing he was right. And those memories she would cherish forever.

Tala stood in the middle of Alexander Avenue. It was warm, and she could feel the sun on her skin, her arms and shoulders bare in her tank-top, and she breathed deeply. As the air filled her lungs, the tips of her fingers and toes tingled, and she felt joy inside of her.

She turned, spotting him standing down the street, a hundred yards or so from her, and she smiled. His back was to her, but she knew him even from behind. She let out a small laugh as she began walking, her feet steadily following the solid line down the center of the street, no traffic to be found.

With each step, the crowd on the sidewalks began to disappear, and soon it was only them and the towering buildings around them. The city was quiet. Tala called out to him, but he didn't move.

A rush of wind pushed past her, her hair whipping around her neck as she continued toward him. She called out to him a second time. He remained still, unmoving. When she reached him, Tala stretched out her hand, setting it gently on his shoulder.

"Ronin," she said, her voice carrying through the air on the breeze.

He finally turned toward her, his eyes soft and calm, his mouth curved into a smile. His brown hair was flopped to the side, hanging just over his brow.

For a moment, she greeted him happily, then she gasped as she saw the bullet wound in his chest, blood spilling from it. His smile washed away and his eyes hardened.

"Help me," he cried out.

Tala's eyes flashed open, her heart racing and her forehead damp. She pressed her hand to her chest, taking erratic deep breaths as she tried to shake the nightmare. She glanced at Kane asleep beside her, a peaceful and contented look across his slackened face.

Her heart rate leveling, she rolled to her side and slid her body backward, pressing herself against him. She reached for his arm, pulling it around her waist. He stirred and mumbled something incoherently, and she pulled his arm tighter, curling into him.

Taking slow breaths, Tala closed her eyes. She felt the steady rise and fall of Kane's chest against her back, and she timed her breaths in sync with his. Listening to his rhythmic breathing, his arm wrapped around her, Tala felt safe, growing heavy with sleep once again. Slowly, the world fell away, and she slipped back into the darkness.

When Tala woke the next morning, Kane's side of the bed was empty. She felt exhausted and groggy, and she struggled to open her eyes. The hatch in the ceiling was open and Tala could hear a muffled conversation from above, recognizing both Kane's and Max's voices.

She sat up, rubbing her eyes and stretching her body, and after a minute, she finally rose to her feet. She crossed the room and climbed the ladder up to the living room, and both Kane and Max went quiet as she emerged through the door in the floor.

She exchanged quiet looks with each of them, an unsettling feeling coming over her as she saw their expressions, both a blend of sadness and worry.

"What is it?" she asked as she approached them in the kitchen, watching as they exchanged furtive glances with one another. "I know there's something," she asserted as she locked her eyes on Kane.

He took a small breath, and she saw his hesitation.

"Just say it," she said.

"This morning, Max got onto the site that listed the victims and missing from yesterday," he said with a pause. "He was looking for anyone he knew," he said as he glanced across the counter at Max. "And a name stood out to us."

"Who?" she asked, afraid of what he would say next.

"Mila," he said. "She's listed in critical, but stable condition in a hospital in Stoughbour."

Tala's heart fell as her chest restricted, dizziness washing over her, and she reached for the counter to steady herself.

"I told her not to go," she gasped.

Kane was quiet as he reached out, his warm hand covering hers.

After watching Ronin die in her arms, the terror on the streets, she didn't think she had any grief left in her. But the thought of Mila now in a hospital stirred it all over again. Tala felt its cold, gripping claws reaching for her, closing over her throat. The ache in her chest was slowly morphing into pain that resonated deep inside her, darkness spreading outward, threatening to consume her.

She closed her eyes and there, in the dark periphery of her mind, she saw an unexpected, faint trace of light. But what she wasn't sure of was whether it was the soft glow of a dying ember or the flicker of a growing flame. She took a shuddered breath knowing that only time would truly be able to reveal that to her.

She bit at the inside of her cheek and opened her eyes. "What if he goes after her?" she asked, looking between Kane and Max. "She won't even know what will have happened to me."

"Maybe I can go to her," Max said.

"Let's get you to safety first," Kane said to Tala.

She swallowed hard, her heart heavy, only more burden weighing down on her. She felt lost in a sea of heartbreak, the current pulling her deeper, and she wondered if she'd ever figure out how to swim before she drowned.

Tala slipped into her jacket, pulled the hood up to cover her blond pony, and slipped the duffel strap over her shoulder. She turned toward Max, her eyes catching his, and she felt a pang of guilt for taking Kane with her.

"I'm sorry," she said, knowing her words were feeble but not knowing what else to say.

"The only reason I'm okay with this is because if there is such a thing as soulmates, and science would say there isn't, but if there is, I believe it's you two," he said, then gave his glasses a nudge.

She gave him a small smile as she reached out and wrapped her arms around him, his body going rigid beneath her grasp.

"I'll always fight for him," she whispered, and he finally brought his hands up, placing them gently, awkwardly, on her back to hug her in return.

"That, I believe," he said when she pulled away. "And you," he said as he turned toward Kane who was watching them patiently. "I haven't harbored you and kept you safe for the last decade so that you can go out there and get yourself killed. Fight when you must, but be smart and know when you don't have to," he said with a knowing gleam in his eye.

"Got it," Kane said, the corner of his mouth pulled into a small grin, and the two of them shifted their feet as silence fell over them.

Tala watched them, her eyes flitting between each of them, wondering who would break first. There was too much history between them to make an easy goodbye.

"Let's just go with, *see you soon*," Max said with a small wave of his hand.

"We could," Kane said. "But if I never have the chance to say this again, you've gotta know, you've always been my brother."

Max nodded with a sheepish grin and shoved his hands into the pockets of his sweat jacket. "You too. Make things right and come back," he said as he straightened his back and stood a little taller, though still a head shorter than Kane.

Tala followed behind Kane as they stepped onto the street, the dark gray sky and heavy, low-lying clouds threatening rain, and she shivered from the chill in the air.

His bag slung over his shoulder, he reached for her hand, and Tala laced her fingers through his. It didn't matter who saw them anymore. Nothing from her old life mattered anymore. And as Kane gave Max one more glance over his shoulder, they set off down the street for Avery's.

Thunder cracked overhead, and Tala pulled her jacket collar tighter, Highland Avenue not far ahead. A single truck whizzed past them.

"Do you know any of Avery's plan?" she asked.

He gave a hard shake of his head. "No. Just don't expect to be comfortable."

"How do you thi—" Tala froze in her tracks, her heart dropping, her body going cold.

She watched as he stepped out from behind a dumpster bin, disheveled in his suit, his tie crooked, his shirt half untucked, and he let out a wild laugh, pulling a plasma gun from the waistband of his pants.

"Vaughn?" she said in disbelief laced with a tinge of fear.

"I can't believe my luck that I actually found you," he said, his words nearly slurred together as he waved the gun through the air. "With all these pods here," he said, looking up at the tall buildings, "I had no idea which one you were in. Or if you were here at all. I thought I'd chance it and wait. And my waiting paid off because here you are," he said with a wicked grin.

"How did you…" she let her sentence fall off as she dropped Kane's hand, giving him a wide-eyed, sideways glance, her gut twisting inside her.

"Find you?" Vaughn scoffed as he finished her thought. "It wasn't hard," he said, bringing his free hand to his face, dark stubble along his jaw and chin. "I knew it," he said bitterly as he looked at Kane. "That night we ran into him outside the restaurant. I saw the look on both of your faces. And you tried to tell me otherwise," he said with a shake of his head. "You kissed me in the car on the way back to your pod, assuring me you didn't know him."

Tala's heart hammered in her chest, and she stole another glance at Kane who was strangely calm.

"You came here after I dropped you off," Vaughn spat.

"You followed me?" she said, her face screwed up. A gust of wind rushed down the narrow street, blowing her hood off. She let her duffel slide off her shoulder, dropping to the ground with a thud.

"Of course not. I had no reason to doubt you then. But," he said, his eyes flaring wide, "you must've forgotten to change before coming here," he said with a caustic grin.

"Change? My clothes?" she asked in confusion. A car passed them, slowing only briefly before speeding away.

Vaughn didn't respond, just raised an eyebrow and studied her. Waiting.

"The bangle," she gasped, it dawning on her.

He gave a low chuckle and a slow nod of his head. "Then imagine my surprise to see you in a lip lock with him at the park yesterday. I saw you both and I knew… I just knew. So I went back to the tracking software and retraced your steps."

"Vaughn," she said calmly as thunder clapped overhead, making her jump.

"Who are you?" he snapped at Kane as he aimed the plasma gun steadily at him.

Kane was silent, his lips pressed in a firm line.

"Are you in love with her?" Vaughn asked with a flash of indignation.

"Yes," Kane said flatly, his body unflinching.

"No, I'm in love with her!" he yelled, his voice echoing off the high walls of the buildings that surrounded them.

"Vaughn, I'm sorry that I—"

"It was all a lie!" he spat, cutting her off. "You just kept putting me off and putting me off, and at first I thought it was because you were nervous, but now, now," he gasped breathlessly, "now I know that you were just keeping me at bay because you were with him," he said, thrusting the gun through the air at Kane. His eyes were full of fury. "And now I'm going to shoot him. Right here. And I'm going to watch you watch him die," he jeered icily.

She looked at Kane, seeing the hardened expression on his face.

"You really think you can shoot me?" he asked coolly as he tossed his bag onto the pavement.

"Of course I can shoot you," Vaughn said with a smirk. "I'm the one holding the gun. What is it you think you can do to me?" he sneered.

"You have no idea," Kane said, his mouth curling into a grin as he stared at him.

Tala's breath caught, and without even seeing him move, Kane was instantly at Vaughn, his arm hooked firmly around his neck and restricting his air as he carefully pried the gun out of his hand. Vaughn clawed at Kane's arm as he struggled for air, making loud, gasping sounds.

"Take this," Kane said as he tipped his head to Tala, holding the gun out. She hurried to him, snatching it from his hands.

"Now, about you," Kane said steadily in Vaughn's ear. His body thrashed wildly beneath Kane's firm grasp.

"Who… are… you?" Vaughn managed through labored breaths.

"Pity you'll never know," Kane said flatly. "I'll let you live, for today. But if you ever come near her," he said as he gestured toward Tala, "I will kill you, slowly, so you can feel every ounce of pain."

Vaughn coughed, his legs kicking as he struggled to break free.

Kane gave Tala a knowing glance, and she nodded as she watched his grip tighten around Vaughn's throat until his body finally went limp. He released his hold, letting his unconscious body drop to the pavement. He quickly tucked him in the corner near the dumpster he'd been hiding behind, then looked up at Tala.

"I think maybe you should hang on to that," he nodded toward the gun still in her hand as he scooped his bag up. "Maybe it'll be good to have a second," he said. She already had her MF-issued plasma gun in her bag. "We've got to go," he said as he reached for her hand.

She quickly slipped the gun into the side pocket of the duffel, pulled her hood back on, then hooked her bag over her shoulder. Grabbing Kane's hand, they took off.

With her head down, avoiding eye contact with everyone around them, Tala let Kane pull her along. They hurriedly made their way from street to street, and after a near jog for twenty minutes, Tala found herself in a part of the city that she was very unfamiliar with, stirring uneasiness in her.

Thunder boomed loudly and Tala's heart hammered with it. Then she felt a raindrop hit her face, another a second later.

She glanced over her shoulder at every turn they made, having lost herself long ago. But Kane steadily pushed on, determined, and knowing exactly where he was.

The East River Channel coming into view, Tala was certain she had never been in this part of the city before. Old, red brick buildings long since converted into pods surrounded them, and her pulse quickened as she felt the eyes of people lingering outside on her.

"Just keep your head down," he said over his shoulder, pulling her closer to him as they continued at their brisk pace.

More drops of rain fell on her face, and the wind was beginning to pick up. She watched a bolt of lightning streak across the sky, followed by a loud crack of thunder. With a layer of perspiration on her back, Tala was beginning to feel exhausted and breathlessly struggled to keep up with Kane.

"You know," she said between deep breaths, heaving her bag higher on her shoulder, "not everyone can move around like you without getting tired."

"Almost there," he said, not slowing his pace.

Tala took in large gulps of air, her legs growing more fatigued with every step as they wound their way between building after building, each looking exactly like the one before. Then finally, he slowed, and Tala took the reprieve to catch her breath.

"Here," he said with a nod of his head toward a ground-level door. They both approached with caution.

Kane gave three hard knocks, paused, then gave three more, and Tala held her breath. A moment later, it cracked ajar, but the person lingered in the darkened background, and Tala could make out nothing about them.

"Who is it?" a male voice called through the opening.

"Phoenix," Kane said. "Here for Boy Scout. With the package."

The door slammed shut, and they waited, Tala's stomach in her throat until it opened again, this time all the way. Avery stood in front of them, a wide grin across his face.

TWENTY

Avery's pod, if in fact, it was Avery's pod, was small and dim, the windows draped and covered with heavy fabric. The furniture was worn and battered, but it was clean, a faint spiced smell in the air.

A loud boom of thunder clapped, and Tala gave a small jolt. Her emotions were running high and just standing in the living room was enough to bring her closer to the edge. Everything felt surreal.

"Tala," Avery said jovially, "this is Bull. He's going to help us today with the first leg of your journey."

Bull was a pasty man, tall and barrel-chested, with a slim face and a head of black hair that was buzzed short. He gave her a nod with a sly grin that made her recoil inside.

"Never thought I'd see this day come," he said, taking small steps toward her.

"You're not the first person to say that," she said. "Guess no one around here has any kind of imagination."

"She yours?" Bull asked, his eyes moving to Kane.

"We're together, if that's what you mean," he responded flatly.

"Well, aren't you lucky? She's a pretty one," he said with a chuckle. "Even more so in person."

"Anyway," Tala said with a shudder as she looked at Avery, catching Kane's flexing fist from the corner of her eye. He clearly was running just as high as she was.

"You weren't kidding when you said that this was big," Avery said as he crossed one arm over his body and brought his other hand to his chin. In his t-shirt, she could see that his right arm was a half-sleeve of black ink with a large dagger on the inside of his forearm.

Tala was quiet.

"You said he mobilized troops to the south before any of this happened," he said. "I reckon he was planning to pin this on DeSoto all along."

"Why do you think that?" she asked.

"Their resources," he said with a shrug. "They've always been reserved when it comes to what they export. And with the Republic's over-population problems only growing, the government has a hard time sustaining when it comes to things like rice, cotton, and sugarcane. Just to name a few," he said with a tip of his head. "Not to mention that DeSoto shipping ports are centrally located with greater access to the Caribbean and Central America, directly impacting international trade. If the Republic could assume power over DeSoto, it would gain control of all those resources. Especially offshore oil reserves and petroleum, which are limited here."

None of this had occurred to Tala. International relations had never been her thing, but as Avery made his points, she couldn't help but see the merits in his argument.

"Now, the mission. We're going to the shipping docks," he said, beginning to outline their plan. "We have a contact there who's going to help. We'll put you in a cargo container that's already cleared inspection and has been approved for shipping. Thanks to our friend. From there, you'll be loaded onto one of the freight ships headed for Bristol tonight."

"Why would we go so far south?" she asked with a raised brow. Bristol was a coastal city over three hundred miles south of Columbia City. "We just said Thias has all kinds of troops down there."

"We'll still be a good four hours or so from the border and it's the best route to go west from. Even if he suspected you were trying to get out of the country and not just in hiding somewhere, he won't expect you to go into southern territory with such a heavily armed presence. He knows you don't know that part of the country. One of our biggest risk factors is that you could be recognized. You need to keep a low profile at all times."

"Think you can handle all that, princess?" Bull said with a lopsided grin. "Traveling in a large steel box can't measure up to your life of luxury up to this point."

"Oh, shut it," she snapped, a rush of anger surging through her. Even if that was true, she wasn't so inured to comfort that she couldn't handle a night in a shipping container, despite what they thought.

"She's about as much a princess as you are," Kane said, folding his arms across his chest and flexing his arms.

"Then you should consider yourself a lucky man," Bull jested. "You get her pretty and tough. I'd bang her too," he said with a laugh.

"What'd you say?" Kane snapped, his arms flailing from his sides as he took an aggressive step toward Bull, his jaw clenched firmly. His hands balled into tight fists.

"Hey, hey," Tala said as she stepped forward, her arms outstretched between them. "He's not worth it," she said as she looked at Kane.

"Oh, look at that. Letting your girl step in to intervene for you," Bull said with a crazed laugh.

This was her breaking point. Too much had happened, and she wasn't going to play nice anymore. Tala turned on her heel, swinging her arm hard and fast, her fist collided with the side of Bull's mouth, and he stumbled backward.

"I'm in no mood to be screwed with," she snapped.

"What the hell?" Bull gasped as he brought his hand to his busted lip.

Tala ignored the pain in her hand as she glanced between Avery and Kane, seeing unmistakable smirks across both their faces.

"Guess that puts the title of princess to bed," Avery said with a chuckle, brushing his hair out of his face.

"You were saying," she said calmly to Avery as she readjusted her shirt.

"You're just gonna let her get away with that shit?" Bull spat.

"I'd say you had it coming," Avery said, a smirk still on the corner of his mouth. He turned away from Bull. "Once in Bristol, you'll be met by Freelancer, who'll bring you to Vulcan, and you'll cross the Mississippi River into the Colonies at Clara City."

"Vulcan?" she repeated.

Avery nodded. "UR leader. That's who approved this mission in the first place."

"And Freelancer?" she asked.

"We always go with codenames. If they want to give their real names, they can. Although, Vulcan is always Vulcan. I don't think anyone knows Vulcan as anything else. Hell, maybe it really is a name. Now," he said with a pause, "on to other matters. All members of the UR take their role very seriously. And it's a commitment for life. We're a tight-knit band of brothers and sisters and once we pledge, there's no going back," he said. "You're no exception to this, Tala. And there's a price for what we're about to do."

Tala eyed him carefully and gave a stern nod of her head. She knew this was coming. "Ink," she said.

"Whoa," Kane interjected as he stepped forward. "Avery, she's already agreed to be one of the faces of your cause."

"It's fine," she said, bringing her hand up. "I was expecting this. But first, I need something from you," she said, her eyes meeting Avery's. "My podmate, Mila, she's about all I have left other than Kane, and I need her to be protected. She was injured in the shooting, and she's in the hospital, in critical condition. If she pulls through…" Tala said with a pause, her mind going to an unconscious Mila.

"Thias could use her against you," Avery said in understanding.

Tala gave a grave nod of her head.

"Done."

She swallowed her rising emotion, relief washing over her. She was feeling more and more conviction in her decision.

"Is there anything else? We've already got an eye on Max. We've got plans for him," he said.

"No."

"From now on, you'll be referred to as Bluebird. That's your callsign. And if there's nothing else, that officially wraps up this conversation. Krys is in the other room, and she's ready for you. When it comes to ink, she's the best," he said as he turned and headed down a hallway that led off the living room.

"Tala," Kane said quietly after Bull left, following after Avery.

"Really, it's fine. I suspected this would happen. And I'm fine with it," she insisted as she reached for his hand, taking it in hers. "If you can have one, then I can." She gave him a coy smile, then turned, heading in the direction Avery went in, pulling Kane along.

"I have to say," Krys, a short, thin woman with long, black hair braided into thin strands, said when Tala stepped into the room, "it's an honor to do your ink." She gave Tala a genuine smile.

The room was lit brightly, unlike the rest of the pod, but still lacked any natural light. The walls were covered in large panels filled with images of all colors and sizes, with no two designs the same.

Tala stepped up to one of the panels, her eyes wandering over each image: animals, faces, geometric designs, words, the options seemed infinite.

"I can do just about anything. But if it's too big, you'll have to have it finished once you're in the Colonies," Krys said. "So. What'll it be?"

Tala slid her hands into the pockets of her jeans as she stole a glance at Kane, his eyes fixed on her. "A phoenix," she said without hesitation as she turned back to Krys.

Her mouth turned up at the corners. "How appropriate," she said.

"In more than one way," Tala said. "I want it here." She moved her hand to the side of her ribcage, under her arm, near her heart.

"That's always a sore place," Krys said.

"I'll be fine," she shrugged.

"Okay, then. You guys," Krys nodded and waved her finger at Avery, Bull, and Kane, "out. This is girl time."

Kane moved to Tala, brushing a small strand of hair that had fallen loose from her ponytail behind her ear, and he smiled, his eyes wrinkling in the corners. "Can't wait to see it when it's done," he said, his voice low and hushed, then he leaned down and kissed her.

They had stayed in the pod until after dark. When they finally stepped outside, Tala stopped, taking a moment to look up at the nighttime sky, a rolling blanket of rainy, stormy darkness. When she finally would see the sun again, her world would be different, her old life gone, dead.

They crouched low at a fence along the perimeter of the shipping yard, rows of horizontal cables that went at least ten feet high. They had left the car blocks away, trudging to the yard through the cold rain, which wasn't coming down heavily, but it was coming down steadily. The petrichor emanating from the saturated ground and pavement was strong in the air. The temperature dropped drastically when night fell, and the wind had picked up, howling around them. In the distance, there was a low rumble of thunder, dull flashes of lightning eclipsed by the city skyline.

Avery slid the backpack he carried off his shoulders and pulled out a small multimeter, carefully touching the nodes to one of the fence cables.

"Damn it," he cussed under his breath. "Power hasn't been cut yet," he said, looking up at Bull as he hovered over him.

A wave of anxiety rushed over Tala, and through heavy, wet lashes, she glanced over her shoulder at Kane, whose eyes seemed to reflect her sentiments. Even under the cover of night, she felt exposed as the four of them huddled along the fence.

"What now?" she asked.

"We wait a couple of minutes," Avery said.

"Think there's a problem?" Bull asked.

Avery gave a firm shake of his head. "We're not thinking like that yet," he said sharply.

Tala took a deep breath, and despite herself, it shook when she exhaled. She shivered, goosebumps raised on her skin beneath her jacket, now soaked from the rain, the wind biting at her face. She could see her breath with every exhale. But it was easier to think about the cold than the risks she was taking to get out of the city. She gave her duffel a heave and readjusted the strap across her body.

Avery touched the nodes to the fence cable for a second time, then cursed again. "Bull," he said quietly but sternly, "I need you to see if you can track down Oracle and make sure there aren't any problems. We're running tight on time already, and if we miss our window, I'm not sure when we'll be able to try again."

A chill unrelated to the cold ran through Tala at the thought of not getting away. Thias would invariably find her if she stayed in Columbia City.

"Watch closely for security," he asserted, though that seemed obvious. "I'm sure they're crawling around this place after what happened yesterday."

Bull nodded, unfazed by his new mission, then turned on his heel and took off in a jog, sticking close to the fence line, quickly disappearing into the darkness.

Tala looked past the fence into the industrial shipping yard. A wall of large, rectangular shipping containers, stacked as many as six high, towered in the distance, the river just beyond that. She could make out the rumbling and beeping of a crane and heavy equipment in the distance as crews worked to load the ship.

Far off to her left stood a tall lamppost, the rain creating a halo around its soft glow, reflecting in the puddles on the ground.

She glanced anxiously around. This was taking too long.

The white beams of headlights suddenly appeared in the darkness from around a corner as an unexpected car approached, and she stiffened, her chest tightening.

"Get down," Avery snapped under his breath. The three of them dropped even lower, each of them nervously watching the nearing vehicle, the tires rolling over gravel that crunched as the car crept forward.

The headlights shone brightly, illuminating the shipping yard beyond the fence. And although they weren't yet in their range of vision, Tala knew that if the vehicle continued its advance, it wouldn't be long before they were spotted. There was nothing to shield them. They were exposed sitting ducks. The urge to run came over her, and her body shook. Kane reached out, putting his hand on her shoulder, giving it a gentle squeeze, grounding her. She dropped a knee to the ground to steady herself, the water soaking through her denim pant, and she stared unblinking at the car as it came to a slow stop, its brakes squealing loudly, the engine knocking as it sat there idling.

"The fence is dead," Kane whispered, his voice deep.

Avery cocked his head to the side as he looked at him curiously. Tala knew he heard the electrical current go dead. Avery reached for the multimeter, touching the nodes to the fence cable again, and sighed in relief. Digging into the backpack, he pulled out a bolt cutter. Bringing the blades to the fence, he gave a hard squeeze, slicing through the thick cable. It snapped back sharply, the tension severed. Without hesitation, he sheared through three more, creating enough space to squeeze beneath.

"Let's go," he said as he tossed the backpack through the opening, then quickly crawled through. Tala chucked her duffel through next, then ducked beneath the overhead cables as she slid through, Kane following after her.

Tala heard the slam of a car door as she reached for her bag, slinking her head through the strap.

"Hey," the deep voice of a man called through the darkness. "Someone out there?" he asked as the beam of a flashlight swept over them.

"C'mon," Avery called over his shoulder as he sprinted toward the mass of shipping containers.

Tala took off in a brisk run, Kane easily in stride beside her as they ran for cover. Slipping between a small gap in the wall of containers, they were quickly swallowed up by the maze of steel boxes.

With Avery just ahead, she ran hard, adrenaline pumping through her veins as they weaved through narrow rows and around sharp corners, and in less than a minute, Tala had completely lost her sense of direction, swimming in a sea of cargo containers.

"Keep close," Avery whispered as he slowed his pace.

Tala glanced around, trying to regain her bearings. But Avery seemed to know exactly where he was. She knew he was no amateur.

As they rounded a corner, Tala heard two men making indistinct conversation, and her breath hitched. Being caught wasn't an option.

"Security," Avery mouthed to them as he brought his finger to his lips, then turned and took slow, quiet steps away from the voices.

Her heart hammered hard in her chest as she followed closely behind him, Kane on her heels. Her shoes sunk into thick mud, and she splashed through puddles, though the cold was no longer on her mind.

As they rounded a sharp bend and slipped through a narrow opening, Tala's shoulder caught a piece of protruding metal from a container, slicing through her jacket and into her arm, and she let out a gasp from the instant pain.

Avery slowed as he looked back at her, but biting hard on the inside of her cheek, she silently waved him on.

She winced as she gripped her shoulder with the hand from her good arm, pain radiating down her arm and into her fingers.

"You okay?" Kane called from behind in a low voice, and she nodded.

Cautiously, they made their way down a wide aisle between the piled high containers, and Tala could hear the heavy machinery close by.

"Okay," Avery finally said as he came to a stop and turned toward both of them. "Home sweet home," he said, slightly winded, as he smirked and gave a nod toward the dull orange cargo box. He gave a hard tug on the ajar door, and it creaked as it opened.

Tala tensed as the loud horn from a ship blared into the night. Inhaling deeply, the chilly air making her lungs burn, she let out a small cough. Still holding her throbbing shoulder, she stepped inside the shadows of the oversized box, her feet shuffling over the steel floor, echoing into the cavernous container. She turned to Avery.

"I don't know what to say," she said quietly.

"Just stay alive, get out of the country, and whatever you do, don't stop fighting," he said. "I'll admit that I misjudged you. You're tougher than I imagined, and your brother is going to regret the day he decided to stand against you. You might not have much now, but you've got us. We don't bet on just anyone," he said, his wet, bleached hair hanging into his eyes, a devious grin curling on the corner of his mouth.

She pursed her lips together and gave him a half-smile in return.

"Right then," Avery said under his breath as he turned toward Kane, handing him the backpack he'd been carrying. "There's a light in here. It has a full charge, so even if you run it the whole journey, you'll still have life to spare from it. There's water and a blanket in here too. It's going to be cold. Especially in this weather. Fortunately, you're heading south. And there's a bucket in the corner inside for, well, you know," he said as he pointed into the darkness behind Tala.

"That's great," she said with a sigh as she glanced at Kane.

"I won't listen," he said with a small chuckle.

"Should take about seven hours to get down to Bristol," Avery said. "Sit tight until Freelancer can get to you. She'll knock hard five times. That's her signal. Don't let anyone else open this door," he said sternly as he eyed Kane. "And don't get too shaken up when the crane lifts this thing onto the ship. It won't be long now. All right. I think you're set. Good luck," he said with a nod, his eyes darting between them.

"What about you? And Bull?" she asked.

"We'll be fine. We know our way home," he said.

Kane tapped his forearm to Avery's, then he stepped inside beside Tala.

"Thanks, man," Kane said, and a moment later, the doors closed, and they were left in complete blackness.

Kane was quiet, and Tala reached for him, grabbing hold of his arm. She could hear his steady breathing, and she stepped closer to him. She felt for the backpack in his hands and took it from him, wincing as she grabbed it with her injured arm. She dug blindly through the bag, feeling the water bottles beneath the blanket, then her fingers found a hard cube, and she pulled it out. Fumbling it in her hand for a moment, she found the power button. Pressing it, the cube lit up brightly enough to illuminate the entire inside of the empty container.

Her eyes met Kane's, dark shadows cast over his face, and he looked at her quietly.

As the seconds passed, their silence grew louder.

"I never wanted this for you," he said finally, his voice reverberating off the steel walls, amplifying it. "I've spent so many years living in the shadows, and this isn't what I wanted for you," he said with a solemn shake of his head, his shoulders falling.

"It won't be forever," she said. "And I'll only be in the shadows until I get out of the Republic. Then I'll be free. We'll be free. Really free, where we can be together without watching over our shoulder. That's worth all of this," she said as she motioned to the space around them.

He was silent again, a pensive look in his dark eyes. "Let me see your shoulder," he said a minute later.

"It's fine," she said dismissively.

"Tala," he said firmly.

She dropped the bag and took a step closer to him. Unzipping her jacket and gingerly sliding it off her shoulder, she revealed her bloodied and torn shirt.

"It's nothing I can't fix," he said as he helped ease her out of the wet jacket. He reached his cold hand under the hem of the short sleeve and cupped her shoulder in his palm.

Tala winced and looked away as she took in a deep breath to clear her head and push away the throbbing pain. A moment later, she felt her shoulder begin to grow warm under his touch, then hot. She remembered the first time he had done this. The exasperation she'd felt. That felt like a lifetime ago.

The pain in her shoulder dissipating, then gone altogether, Kane slipped his hand out from under her sleeve and took a small step back. When his eyes met hers, there was a flutter in her belly. He had a way of stirring something in her with only a single glance.

Tala sprawled her wet jacket out on the floor, not too hopeful it would dry in a dark, cold shipping container, but it was worth trying. She dug into her duffel, pulling out a thick sweatshirt and slipped into it. The dry cotton was soft on her skin as it took away the bite of the chill in the air.

Kane slipped off his wet leather jacket and laid it beside hers.

She reached for his hand, and he took hers eagerly. He grabbed the wool blanket from the backpack, and they took a seat, the steel floor cold beneath them, their backs against the wall. Tala shivered as he slipped his arm around her, pulling her closely.

"We're going to be okay," she whispered as she pulled the blanket up to her chin.

"I wish I had your confidence," he said.

"You used to run around with the Rebels and have managed to live secretly under the Republic's nose for years. Since when do you think you can't go up against them?" she asked as she stole a glance up at him.

He lowered his head and kissed her softly on her head. "Since I had so much to lose."

She was quiet, sinking farther into him. She had made a mess of her life and was pulling him into it. He had been off the radar of the Republic for over a decade, and now, he was likely to be discovered. Vaughn had seen what he could do, and she was certain he wouldn't rest until he identified him. Until he found him. This very thought filled her with dread. He was all she had left. But was she being selfish by holding on to him?

She thought about Thias, not as the murderer he was now, but as the twenty-one-year-old version of himself. She was sitting in Command, in what was now Captain Kole's office, on a small couch with a blanket wrapped around her, the weight of emotion heavy on her heart. As she tried to rub a streak of soot from her bare arm, Thias came into the office. He stood tall and strong as their gazes met from across the room.

"Tala," he said as he approached, his blue eyes soft and gentle, and he took a seat beside her. "I'm going to take care of you," he whispered. "I'll always protect you."

She had leaned into him. Despite her breaking heart, she felt safe beside him, believing he would be true to his word. They no longer had their parents, but they had each other.

Now she knew the truth, and it tainted this very memory. She was supposed to have died in the fire; she was the upset of his plan. Though she couldn't help but wonder if, despite it all, some part of him meant what he said. Even in some warped way. He had been all that she had left, and she clung to him. Of all the things she regretted, even as she sat in a cold shipping container trying to get away from him, loving him as her brother wasn't one of them.

"My parents are dead, and my brother betrayed me," she said quietly as she broke the silence that had settled between her and Kane. "I have no family," she said, hearing the sadness in her voice.

"You have me," he said, his chin resting gently on her head. "I will never betray you, and I will never abandon you. I'll be your family," he said resolutely.

Tala felt a rush of warmth come over her as she looked up at him, their eyes meeting, and she felt calm, she felt safe. He was all that she needed. Despite everything, she had managed to gain just as much as she had lost. Even more.

Kane brought his face down, his lips brushing gently over hers. She reached up, her hand sliding behind his head, and she pulled him to her and kissed him earnestly. Even if it was selfish, she was never going to give him up.

TWENTY-ONE

The cargo container was frigid, Kane's breath rising in puffs, but after the many hours they'd spent hidden away, his body had acclimated. He peered down at Tala, asleep in his arms, their bodies intertwined and wrapped tightly in the wool blanket. While he longed for unconsciousness, if only to pass the time, he didn't think he would be able to sleep, but he had managed to doze off at some point. At least for a little bit. But he was awake now, his brain regurgitating the frenzy in his mind. He wondered what time it was. How long had they been hidden away? He had nothing to tell the time with, and he sighed.

His tension wore on him. He felt it in his muscles, he felt it needling into his bones. His head was throbbing, he could feel the pulsing in his temples, and he took a ragged breath, letting it fall into his hands.

The silence within the shipping container was a false reality playing with his mind, taunting him. It made it seem like the outside world had simply disappeared. But it was still there, and it was just as dangerous for them as ever.

Fear had rarely been a driving emotion in his life. Hatred, yes, but not fear. Until now, that was. Things had been easier living in the shadows. And then Tala entered his life, and while she was worth everything, things had become a hundred times more difficult. She made him vulnerable. Max mattered to him, greatly, he was the true definition of family, but what he had with Tala was strong enough, rare enough, to change the tides in the sea.

While physically, Tala was ten times more capable than Max, he never worried about him. And now he lived in a state of constant fear, fear that something would happen to her. Fear that he wouldn't be able to protect her.

She was his whole world, and that terrified him.

Looking down at her now, she looked at peace. Sleep was her only reprieve from all the turmoil. He loved her more than anything, and yet he knew that somehow, he would love her more tomorrow. She had given him a reason to hope for the future, and that was dangerous. He reminded himself, almost scolded himself, that the present was all he could afford to think about. Tomorrow was so far away, a million things to do between now and then, with a million things on the line, and a million things that could happen to ruin it all. But she had given him hope, and despite himself, he found that he still looked for tomorrow.

A loud creak of flexing steel screamed into the silence, followed by an even louder clanking, and Tala jerked awake. Sitting up abruptly, she looked up at him, shadows from the lamplight playing across her face, and he gave her a weak smile. They had arrived. The easy part was over. Now they had to get off the ship. Now they had to drive across the country, at least twelve hours to the western border.

Tala's eyes were wide and alert, and he heard the quickening of her heart.

"It's okay," he said softly with a small chuckle from deep in his throat as he slid his hand down her back. "I think we're here."

She yawned, stretching her body.

"Did you sleep?" she asked.

"I did," he said. Though he wasn't about to admit he'd been awake most of the night with worry gnawing at him, that he was filled with dread over everything that came next. He had abilities that made it hard for others to come up against him, but he wasn't indestructible, he wasn't infallible. Even he had his limits, and even he could die just like everyone else.

Tala was his priority. The fear aside, it was anticipation that left him the most unsettled. Anticipation of the problems they were sure to encounter. And while he was smart enough to know they would encounter them, he had no way to predict them. He could only plan so much. And that's when the fear crept in. That fear owned him. But despite that heavy demon upon his shoulders, he was prepared to take on anything. She was all that mattered.

This was the dawn of a new revolution, proving only that mankind would always be doomed to repeat its mistakes. Walls could be built and borders drawn, but countries and governments would forever be run by people, and people were imperfect. There would always be greed, anger, selfishness, and that meant that peace was invariably and eternally going to be fleeting.

Kane switched off the light that had burned through the night, enshrouding them in complete darkness, and they held each other close in the tense silence. But it wasn't complete silence for him. He could hear her pounding heart and shallow, quick breaths, and it was distracting. She was a warrior, but it didn't mean she wasn't afraid. And she was made higher in his eyes because she forged ahead in the face of those fears.

The thick steel walls around them made it nearly impossible to hear anything beyond the shipping container they hid in. Kane wasn't sure how long they sat in the silence, in the dark, clinging to each other, but the knocks finally came. Like Avery had said. Five hard, steady knocks. He rose to his feet and knocked back, and a few seconds later, the doors opened, a rush of warm, humid sea air washing over them.

"Phoenix? Bluebird?" a woman asked, appearing before them, the sky still hidden by the darkness of night. They were up high, Freelancer clutching the door, balancing carefully on the bars of the door on the container stacked below them. She was a small woman with long, brown hair pulled back into a loose pony, thick tendrils falling around her face. She was dressed in dark clothes, a heavy leather vest, leather tactical gloves on her hands, and a leg holster secured tightly around her thigh holding a handgun and a sheathed knife. She was young, maybe younger than Tala, and he wondered how it was that she'd gotten involved with the UR. How someone so young would be entrusted to carry out such a high-risk mission.

"I'm Freelancer," she said with a firm nod of her head. "This ship is in line behind two others to be unloaded, meaning that for the next little bit, there will be few people walking around. The crew is still in their bunks. But it's not safe to go below deck. MF are around here, so stay alert." She reached behind her, pulling leather tactical gloves from her back pocket and handing them to each of them. "You'll need these when we take the mooring line off this ship," she said casually, then easily began to climb back down the cargo doors she had scaled to get to them.

Kane let Tala go next, taking the rear as they eased their way down to the vessel floor. They followed quietly, light on their feet, behind Freelancer as she wound her way through the narrow spaces between the towering stacks of cargo containers in the dim light of the docks. She navigated the deck easily.

They came to the bulkhead wall near the bow, and peering fleetingly over her shoulder, Freelancer swiftly scaled a ladder, then dropped to the floor on the opposite side. Tala, then Kane, followed after her.

In the bow of the ship, Kane sighed with brief relief knowing they wouldn't be as easily spotted in the area that was sectioned off from the rest of the vessel. It was the lights of the dock and the moon above that made it possible to ease around the massive chains and winches rolled with thick cables as they approached an opening in the sidewall, a mooring bowline strung down to the dock below, anchoring the ship.

Freelancer looked at them, her face shadowed in the dark. "We're taking the line down," she said, hushed. "The crews on the docks are down that way," she said, pointing to the right. "And we're going that way," she said, inclining her head in the opposite direction.

He and Tala slipped their gloves on, their fingers exposed at the tips.

"I'll go first. And I'll whistle from below when the coast is clear," Freelancer said, glancing between them, then turned on her heel. Crouching low, she eased her body through the gape in the side of the ship's wall. She pinched the thick rope between the soles of her boots, then using the strength of her arms, she began to descend, slow and steady at first, then gradually picking up speed. Her hands went one-by-one below each other, gripping the rope tightly, until finally reaching the bottom where she hopped over the hook the rope was tethered to, her feet firmly landing on the dock.

Kane watched Tala as she gazed down below, her eyes wide. He could hear her nervous heart hammering. "You've got this," he said with a small pump of his fist for encouragement. "Give me your bag," he gestured to the duffel slung across her chest. She also wore the backpack Avery gave them. "I can take yours down with mine."

She handed it to him, their eyes meeting, and she gave him an uneven smile. "It's been a while since I've fast roped," she said, then let out a nervous laugh under her breath. Tala eased her body through the opening, pinching the rope between her shoes as Freelancer had done, and in her ready position, she waited for the faint whistle that came a moment later. She nodded at Kane, then eased herself down the rope. His chest was tight as he watched her, her body suspended above the dark ocean below.

Though not as quick as Freelancer, she made her way down the rope with relative ease, and as her feet hit the dock below, he sighed in relief. He was next. He wanted to just hop over the side of the ship. It would be a long fall, though still manageable. But that would most definitely alarm Freelancer. So instead, he eased himself down the rope like they had.

Without a word, Freelancer gave them a wave of her hand, then took off in a jog across the dock as she headed for cover in the mass of shipping containers not far ahead. As they were slipping into the safety of the massive labyrinth, a voice yelled out to them.

Kane's mouth went dry, and he picked up his pace, right on Tala's heels as she closely followed behind Freelancer. But even as they were swallowed up by the mass of shipping containers, he could hear footsteps not far behind, a racing heartbeat that trailed them closely.

"I'm in pursuit," the person, a man with a scruffy voice, called. "I don't know how many. Spotted two for sure." He already sounded winded.

"We're coming in from the north and west," another voice cracked through a radio.

Kane and Tala followed Freelancer around a corner, and then he could hear them, more heartbeats, at least four of them. MF were near and closing in fast. At any moment, he knew they would be surrounded.

Freelancer slowed her pace, then came to a stop in a narrow, dark space between two rows of containers.

"Shit," she mouthed as she stole a glimpse around a corner, then abruptly sunk into a crouch, reaching her hand out and steadying her body with the steel wall of a container. Tala and Kane dropped down beside her, and she lifted her finger to her lips, then pointed silently to her left.

Kane couldn't see him, but he could hear him, he could smell him.

"Anyone have a visual?" a voice called statically through the radio.

"Negative," the man around the corner from them responded.

Kane's eyes met Tala's, dark and shadowed, but the alarm in them was unmistakable.

Tala gave him a hand signal of a gun, reminding him of the two plasma guns in her duffel. But he also knew there was no time to rifle through the bag.

Adrenaline pumped through his body like a wildfire raging in a dead forest, and he watched as a man, an MF agent, walked slowly past them, his back to them as they crouched in the small space, covered only by darkness. His plasma gun was drawn, ready for them. A moment later, he turned a corner, disappearing from sight.

Kane knew this was a shoot-to-kill scenario. If they were spotted, this would be it. They were outnumbered and outgunned. He gave one last look at Tala, leaned in and kissed her cheek, his lips lingering for a moment, then looked at Freelancer. He gestured with his hands and fingers, telling them to go as soon as the coast was clear, then he slipped out of their hiding space and around a corner. With his eyes no longer on Tala, his heart was caught in his throat, and he desperately hoped he was making the right decision.

It was their only chance. He had to attack first. All he knew was that if he was able to distract the MF enough, maybe Tala and Freelancer would have a chance.

Kane approached the end of the row with caution. He knew an agent was standing just around the corner. It was more than just hearing him, than smelling him, he could actually feel his presence. He had to be swift. He couldn't hesitate.

He took a deep breath and rounded the corner, the agent quick with his gun. But Kane was quicker, slipping his arm below the agent's chin, around his neck, and he tightened his grip. The man's body thrashed wildly. Dropping his plasma gun, he clawed at the sleeve of Kane's leather jacket, just as Vaughn had. Kane tightened his grip, and after a few seconds, the agent's body went limp with unconsciousness. Quickly, Kane took the cuffs from the agent's pocket, then pulling the man's arms behind him, he restrained him at the wrists, looping the cuffs through the steel bar of a container door. He kicked the gun out of his reach and tossed his radio, then turned on his heel, disappearing farther into the maze.

Kane rounded corner after corner, losing himself deeper into the web of cargo boxes until finally, he picked up the sound of labored breathing. He slowed his pace and stole a brief peek around a corner to find a second agent easing slowly down a row, his back to him. And like he had with the first agent, Kane rushed him, subduing him and cuffing him to a container door.

His senses alert and in overdrive, he hurried down the narrow aisles and around corners, and in the distance, he could make out the faint sound of beating hearts and footsteps. More than one. He turned in circles, trying to find his bearings, unsure whether he was even hearing Tala or Freelancer.

Closing his eyes, he exhaled deeply to clear his head, even his thoughts of Tala slipping away. His mind homed in on the sound of a single heartbeat. Taking a slow, long breath, he fixed on it as he let his senses do what they had been designed to do.

And then he heard them, loudly and clearly.

His breath caught.

First was the deep electrical blast of a plasma charge, followed by two gunshots.

Kane's heart dropped, and without a second thought, he took off, his body blurring through the maze. He had no idea where he was going, but those gunshots only meant one thing: someone had found Freelancer. Someone had found Tala.

Rounding a corner, his breath hitched as he spotted the lifeless body of an MF agent lying on the ground, blood pooling around his head, a bullet in the shoulder and a second to the forehead, and for a fleeting moment, relief came over him.

He looked around, narrow aisles between towering rows of stacked containers leading off in three directions. He glanced frantically down each one, desperate for any clue to point him along. In the distance, he could make out the faint sound of feet receding from where he stood. His only hope, he turned to follow in their direction. His mind went to Tala, somewhere in this labyrinth without him, and his gut twisted with anxiety. He wouldn't let this be the end. He couldn't.

Kane slowed his pace, taking cautioned steps, rounding a corner, finding the next aisle empty. The footsteps were growing fainter.

With nothing left to do, he took a guess, turning left and taking off in a jog, his ears and mind alert, straining for anything.

Then he heard them. Heartbeats. Three distinctly different beats.

"Don't move!" he heard, a deep voice calling loudly into the night.

Kane's breath caught as he picked up his pace.

"They said we might run into trouble," the voice yelled. "And look what I've found." The stranger's voice echoed off the steel walls, making it difficult to pinpoint the direction it came from.

Kane turned corner after corner, only to find more empty rows. His heart raced frantically as he tried to focus on the sound of the man's voice, but thoughts of Tala in trouble clouded his mind.

"I said don't move," the voice called out again. "I've got them in the open lot on the north side," he said, likely into his radio. But no response came back to him. "I said I've got them," he repeated.

"What'd you do?" the man hollered angrily. "You think you can take down my team and that I'd let you walk away?"

His voice was growing louder, and Kane knew he was getting closer, but around every turn, he came up empty. Every step he took, every passing moment when he couldn't find them, he was one moment closer to completely losing everything. Maybe leaving them had been a mistake. He was so close now, he could feel her in his chest, but she was still out of reach.

Time was running out.

"Wait a second," the man yelled. "You're Alexander," he said, and Kane could hear the unmistakable pleasure in his voice as her identity registered. "You're wanted for questioning in the attacks in Columbia City."

"If you think you can take her alive, you've got another thing coming," Freelancer yelled back, her voice steady and firm, unwavering. "There's no way she's going back."

The agent let out a mirthless laugh, sending a chill running through Kane's body.

He was so close. He could feel it.

"She's supposed to be taken alive," he called back. "But I'm more than happy to make sure she doesn't go back if that's what you really want. No one would blame me if I said she was about to attack me."

Kane's heart hammered so loudly that it was almost deafening in his ears. There was a tightness in his chest making it difficult to breathe. He was going to fail her. Everything will have been for nothing.

He turned another corner to find only another empty row. His panic was visceral. His chest was now threatening to explode, adrenaline and fear surging through him. And while the sound of two heartbeats pounded rapidly nearby, the third was slowing.

Kane rounded a corner, an open lot sprawling out before him. Tala and Freelancer stood beside each other, opposite him, and he watched as Tala lifted her chin high. Freelancer steadily held her gun in her hands, pointing it keenly across the empty lot. Kane's eyes followed its aim, looking to his left to see the MF agent with his plasma gun drawn, his sights directly on Tala. His heart all but stopped.

Time seemed to stand still, the scene before him freezing for a fleeting moment. Then he heard it, the sound of the agent sucking in a slow breath. Kane's eyes flared. Without hesitation, he rushed the agent. Kane was at him in the flash of a second, clasping his hands around the man's head. With a sharp snap, his neck broke, his body dropping to the dirt with a dull thud.

Breathlessly, Kane looked down at the lifeless body. Then he swallowed hard as he steeled himself and looked up, relief washing over him like a tidal wave as Tala ran for him, Freelancer standing in the background, the hand holding her gun dropping to her side.

Tala threw herself into his arms, and he gripped her hard, his heart racing, his fingers tingling.

"Guys," Freelancer called in a hushed voice. "We've gotta go! You can hug later."

They released each other, and Kane took a breath, his eyes locking onto hers. In the blink of an eye, he had nearly lost everything, and he knew that in that moment, he'd never been more grateful for anything in his life.

Tala lay flat across the backseat of the small car as they sped down a nearly deserted highway. Occasional headlights meeting, then quickly passing them. Kane repeatedly glanced over his shoulder at her from the front seat, the relief on his face palpable, and she gave him a reassuring smile each time.

They rode in silence, the three of them, the hum of the car playing like quiet music. Tala gazed up out the backseat window, the sky like a black ocean above them, the moon a beacon in the west that guided them along. She had never seen it so big and full, its light spilling across the backseat and casting a soft and silvery glow over her pale skin. It was so much brighter without the lights of the city to dull it, dimming even the stars around it. She propped herself up, just high enough to steal a full glance out the window, and she gazed in wonder. Where she was used to seeing buildings, there now stood trees, trees spreading densely over the land as far as she could see in every direction. It was surreal, the realization hitting her that she really was out of the city, that she was never going back.

"Keep your head down, Tala," Freelancer said quietly as she glimpsed her in the rearview mirror. They were the first words spoken in nearly an hour.

"You know my name?" she asked quietly, and she watched Freelancer nod, glancing at Kane and then back to the road ahead.

"You're my mission, of course I know your name. Besides, you're hard to mistake for anyone else," she said with a small grin.

Tala sighed. She was an Alexander, and it was her blond hair and blue eyes. She'd stood out her entire life. She could never be safe in the Republic.

She studied Freelancer. She wasn't a big person and looked young, but she was more than capable. She knew what she was doing when she got them off the ship, got them out of the shipping yard. And even when the MF agent had discovered them, she showed no fear, her only priority being Tala.

"Your picture has been plastered across every National Statement coming out of Columbia City," Freelancer said. "You're wanted for questioning in connection with the attacks."

"Will that change things?" Kane asked, his voice deep and rough.

Freelancer shook her head. "We're proceeding as planned. The three of us will drive to the western border, where Vulcan will be waiting for us to get us into the Colonies."

"Who is Vulcan?" Tala asked with hesitation.

"A top UR leader. A tough one, but a good one," she said, her voice trailing off.

The car went quiet again, and Tala looked back up at the moon. It would be daylight soon, which would only make it that much harder to hide her.

"We're going to a safe house right now," Freelancer said. "We'll get you both cleaned up and fed. You'll undoubtedly attract attention in public if you're both as dirty as you are now. I'm guessing it was muddy back in the city?"

"It was raining," Tala said.

Freelancer nodded.

"What about me? My hair. If you think I'm going to stand out with a little dirt on me, I'll stand out ten times more as a blond traipsing around."

"First of all, it's not just a *little* dirt," she said with a low chuckle under her breath. "And second, yes, we need to do something about your appearance."

"Who announced I was a person of interest?" she asked.

Freelancer was quiet for a moment, and Tala felt her heart sink a little.

"It was Thias, wasn't it?" Tala said and watched as Freelancer nodded.

"I'm sorry," she said with contrition. "I can't imagine any of this is easy."

"No," Tala mumbled. None of it was easy.

"Cara," Freelancer said firmly. "Figure if I'm going to know your name, it's only fair you know mine," she said with a glance in the mirror again, and Tala gave her a half-smile.

"Kane," he said as he turned toward Cara.

"Well, we're all officially acquainted," she said. "And I guess I should also say thank you for your help back there." Her eyes didn't leave the road, but Tala saw the tension in her outstretched arms on the steering wheel. "Even if I have no idea what I saw."

Kane glanced quickly to Tala, then turned forward. "I just did what I had to do," he said flatly.

Cara solemnly nodded her head. And that was the end of that conversation.

Tala woke to the sunshine streaming in through the windows, nearly burning through her eyelids, and she brought her hand to her face to shade them as they fluttered open. Her body was stiff, crammed in the small backseat of the car, her head pressed against one door, her feet wedged against the other.

Kane turned in the front seat, peering back at her with a small smile that didn't meet his eyes. "Morning," he said.

Tala offered a weak one in return, then yawned, stretching her arms up. She saw the exhaustion on his face, in his posture, the way his shoulders slumped forward, and she knew that despite what he said, he hadn't slept.

"Can I sit up yet?" she asked.

"Soon. Sorry," Cara said, her eyes flickering a glimpse back at her through the mirror.

Tala couldn't see much out the windows, the blue sky above and the tops of rolling, tree-covered hills just above the tips of her shoes, and she sighed with anticipation. She wanted to look around. She wanted out of the backseat.

Time ticked by slowly, one minute dragging into the next at half-time. The tedium of the ride flat on her back was boring. But Tala quickly reminded herself it was better than action or excitement, which only meant trouble. So she lay there, crammed, without complaint.

"We're here," Cara finally said as the car turned off the smooth, paved road onto loose gravel that crunched below the tires. Tala was tossed across the seat, her head bouncing hard against the door as they hit pothole after pothole. She breathed a sigh of relief when the car came to a stop.

"You're in the clear," Cara said as she looked over her shoulder. "We'll get you two fed and bathed and then get back on the road."

Tala crawled out of the backseat of the car and stretched her cramped legs. She glanced around, feeling her mouth gape as she took in the sight. It was the most beautiful thing she had ever seen, her senses converging in a surge: the sound of the rushing water in the river before her, a woodpecker somewhere in the distance pounding loudly, his rhythmic tapping echoing through the still, warm air on her face. The sky was a vibrant, deep blue with puffy white clouds on the horizon. A smell that was entirely foreign to her hung in the air, sweet and smoky at the same time, and beyond the lush and colorful forest surrounding her, small plumes of smoke rose above the treetops. She bent down, running her hand across the thick grass that was covered with a thin layer of lingering morning dew, wetting her hand, the long blades tickling her wrist. The unfiltered world around her brought happiness to life inside of her, giving way to pure amazement over its splendor.

She rose to her feet and looked sheepishly at Cara, who watched her intently, and she felt her cheeks redden. "Sorry," she mumbled.

Cara's mouth curled into a smile, and she shrugged. "It's a little different than the city," she said, and Tala nodded.

Kane reached his hand out to her, and Tala took it, his skin warm and dry against hers, and they turned, following Cara to the door of the log cabin-looking house, a worn porch wrapping around it on two sides.

Cara knocked hard. "It's Freelancer," she called out loudly.

A moment later, a middle-aged woman, tall and stocky with deep ebony skin, thick waves in her short hair, and wide, gentle eyes, answered the door. She looked both strong and beautiful, and she smiled kindly at the sight of Cara, then took a step back to let her in.

"Well, aah'll be," the woman said in a booming voice as her eyes fell upon Tala. "This is a real turn of events."

Tala followed Cara into the house, Kane, still holding her hand, following behind.

"Aah'll be honest," the woman said, "Aah wasn't too keen on letting y'all in now, but Cara assured me there'd be no problems." She spoke at a leisurely pace, drawing out her vowels with a semi non-rhotic accent. Tala had never heard a true southern accent before, and she couldn't help but find it completely charming to listen to.

"I mean no trouble," Tala said, feeling small beside her.

"Tala, this is Clarke," Cara said with a nod between them. "And this is Kane."

Clarke eyed them carefully, and Tala couldn't tell if it was skepticism that she saw in her eyes or approval.

"Well," Clarke said after a moment, "let's git yeh both cleaned up. Caint have y'all runnin' round covered in mud."

Tala glanced down at herself, the bottoms of her jeans brown, painted with dirt, splatter as high as her thighs, the soles of her shoes with thick, caked-on mud, and she looked up at Clarke and nodded.

She and Kane slipped off their shoes, then followed Clarke down a short hallway. She turned in front of a door and tipped her head to the side.

"Bathrum's right hee-yah. Plenty of water. And y'all can change in this bedrum," she said, pointing to the door across the hall.

"Tala, yeh don't need to wash yeh hair. We gonna dye it first. Yeh runnin' round here with that pretty blond hair is tantamount to holdin' up a sign with yeh name plastered cross it. MF been all ovah the place lookin' for DeSoto nats, and now with yeh labeled a person of interest in the attack in the capital, it's even more dangerous."

"I'm grateful for your hospitality," Tala said, knowing she sounded feeble. She wondered what you said to someone you've never met who was going out of their way to save your life.

"You take the first shower," Kane said. "I'll grab our bags from the car." He gave Tala a small smile and nodded at Clarke, then turned quickly and retreated the way they had just come.

Tala stepped into the small bathroom and closed the door. Despite her stints of sleep in the shipping container and the car, which had been fitful at best, she was tired, her body exhausted. But she couldn't let that drag her down. She had come far, but she wasn't there yet. People were counting on her, and she refused to let them down. She refused to let herself down.

Her mind wandered to Mila, back in the city, lying in a hospital bed. She thought of Max. And even Avery. These people were relying on her, they believed in her.

She reached for the shower faucet and turned it on, the water taking a few minutes to heat up, and she stepped into it eagerly before it was completely warm. It felt good on her skin. Refreshing. The quiet, only the sound of the water, filling her soul, calming her body and mind, the respite fortifying her for what was coming next.

She wasn't sure how long she stood there, the hot water cascading down her, her skin bright red from the heat, and she finally leaned over, shutting the water off. A rush of cool air came over her, and she shivered. She reached for the towel and stepped out of the shower as a knock came at the door, and Kane's face appeared as he cracked it slightly open.

"I'm finished," she said as she pulled the door open the rest of the way.

"Your bag is in the bedroom. And they're ready to color your hair in the kitchen," he said.

"Think I'll look as good as a brunette as I do as a blond?" she teased.

He smiled. "Absolutely."

"Is it weird that I think I'll miss it? My blond hair, I mean."

He shook his head. "It'll wash out."

She nodded, then leaned in and gave him a small kiss. "Hope I didn't use all the hot water," she said with a smirk as she pushed past him, but he caught her hand, stopping her. She spun toward him, and he slipped a hand behind her, pulling her against him, and kissed her. Tala melted into him, and when they finally separated, she smiled. Kissing him was the greatest thing. Her heart swelled, her body tingled, and happiness pumped through her veins. She never wanted to imagine a day without him.

Tala found Cara and Clarke right where Kane said she would, in the kitchen and ready to color her hair.

"Take a seat," Clarke said with a nod toward a chair, and Tala followed orders. Clarke grabbed at the ponytail, pulling the band out of her hair, her long locks falling down her back and over her shoulders.

"Aah'd cut it if aah had any skills with a scissors," Clarke said in her booming voice that filled the room as she handed a small, handheld mirror to Tala. "But aah'd make yeh look somethin' awful, and that'd only draw attention to yeh." She grabbed the hair, sectioning it into three parts, then took a bottle with a pointed tip and squeezed the brown cream along the parted hairline. With her fingers and the help of a comb, she pulled the color through her strands, the blond quickly disappearing as Tala watched in the mirror.

"Yeh got lots a hair, gaarl," Clarke said with a chuckle a while later as she reached for the last chunk of sectioned hair. Tala gave a small nod, watching quietly, feeling a small emotional tug. Kane was right, it wasn't going to be forever. A few washes and she'd be back to normal.

Kane appeared in the kitchen dressed in clean clothes, and Tala noticed his trimmed facial hair and freshly shaven head and she smiled. She couldn't help but find him so good-looking. A combination of handsome and rugged and sexy, and she felt a flutter in her belly.

"Wow," he said with big eyes.

"Hope that's a good wow," Cara said with a laugh.

"Of course it is," he said as he crossed the kitchen and took a seat near her. "What's our plan?" he asked, squaring his shoulders to her.

"That sandwich is for yeh," Clarke said with a nod to Kane as she pointed to a plate on the table.

"We'll leave here when she's ready," Cara said.

Kane reached for the plate, then took a large bite of the sandwich. "Home baked bread reminds me of my mother," he said between bites.

"Plenty more for y'all too," Clarke said.

"Our goal is Waterford. About eight hours from here," Cara said as she leaned back in her chair, folding her arms across her chest. She was still dressed in her black pants, gray top, and brown leather vest. But she had removed the leg holster that held her gun and knife.

"Patrols are heavy now," Clarke cautioned. "Y'all need to stay alert at all times. Everyone is on edge after that attack in the city. People will report anythin' 'spicious. Now," she said with a heavy breath. "Tala, yeh wash yeh hair out. Y'all need to git going sun."

Tala rose from the chair and made her way down the hall, Kane following after her.

"I'll help," he said as they stepped into the small bathroom and closed the door, pressing it hard until they heard it latch.

Tala knelt and leaned her head over the edge of the tub. The water ran over her scalp and through her hair, dark brown washing down the drain. Kane rubbed his fingers firmly through her long strands and scrubbed at her scalp, and she watched as the water slowly ran clear. He helped her shampoo and condition it, and rinsed it a second time, then turned off the water, and she wrapped a towel around her head.

She sat on the edge of the tub, brushing through her snarls, and they stared quietly at each other. Anticipation was beginning to build as their time on the road grew nearer.

"I'm nervous," he finally said. "We don't know the area. What's the plan if we're spotted?" he asked, taking a seat beside her. Between the two of them, they took up the entire length of the tub.

Her eyes met his, they were unsettled, and she saw the stress-lines across his forehead.

"We don't separate. You and me. I know Cara can handle herself. But no matter what happens, we don't separate," she said firmly, then pressed her lips together.

He nodded. "I won't leave you," he said quietly.

"And I won't leave you," she said as she reached up and stroked the scruff along his jaw with her thumb. It was coarse to the touch. She gave him a small smile, more sad than happy.

"Vulcan," she said quietly. "What do you make of this person?"

"I really don't know. But the name alone leaves me a little uneasy," he admitted.

"You know it?" she asked.

He shook his head. "Only the mythology behind it. I read about it years ago when I was in the facility."

"Mythology?"

"Ancient Rome, all the way back to the first century," he explained. "Vulcan was the god of fire."

She was quiet as she considered this.

"We'll feel this person out together. But you're right," he said with a firm nod, "we don't separate."

TWENTY-TWO

Although Tala now had a full head of dark, coffee-brown hair, she was still made to sit in the backseat of the small car. But she was at least able to sit, rather than ride flat on her back.

She quietly gazed out the window, the diffuse of low-lying mountains fading into rolling hills as they pressed farther west. They'd gone through just one large city, large being relative as it was nothing in comparison to Columbia City, but otherwise, they had passed through only small towns, many with old buildings that likely predated the Great War. The world outside Columbia City was a vast contrast from anything she'd known.

Tala had only been allowed to leave the confined car twice to use the restroom, and even then, she'd worn sunglasses and been instructed to speak to no one and keep her head down.

The closer they got to Waterford, the more MF they encountered on the roads, and they had narrowly missed a traffic stop as they were waved through a security checkpoint. Tala had fake identification programmed into a palm pad, but that didn't mean she wouldn't be recognized. The dark hair would only get her so far.

Her heart had been in her throat when their car slowed, Kane squeezing her hand tightly, and all their relief had been palpable once they made it through.

It was dark now, and it seemed like their car was the only one on the road. Unlike the previous night, the moon was muted, a soft, white glow far off in the eastern sky, partially obstructed by the clouds. The stars were so brilliantly lit that she couldn't help but lift her eyes to the sea above and stare. The view she'd had her whole life couldn't compare on even its best night with the one from the little backseat. In the city, the stars teetered on the edge of visibility, but out here, they were bright and bold and completely mesmerizing. The flickering radiance of all those stars in the black velvet sky pulled at something deep inside her. She felt small in comparison to the greatness around her. Gazing out the window at those distant lights silenced the worries in her mind, letting her simply forget.

She was brought back to reality by the ringing of Cara's palm pad. Reaching for it from the center console, Cara answered it quickly, bringing it to her ear as she continued to drive, her eyes fixed straight ahead.

Tala watched Kane carefully, seeing the strain in his neck, and she knew he was listening to the call. He reached his right hand back to her, and she laced her fingers through his. She could feel his tension in his grip.

Cara gave nothing away as she spoke.

When the call ended, she carefully set the palm pad back in the center console, her attention never leaving the road. Tala's eyes darted between both of them, staring at the backs of their heads, the silence settling throughout the car unnerving. Kane gave a single squeeze of her hand before releasing its hold. Dread flooded her veins, filling her up.

She knew Kane was going to say nothing in Cara's presence. He wasn't about to give away that he had been able to hear her conversation. And Cara silently stared at the road, picking up speed, the engine revving as she pushed the little car harder.

"What is it?" Tala finally asked, impatient and unable to wait any longer.

Cara stole a brief look at Tala through the rearview mirror, their eyes meeting, and she sighed.

"We won't be making it to Waterford tonight," she said, her voice deflated. "That was a call from one of my contacts. MF have security checkpoints all around the city. They've implemented a curfew. We're only about a hundred miles from the DeSoto border, Waterford being the biggest city. They're checking everyone."

"So now what?" Tala asked. Her chest was tight.

"We need to find a place to pull off. Hide for the night. It's too late to backtrack and take a wide berth around the city. It's after eleven, and we're about fifteen miles away. I don't want to be out later than we need to be. Our lone car on the road in the middle of the night will draw unwanted attention," she said, then suddenly braked hard, their bodies lurching forward, and took a sharp right turn onto a small road, a forested area ahead. "I'm not taking any chances of being found by patrols. I'm not a hundred percent sure of what they're looking for, DeSoto nats, UR, you," she said with a pause as she glanced back at Tala. "Which means I don't know how far outside the city they're looking. We'll take cover there," she said, pointing ahead.

Intent on reaching the fringe, they drove past open fields and a large pond, and Tala gazed at a handful of houses they passed, their windows lit brightly from inside. They turned down a gravel road heavily lined with trees, the stars disappearing behind their boughs, and Cara slowed the car, her headlights on bright.

Continuing ahead, Cara's head was on a swivel, quickly looking left, then right, then left again. "Ah," she said a few minutes later, quickly cutting her headlights, then turned the car off the road onto what was more like a wide trail with vehicle treads than a road. She drove slowly, trying to navigate in the dark as they went deeper and deeper into the thicket until she was satisfied they were far enough off the main road, even though there were still tire treads in the earth that led deeper yet.

She parked the car and turned off the engine, then looked over her shoulder at Tala. "We're camping here for the night," she said matter-of-factly.

Kane turned in his seat, looking back at Tala, a hardened expression on his face.

"It won't be safe for the three of us to sleep at the same time," Cara said. "We'll take it in shifts."

"You've been driving all day, and you'll be driving again tomorrow," Kane said as he looked across the front seat at Cara. "I'll take the first shift."

"I can do it," Tala offered. "You haven't slept much."

"I'll sleep once we're across the border," he said, shaking his head, then he opened the car door, the dome light flickering on, but he closed it quickly, the light going dark again. Tala watched him walk around the front of the car, the faint flickers from fireflies playing in the trees behind him. He opened the door to the backseat, a litany of chirping crickets and croaking frogs echoing through the quiet stillness around them, and crawled in beside her.

"All right then," Cara said with a shrug as she reclined the seat. "Will this bother you?" she asked over her shoulder.

"It's fine," he said. He reached for Tala, pulling her close to him, his arm slipping behind her, and she leaned into him. "Get some sleep," he mumbled as he tipped his head down, her hair catching on the scruff on his face.

Tala glanced briefly up at him, kissed him, then settled down in his arms. There was something about the way he held on to her that made her feel like he was holding her together, keeping her from falling apart. Closing her eyes, she let her exhaustion take over, and it was only minutes before her body surrendered to sleep.

Tala was shaken awake, and she opened her eyes to see Kane gazing down at her, his face enshrouded in shadows. She sat up, stretching her arms through the small backseat.

"I didn't want to wake her," he said quietly with a nod toward Cara, still asleep in the driver seat. "But I can't keep my eyes open any longer." She saw his fatigue in his face, his eyelids heavy.

"It's okay," she said, pushing back her grogginess. "Get some sleep," she whispered as she stole a glimpse up at him.

Kane slipped his hand behind her head, his fingers lacing through her hair, and pulled her to him, gently kissing her. She slipped her arms around him and leaned into him as she kissed him back.

His hand traced down her back, raising goosebumps across her arms. He kissed her deeply, thoroughly, waking her up. He made her heart both race and stand still simultaneously. He made her forget to breathe.

Her hands roamed over his shoulders, feeling his sinewy muscles below her touch. She was hungry for him. She wanted him more than anything.

She took a breath and pulled away, her eyes meeting his, and she knew he wanted her just as badly. She gave him a knowing smile, then ran her hand over his head, smooth to the touch, and he smiled back.

"How am I supposed to sleep now?" he asked under his breath.

"Well, it'll keep me awake," she teased.

He shook his head, his mouth curled into a smile, and he leaned in, kissing the corner of her mouth before he stretched back, propping himself between the corner of the seat and the door.

She slipped out of his grasp and watched as he folded his arms across his chest, dropping his head back, giving a small wiggle of his body as he adjusted to a comfortable position.

Reaching for the door, she opened it and stepped into the darkness, the air cool on her bare arms, and she shivered. She took a few steps away from the car, the trees thick around them, and she glanced aimlessly down the faint tire treads on the ground, both behind and in front of their car. She wondered what time it was, and with the moon out of sight, there was no way to guess based on how high or low it was in the sky.

Night this dark was a new experience, and she didn't let herself roam far, her feet stepping over dried leaves that crunched and twigs that snapped. The cool air helped push away her sleepy mind, and she slid her hands into the pockets of her jeans. She glanced back at the car behind her, then kept walking, the blackness around her like a heavy cloak that hid them from the rest of the world.

She tipped her head back, looking above her, longing to see the millions of stars. But she couldn't find even a glimpse of them through the thick tree canopy and sighed.

A flash of light on the trees around her caught her attention and she spun quickly on her heel, the white beams of headlights appearing in the distance between the trees from an approaching vehicle. Their lights so bright they stung as they shone in her eyes.

Her heart stopped, and her stomach dropped as she sprinted back to the car, yelling loudly, her voice piercing the peaceful quiet around them. She reached for the car door, throwing herself inside the front seat beside Cara.

"Someone's here!" she yelled as Cara and Kane shot upright.

"What?" Cara gasped in brief confusion as she looked around.

The vehicle came to a stop behind them, and from the side view mirror, Tala watched as two men stepped out of the car. It took only a moment for her to register who they were. Militia Forces.

Cara turned the key in the ignition, the car springing to life. She threw it into drive, her foot slamming on the gas pedal, and they took off with a jerk, driving deeper into the dark forest around them.

Tala turned over her shoulder, catching a glimpse of Kane, his eyes wide with panic.

"Tala, get in the back!" Cara yelled as she stared straight ahead and pushed the gas pedal harder. They were thrown up and down and side to side, the car barreling through the woods across uneven ground.

"Get in the back!" she yelled again.

Tala braced herself as she stepped onto the front seat, clutching the headrest to keep herself from careening into Cara. Through the back window, she saw the headlights as the MF prowler struggled to catch up from their head start. It flipped on its orange and red lights, telling them to stop. Tala's body was tossed around as she slid a foot over the center console and into the back, and Kane reached for her to help steady her as she brought her second foot into the back, hurling herself onto the seat beside him.

"Kane," Cara called over her shoulder. Her voice was filled with urgency. Though Tala couldn't help but notice there was no hint of panic. It was steady, controlled. "Grab my palm pad and call the number six."

Kane reached up to the front seat and grabbed the device, making the call.

"Put it on speaker," she instructed. "And hold it near my face."

Kane extended his arm forward, the palm pad only a foot away from Cara's head, and the three of them sat in tense silence as they listened to it ring, over and over. Tala held her breath, her chest tight, and her heart racing, and a male voice answered.

"Freelancer to Shotgun. I'm being pursued. I'm in possession of Bluebird," she said, her eyes never leaving the road in front of them.

With the treads on the ground growing fainter, the terrain grew rougher, and their small car labored over roots, rocks, and deep potholes. But even as their bodies thrashed around, Cara's foot never relented on the gas.

"Identifying your signal, standby while I locate you," Shotgun said.

"Westbound on an unmarked," she called into the palm pad. "North of the twenty-seven, approximately fifteen miles from Waterford."

The trees around them began to thin, and Tala caught the glimpse of the fading moon, the sky beginning to brighten in the eastern sky. She turned over her shoulder for another look at the MF behind them, who were now right on their tail.

"How many are on your six?" Shotgun asked, the volume turned loud on the palm pad.

"One," Cara said, and they drove into a clearing, tall grass on both sides of the car. "I'm running out of road," she yelled, and for the first time, Tala caught the edge of distress in her voice. Their car wasn't built for all-terrain.

"I've located you. Keep going. You're about to hit the highway in a few seconds," Shotgun said.

The grass around them only seemed to get thicker and taller, and Tala stretched her hand out, gripping Kane's thigh, her mind playing back their conversation from the day before.

"No matter what happens, we don't separate."

Her heart pounded, and she could feel her pulse in her fingertips. Adrenaline coursed through her, her body on fire, and she stole another glance behind her.

"Where's the highway?" Cara asked unsteadily into the palm pad, but as the words came out of her mouth, the grass cleared, giving way to a paved road. The front of the car hit the ditch-approach with force, then lurched onto the highway, and she cranked the steering wheel hard as she fought to keep the car on the road, the sound of their dragging front bumper screeching across the asphalt, kicking up sparks outside Tala's window before falling off completely.

The MF pulled onto the highway after them, their lights still flashing, keeping close on their tail with ease. Just as Tala looked over her shoulder, the rear window shattered with an explosive sound. Small fragments of glass rained down on them, and she ducked, instinctively bringing her hands above her head.

"Stay down, both of you!" Cara yelled over her shoulder. "I'm being shot at," she yelled into the palm pad, Kane's arm still outstretched, holding it close to her face while he kept his head low.

"Another mile. There's a row of tobacco barns to your right?" Shotgun asked.

"Yes," Cara confirmed as she stole a glimpse out the window.

"Yes. One more mile," he repeated.

Their car gave a sudden jolt as the MF vehicle rammed into their backside. Cara's knuckles were white as she gripped the steering wheel, fighting to maintain control of the car as they were rear-ended a second time.

Cara pressed harder on the gas pedal, pushing the car and everything it was capable of.

A plasma charge blasted through the car, Tala feeling the heat of the pulse as it blew past her head, hitting the windshield, the glass splintering around the hole it made, and Cara sank lower in her seat.

"I don't think I've got a mile!" she shouted over the noise of the air rushing through the car.

"Just hang on, Freelancer," Shotgun said.

"Tala," she called over her shoulder. "Lift your seat. There are two handguns. Use them!"

"I've got plasma guns," Tala yelled above the whirring of the wind as she fumbled for her duffel on the floor.

"No!" Cara yelled. "If they don't know you're in the car already, they will after using a plasma!"

Tala slid off the seat and gave it a hard tug, the cushion lifting to reveal a compartment, two handguns sitting in the middle of it. She reached for them, handing one to Kane. It was heavier than a plasma gun and cold in her hand.

"The safety is engaged," Cara called loudly as she took a hand off the steering wheel, taking the palm pad from Kane.

Tala looked down at the foreign gun in her hands and toggled the small switch. She sucked in a sharp breath, her knees on the seat, and bracing herself, she lifted her head just high enough to catch a glimpse of the MF prowler behind them. She reached forward, the gun firmly in her hand, and fired three rounds, the gun recoiling terribly between each shot. Kane fired his gun beside her, all of their bullets ricocheting off the windshield, not so much as puncturing their glass.

"It's bullet-proof," she yelled to the front seat as she crouched low. Another plasma charge pulsed through the car and drilled through their windshield, this one shattering it entirely, glass shards everywhere across the dash and Cara's lap.

"Damn it!" Cara blurted out. "Shotgun, where are you?"

"Next overpass. Less than a quarter mile ahead."

Tala stole a look forward between the two front seats, spotting the mentioned overpass as they approached. There was just enough daylight now, and she watched as a figure came into view above the bridge's sidewall. Lit up by Cara's headlights, Tala watched as she registered a person pulling up something long and thin, resting it over the top of their shoulder, and her eyes widened with realization. As they passed below, Tala turned over her shoulder just as the prowler exploded into a fury of flames, a boom clapping loudly as the inferno flipped through the air and slammed back into the pavement in a heap before sliding across the road and into the ditch.

"Direct hit!" Cara exclaimed, then laughed into the palm pad, a wide smile stretched across her face.

"Freelancer, you've got to get off the highway," Shotgun commanded. "I see two vehicles approaching, one from the east, the other from the west. Could be MF backup."

"Where the hell am I supposed to go?" she snapped, her smile quickly gone.

"There's a dirt road ahead. On the right. Take it," he said.

Cara spotted the road and slammed on the brakes, Tala and Kane careening into the back of the front seats.

The car turned sharply, its tires screeching, and Cara hit the gas hard, a plume of dust left in their wake as she sped down the dirt road.

"In a half mile is another dirt road to your left. Take it," Shotgun directed.

"Are you kidding me?" Cara spat into the palm pad. "They're not going to help!"

"They're your only shot right now. You stay in that car and you'll be arrested before you make it two miles down the road. I've got Evergreen reaching out as we speak," he said calmly.

Cara shook her head, a grimace across her face. Tala glanced with uncertainty at Kane, and he shrugged as he shook his head.

"They're not going to help!" Cara yelled.

"Make them help," Shotgun said firmly.

Cara slowed the car as she turned left, then quickly picked her speed back up as they floored it across the dirt road.

"Is there anyone on my tail?" Cara asked with a steady voice.

"No. You're still in the clear," he said.

"Well, I guess I can take it from here," she snapped. "But when this falls to hell—"

"Make it happen," he said, abruptly cutting her off.

Cara slammed her head into the headrest. "Fine."

"Shotgun signing off," he said, and then the line went dead.

Cara tossed the palm pad onto the passenger seat and let out an audible grunt.

Kane glanced over his shoulder, out the busted rear window. He caught Tala's eyes as he sat down, looking as unstrung as she felt.

The car turned again down another dirt road, then slowed, Cara taking in long, slow breaths, bringing the car to a near stop, inching across the gravel before she finally turned up a driveway that led to an old farmhouse.

Tala peered out the window, the night sky still fading, giving way to the sun rising on the horizon. She looked over a harvested field, then spotted a large, bare-wooden barn with plumes of smoke emanating through the top.

She inhaled deeply, catching the same hint in the air from Clarke's, sweet yet smoky.

"What are those?" she asked, pointing.

"Tobacco barns," Cara said, her voice taut.

Near the house, she pulled the car up beside a row of other vehicles, shifted it into park, then killed the engine. Tala watched in the rearview mirror as Cara steeled herself, taking another deep breath, then opened the door.

Tala crawled out of the backseat, giving the car a once-over, assessing its destruction. The rear-end was smashed, the broken taillights crunched up into the trunk, slices cut through the hood and bumper where they were hit by plasma charges. Then there were the busted out back window and windshield and the missing front bumper.

She spotted two men approaching from the house, a white two-story in desperate need of a painting, the front porch sagging to the right. Both had their eyes fixed on Cara.

"I'm sorry to have come," she said, her voice low. "I had no choice."

The two men were silent, the tallest between them studying her intently, his brows furrowed. "You've got some nerve," he finally said, the other looking timidly at Tala and Kane.

"Really, Finn," she asserted. "I had no choice."

He studied her for another moment and then sighed loudly. "I spoke to Evergreen," he said finally.

"Hi, Colt," Cara said to the second man, who looked at her with warm eyes, then quickly averted his gaze. He had sandy brown hair and freckles on his cheeks that gave him a youthful appearance.

Tala's eyes darted to the nearby house as a woman dressed in a fuzzy, yellow robe appeared outside the door. She folded her arms across her body as she looked over all of them.

"What's she doin' here?" she called out to them as she pointed her finger at Cara.

Tala glanced at Kane, his jaw set, a crease between his brows as he watched the strangers carefully.

"I wouldn't have come if I had another option," Cara insisted again.

Tala watched as the woman, her brown hair pulled into curlers, with gray wisps around the crown of her face, neared, a heavy scowl on her face.

"What's she doin' here?" she repeated, her eyes staring Cara down. She spoke with a quick tongue and a sharp twang, her accent a stark contrast from Clarke's.

"I'm sorry," Cara said firmly, straightening as she looked at the woman. "It's an emergency."

The woman scrutinized the destroyed car. "First you show your face 'round here, which is brave of you considering the last time you were here, then you drive up in this piece," she spat as she gave a hard kick to the front tire, "and with strangers in tow," she said as she looked at Tala and Kane.

She stared at them through narrowed eyes, her brows knitted together tightly. She looked back at Cara, but only for a brief moment before her gaze returned to Tala. Her head cocked to the side as she looked at her over the top of the car.

"Wait a sec," she said, her voice losing some of its bite as she walked around the back of the vehicle.

Tala stiffened, and Kane took a step closer to her.

The woman got close to Tala, her eyes studying her quietly. She looked briefly over her shoulder at Cara, who said nothing, then back to Tala.

"You who I think you are?" she finally asked.

"Yes, she is," Cara said.

The woman hung on to her scowl for another moment as she fixed on Tala. "You're brunette now," she said flatly as her face relaxed. "I like the blond better, but I guess a girl's gotta do what's she gotta do. MF are lookin' for you, you know that, right?"

Tala nodded. "That's why we're here."

The woman glanced back to Cara, who also nodded.

"They're saying you had something to do with that terrible tragedy in the capital. That you were working with DeSoto," she paused as she looked Tala up and down. "I don't believe any of it. Most people don't either," she said, raising her chin.

"I told my boys that I'd watched you on the National Statement," the woman continued, "that I'd read 'bout you over the years… I thought you to be genuine. Could feel it. Sometimes you just know these things. Some people call you the princess, but I reckon no princess would ever be MF."

"Then you'd be right," Kane said, his voice deep, guarded.

"And who're you?" the woman asked, her eyes darting to him. "You with her?"

He nodded.

"What're y'all doin' with her anyway?" she asked Tala with a nod at Cara.

"I can't give you any details," Tala said hesitantly, unsure of the woman before her.

She nodded, her eyes wrinkling in the corners. "I think I've got a clear enough picture," she said. "I don't like the idea of you being back here," she said as her head snapped briefly to Cara. "But you," she said as she looked at Tala, again, "I'll help you."

Tala wasn't sure if she was relieved or not. Though she did seem to be their only option.

"Come in," the woman called over her shoulder as she set off toward the house. "All of y'all," she demanded with a wave.

Inside the house, the woman motioned for everyone to take a seat around a long dining table that was far too big for the room it was in. A large portrait of a man hung on the wall, his eyes seeming to linger on everyone in the room.

Tala watched as the man they called Colt made furtive glances at Cara from across the room, giving her a small, inconspicuous smile.

"I'm Lilian," the woman said with a nod toward Tala. "And these are my boys. Finn and Colt. And you," she said as she turned toward Kane. "I don't wanna know no more than I've got to, so if you don't mind, I'd like to keep your name out of it. It's nothin' personal."

"Probably best," Kane said, then pursed his lips as he folded his arms.

Lilian turned toward Finn, the taller of her two sons, with thick chestnut hair that curled on the ends. "Go hide that car. Put it in the back shed. I don't need to be attractin' any MF with that thing parked in my yard."

Finn nodded, then hurried from the room.

"We need a car," Cara said, her eyes meeting Lilian's.

"To get to the border, no doubt," Lilian said. "It's not safe for her 'round here."

The room was quiet, Cara's gaze not faltering. "I'll make sure you get it back."

Lilian turned to Tala. "I wanna hear you say it," she said, and Tala's face screwed up in confusion. "I wanna hear you say you had nothin' to do with that awful mess."

Tala swallowed hard and nodded her head. "I tried to stop it," she said forcefully. "I could never be complicit with something like that. Those were my people."

Lilian nodded her head slowly, her gaze falling briefly to the floor. "That there was my husband, Lee," she said as she tipped her head toward the portrait on the wall. "He was a good man. Hard worker. Maybe cussed a little too much. He took pride in this farm, despite how it might look. Two MF and another guy in a fancy suit showed up here one day to tell us they were cutting the price of what they paid for our cured tobacco by almost half. We were already scraping by, and they wanted to take even more away from us. Said it was our duty to the Republic," she sneered, her eyes wandering off somewhere in the vacant distance. She shook her head. "He tried to argue with 'em, but they didn't care 'bout nothin', and when they were leaving, he followed 'em outside. Let 'em have it. Let 'em know what he really thought of 'em. They gave him one chance to take it all back, and he just stood there with his arms folded, not backing down. And that one MF agent, he just walked right up to my Lee, drillin' a plasma charge right through the head," she said with a shudder, her nightmare playing in her eyes. "But the way I see it, we were the lucky ones. So many just go missing, leaving their families to always wonder. 'Least I know."

Tala's heart sank watching the emotion on Lilian's face as she gazed up at the portrait on the wall. Lilian took a breath. After a quiet moment, she turned back to Tala, a hardened expression on her face.

"I didn't want my boys gittin involved with this one," she said with a nod toward Cara. "Too risky. I'd already lost one. But hatred and resentment run thick down here. Your brother is a ruthless leader of the MF. Oh, I know there are good ones too. But no doubt the man will be even worse as our new president. Laws are supposed to be a weapon against injustice, not for it. There will never be justice under his tyranny. Things are changing though. People are afraid, but the right kind of leadership can be a call for action. There's a storm brewing. And at the end of the day, we're all gonna have hard choices to make." Her eyes were cold as they fixed on Tala. "You... you could just be the one to make a difference."

"Why me?" Tala asked soberly. "What makes you think it could be me?"

"We already all know you. You know loss, like so many of us. And you've lived with the devil himself. That brother of yours. No one knows him better than you." Lilian went quiet, her lips pressed as she fell silent for a minute. "You can take whatever car of mine you want. And if they come knockin' on my door, I'll be happy to lie through my teeth," she said with a wild flicker in her eyes.

Tala felt relief wash over her as she glanced across the table at Cara, whose mouth curled into a small smile, then disappeared in an instant as Lilian turned toward her.

"Just get her 'cross that border," she said firmly. "And I'll do what I can from here to rally. Like I said, we're all gonna have hard choices to make."

Tala was back to riding flat on her back in the backseat, watching a world of treetops full of vibrant autumn colors pass her by, the reds, oranges, and yellows going by in a blur. She stared up at the vast sky overhead, the clouds drifting above her as if in slow motion. Occasionally, she propped herself up just high enough to sneak a peek out the window to catch brief glimpses of wide-open farmland. And then she would settle back down. She was still cramped in the backseat of Lilian's car, wedged between both doors, unable to stretch out, but it was slightly roomier than the other one had been.

The Colonies, she thought, they had to get to the Colonies. Only there would Thias's power be diminished, only there would his impunity no longer reach.

"How do you know them?" Tala asked, knowing it was none of her business, but they needed something to talk about. The silence let her mind wander too much.

"Colt and Finn?" she asked not taking her eyes off the road.

"Yeah."

"I met them both in a bar about a year ago," she said.

"And you and Colt?"

Cara nodded. "Yep. Me and Colt. Until Lilian figured out what was going on and that he was helping me. I get it though," she said generously. "She hates the Republic. But she wasn't willing to risk anyone else in her family."

"Avery said the UR wants to bring back the United States. Do you really think that's even possible? That was another time. Doesn't that seem like going backward?" Tala asked.

"You heard Lilian's story. And there's a thousand more out there just like it. Every tithing hike, every MF brutality and show of force amplifies the unrest building in the people. The United States isn't just a country, it's an ideal. It's a place where democracy thrived and people had a voice. There's nothing *republic* about this country. Maybe in the very beginning, but that was short-lived. Mankind can destroy anything. But we can also rebuild almost anything. The power is truly ours. We just have to choose how to use it."

Kane stole a look back at Tala. In the world they were in, he had no voice, and the people's, like Lilian's, didn't matter. For the first time, she saw the real need of the people. Tala had lived beneath a veil of ignorance, and she was awakened to a harsh reality. Her love for her country and for her people ran deep, it's what had motivated her and why she had taken an oath as a Militia Forces agent. This was the ultimate call to fight, to defend, to protect.

The deepest parts of her soul, the strength of what lay in the very core of who she was, was being challenged. She felt her resolve shifting. She was standing at the base of a mountain, and she was more determined than ever to show that it could be moved.

The darkness was heavy and all-consuming, but all it took was a single spark and everything could be different. Seeing the other side, she had seen it in Lilian's eyes: hope. Tala's character and dedication were being tested, and she would not cow in the face of adversity. It was no longer about being brave for herself, she had to be brave for her people so that they could live a better tomorrow. She didn't have to be the entire blaze, she just had to ignite the fire within the people. A flicker of hope could be just what was needed to change it all.

♦♦♦

They arrived in Clara City, which was a bustling city along the Mississippi River, a border city, in the late afternoon. As they turned down a rough, unpaved road, Tala once again stared at a canopy of dense trees, her body tossed haphazardly around the backseat.

When they finally stopped, she was eager to escape her confinement. She stretched her aching body, her muscles cramped, and took a look around. Cara had taken them to a clearing deep within a heavily wooded area, the sound of rushing water nearby.

There was something about the beauty around her that seemed to wake her up in a way the city never had. The way the breeze made the leaves dance, the sun lighting up the fall foliage, the chirp of a crimson red cardinal as it fluttered past. It was all seemingly simple, yet complicated, separate but connected. It was untouched, unhindered, and uncontrolled by mankind, occurring naturally and on its own, all of it singing a melody that only Tala's heart could hear.

"What're we doing here?" Kane asked as he looked around the vacancy of the clearing.

"This is where we're camping tonight. Vulcan will meet us here," Cara said casually as she pulled bags from the trunk of the car and tossed them onto the hardpacked dirt. It had taken a crowbar, and some assistance, unknowingly to the others, from Kane, to pry open the trunk of their other car to retrieve the things Cara packed. There was a ring of large rocks and charred logs that made it obvious the clearing had been used as a campsite more than once.

"And when will Vulcan be here?" Kane asked. Tala heard the apprehension in his voice.

Cara must have heard it too as she looked up at him through narrowed eyes. "Vulcan is one of the best. Strategically smart, tactically skilled, and provides our people guidance."

"I just need to know that they can do this. It's one thing to get across the country, which we nearly didn't on a few occasions, but it's another to get across the border," he said firmly.

"I get it," she said without malice. "You've got a lot on the line. But we all do. Our vision is larger than any one of us. Great reward doesn't come without great risk. They go hand-in-hand. You've come this far. If there's anyone who can get you across that border, it's Vulcan. The way I see it, this is your only option. Actually, it's her only option. She stays, they will find her," Cara said adamantly.

"I'll make sure she gets across that border," he said, his jaw flexing. "No matter what it takes."

Cara was quiet as she gave him an understanding nod.

Dread opened like a black hole inside Tala. Cara was right, this was her only chance. But she wouldn't do it without Kane, she couldn't. He was the calm in her chaos, he was the tenderness in the harshness around her. He was in the very breath she took, fortifying her and dividing her grief, her worries, her fears. What was coming was going to come, this she knew. She couldn't stop it, reverse it, or slow it down. She had to be prepared to take it all.

They pitched two tents, each tucked just slightly into the tree line on opposite sides of the clearing, tossing in a few blankets and a deflated pillow for each of them. As dusk began to creep in, Cara was stoking a small fire while Kane nervously paced the woods around them under the pretense of looking for firewood when a truck with a large flatbed appeared in the woods, its loud engine drowning out the sound of the nearby stream, making its way toward them in the clearing.

Tala tensed, her body going rigid, and her breath catching. She rose to her feet from the downed tree trunk she sat on, Kane rushing into the clearing, and she stole an anxious glance at Cara.

"Relax," she said calmly, not moving from the log that she sat on around the firepit.

"Vulcan?" Tala asked, her eyes meeting hers.

Cara nodded, and Tala watched Kane drop the wood in his arms, then make his way toward her as the truck parked on the edge of the clearing.

Tala's hands shook with anticipation, and she glanced up at Kane as he stood beside her. Her body was in a hyper-state of fight or flight, and in the moment, all she wanted to do was run. But she knew she wouldn't. She felt strong in her resolve that this was what she had been built to do. It was for her parents, it was for Ronin, it was for Mila, and for every life she'd never know.

Their camp went quiet, and Tala watched with a racing heart as a man got out of the truck and started his way toward them. He was dressed in dark, tapered cargo pants and an olive-colored t-shirt, the sleeves rolled and bunched around his shoulders. He was fair-skinned and thin, but sinewy, with a thick head of long, dark brown dreads that hung to the middle of his chest. He had a stern brow and defined jawline, ink covering the entirety of one arm, and a hoop piercing in his nose. And as he approached, she noticed his gaze lingered only on Kane.

Tala stole a sideways glance at Kane to see his wide eyes. Confused, she looked back at Vulcan as he came to a quiet stop only feet away from them. A sense of familiarity washed over her. She looked back at Kane, his forehead puckered, his head cocked slightly to the side.

"Addox?" he finally said, breaking the silence around them.

Tala's breath caught as she let out a muted gasp, her head snapping in Vulcan's direction.

"I wondered when this day would come," he said coolly. It was clear by the lack of incredulity on his face that, unlike Kane, he had been expecting their meeting. He stepped forward and outstretched his hand to Kane.

"No," Kane said firmly, his voice low and angry. "There's no way you're our contact."

Vulcan retracted his hand, shoving it casually into his pocket. "But I am, brother."

"You don't get to call me that," Kane snapped loudly. "This is a mistake," he said, his head turning toward Cara. But she only nodded in confirmation. "No," he boomed. "The Addox I knew was a coward. He didn't have it in him to be any kind of leader for a rebel movement."

"Just because I was quiet doesn't mean I was a coward," Vulcan said calmly, his voice steady. "I've spent the better part of the last ten years looking for you."

Kane shook his head feverishly. "You must think I'm crazy if you think I'm going to trust her life in your hands for even a second."

"Kane," Tala said gently as she reached for his arm.

"No," he snapped again as he looked at her. "You're not going with him. I'll get you across."

"And how do you plan on doing that?" Vulcan said. "The borders are closed and MF are everywhere. News of your little car chase, ending in the death of two agents, has been circulating everywhere. Though no one knows it was her they were chasing. The big questions lingering on their minds now are where she's at and where she's going… south or west. There's a bounty on her head," he said sharply.

Tala felt her stomach drop. "A bounty?" she asked quietly.

"That's right, a bounty," he said, his eyes settling on her. "We've got allies all over down here, but you better believe me when I tell you that someone would sell you out for so much as a hot meal in these parts. Any chance you have for anything is to get across that border. And I'm your only way across," he said, his eyes, hazel and stern, boring into her with the same intensity she often saw in Kane's.

Tala was sure Kane could hear her racing heart, which pounded loudly in her ears. She was putting the lives of everyone around her at risk just by being near them. She felt the color gone from her face. Regret, anxiety, devastation, it all threatened to consume her. She looked at Vulcan through heavy eyes. She had been foolish to think Thias wouldn't go to extreme measures to find her. She silently scolded herself. He once again went one step further than she planned.

The clearing was growing darker by the minute as the sun was dropping lower in the western sky, just beyond the heavy woods that enshrouded them. It was also getting cooler with the more daylight they lost, and Tala pulled her jacket a little tighter. "You can hate me all you want," Vulcan said as he looked at Kane. "But I'm it. I'm her only chance. And this either happens tomorrow, or it doesn't happen at all," he said flatly.

"Let's sit and talk," Cara said calmly, speaking for the first time since Vulcan had come.

Tala felt numb as she walked toward the fire, sitting on one of three tree trunks that surrounded it. Her hands shook, but not from the chill in the air. She felt emotionally exhausted, fatigued from every blow, a profound sadness falling over her.

Kane sat beside her, taking her hand in his, but she didn't dare look at him, afraid all of her emotions would rush to the surface and she would be unable to stop it from spilling over. Instead, she stared silently into the fire, the orange flames licking the logs in the stone pit, the hot coals simmering at the bottom.

"So, tell me," Kane said, and Tala could hear the stress in his voice. And while she didn't trust her eyes to meet his, she leaned into him, his body warm against hers. "If you're our only shot, how're you going to get us across that border?"

Vulcan didn't immediately respond, and Tala looked up, his face appearing just beyond the flames, and she heard Kane's voice in her head:

The god of fire.

A chill ran down the length of her spine, suddenly realizing who had been responsible for their father's death: unsolved murder-arson case. Vulcan didn't just choose this name for himself, he'd earned it.

"That's just it," Vulcan said seriously as he looked across at them. "With the borders closed, things just got exponentially more difficult. I can't take both of you. Only her."

TWENTY-THREE

"I can't get both of you across the border," Vulcan said, the flames of their fire brightening his face with an orange glow. "I don't have enough room in the hidden cargo hold. And I don't have solid enough credentials that could get Kane through a closed security checkpoint. It has to be Tala. I'm sorry, but she's been the goal all along." He leaned forward, his elbows on his thighs, his long dreads falling in front of his shoulders.

"No way. It's both of us or neither of us," Tala urged. She felt Kane's hand slide across her leg, and it was warm to the touch.

Vulcan shook his head. "There's a bounty on your head, Tala. You stay, you will be found. Kane will be fine on his own. No one is looking for him. You stay together, and you're both certain to die."

Cara prodded at the ash beneath the logs in the fire with a branch she'd grabbed from nearby. "Kane's managed to slip under the radar of the Republic for years," she said. "Eventually, we'll get him across too. But it's too risky right now."

"Can't we get a second truck? Or come back? Make two trips?" Tala asked, ignoring Cara. As Kane's hand gave her a gentle squeeze, she noticed his silence.

"I already told you, the borders are closed. I'm pressing my luck to get through that checkpoint this one time," Vulcan asserted.

"You're awfully quiet," she said, turning toward Kane.

His eyes met hers, and she knew he was calculating his words. "He's right. You stay, you're dead. Arrested at best. It would be only a matter of time before you're recognized by someone."

"No," she said, hearing the rising emotion in her voice. "We've come too far. Together. I'm not leaving you." There was pressure building in her chest, and she struggled to breathe, as if her lungs forgot how.

"The only chance you both have is to separate," Vulcan said. "Your brother will stop at nothing to get to you. Don't drag Kane down with you," he said, his eyes on Tala.

She wanted to throw the large rock that lay at her foot at him. There was little emotion in his voice, and she couldn't understand his detachment. This was his brother. How could he not understand why they needed to be together, why she needed Kane? She was seething and bit the inside of her cheek to keep her gathering tears at bay.

"Looks like you have some things to consider," Vulcan said. "We leave at first light. And it will be your only chance." He stood, gave a lingering look at Kane, then he turned and headed to his tent across the clearing.

Cara frowned as she looked at them. "I'm sorry you guys," she said after a quiet moment. Tossing the branch into the fire, she stood up and gave them both one last glance. "Good night," she said and walked off toward the tent Vulcan had gone into, leaving Tala and Kane alone.

The heat of the fire had been warming her face and the front of her legs, but now Tala felt nothing but the cold.

Once Cara was out of ear shot, she turned to Kane, a pleading look on her face. "I won't leave you. I can't," she said, her emotion bubbling up.

"Tala," he said in his deep, firm voice as he took both of her hands in his, his thumb brushing over the inside of her wrist. "You have to. They're right. If we stay together, there's no chance for either of us." He tried to keep his voice steady, but she heard the subtle crack in it.

"The only reason I've made it this far is because I've had you," she said.

He shook his head. "You're strong enough. You underestimate yourself. And believe me when I tell you that you can go on. You have to leave me behind."

"No!" she said adamantly. She was on the brink of completely falling apart. "We agreed that we wouldn't separate. I need you," she pleaded.

"Tala," he said gently, the look in his eyes telling her he'd made up his mind and nothing was going to change it. He was going to make her go on without him. "I'll be with you wherever you go. You have to continue to move forward, and if you stumble, let my presence in here sustain you," he said, tapping her chest near her heart.

She took a ragged breath, a single tear breaking her resolve and falling down her cheek. He instinctively reached out and gently wiped it away.

"Come on," he said as he rose, pulling her up alongside him. He gave the logs in the fire a firm kick, letting them fall away from each other, and instantly, the bulk of the flames dissipated. He gave her a small tug, and together they made their way to their tent, pitched opposite Cara and Vulcan's.

The bite of the nighttime air was less apparent inside the tent, despite its thin walls, and Tala crawled inside after Kane, taking a seat beside him. She leaned into him, the only light a soft glow from the straggling fire outside.

She turned to him, her heart full: love, anger, heartbreak. She let his dark eyes look her over, and she couldn't help but think that he was the most beautiful thing she had ever seen. She choked up telling herself that what connected them was greater than any distance that could separate them. She swallowed hard as she brought her hand to his face. The stubble along his jaw and around his mouth was rough to the touch, and she leaned closer, letting her lips brush against his. They lingered there for a moment before his hands slid around her, and he pulled her into him, their kiss deepening.

Desperation washed over her, and she kissed him harder, her mind frantically taking in everything about him. She wanted to hang on to every piece of him.

She unzipped her jacket, willing herself to slow down, to let herself live in the moment between them, to let herself feel everything that only they could share. She let the jacket fall behind her, her bare arms now exposed to the cool air, though she felt none of it. She pushed Kane's leather jacket off him as she slid her body onto his lap. She felt his chest press against hers, and he leaned in, his lips brushing along her neck as he slowly gave her soft, tender kisses down to her collarbone.

Tala let out a low exhale as she reached for the hem of his shirt. She lifted it, gliding it up and over his arms, tossing it aside.

With his arms wrapped firmly around her, in a smooth, swift movement, he gently laid her on her back on top the thin blankets. Hovering over her with bated breath, she felt a charge rush through her, feeling intoxicated as she drank him in. She kissed him, letting every ounce of love she had for him spill over, feeling it race with exhilaration through her veins.

She loved him truly, knowing there was no better match for her in the world. She hadn't planned for him, nor saw him coming, yet here they were in each other's arms, and it was the most honest and natural place she'd ever been. To love someone is to make a warrior of them. As long as he was, there would always something for her to fight for.

A while later, her body curled up into him, she listened to the rhythmic beating of his heart, which had been frantic and quick at first, but had since slowed and pounded softly, just a whisper in her ears. She felt him drift off to sleep as his body went lax and his breathing grew light. She was just glad he was finally getting some sleep.

She lay next to him for what felt like hours. The air growing colder around them with every passing hour, she slipped out of his grip and pulled on her clothes and jacket, but it did little to warm her. The real cold was inside her, buried deep within her bones.

She'd sworn she would never leave him. But looking at him in this moment, so peacefully asleep, she realized she had been wrong to promise that. Now, as she stood in the fire, her life burning around her, she knew she couldn't let him burn as well. Leaving him behind was the only way to keep the flames from consuming him too.

Falling back into him and pulling his arm around her, she knew this was all that was left. And even if it was the last time he would ever hold her, he would always touch her, his hand on her soul.

Only drifting in and out, Tala hadn't truly fallen asleep. She had been content simply listening to Kane breathing beside her, feeling the rise and fall of his chest while she pressed herself against him, keeping his arm snug around her.

The first rays of light flickering through the trees began to brighten the inside of the tent. Tala studied Kane, his smooth, brown skin, his full lips, his sharp jawline. Everything about him was perfect, and her heart swelled.

He stirred, the voices of Vulcan and Cara talking outside reverberating inside their tent. His eyes fluttered open, meeting Tala's in a sleepy haze. A moment later, he gave her a bleak smile.

"You didn't sleep, did you?" he asked knowingly, his voice raspy.

She said nothing.

"You ready?" he asked as he gently brushed a strand of hair away from her face, his fingers grazing her cheek.

"No," she said, realizing they had never actually discussed what they both knew was going to happen. "I could never be ready for this."

"Time to get up," Vulcan's voice called through the tent. "We're leaving in a bit."

Tala pulled Kane's arm tighter around her waist, and he pulled her firmly against him.

"Be right out," he called out as he buried his face in her hair.

She lay in his embrace as long as she could, breathing him in, her heart heavy and her sorrow draining through her.

"Time to go," he finally whispered. He gave her one last squeeze, then released her. He sat up and reached for his clothes, dressing quickly.

Opening the door, a rush of cool air swept through the tent, and together they crawled out, their temporary campsite now lit by the rising sun. Vulcan and Cara's tent had been taken down, and Cara stood by the truck dressed in a standard-issue Militia Forces uniform, catching Tala off guard.

"We've got good credentials for her," Vulcan said with a glance over his shoulder, no doubt seeing the startled look on Tala's face. "We get hassled less this way. Just need one of the plasma guns I hear you have."

Without a word, Tala pulled one from her duffel, giving it to Vulcan.

Cara loaded bags onto the truck alongside a dozen barrels, supposedly of a fine wine made only in the northeast. Vulcan had false government documents that showed it was a special transport approved for passage, despite the closed borders, by request from Central Colonies Governor Hutton. But those barrels would never make it to him. Their actual journey would take them across the Mississippi, and then they would make their way northwest the five-hundred miles to Hatfolk, Tala's final destination. Though she didn't know what exactly was waiting there for her.

"All right," Vulcan said firmly. "We've got to get going. We can't delay any longer. Kane," he said, approaching, a palm pad in his hand. "Stay in this clearing. Keep the tent. This," he said, holding out the device, "has some money on it as well as fake credentials. Though I wouldn't suggest testing them against MF. We'll get in touch as soon as we have an exit plan. Its service is only good for three days. Hopefully things settle down a little and we can be in touch before that."

"Thanks," Kane said, taking the palm pad. As Vulcan walked away, he turned to Tala. He reached for her hand and pulled her into his arms. Their bodies pressed so tightly together it was impossible to know where one ended and the other began.

She heard him take in a deep breath, and when they pulled apart, she saw his eyes glossed over. There was a tightness in her chest, and she exhaled hard, unsure how she was ever going to walk away. It felt wrong.

"I'll find you. I will," he whispered to her, pressing his forehead to hers.

She gave a small nod, her words failing her. She didn't know how to say goodbye, and she didn't trust her resolve. She knew she would crumble to pieces if she opened her mouth. Instead, she kissed him, regret and heartbreak flooding her.

They made their way to the truck where Vulcan had pulled loose some wooden boards on the platform of the bed, revealing a small compartment she never would've guessed was there. He motioned for her to climb into the narrow space.

"It'll be a rough ride," he said. "And I'm sorry about that. It'll be chilly too. So, I've got a blanket for you. Once we're about sixty or so miles inside the Colonies, you'll be able to come out. Republic MF don't typically go in any farther than that. They're not welcome there in the first place."

Setting his hands on Tala's hips, Kane lifted her swiftly onto the bed. She turned to look at him, tears clouding her eyes. She had never wanted to give him up, to let him go, yet that was what she was doing. "I love you," she whispered. He was trying to be strong, but she saw the pain in his stoic eyes. She swallowed hard, then turned away, desperate for it to not be the last time she'd ever see him. With an uneven breath, she lowered herself into the tiny space in the floor. The grooves in the metal floor pushed uncomfortably into her back. Vulcan spread a thin, black blanket across her body, stuffed her duffel near her feet, then gently replaced the wooden floorboards. Covering her entirely, he nailed them down, then slid barrels over the top of her.

Tala could hear a faint conversation between Kane and Cara, though she couldn't make out what they were saying. The leaden weight of reality pressed down on her, and her emotion caught in the back of her throat.

Narrow slivers of light shone through the cracks in the planks above her, and sucking in the cold air, she closed her eyes. Tears slipped from the corners of her eyes and down the side of her face, into her ears, muffling the sounds around her, a chirping bird in the distance, the quaking of the leaves on the breeze. She felt the truck roar to life. She wanted to scream for them to stop. That she couldn't do this. She wanted to see his face one more time. She wanted to touch him, and hold his hand, and kiss his mouth. She wanted to hang on to him for just a moment longer.

But then the truck gave a hard jerk as it began to drive away, leaving Kane alone in the empty clearing.

Kane watched the truck as long as he could, and when the last flicker of the taillights disappeared from sight, he dropped to his knees in the dirt, struggling for breath. For only the second time in his life, he felt the weight of loss paralyze him.

He cursed himself for falling asleep in the night. It was perhaps the last night he'd ever spend with her, and he had slept it away.

He wanted to tell himself that this wasn't the end. But he couldn't bring himself to even think it for fear that he would believe it. Because if the day never came for them to be together again, his devastation would be even more crippling.

He felt the overwhelming swell of emotion in his throat, choking him, suffocating him. It was as though time stood still. He knew he didn't deserve her, yet he was certain that they had always belonged to each other.

Tala once said that grief wasn't a single place but rather a journey that would forever be walked. In that moment, he was desperate for it to be just a single place. He needed it to be where he stood now so that when he walked away, he would be able to leave his pain rather than carry it with him. It was a heavy burden. But he was prepared to carry it nonetheless, it would forever be a reminder that he knew the greatest love.

He was sure that everything in his life led him to her, and in loving her, his journey was complete. But as he had stood at the precipice of their goodbye, he wondered if some people were only ever meant to be part of history rather than destiny. He desperately hoped this wasn't true. The only future he wanted had her in it.

His chest was tight in those last moments as his eyes had lingered longingly on hers, those beautiful blue eyes, not wanting the moment to end. But this was the only way she could have a future. And regardless of the uncertainty of his, he knew one thing to be absolute, in finding her, he had found himself. He had to move forward, if not for his sake, then for the very possibility of finding her again.

The ride, as Vulcan had warned, was rough. Tala was tossed between the walls of the compact, hidden compartment. Her head bounced on the metal bottom, and she had a raging headache that only grew stronger with every bump, large and small. And it was cold, so cold. She gripped the blanket hard. In the distance, she heard the faint sound of a train horn, and she could hear traffic rushing past them, the world passing her by.

After what Tala guessed had been about twenty minutes, though she didn't know for sure, the truck slowed, then stopped completely. She heard voices that pounded in her ears as her heart began to race.

"Border's closed," a man with a rough, gravelly voice said loudly.

Tala couldn't make out the next words, although she could tell they were Vulcan's.

Then she heard Cara's voice, her words lost on the breeze.

"Let me see your documents," the gravelly voice said. Tala heard footsteps scuffing across pavement, and she willed her breathing to keep steady.

"Get out of the truck," a fourth voice said curtly. Tala could hear the loud creak as the cab doors opened. There were two thuds on the ground, then more footsteps, this time nearby.

As someone crawled onto the bed of the truck, she felt her body go stiff, and she held her breath. Through the small cracks in the floorboards, she could make out the bottom of a pair of boots, and she squeezed her eyes closed. Then a second person crawled onto the truck. She felt panic taking over as her heart raced so fast that she began to feel dizzy.

This was it. Everything boiled down to this very moment. She would either be caught and caged or released and set free.

She took a small breath, masked by the sound of the large barrels being slid across the floor above her.

"Open those up," a voice croaked. As the pairs of feet above her slid around the false wooden floor, gravel and dirt fell onto her, and she inhaled the fine dust. She bit down on the inside of her cheek, holding her breath, tasting the blood. She bit harder, giving herself something to concentrate on rather than the tickle in her nose.

A moment later, Tala heard thuds on the ground as the men jumped off the truck bed, and she let out a small exhale, but still bit at her cheek to keep her sneeze at bay.

"Let them pass," she finally heard. With her heart drumming loudly, she let out a sigh of relief.

The truck squealed as it was put into gear, then lurched forward, tossing her body to the side, her head hitting the metal, and she let out a small gasp that was drown out by the loud growl of the truck.

The sound of rushing water filled her ears, and she knew they were crossing the river, traversing the divide. Once the river was behind them, they drove over uneven ground, her body haphazardly thrown from one side of the compartment to the other, then after what felt like a lifetime, Tala heard Cara's voice call through the open window at the back of the cab.

"Tala, we're through!" she proclaimed, and Tala finally sneezed. "Another hour or so and you can come out. You're going to be okay," she yelled over the roar of the engine and wind as they picked up speed.

Okay?

Was she really okay?

The weight of betrayal and loss was heavy within her. Her life had converged with Kane's most unexpectedly and extraordinarily, the stars aligning for them for a single moment, bringing them together. But now she had to go on without him, if it was even possible.

Kane said it was. But did she have it in her to continue? The very fact that she had come this far, after everything, seemed to be proof that she did have it in her to go further. She took a shaky, uneven breath. She was no longer a reflection of her former self. And even if it was possible to go on, as she knew she must, she wasn't sure she would ever be truly okay.

ACKNOWLEDGMENTS

This has been a long road and a great adventure for me and my writing. I have so many people to thank for their support along the way. I couldn't have done it without you all. I am eternally grateful.

Thank you to B.B. Scott for your critique and advice, every ounce of it was invaluable. You helped give me the moxie to persevere in this difficult industry. And thank you for your keen editing eye.

Thank you to all my beta readers, especially Becky Lytle and Christy Saute, for giving me fresh perspectives, asking the hard questions, and pushing me to make this story that much stronger. I carefully pored over all of your notes and comments and am so grateful you took the time to read this story... and to encourage me to see it through. Becky, I couldn't have done this half as well without your brilliant insightfulness and editing skills. Your enthusiasm and belief in me helped bring this to fruition.

To my writing community, thank you for the oodles of guidance and support for success. Even the smallest amount of counsel and direction went a long way: 20BooksTo50K, The Write Life Community, Writers Helping Writers, and Inner Circle Writers' Group. The knowledge gleaned through these groups and the writers participating in them has given me the ability to make this book and its publication possible.

Can I just tell you how much I love the cover design? Britani and Casey Christenson have skills and imagination that are boundless. And to take my fragmented ideas and turn them into this masterpiece is nothing shy of incredible.

A monstrous thank you to Mel Miller for keeping my head in check when I had not-so-good offers on the table and for seeing my dream and running with it – marketing and promoting the heck out of it. Your genius is my blessing. How lucky I am to have you, in oh, so many ways. Thank you to my husband, Tim Ahles, for helping me get in the head of a male character, as well as offering your engineering brain when it came to the science and logistics of so many things in the story. And thank you for always making sure I had the time to write and for supporting me when I may have been going a *little* crazy in the process. You keep me going in life. A never-ending and tremendous thank you to Kristin Elswood. You believed in this story before it was even a story and pushed me to stick with it and see it through. You read through my early drafts, helped me muddle through the thick of it, and never let me give up. I know this story would never have come to be without you. You believe in my dreams as much as I do, and I am grateful. You are a treasure in every way.

And the biggest thank you of all to God for giving me these people to make all of this possible and bestowing upon me my writing skills and passion.

The story continues…

Tala's harrowing escape from the Republic of Columbia is far from the end of her story. The Republic turned out to be nothing like she expected, but outside its borders, she discovers that neither is the rest of the world. Her country has erupted into war, and she's aligned herself with the last group she ever thought she would, the Revos. To restore and rebuild a democracy she thought was long gone, Tala must be the catalyst for change, inspiring hope in her people. When devastation finds Tala and Kane, she realizes she is the only one who might finally be able to take down her tyrannous brother. No one knows him as she does. But he's a master of manipulation, and she must find a way to play his psychological game without falling victim to his endgame.

RESURGENCE

ABOUT THE AUTHOR

Originally from small-town Minnesota, Nicole currently lives in the greater Salt Lake City, Utah area with her husband, two children, and a very fluffy dog. She is a graduate of the University of Minnesota, Morris. In addition to having an addiction to writing, she is an avid reader, a baseball enthusiast, and has an affinity for novelty coffee mugs. Nicole is also the author of *The Cape House*, *What I Am Made Of*, and *Resurgence* – the thrilling sequel to *Convergence*.

Find Nicole on social media.

Facebook.com/AuthorNicoleAhles

Instagram: NicoleA_Books

www.NicoleAhles.com